Readers' love for THE BOOK OF ECHOES

The Book of Echoes

Rosanna Amaka

BLACK SWAN

TRANSWORLD PUBLISHERS
Penguin Random House, One Embassy Gardens,
8 Viaduct Gardens, London SW11 7BW
www.penguin.co.uk

Transworld is part of the Penguin Random House group of
companies whose addresses can be found at
global.penguinrandomhouse.com

First published in Great Britain in 2020 by Doubleday
an imprint of Transworld Publishers
Black Swan edition published 2021

Copyright © Rosanna Amaka 2020

Rosanna Amaka has asserted her right under the Copyright,
Designs and Patents Act 1988 to be identified as the author
of this work.

A CIP catalogue record for this book
is available from the British Library.

ISBN
9781784164836

Typeset in Adobe Garamond by Integra Software Services Pvt. Ltd, Pondicherry.

Printed and bound in Italy by Grafica veneta S.p.A.

The authorized representative in the EEA is Penguin Random House Ireland,
Morrison Chambers, 32 Nassau Street, Dublin D02 YH68.

Penguin Random House is committed to a sustainable future
for our business, our readers and our planet. This book is
made from Forest Stewardship Council® certified paper.

This book is dedicated to my mother, my Jamaican and Nigerian grandmothers, and my ancestors.

1

The Beginning – London

West India Docks, London, 1803

THEY DRAGGED ME from the ship, kicking and screaming.

I heard them enter the hold, heard them begin to search. The two voices grew louder as they approached the hole where Wind had hidden us. I held my hand over my mouth to stop the nausea, the other over my heart to calm its beating, felt the dead boy beside me, smelt him, cowered downwards, deeper, towards the spot where I could feel a little breeze coming through. I prayed then for freedom, for Wind, for our precious belly, for the dream that Wind had forced me to believe in. Then I heard someone walk off, heard his footsteps die away on the deck, heard the other follow. My heart lifted. Then he stopped, paused, as if he was having one last look around, sniffing the air, and turned right around, his footsteps became louder as he drew closer. He jerkily shoved the barrels aside, kicked the board covering the hole, bent down low, peered in – his eyes seemed to glitter.

I screamed.

'In here,' he called, 'quick.'

He reached into the hole and grabbed hold of my arm, my dress, my ankle, pulled me feet first out of that hole. I shrieked, felt the pain as our precious belly dragged against the sides of the hole, knocking my head. I clung to the edges for dear life, felt the pain as he yanked harder at my ankle. Then he dropped it, came over to bend my fingers back, and I kept crying 'No!' as he loosened my grip, before dragging me out by my collar, along the deck, up the stairs, each step striking my belly, my head. I felt the splinters in my palms sting as I tried to resist, tried to get a grip, felt the cold night breeze on my face as they hauled me out on to the top deck, down the gangway, before smashing me, and our belly, against hard cobbled ground. The pain shot through me and I emptied my stomach of the little I had left in it.

It must have been the smell of the boy that led them to us; the gangrene had got him the day before.

Earlier, Wind had hung his head like it was too heavy for him to carry, when he realized he was too late. He took his cap off, kneeled and reached in to close the boy's eyes gently, then prayed like the white sailors do. I placed my hand on his shoulder, tried to console him, but he shrugged it off, then turned to lift me into the barrel, but I wouldn't let him. I grabbed his face between my hands, stared into his eyes, forced him to look into mine, placed his hand on our belly. And he finally understood. She was tender. I did not think she could take the rolling. He did not want to let me go, so I kissed him on his mouth, breathed my strength into him, like he had breathed his into me, and he promised with the twitch of his eyes to return, to come back with a sack and fetch me from the hole.

He took the young man first, a man he had found running from the British soldiers just before we set sail from the Island, Jamaica. He rolled him off the ship on to the docks like he was a barrel of rum, and he, the young man, disappeared into that London night, finally free from the plantation where he was born, swallowed among the black poor of the East End. Wind saw him safely on his way, left him in the hands of folk in Canning Town, and as promised turned right around to get me. There were three of us he had tried to save: the boy, the man, and me. Four including our belly.

Outside by the docks where they had thrown me, I tried to crawl away from the voices shouting above me, but the pain from my belly pierced me and my body convulsed with nausea but gave up nothing. I heard more voices surround me, and as I looked upwards from the cobbled ground, the crowd parted to reveal a man who descended upon me like a white-headed eagle, dressed in layers of black cloth, his hair as wiry and white as cotton. He held a flaming torch in his raised hand and a stick in the other. I cowered away from the devil, tried to crawl with one arm towards the dock waters, holding our precious belly with the other, but he would not let me. He shoved my shoulder hard with his stick. I fell backwards, landed flat against the hard cobbles. I looked up at the night sky, at their angry white faces peering down at me, and wondered why I had come to this hell.

'Stowaway, sir. I saw the negro, James Jones, rolling a barrow off the ship, sir.'

'James Jones?'

'Yes, sir – you know, the sea hand? They call him Wind. Tall, sir.'

'Yes. Yes, I do.'

'I was coming out of the alehouse, saw him rolling an empty barrel off the ship and something about it seemed strange, so I went investigating, sir. Found her and a dead negro boy, sir.'

'Where is the sea hand now?'

'Don't know, Sir.'

'Paul, send out a search party. Find this negro.'

'Yes, sir.'

'Search the docks.'

'They say he resides in the East End, sir. Maybe Canning Town.'

'Paul, send a few men to search there too.'

'Yes, sir.'

'Sir, what do we do with the negro woman?'

'Put her in the warehouse. We can deal with her later.'

And I felt a wetness soak my clothes, tried to look down at our precious belly to see if she was all right, but I could not. So I lay upon that cold ground, fighting to breathe, for the life within me was our hope, the only choice I had made since being taken from my homeland, for she was made in love, in hope, my lone flower. I heard the water lap against the quayside, the faint sound of the horses' hooves, the squawk of a seagull above, and I breathed deep and hard and fought to stay alive.

Two hundred years Wind and I have roamed. Two hundred years we have waited by these docks, and in that time we have seen many changes, watched many beginnings.

I am their beginning, the womb whence they came. It was not out of choice that my children were separated, not out of choice I was joined with their fathers.

Uzo, my firstborn, was a round and healthy baby who giggled when I tickled him under his chin. Eze, my husband, was proud. We were happy in our small village, surrounded by the lush green bush, which shaded us from the African sun. We woke to the sound of the cockerel, and each morning I rose from the mat where we lay to clang my pot on top of an open fire and fetch water from the stream as Uzo slept peacefully on my back.

Eze, my husband, was a kind man whom I grew to love. I was sixteen, he much older. I remember the day he came to carry wine, and I became his wife. That day we heard the *oja* flute in the distance and it soared like an excited bird in flight, before being joined by the rhythm of the *ogene* gong and the beating of the drums drawing nearer. My mother fretted, but my friends poked their heads out of the hut, eager to see what was happening, and reported back happily on their first impressions of Eze and his family. I sat while my aunts added my final adornments. I could hear so much fanfare outside that my spirits soared and when, some time later, I finally handed Eze the cup to drink from, he took it in such a gentle manner that I was happy with my parents' choice.

I thought . . . Well, I thought many things. Back then, my future was young with fresh virgin cheeks. I thought I would grow old. I thought our lives would be entwined for ever, that I would wake each morning to Eze's smile, and the warmth of our baby between us. That I would rise each morning to clang my pot on top of the open fire, stir the food to feed my husband and send him on his way to labour in the far fields with, as he would say, my 'sweet cooking' wrapped in banana leaves, securely placed in the pouch by his side. I thought I would die in our small village surrounded by the green bush, not far from my father's land, and the people who loved me. I could not see into the future, nor could I have imagined what it held. I did not know how the disease of others would infect my life. It killed me. I was twenty-five.

Wind and I have never known that kind of happiness – there was never enough time – or laughter, or peace, or words. You see, at first he could not speak my language, nor I his, for although his skin was black like mine, he came from their land.

But we held on, Wind and I, from the moment we locked eyes. There was comfort in his gaze, a strength I needed that day as I walked unsteadily on to that ungodly ship with its huge wooden spears that rose into the heavens and the layers of white cloth at its feet. My back was in pain from the weight of the shackles at my neck and wrists, as I prayed for my son Uzo I had left in the shrine. I looked up and there was Wind, scaling down the pole with such agility. His black face seemed strange among their ghostly ones. I wondered how and why he could betray us so. Then he looked up, right at me, and our eyes met and he willed me on, willed me to fight. I could not look away. He held my gaze as I descended into that hell, giving me strength. I never let go.

That was the last day I ever saw Africa while alive.

It was a simple decision that changed my life – to go to the near field to collect yams to feed my family. The harvest was good and there were more yams to dig out than usual that day, so we returned home later, and on our way back I insisted on stopping at the shrine to thank the Goddess Ani for my blessings: for Eze, my husband, for Uzo, my son, and for the abundance of yams harvested that day. The others, my sisters-in-law, went on ahead. Uzo was dozing; I could feel his heartbeat, his warmth, against the middle of my back. It was a simple decision and my world, our world, was changed for ever. As I knelt and made my offerings, I heard a rustle in the bush, looked up to see three strange men creeping towards me. I screamed for I knew in that moment that I had made a mistake. I did the only thing I could do to save my child. I threw him towards the boundaries of the shrine, in among the deities, shielded from the sun by its thatched roof. And as they dragged me away screaming I prayed for the others to hear me, for them to come quickly and at least find my baby Uzo, lest the bush rats or snakes should do him harm, lest the priest should find him and think him a sacrifice, a dedication, make him *Osu* – an outcast among his people. I prayed directly to Chukwu, the supreme God, creator of all, to save me, save my child, for I could not trust the Goddess Ani any more.

Now, two hundred years later, we – Wind and I – sit and stand among the people of these docks, follow them inland, into front rooms, into supermarkets and malls, into big dance halls with strange names and strange ways. I watch the people of London speed past; they make me dizzy with their haste. I catch their energy, hear their jumbled sounds, and pick up ends of conversations, which

I chew and then swallow. This keeps me young, younger than the day I died.

We wait here, joined by the same destiny that stole us from our lands, the death we shared, and the daughter he put in me. I think she was a girl – I always think of her as a girl. I did not see her properly; they took her away too quickly. But I remember her smell, like ginger, and the half-moon on the side of her face, like her father, and the steam that rose from her little body as they opened the warehouse doors and hurried her away into the cold. They say she did not make it further inland to the East End but was shipped out to the Islands, or maybe to the Americas, to Brazil, to Nova Scotia, to Virginia, to . . . We do not know.

My heart cries out for the two, Uzo, my baby boy, and my baby girl, taken from me that morning while I lay dying over there among the barrels of sugar, spices and tobacco, the feel of the cold hard floor against my back.

Each day I search for them, look for them, hunt for them. I did not choose to leave them. I am and will always be their mother, their African mother. Sometimes I hear them cry for me and each day I look, from here to Virginia, to Barbados, to Haiti, to Cuba, to Jamaica, and back again to the Bight of Biafra and the Bight of Benin, and further inwards to my homeland. But every day I return to these London docks, hoping they will, she will, remember and return. And in between, I watch people. I sit and stand among them, watching their beginnings and sometimes their ends.

PART I

Michael

2

So They Come, So They Go

Brixton, 1981

THIS MORNING AT eight o'clock, I saw Delores open her eyes and smile. That smile started from deep inside and it spread out to the tips of her fingers, to her toes and the roots of her hair. Her spirit pushed the weight in her heart, pushed it aside like the great man Hercules. And that joy, that release, shone out like early morning sunshine.

I've not seen Delores, or Ms Lorez as I've heard them call her, smile that deep in a long time, not since Mr Watson, her husband, left – well, ran off – with a sixteen-year-old, or maybe even as far back as when her daughter, Marcia, was born. In those days she seemed happy. Michael and Simon, her stepsons, were still little boys, and they used to watch over Marcia like she was a pup. Ms Lorez didn't have to worry about warming up the milk when Marcia cried – those boys were already boiling the kettle before she could even ask. They fought over who should do it, but still they did it. I suppose that is when Ms Lorez's love for those boys really started.

But maybe I'm wrong. Maybe the last time she smiled that deeply was just before her husband turned funny over the schoolgirl. For some reason he stopped trying to be the master of their family and started being a part of it, doing small things around the house. He even fixed Michael and Simon's old wardrobe, which had needed mending for months. Simon, the older of the boys by two years, watched on, passing over the tools, glad to be spending man time at last with his father. Mr Watson even helped with the washing-up and brought home yellow daffodils, which Ms Lorez lovingly arranged on the dining table.

Anyway, as I was saying, this morning Ms Lorez opened her eyes and smiled. And as she got out of bed, Michael slammed the front door, his shoes making cracking sounds on the concrete corridor as he hurried off to work. And I saw Ms Lorez walk over to the window, draw the net curtains apart to see Michael's small form appear in the courtyard below. She watched him hurry into the cold morning, along with Mr Clark and the others, to start the new day. 'Happy birthday,' she sang as Michael disappeared behind the adjacent block. Then she turned to wake up Marcia, picking up laundry from the floor as she went, and just before leaving her bedroom she stopped in front of the wardrobe mirror. I've never seen her do that before – I mean, look deep into her eyes to see herself inside. It's as if on past mornings she had been frightened of what she had become, of what she would see if she looked too hard, so her glances were always fleeting, done quickly enough to check that her blouse was tucked in, or her skirt was straight, or her lipstick was not too thick, but never to look at who she actually was. This morning she stopped and looked at her face, examined the puffiness around her eyes, looked deep into her soul, and I heard her say, quite adamantly, 'Life begins at forty-nine.' And as she said it, the grey streaks in her hair shimmered like comets and I felt a new energy, a fresh hope, surge through her, and I hurried off, smiling to myself on my way to meet Wind.

It's a few hours later and she's no longer at home. The clouds have gathered, and Big Ben chimes in the distance. The room she is in is quiet. She lies still on the bed, her face swollen, moon-shaped, so bruised she is barely recognizable. Her head rests against a white pillow, the words 'St Thomas' Hospital' printed in the inner fold. Her hair is wild, and hidden in it, barely visible, are specks of dry blood, and at the root of each of her comet-like strands is a nucleus that seems to suck the energy pumping through her veins. Stealing it away, driving it up through the hair follicle, past the dermis, past the epidermis, losing it into this whirlpool called 'the World'.

The objects in this room – the grey pedal bin near the door, the blue plastic folder on the side cabinet, the clear water container on top of the table – are so normal, so commonplace that at first glance they hide her battle. Four hours ago she had taken her best dress from her wardrobe, put it on, and danced with a new freedom. That is before . . . before the screams and the blood, which spurted out of her like a geyser, shooting high into the air, then down to trickle along the slopes of her body, past invisible slashes and exposed sore pink flesh, staining the yellow flowers on her dress, soaking into the carpet beneath her.

Her children, Michael and Marcia, sit with her in this room. Emergency surgery has been carried out. I watch Michael, this lanky boy still growing into himself, holding his mother's hand tight. Marcia, her eleven-year-old, the youngest, sits quietly beside him. Her eyes wide, darting, taking it all in.

Inside I hear Ms Lorez say, 'Give me more time, please, me pickni dem, oh please, me pickni. I ain't shown dem how to live. How Marcia goin' survive, seeing what she seen? Who goin' keep Michael from trouble? He ain't got no proper sense. Please, me pickni.'

There is a noise, a slight sound, a hollow sound, it comes from behind. It screeches, its pitch getting louder as it approaches. Like a dart – no, a bullet – it travels through the universe, faster than a meteorite, it travels through the heavens, on a mission, bursting through the sky into the light. Time, time, a millionth of a second, it flashes through the window, pierces into her body, lifts her soul, and in this millionth of a second, she gasps, '*Protect dem . . .*' In that moment she sees me. I see her. Our eyes meet. Then tension, life, leaves her body.

And in that moment the air is stagnant, but alert. I hear a man's booming laughter drift through the corridor, the click-click of a wall clock, the muffled voices of visiting relatives, the sound of fresh-mint-flavoured adverts from the TV room and Adam Ant's 'Stand and Deliver' song seep under the door and through the pores in the walls, invading the silence.

The air molecules surrounding the two young people float like a leaf and settle on their shoulders. Marcia jumps, the metal chair legs squeal against the green lino; it plays a discordant tune. She raises her hands into mid-air and shakes them in a drying motion over her mother's face. Michael doesn't move, he can't move.

'Mum, Mum, Mummy,' says Marcia, looking at Ms Lorez's cold eyes.

Her mother's arm swings freely down the side of the bed. Marcia bends over and gives her a shake.

'No,' she cries. 'No!'

Marcia's scream travels through the room; it slaps her brother across the face and runs down the corridor to grab two nurses and a policeman at the reception desk. They freeze, then go running towards the sound.

'You promised!' cries Marcia, holding her mother's hand to her small chest. Her thoughts run back to last Tuesday.

'Mum, when we gonna have our day together?' she'd asked Ms Lorez.

'I'll take a day off next week, Marcia. I won't go anywhere, baby. It'll be just you and me.'

'But Mum, you always say that.'

'I know, but honest, baby, this time I promise.' She cupped Marcia's chin in her hand. 'I promise.'

It's my fault, thinks Marcia. *It's my fault she wasn't at work. She should have been at work. It's my fault she's dead.*

The two nurses and the policeman run into the ward. They see Michael sitting calmly in his seat and Marcia bent over Ms Lorez's body, the tears streaming down her face. The Sister goes over and takes Marcia in her arms; her touch, not yet warm as she's just come on duty, removes any control Marcia has inside.

'Mum! Oh, Mum. No way. Get up, please! It's me – it's me.' So there she is just standing and screaming for her mother, the ordeal of the morning, the terrible event playing in her mind.

The Sister holds her, while the tears keep pouring down her cheeks, nothing to stop the hurt, the memory, the Sister holding on, holding her tight, patting her back trying to soothe away the pain, but there isn't anything you can say, nothing you can do to ease the pain of losing your mother. But now this little girl, Marcia, can't scream any more and collapses against the Sister.

'Are you okay?' asks the Sister.

Marcia nods her head.

'Would you like a nice cup of tea?'

The Sister sees the puzzled look on Marcia's face and glances over at the policeman. He turns to Michael, standing quietly near the bed.

'How old are you?' he asks.

'Sixteen.'

'Can we contact your father?'

'I don't have one. He left years ago.'

'What about another adult I can call?'

'Uncle Fred. I've called him,' says Michael.

'Your mother's brother?'

'No, family friend.'

'Family friend?'

'Yes. My mother and his wife were friends as kids.'

'Can I have his number?'

Michael gives it to him.

'By the way, where were you when it happened?'

'At work. Marcia phoned me.'

'And what—'

'That will do, Constable. You can ask questions later when their uncle gets here,' says the Sister.

The constable frowns.

'You two go with Nurse Iris now and she'll get you a nice cup of tea,' says the Sister.

Nurse Iris holds the door open, gives the two a warm smile, and Marcia and Michael follow her silently out of the room.

'It's so sad,' says the Sister.

The policeman shakes his head. 'It doesn't surprise me.' He flicks through his notes. 'Caribbean, about forty, single parent. Could be a boyfriend that did it. It's sad. That little girl's probably seen a lot already.'

'You know much about them?' asks the Sister.

'See it day in and day out in my job, and their area of Brixton isn't the best. Only have to look at the statistics. Lot of crime there. I'm out every day on patrol.'

'*Statistics*,' thinks the nurse and she nods her head. *It's a shame about these people.* Then she hurries out of the room to get things sorted.

Drawn curtains darken the room, clothes litter the floor, and the pungent smell of excrement fills the air. In the far corner of the room is a single bed on which he sits rocking back and forth, while he uses his shit to write cryptic messages on the wall. Sweat pours from him, leaving damp patches on his dirty navy tracksuit. His eyes dart from left to right, following the sound of the traffic coming in from the street; it speaks to him.

He jumps off the bed and laughs. It will be all right now, *he thinks. He's done his duty. All will be good.* Time is alive. The maggots within will no longer take away my soul.

Voices congratulate him. 'Yes,' *he says.*

Now is the moment he has restored peace. No more evil exists now he has made the holes to set it free. The evil spirit has escaped from the prison of her body. She'll be okay, *he thinks. He is her saviour. The evil of fathers, of abandoning loves, of unspoken words, of decaying insides and wanting will no longer hurt her. She will no longer carry the evil spirit inside her, as he carries it in him.*

He picks up a knife, ready to puncture more holes, to free the evil left behind by the deprivation of recognition, the wanting and hunger for love from his father, from his birth mother, from the world, for the empty promises that never bore fruit and the silent dull ache that hums ever so quietly, barely noticeable, within. He holds the knife high above his head, but the voices in his head speak. 'You must not sacrifice yourself, it is not time to die, if the evil escapes it will enter someone else. You must not allow it to escape, you must protect others from the evil. He, the Evil, the Father, will escape.'

And I see the layers of abuse, of unknown struggle, unaddressed pain, passed down from generation to generation, not understanding, not comprehending. Buried deep, it bubbles inside, pushed down, but it oozes out, into this.

Uncle Fred paces the sitting room, occasionally fidgeting with the net curtain to see if he can see Eliza, his wife, making her way up the tree-lined road from her job at the old people's home in Clapham.

He looks up and down the row of Victorian terraced houses on the Brixton–Clapham borders. They live in the end house, with a garage. He looks across the road over the tops of the parked cars; he can only make out the heads and shoulders of two youths deep in conversation walking by. He lets go of the curtain and goes upstairs to the bedrooms to glance in at the children and they are sound asleep, worn out from a hard day's play. He takes a look at his watch. She'll be back any minute. He grabs his keys, leaves a note and hurries out of the house, jumps on a number 88 bus as it passes the bottom of the street.

He gets off near Westminster Bridge and makes his way up to the ward. A young nurse shows him into the room. He notices the policeman standing at the window first, then Michael holding Marcia on the two-seater, and then their eyes. His eyes are as dry and hot as the Skeleton Coast. Hers are ransacked.

Before Nurse Iris can open her mouth to say the words, he knows. Maybe it's the way she ushers him in and closes the door, or the way the policeman stands so solemnly at the window, or what he sees in Marcia's eyes, or the way Michael can't quite look at him, but the truth is that it's his age. Age has taught him to know death's scent and he smelt it as soon as he came out of the lift – these things are simple confirmations. Fred wraps his arm around Marcia, then reaches out to rub the boy, Michael, on the back.

The policeman speaks: 'I'm afraid I have to ask Marcia some questions. She's the only witness.'

Fred nods his head.

'Can you tell me what happened?'

'Mum sent me to throw away the rubbish but when I came back, he . . . he—'

'It's all right, Marcia, it's all right,' says Uncle Fred as Marcia buries her face into his chest. 'Hush now, hush. Who is he, Marcia?'

'Simon.'

'Simon?' Uncle Fred repeats.

Marcia nods and buries her head deeper into his chest, sobbing uncontrollably.

Uncle Fred looks up at the policeman and says, 'She's had enough for today. Can me and you continue this outside?'

'I suppose I've got most of what I want. She gave a statement to my colleague on-site but that was before it turned into a murder investigation. I'll talk to him to confirm things. We'll do our best to find him.' The policeman puts on his helmet and leaves the room with Uncle Fred. Five minutes later Uncle Fred returns.

'Can I see her again?' Michael asks Nurse Iris. It's almost two hours since he last saw his mother's body and he wants to check that there are no mistakes, that she's really dead, that this is not a joke.

'I don't know if—'

'Please.'

The nurse looks at Fred, he looks at Michael and sees the pleading in his eyes, and he turns and nods.

'Okay. We've moved the body. If you wait I'll try and sort it out.'

'I'll go too,' says Marcia.

'I don't think that's a good idea,' answers Nurse Iris.

'I was there when she died. Please.'

Nurse Iris looks towards Fred and Marcia squeezes his hand.

The three stand in the dim light of the morgue. Fred holds back and allows Marcia and Michael to go in front. Ms Lorez's body lies on a metal gurney, still, not the way they remember. There is hope in their hearts that this drugged-up haze isn't real. That their protector, the one who spread her arms and let them climb into her warmth, who laughed and barked, isn't lying in front of them with that stillness. Not a sleeping stillness, there is peace in that; not a thinking stillness, there is continuation in that; but this cold, empty stillness that leaves nothing.

Michael picks up Ms Lorez's heavy hand and squeezes as hard as he can to wake her up. Marcia clings to his arm. He sees it in Ms Lorez's eyes; death in her eyes. Marcia holds on to Michael even tighter, stopping the blood flow in his arm. He feels her grip and her weight begins to drown him. He feels the water flooding his mouth; he opens wider and tries to breathe harder. In an instant, he shoves his sister aside, and runs out of the morgue. 'He did this – I'll kill him!' he shouts. 'I'll kill him. I'll kill him.' His cries echo down the corridor.

Michael jumps on a passing bus. Fred is chasing behind but gives up, bends over, clutching his chest, as he watches Michael and the bus disappear down the road. Hospital staff come running on to the pavement. Fred nods his head towards the bus as it disappears under the arches on Westminster Bridge Road.

Michael heads to the hostel on Landor Road, not far from the South Western Hospital. Big Charlie, a local and owner of the café under the Brixton railway bridge, has told Michael he'll find Simon there.

'Charlie said he might be here,' says Michael to the hostel clerk.

The old clerk at the grimy reception desk shakes his head. 'Ain't been back here since the police came lookin' for him. Left his room in a real state. Have to repaint it,' he shouts after Michael as he hurries out the door.

Michael heads into Brixton on foot. Down Electric Avenue, up Acre Lane, down Ferndale Road, Railton Road, asking the men on the Frontline if they've seen him. Searching for him at friends' houses, at old hang-out joints, among the faces he passes, through shop windows and in cars that linger at traffic lights. Searching till the soles of his feet hurt so much that he can't take another step. Then, and only then, does he slide down on to the pavement outside the Fox & Hounds, opposite the Ritzy, and sit back against the pub wall, holding his head in his hands. He lets out a wail. Pedestrians cross quickly to avoid him. But the tears don't come. They won't come. He can't let them go. Anger and frustration all crunched up like waste paper, soaking up the tears in him till there's nothing left to flow out. And when it's crunched up like that, soaking it up like that, if it doesn't come, it stays and mutates, and changes into something hard but brittle, and it's the something left behind that really makes you worry.

A police car slows and hovers at the kerb near Michael, hesitates, before moving on to stop and search a group of three black lads hanging out further down the road.

Michael dials a number in the red phone box, a faint tang of urine in the air.

'Uncle Fred.'

'You calmed down yet?' asks Uncle Fred.

'Yes, sir.'

'Just as well. You never know what injury he might have done you. I just hope the police find him before he injures anyone else. You better get some things over at the flat for you and Marcia and come on over here.'

'Yes, sir.'

Michael's key rattles in the lock and clicks into position. He pushes open the door, breaks the police tape and stands for a second. He holds his shoulders up, shivers a little, wishes for his uncle. This is déjà vu. How many times has he stood at this door opening it as he just has, but he didn't pause then, then it was home, inside there was warmth and a rough peace that he belonged in. He wanted to rush in and share stories about people and friends he met out in the world beyond the estate, at Clapham Manor College, or Dozers raves at the youth centre, or his part-time job at the local supermarket. He would open it eager to tell, the words clattering out like table tennis balls, rushing into the kitchen or sitting room or bedroom to spark off Ms Lorez and feed from her nods and chuckle laugh. But this is déjà vu – not the proper déjà vu, but the kind you have in the middle of a nightmare.

He closes the front door behind him. Ahead is the door to the sitting room, and around the corner from that are the kitchen and bathroom. Ms Lorez's bedroom is the first on the left; their rooms are further on. On the white walls leading from Ms Lorez's room is blood – a handprint is stencilled among the stains. He wanders towards his room at the far end of the hall, past Ms Lorez's open door, avoids looking in, opens his wardrobe, pulls down the navy carryall, packs his clothes, then moves to Marcia's room and packs her things. But like Lot's wife, before Christ, before England was born, he cannot help himself. Warnings whirl in his head crying for him not to look in the room – the problem is they draw attention to it – and his head is dragged like iron towards a magnet. He looks inside.

Everything is left as it was, folded clothes remain on the bed and floor, a broken chair lies on the carpet, three legs sticking up in the air, its back split in two. Her creams and bottles are scattered at the bottom end of the dressing table, its mirror shattered into pieces.

And there is blood on the carpet, mixed in with the broken glass. 'Oh God,' he breaks into a sob. And then he runs. Out of the flat, through the estate, past the swings and the small patch of green in the centre of the U-shaped courtyard, down the road, jumps on to the 37 bus that waits, as if it knows, as if it has heard him calling. *Ding ding.* It starts up. He peers through the back window as the estate disappears into the night. The other passengers speculate at his haste and the blood stains on his carryall. He wonders if his life will ever be the same again.

3

Walk Good

TWO WEEKS LATER the police are still looking for Simon. The question is, will he hurt anyone else before they get to him? But that is not on Michael's immediate mind. They – Michael and Eliza, Uncle Fred's wife – sit in the funeral directors', picking out coffins to bury Ms Lorez in. The room is at the rear, lit dimly with a sixty-watt bulb, but no windows. Decorated well enough and pleasantly enough for a Mavis or a Daisy wanting to bury their husband of sixty-five, seventy years, but not for a sixteen-year-old boy whose biggest concern should be, like for so many others, who will win the FA cup. Instead he sits at a desk with his Auntie Eliza, listening to the latest in coffin designs.

'You'll like the silk interior – it's one of our bestsellers,' says the assistant.

'How much?' asks Auntie Eliza, leaning forward to look more closely at the brochure.

The assistant names a hefty price.

'These things are expensive. What do you think, Michael?'

Michael isn't sure. He has one hundred and fifty pounds he was saving to go on holiday to Wales this summer. It would have been his first ever holiday, his first time leaving London. Four hundred from his mother's savings account, plus three hundred from Uncle Fred and Auntie Eliza. In total eight hundred and fifty pounds. It's not enough to also pay for the hearse, the flowers, the food and the coffin. His cheeks glow red with embarrassment; it cuts away at his manhood.

'What about the other one in that brochure?' he asks stiffly.

'You mean the Royale?' A further hefty price is quoted.

He scratches his head. His hair needs a cut, but these things go unnoticed. Ms Lorez would have noticed it; she would have made him cut it. He's confused about everything – norms are not norms, constants are no longer constant, and the uncertainty of money and all its implications hit him. The electricity bill and the gas bill and the phone bill and the water bill and the TV licence and food and clothing and Marcia's fees and all the other bills that Ms Lorez took care of now fall on his shoulders. But the question that runs through his mind like a sprinter in a hundred-metre race is: how are they going to survive on his weekly wage of thirty pounds from the supermarket?

He wants to laugh at the madness of it all and break this glass balloon cocooning him from the shrillness. Eliza reaches over and touches his hand.

'It's expensive. You have anything else?' she asks the assistant.

He can just make out the sound of the busy traffic on Brixton High Street and above it two male voices in heated argument. He smells the tension and starts to feed off it, taking little baby bites. After all, he's a baby – a sixteen-year-old baby who has to grow up.

'I don't like the metal,' says Michael, shaking his left knee.

'Sorry, what you say?' says Eliza.

'I don't like the metal. It's rigid. My mother wasn't rigid – firm but not rigid. I don't like the metal.'

'All right, we won't have the metal. Can we see the ones in wood again?'

'Yes, madam. We also have an all-inclusive package if you want, with a choice of the two coffins in the picture over there, and we will embalm the body and dress her nicely. It also includes delivery to the home address for the wake and then on to the cemetery.'

'We want to do the final dressing ourselves,' says Eliza.

'We can arrange that too.'

Michael fidgets in his chair. He clears his throat to hear the sound, to confirm its reality.

'Can we take the brochure with us and then decide?' asks Eliza.

The assistant hesitates, looks quickly at the two in front, Michael and Auntie Eliza, then says, 'I'm afraid it's my only one. If you want, there's a place that does copies off Atlantic Road – you could make a copy of it there as long as you bring it back.' She emphasizes the bringing back.

It pushes something in Michael. He leans forward. 'You want me to photocopy coffins to bury my mother in? You want me to stand in a queue like I'm photocopying a menu or a flyer and photocopy coffins to bury my mother in?' His voice rises as he speaks.

'Michael, calm down.'

'What do you mean "calm down"?' he says, starting to shake. 'I'm calm – I'm fucking calm.'

'Since when did you start using that kind of language? The lady's only trying to be helpful. Calm down.'

He falls silent. 'Sorry, Auntie Eliza. I'm sorry, I'm so sorry.' His voice cracks. Suddenly he gets up and rushes out of the little room. He throws open the front door leading on to the road, but there are people blocking his way. He squeezes by, weaving his way out through the crowd building outside the funeral parlour, which is opposite the police station. He spots a line of police cars across the road. A young black man sits in the back of one of the cars, his face bruised and scrunched up in pain. A Rasta behind Michael shouts,

'That boy ain't done nothing.' Another voice shouts, 'Get the boy to hospital!'

'Move along now. There's nothing for you to see here,' says a policeman.

'Can't you see the boy da bleed?' calls another man in the crowd. 'It don't take eleven policemen to hold an injured youth. He ain't done nothing. Take him to hospital.' But somewhere else across Brixton another black boy is being stopped and searched, and another black mother's house is being ransacked. The quiet tension murmurs, it hums and builds.

Michael ignores the commotion and pushes his way through the crowd, turns left, crosses the road and walks briskly up the high street. He thinks, he doesn't think, as he bumps into other pedestrians, who glare after him. Then he stops, stands in the middle of the pavement, at the point where Brixton High Street becomes Brixton Hill. Across the road, in the centre, stands St Matthew's Church, majestic and gothic with its graves and opulent stone carvings. The church building is in disrepair. It acts like a roundabout splitting the high street in two, sending traffic off in three different directions, one to Tulse Hill, the second to Streatham, and the last redirected back into Brixton. Further up the hill on the opposite side, three people wait at the bus stop, and beyond that is a park area belonging to the estate, with trees and hedges hiding the block of flats from view. Michael stands on the busy road as traffic passes, and looks up through a gap in the trees towards his block. He can make out the top half of his window. He wants to go home, to open its door just like he's done so many times before and feel its warmth welcome him in. He wants to go home, but home is no longer home now she's not there. He wants to go back there, for he's tired of being cooped up in Uncle Fred's house, tired of people's sympathy and their carefulness and the constant tension that fills the air.

'Michael!' calls a voice. 'Michael, you all right there?'

It's Devon. Devon was Michael's best friend at primary school. Ms Lorez never warmed to him. She said there was something short about his smile, it didn't show all of him, but instead he seemed to want to hide himself in it. They, Devon and he, have grown apart over the years but they often bump into each other on the street or at parties, or on the Frontline among the guys who controlled the area as Michael passed by.

'You all right there, mate?' he calls again. He comes over, hands in pockets.

'Sure.'

'Where you heading?'

Michael scratches his head.

'You're walking there like you're a zombie, mate.'

'I don't know, I . . . The market – I'm going to the market.'

'You sure? You seem a bit confused.'

Michael nods. A lorry clatters past, drowning anything he might have said.

'You want me to come with you?'

'I'll be fine.'

'Sure now?'

'Yeah, don't worry.'

'I tell you what, why don't you pop round mine when you've finished? We can talk about old times.'

'Yeah, I'll do that.'

'Laters, right?'

'Yeah, laters.'

'Come in, come in,' Devon says, opening the door wider. 'I didn't think you'd come. Not so soon.'

Michael nods his head and looks quickly over Devon's shoulder into the hallway and hesitates. Now he's here he's not so sure. He needs a break from the closeness of Uncle Fred's place, so he enters. Devon shuts the front door behind him with a loose click.

Devon is much shorter than Michael but stockier. The best way to describe him would be to say that whereas Michael is like a bullet, Devon is like a hammer. There's no mistaking Devon's presence: his muscular frame comes from his father's side, but his skin is very pale and his brown Afro hair has a hint of red in it, which comes from his Irish mother. These two, Devon and Michael, were notorious at school. They were the only ones in their year able to emulate Starsky and Hutch routines. Simon taught Michael well, made him practise by sliding across random car bonnets parked downstairs on the estate. They were the two that girls wanted to be caught by during kiss-chase. The ones that Stacey Nathans, the most experienced girl in the school, showed her six-million-dollar knickers to in the girls' toilets behind the gym. They were a team. But that was before Michael's father left and the fear of losing Ms Lorez and wanting to please her caged his wild spirit.

The flat is almost identical to his, built on another part of the estate further in from the main road than Michael's. Its shape is home, its smell isn't, but the familiarity of the space puts him at ease. He follows Devon down the hallway into the sitting room. It's mid-afternoon and the curtains are drawn. Devon reaches over the couch and clumsily pulls them open. The air is stale from old socks, trainers and bits of sensi scattered over the coffee table and sprinkled on the carpet. A half-smoked joint lies in the ashtray. Devon picks up the joint, motions for Michael to sit and lights it, taking a long hard drag. His eyes crease into a smile. There are small dark freckles on the bridge of his nose.

'Breakfast,' he jokes. 'You want some?'

Michael gives a weak smile. 'Don't smoke.'

'You always were square.'

There's a silence. Michael begins to wonder why he came.

'But I've always admired you. It didn't matter what me and the others decided to do, like the time at school we decided to take those tyres from round the back and you wouldn't have any of it, or when we teased those woola woolas – you know, the African kids. You always knew your own mind.'

'Did I?' says Michael.

'But your mum, man, I was frightened of her. She wouldn't let you play out like the rest of us. Maybe that's why you never got in trouble like us. She's a good one.'

When Michael's mother ran out on them when he was four, and three years later, after two years of marriage to Ms Lorez, his father did the same, he thought if he was good, if he did the things Ms Lorez wanted him to do, if he only behaved, that she would stay, that somehow it would make a difference. It controlled him, but the truth is it didn't matter what he did or how he was, Ms Lorez was gone, and it hurt badly. It tore him in half each night and each day and each hour he was awake – the anger at her death, at the fact that none of it mattered now, and at the end of it all what he did, who he was, how he was, couldn't have stopped her death, like he couldn't have stopped his father or his mother. He reacts against it all, against her or him up there that took Ms Lorez away, 'cause it didn't matter any more, it plain didn't matter.

'You know what, I will have a puff.'

Devon hands him the joint. He holds it between his two fingers contemplating it. He sees God's face, Ms Lorez's God, and his disapproving nod, and takes a drag in reaction to it, then coughs and splutters.

'Easy, man, easy,' laughs Devon.

Michael smiles back through the haze.

'I miss those days,' says Devon.

'I miss them too.'

Michael hasn't realized until now how much he missed their friendship, and God knows he needs it.

'I tell you what, there's a good night next Friday at the club down the way. I've got some business happening there. Do you wanna come?'

'What kind of business?'

'A bit of this and that. Why you so interested?'

'I don't know. I'm just curious.'

'Well, anyway, you coming?'

'I've got—' Michael thinks of his part-time job at the Spar supermarket and his college course, which he's not attended this past week. But none of that matters now. He thinks, *Thirty pounds isn't gonna get us very far and I'm gonna have to give up college for a while.*

'Yeah, definitely,' he says.

'So how's your old lady? I thought she didn't like you hanging out with the likes of me.'

'Well, things change.'

'What do you mean?'

'Nothing.'

Michael doesn't know why he said it that way or didn't say it at all. Maybe for once, since her death, he wants to be somewhere or with someone where he can pretend that everything is all right, that the last two weeks didn't happen. Or maybe he's saying it indirectly, subconsciously, as it came, as death came, as casually as it's now destroying him, as if his own wishes, his wants, his needs count for nothing.

'Nothing. It doesn't matter. I'd better go. See you Friday then,' says Michael. He gets up and leaves, makes his way over to Uncle Fred's flat and the awkward silences that await him.

*

Delores Sonia Watson will be buried today in Streatham Cemetery, plot A of row 679. The hearse makes its way up Streatham High Road, a succession of black cars following on behind. At the church, old-time friends meet again, their talk subdued, some laughing at past memories, at brief glimpses of Ms Lorez remembered before silence descends.

Marcia sits in the Rolls-Royce, her forehead plastered to the window, watching the dreary clouds high up in the sky and wondering if they too have had enough. She clutches the scarf around her neck, her mother's scarf, the only thing she grabbed from the flat, from the hooks where they hung their coats. Auntie Eliza said it might be cold by the graveside. She smells it, buries her face deeper into its folds, then lets go and gazes out the window again. Tears have fallen outside and in, dripping down through her throat into the pit of her stomach, filling her up with grief. The other women in the car find it awkward but Auntie Eliza understands. She reaches out and holds her hand, not offering wise words like the others, just holding her small hand between hers.

The cemetery gates are ahead, the cars make their way to the plot, some reverse in, doors slam, over two hundred people are already waiting around Ms Lorez's graveside.

The gravediggers stand two hundred yards away observing the crowd, impatiently waiting, half wanting them to leave so they can get on with the job, but looking forward to the collection that will be taken after the funeral. In the distance, a middle-aged English couple stand burying their beloved eighty-six-year-old aunt.

When all the mourners appear to have arrived, the local Church of England vicar, short and stout in stature, stretches up to see over heads, checking for anyone else still making their way up the hill. His balding head shines and small droplets of rain bounce off his russet-freckled crest. He begins.

'We are gathered here today to lay to rest . . .'

The crowd listen to his words. His clipped English manner gives them a cold, regimented tone, totally unlike anything Ms Lorez was. She's not yet faded in their minds, her image is as warm and round as it was three and a half weeks ago when she was still alive.

'Happy are the dead who die in the faith . . .'

A faint musty smell of ginger and cooked kidney beans drifts through the air; a butterfly lands on top of the wooden coffin and flutters its wings, before lifting off. Eliza smiles.

'. . . for he knows of what we are made; he remembers that we are but dust . . .'

The coffin is lowered. 'We commit her body to the ground: earth to earth, ashes to ashes, dust to dust.'

Michael and Marcia come forward slowly, peer over the side, and throw soil on to the coffin. The vicar closes the Bible in his hand, signalling the end of the funeral. The crowd stands waiting for more; it's so short, they don't feel they've given Ms Lorez a proper send-off. Fred Bailey, wearing a black jacket, begins to sing a slow song, his bass voice growing more resonant with every beat. His wife Eliza, dressed in a black suit, a gold chain twinkling at her neck, and small black pumps, joins him. They both sing Ms Lorez's favourite song, reminding everyone of church back in Jamaica.

'It soon be done, all my troubles and trials
When I get home, on the other side
I'm gonna lie down beside my sweet Jesus
I'm gonna . . .'

One by one, members of the crowd join in the singing until they are all captured in the moment, their voices trembling in the wind. Those who knew Ms Lorez well, and even those who did not, cry for their own individual reasons. This is a time for contemplation, a time for evaluating their own meeting with death.

Marcia weeps uncontrollably, her narrow shoulders heaving up and down, and Auntie Eliza hugs her tightly to her bosom, restraining her from jumping in with her mother's body. Michael is dangerously calm. Uncle Fred sees a redness to his eyes and pats him on the back trying to comfort this boy–man as best he knows how. As another song begins to rise up, Fred notices the shovels standing in the heaped earth to the side of the grave. He hands one to Michael. 'You're a man now,' he says.

Michael stiffens his shoulders, takes the shovel, and begins to hurl dirt on to Ms Lorez's coffin. Fred removes his jacket, carefully rolls up the sleeves of his white shirt, and joins in. His sons Stanford, Leroy and Mark join their father in covering the coffin.

Michael's friend Devon makes his way forward and whispers in his ear. 'I didn't know, mate, when I saw you last week. Why didn't you tell me? Stanford had to tell me.'

'I don't know.'

'I wish you'd told me: you and me are spars,' says Devon, and hugs him tight.

Michael hugs Devon back and neither wants to let go. 'Yeah,' he says, trying to hold on to it all. After all, he's a man now, not a boy.

Devon takes the spade from his senior, Stanford, and stands beside Michael to help him shovel dirt. The crowd continues to sing, in harmony now, until the coffin is properly buried.

'Come, baby. You cry that hurt out. Come now, it's time to go home.' Eliza guides Marcia to the hired car and they drive in silence to Uncle Fred's and Auntie Eliza's house, where food Eliza has prepared for the wake lies waiting.

Michael heads in the opposite direction, to their flat, his home, to get away from the two hundred guests, the tight space, their pitying looks, and the useless conversations that only make him want to cry and during which he never knows what to say or how to behave. Embarrassing silences and condolences which won't bring her back. Devon follows him.

'Wait up, man, I'm coming with you.'

At the same time as Ms Lorez is buried, in this year of 1981, I can see a riot begin to boil in Brixton. The many stop and searches fuelling it, like a pot of water over fire. Rumours spread like the sound of whispering trees. They gather momentum like the distant hum of a speeding train.

'The police kill dat bwoy. The one wey dem stab upon the Frontline. The police kill dat bwoy. Dem kill him; dem kill we. Kill him!' Bang! Impact. The riot erupts.

On one side are the police, marching on the crowd with riot shields and dustbin lids. On the other side are angry young men hurling bricks, bottles, petrol bombs, pieces of metal, and anything else they can get their hands on. Cars burn, shop fronts are smashed in and the streets are aglow with orange flames.

And I look on, remembering that night in Trelawny way back then, on the Island of Jamaica when I was alive, the fields of sugar cane ablaze with the revolts, burning, the fever for freedom, to fight till we lay down dead. I lifted my skirt and ran, torch in my other hand, setting alight whatever I could. I opened my mouth wide, screaming to let out the pain of working that plantation, of being treated as less than human, of being kept penned on that plantation like an animal. The tears streaming down my face, my hair as wild as they had made me, screaming out that madness, as the British troops tried to contain us. I understand what being under siege can do to a person. I felt it coming when the police descended on this area, knew it was coming. But I wonder if they even truly understand. I know it echoes inside them, that recognition of freedom being taken away as that baton of pain is passed on. So I watch the riot rage, its angry flames licking, pushing thick black smoke high into the South London sky.

Marcia watches from the Baileys' kitchen window as fire and smoke flicker on the horizon; it's as if the whole world is raging against her mother's death. She senses the chalky taste of fear and wonders if Michael is okay over there in the old flat.

The police appeared at the door just two hours after the funeral to give him the news. He took it with a nod.

'Just wanted to let you know that we arrested him this afternoon. Looks like he might have had an episode,' they said. 'We were passing by and saw the light on, thought it best to let you know in person.'

'Thanks,' he said, his face expressionless as he closed the front door.

But now Michael is pacing up and down, and something inside him simmers; it simmers until it begins to bubble, and bubble, and bubble.

'He killed her, Devon. Took a knife and stabbed the life out of her.' He clasps both hands to the top of his head and closes his eyes; his cheeks quiver.

Devon can only nod.

'Marcia has nightmares; she can't sleep, can't eat. I had to hold her for two hours last night.' He's shaking now, walking round and round the room, his voice uneven. 'Oh God, how could he do this to us? And all those lies, those damn lies he told – said he was off the stuff.'

'Calm down. It's gonna be all right.'

'How can it be? She's gone and I couldn't do anything. What were they doing? Ms Lorez warned them. I warned them. And now they come to tell me he's been arrested. It was so easy for the police to harass him whenever he went to pick up Marcia from school or as he walked the streets, wasn't it? A black man can't move out there without being stopped and searched every ten yards. But when we needed help, where the fuck were they? They couldn't keep an eye on him for just one week. One lousy fucking week.'

'Calm down.'

'Don't tell me to calm down!'

'I didn't mean it like that – I just mean you're not alone, Michael,' says Devon. He places a hand on Michael's shoulder, but it's shrugged off.

'I'm so fucking angry with all of it. Tell me, for fuck's sake, why it had to happen?'

'I don't know,' says Devon.

'All they had to do was keep him in. And look what they've fucking done to us.' Michael's voice cracks. In one move, he's grabbed a cup and smashed it against the sitting-room mirror.

'Calm down, mate. If you really have to start throwing things, then you're better off out there with them. Don't wreck your own place.'

Michael hesitates, looks over at Devon, his eyes dark. 'Then let's go.' He steps towards the door. Devon is still sitting. 'You coming?'

Devon sits, shaking his head, then he gets up and follows Michael into the hallway.

Michael hurls open the front door and sprints down the street to join the hot fury of young men.

Devon shakes his head again, throws his hands in the air and follows.

Outside, late afternoon, the riot still rages. A line of police charge the crowd, dispersing them. Michael and Devon dart down a side street towards the back of Ferndale sports centre, straight into a waiting police van.

'No!' shouts Devon. 'The other way.'

But Michael isn't fast enough. 'Leave me alone!' he shouts as a police officer pins him against the net fencing, spreads his legs apart and thrusts his arm halfway up his back.

'Why don't you pick on . . . ?' Michael winces in pain as the police officer forces his arm further up his back. Michael resists, but the officer wrestles him to the ground. Michael's body hits the ground hard.

'Bastard!' he shouts.

The officer presses his knee into his back. 'Shut your fucking mouth, wog, or I'll shut it permanently. If I had my way I'd send the whole bloody lot of you back on the next banana boat. Now get up.'

They force Michael to stand up, bundle him into the back of the van and slam the door. Inside, it takes a while for his eyes to adjust to the lack of light. He senses a presence to his left.

'You all right?' asks a deep voice.

It's Rizzlar, a big and fearless man and a legend on the Frontline, down by Railton Road. Michael breathes out with some relief and smiles a half smile. Rizzlar smiles back, reclines and begins to hum a Freddie McGregor tune. After the speed of recent events, Michael feels calmed. The doors open again. Three more men are piled in, secured in their seats. The doors slam. The van moves off through the pockets of rioters as bricks and insults are hurled at the windows.

They drive steadily for ten minutes. Eventually the van doors burst open and they are ushered into the station. The light hurts Michael's eyes.

'Name.'

'Michael Watson.'

'Address.'

'43 William House, Benny Estate.'

'All the cells are full up here. Put them in the basement.'

The basement's brick walls are painted over in yellow as if to disguise its purpose. Rizzlar takes the hard bed and laughs at him.

'This your first time here?'

'Yes.'

'Don't worry, it's worse than it looks. Just find somewhere to lie down – we're in for a long night.'

Michael gives him a small smile. They chat a bit and Michael is grateful for his presence.

An hour later I watched as they came for Rizzlar.

Fear was Michael's saviour that night. Fear sat fidgeting by his side, his only companion in that room. 'Go on, jump, wog, jump,' so he did, and fear helped him achieve the height, and with each jump he felt the yank in his balls, like someone trying to pull them off. And he felt powerless, less than, smaller than. Fear, shame and that feeling of being powerless will be his silent companions from now on. They will shadow him, and once in a while when he forgets, in the middle of laughter or in joy, they'll tap him on the shoulder and Michael will reach for his balls, making sure they're still there. Yes, that night, he was saved by his own fear.

Rizzlar never went home; he died in his cell. According to the police report he tripped and banged his head.

'One less wog to worry about. Shouldn't have tripped and killed himself.'

4

What Will Be?

MICHAEL WATCHES DEVON as he takes out nine empty plastic pouches from the glove compartment of his brother's Mini and carefully places an equal amount of weed in each. Michael shifts awkwardly in his seat, rubs his hands against his jeans and looks out the window. They're parked in the darkest part of the street; a little light shines from the street lamp further up the road. He sees a group of revellers making their way towards the club.

There's a knock on his window. Gary, a ginger-headed Scotsman brought up in the East End, stands outside. Devon gestures to Michael to unlock the door.

'All right, mate?' says Gary. He stands on the pavement leaning in. 'There's a good crowd tonight. The birds look real tight. One bird, she had legs right up to here.'

'Michael, Gary. Gary, Michael,' says Devon. 'Good friend of mine.'

'Pleased to meet you, mate,' says Gary, then turns back to Devon. 'Where's your brother?'

'Club down Clapham way.'

'Got the stuff ?'

Devon hands over the plastic packets.

Michael looks away and watches the club in the distance; a long queue is forming. 'Mr T's' is written in bold on the sign over the entrance. His eye wanders down the line at the men's suits, at the women's white stilettos. This is not the usual club Michael goes to, it's an older, wealthier crowd, with more white people than he's used to at the club nights at his local youth centre.

'Michael, do me a favour and lock up. We'll wait for you just outside,' says Devon as they get out the car. He heads off with Gary, the two of them, hands in pockets, deep in conversation.

'Yeah,' says Michael after them, and pulls on each door handle to check it's locked. He sees Devon and Gary separate. Gary starts to tout for business among the clubbers waiting patiently to go in, and as Michael watches Gary weave in and out, there's a worm of discomfort in his belly. And it's not the weed that makes him feel this way, for he grew up seeing it in his mother's, Ms Lorez's, medicine cabinet. Watched her stand over the stove, bring their old blackened kettle to the boil, to brew it in a tea and carefully hand a mug to friends and family seated at their kitchen table, to help ease away a pain or an ache that paracetamol couldn't reach. A recipe handed down to her from an ancestor long ago, before there were painkillers on the Island to numb the pain of the sugar planta-tion. And that ancestor learnt what she knew from her mother, a healer from the motherland, Africa, where she foraged in the bush, searching out plants: to brew on open wood fires; to give to the sick to soothe their aches away; to steam in huts while cradling babies to ease their coughs; to mash and compact and place over open wounds with a comforting word. Urgently called upon. Always welcomed. And as she sat upon that ship heading away from her home to the new land, sick from the beating and in sheer despair at her plight, little did she know there was even greater need for her awaiting her on that Island. No, it's not the weed, but their move-ments that disturb him, and as he catches up with Devon he hears

Ms Lorez in his ear, 'Can't trust a man whose smile is short.' And in that moment, Michael longs for his old life back. But life has changed; Brixton has changed.

This morning he had wandered through his neighbourhood looking at the debris left behind by the riot. The broken bottles and bricks lining the pavements, the smashed shop windows and mangled shutters, the burnt-out cars and the soot that seemed to cover everything. He stood outside the old supermarket where he used to work and examined the burnt shutters, wondered if it would ever open again, how he was going to pay the mounting bills, keep together the only family he has left. Devon had promised he might find work for him here at Mr T's. His mind wanders to the unopened bills lying on the kitchen table, to Marcia's social worker, her school fees. Then he breathes in deep and follows Devon down the stairs into the club.

It's Devon's home away from home. In here, men and women disconnect from families, jobs, bills, routine, or the disappointment of manhood, or the disappointment of womanhood. In here they dance, trade quick pleasures with one another, to ease away the pain of reality.

Michael looks around the space – it's dark and pulsates with big speakers at each corner. He stands with his back to one of them and allows the heavy bass to vibrate pleasantly through his body. A mirrorball hangs above the dance floor. Red, yellow and green lights randomly illuminate the clubbers.

'Wait here,' says Devon, raising his voice over the music. 'I'll be back.'

Michael stands near the entrance, watching. It's like a stage, and, like on a stage, the essential action takes place in the wings, in Tom the manager's office, or among the club hands that work behind the bar, or outside in the queue. Michael makes his way through the crowd to the bar on his left.

'Coke, please,' he shouts to the bartender, and leans on the bar to watch people around him. He guesses the majority to be around thirty. This makes him feel younger than his sixteen years. He clears his throat, tries to bulk out his shoulders.

'Sorry, mate, the pump is out. Only got beer at the moment.'

Michael agrees to the beer.

'Blue Arrow?'

'Yeah.' He collects his beer, takes a sip and winces at the bitter taste, but forces himself to drink it anyway.

He bobs his head to the music. Stevie's latest, 'Master Blaster', is playing. He hums, sings, looks over to the far corner and notices Devon in conversation with two white men, one in a suit, the other more heavily built, dressed all in black, a guy he presumes to be a bouncer.

It's a mixed club, and in his corner he's mainly surrounded by black men and white women. He watches the unspoken inter-actions. Catches the eye of a blonde. She smiles. He smiles back awkwardly. He guesses her to be roughly twenty-five, but her stare doesn't say 'little boy', like it would have if she'd been one of the older girls at his local youth club. Her stare adds power to him, power he doesn't have, stolen from watching shirtless black athletic muscle on TV, sprinting, pounding, winning, and as she'd watched those men while sitting on her couch at home, she could barely contain her own desires. So, here she is giving him a stare, brushing up against him. And he likes it, likes the reflection in her eyes; it gives him back a little of what he lost the night of the riots, that night Rizzlar died. Michael stands taller, he drinks from her desire, grows with it, it makes his dick harder, and he puffs out his chest to reflect that fantasy in her eyes. He doesn't see how she grips the drink tight in her slim hand. If only he'd seen her last Saturday night, lifting herself out of her own vomit, drinking away the pains of her own life, then maybe he would not stand here with such expectation.

'Sorry, mate, I didn't mean to leave you for so long.'

Michael tears his eyes away from hers to see Devon hovering beside him.

'Come over. Tom wants to meet you.'

Michael mouths an excuse to the girl and follows Devon. 'Did you take care of the business you said you had?'

'Oh, that. Yeah, yeah, no problem, mate,' he says. They enter an office at the back of the club.

'Tom, this is Michael, my mate I was telling you about. The one that lost his mum.'

'I'm sorry to hear that, son. I lost mine when I was thirteen. I know how hard it can be. Here, take a seat.'

Michael takes a seat.

'Devon here is a good lad – known him a long time. He's the son I never had.'

Devon grins widely.

'Used to date his mum in the old days, before she turned tricks . . .'

Devon's face falls.

'Had the most beautiful skin, white like porcelain, and hair as red as a sorrel horse – she was like an Irish mare. How is your mother these days?'

Devon shuffles his feet and looks at the ground. 'Fine, just fine.'

'You seen his brother Afton – as white as me he is, and this one's almost black like his father.' He laughs. 'Strange, isn't it? Oh, by the way, he turned up late again at the weekend. Do me a favour, Devon – push him out of bed, will you? Eight sharp he's supposed to start.'

Devon laughs. 'I think he's permanently attached to his bed.'

Tom laughs at the private joke, referring back to the months when he lived with them and tried to play stepfather.

'Devon tells me you might need some work,' he says to Michael.

Devon clears his throat and pipes up. 'Yeah, Michael's a bit of a square one, a casual job, like. At the door or helping with this and that around the club.'

Tom raises his eyebrows at Devon. They exchange a look.

'Yeah,' says Michael.

'You're not big enough to work on the door and not old enough for the bar but I could use someone to help with collecting the glasses, or shifting things or helping out in the cloakroom now and then.'

Michael looks hopeful.

'When you ready to start?'

'Now.'

'Seventy pounds for the Saturday and Sunday at the weekend, cash in hand.'

Michael grins happily.

'Welcome to the family, son.'

Michael moves back into Ms Lorez's flat today. Auntie Eliza and a friend came round to help clean up. Moving back in was easier than he thought. It's a month and a half since she died but there are moments when it seems, to him anyway, a lifetime ago. He's like force-ripened fruit: he's grown older but not sweeter, mature but not wiser, experienced but naive of the lessons to unfold.

'Now, you'll be okay, won't you? I don't know why you insisted on moving back here,' Auntie Eliza says, giving the small kitchen stove a final wipe down.

'I need to start getting on with things.'

'Well, we weren't stopping you.'

Michael doesn't know how to tell her how much he needs this space. He doesn't need the reminders, or the small talk with people he doesn't know, or to listen to their descriptions of his mother that he doesn't recognize. He especially doesn't need the charade, to tell the constant lie about what really happened the day she died, the pretence that some random stranger killed his mother, and every time he utters this lie it kills a little bit of him inside. What he really needs is to be alone and there is no other place than in this flat.

'You know Marcia will want to come back with you now you're here.'

'I know, and once I've settled, she will.'

'Don't be silly. How are you and her going to manage? You're a kid yourself.'

'We'll find a way.'

'It's bad enough that you've moved in here, let alone wanting to move Marcia in as well. How are you going to support the two of you? Do you think the social will let you take care of a child, when you're barely out of nappies yourself?'

'Marcia is the only family I have left and I'm the only one she has.'

'And now you gone and given up college. Ms Lorez—'

'I need the money, Auntie.'

'But still, Ms Lorez wouldn't—'

'I can always go back, but now I just need to show the social I can do it – keep Marcia and me together. I was hoping with your support, Auntie, we could do it.'

Eliza goes silent, then smiles weakly at him. 'You have my support, son.'

'Thank you.'

'Look at you. I know I keep asking you the same thing but, boy, why you do that to your hair?'

Michael touches the beginnings of locks on his head. He laughs and starts to gently push her towards the door. 'See you later, Auntie.'

'You've got the number, haven't you?'

'Yeah, I've got the number. See you later.'

'Call if you need something.'

'I will.'

He gives her a kiss and then she's gone.

'I'll be okay,' he says to himself as he makes his way back into the sitting room. He falls on to the couch, plays with his thumbs, switches on the television, switches off the television, rolls up a joint that Devon gave him, lights it and takes a few drags to steady his nerves. 'I'll be okay,' he says, his left knee shaking. 'I'll be okay.'

PART II

Ngozi

5

Awakening

Nigeria, 1981

IT IS SIX in the morning and the village of Obowi awakens. It stretches the sleep from its body and gives out little morning coughs and slipper shuffles. At first glance, not much has changed in Obowi, not since – well, not since I left my baby boy Uzo in the shrine, way back then when my yesterdays began, as far back as one of the village folk songs remembers. You see, roosters still flap their wings on top of yam hills to crow in the day. Women still rise to clank their pots on top of open fires. Children still scurry to fetch firewood from the bush and water from the stream. But underneath, hidden, that is where the changes are, dispersed around the village in objects that have been there so long they have become part of the landscape: in the cast-iron cannon and shackles that live in the grounds of the newly rebuilt Catholic church on the path to the village; in the World War II wireless, which sleeps quietly in the bush; in the old military tank sitting under the *ekpili* tree, swallowed among the cassava fields; in the satellite dish attached to the yellow hut over there. These things hint at the villagers' past and present, at the sweat and tears, and at the ghosts and souls buried beneath the dust.

It's in this village, eleven years ago now, that I met Ngozi. It was her eyes that held me the night she came yelling into this world. Those big bright eyes shaped like teardrops, which reminded me of my baby girl. They shimmered like silver, reflecting her might, and I could not help but marvel at the ferocity in her cry as this tiny girl opened her mouth wide and screamed for life. I'm telling you, she fought, fought through the fever that killed five the day before, to be born into this dirt.

Ngozi lives in the small hut over there, the one covered with crumbling plaster and with the rusty zinc roof. The walls were once white but the red dust tamed it long ago, like it does most things. You can see the conquests of this soil in the old, whose backs are crooked from sowing empty dreams; in the poor, their skin turned to leather from bending in the feverish sun; in the young, whose eyes are bloodshot and irritated by a harvest of frustrated desires. The only ones who escape hang inside the huts like pop stars, captured on Obowi society calendars, smiling down like deities – the doctors, the lawyers, the businessmen and -women, who no longer live among them but somewhere, out there, in the cities where they went to be educated and from which they never returned.

Inside the hut, Ngozi lies quiet beside her three sleeping siblings: Blessing, Emeka and Ike. She listens to the old familiar sound of Blessing's breath in her left ear, her mother's humming which waltzes in from the yard. Tucked discreetly within the folds of the hum is the crackle of *akara* as her mother places more mixture into sizzling oil.

'Blessing,' she hisses in the dark.

Her younger sister mumbles and turns away.

'Blessing,' says Ngozi.

'What?'

'What do you mean "what?"'

'Ngozi, I'm sleeping.'

'I need to talk, O,' she says and nudges Blessing in the ribs again.

'Leave me now!'

'Please.'

'What?'

'I want to talk.'

'Then talk.'

Ngozi hesitates. 'It's going to be strange.'

'Is that what you woke me for?'

'I'm scared, O.'

'Scared of what?'

'What if . . . what if I . . . I mean, I don't know them – they're strangers.'

'Don't worry. Mr Tobenna said the Asikas are nice people.'

'I know but . . . but the stories I've heard . . . I wish I didn't have to go.'

'I wish you weren't going, too. You know once you're gone Mama will expect me to take over.'

'Yes, but I've shown you how to do it all now.'

'But it's not the same.'

'I know . . .'

'And she'll expect me to go with her to the market.'

'I know, but you and Emeka will share.'

'It's not the same. Besides, when I get to secondary age does that mean Mama will want to send me away too?'

'I don't know. At least you still have two years before then,' says Ngozi.

'Are you excited?' asks Blessing. 'Enugu is such a big place.'

'I know. Mr Tobenna said it was three times, maybe four times bigger than Obowi.'

'I was wondering,' says Blessing, 'in a place that big, could you get lost?'

'Don't be silly.'

'What if you do?'

'I don't know.'

'I heard Mr Tobenna and Mama talking yesterday – he said there are armed robbers there.'

'And so?'

'What if they come after you?'

'Blessing, you're not helping, O.'

'I'm only saying what Mr Tobenna told Mama.'

'Blessing, just go back to sleep.'

'I was only—'

'Never mind. Just go back to sleep.'

Blessing snorts, glares at her sister in the dark, then turns. 'One minute you say you want to talk, the next you want me to go back to sleep. Make up your mind,' she mumbles, curls up and closes her eyes.

Ngozi rises from the mat and feels for her little brother. With a tug she pulls Ike up from the mat on to her hip. He stirs, moans, then nestles his head back on to her shoulder.

Out in the cool breeze of the yard, the smell of burning firewood greets her and flames from neighbouring compounds wave at her through the bush-and-stick partitions. She hears the neighbours' quiet chatter, Mama Nkoli's shriek at her daughter and the squeak of metal buckets as others prepare to fetch water.

A fat mosquito buzzes in her ear and she lifts her hand to swat the bully.

The dreaded morning looms ahead. She holds her little brother a little tighter. Giant shadows sway over their heads, threatening to swallow them whole. Mr Tobenna, Stella's father, has told Ngozi that everything in the city of Enugu is louder and faster and bigger, and out in the hugeness of the dawn darkness this thought sends a shiver down her spine.

'Morning, Ma,' says Ngozi as she adjusts her little brother, then bends to kiss her mother who squats by the fireside.

'*I boola chi*,' greets Nneka with a sad smile. 'Are you almost ready?'

'Yes, Ma. I've shown Blessing what to do when I'm gone.'

Nneka smiles again. 'I heard.'

'Are you sure you'll be okay without me? I mean . . . I want to learn but I don't want to leave you.'

'Don't worry, we will manage.'

'But, Ma, who is going to help you in the market?'

'Blessing.'

'But Blessing has school.'

'Ngozi, don't worry. You'll be of more use to me once you have an education.'

'But what if they don't like me? What if I don't know how to do the things they want?'

'Hmmm, O. Ngozi, come here.' Her mother reaches out and touches her face. 'You know if I had the money I wouldn't send you away, but I want more for you than I can afford, and this is the only way I know how. Now, please, just try your best.'

'Yes, Ma. Ma, what is Enugu like? The Asikas' house, is it big? Is it small? Is—'

'Ngozi, enough, O, hurry and bathe your brother.'

'Yes, Ma.'

Ngozi watches the side of her mother's face as she pokes the *akara* in the big frying pan. It crackles and spits. The flames from the open fire flicker, shadows march across her mother's face – light, shadow, light – and in that moment before shadow crosses again, in that flicker, Ngozi hugs her brother even tighter. You see, she – her mother – will not be there every morning when Ngozi rises or every evening when she sleeps. She'll not see her smile, or hear the words that have nourished her mind, a little each day, enough to grow. In that flicker, as if storing harvest for the dry season, she locks the wise words she can remember, like pearls, in her treasure trove. When she's older, she'll unlock it and admire her simple inheritance.

Ngozi puts Ike down at the corner of the house and throws a cloth over the line above her head to create a bathroom, collects water from the rain drum and begins to scrub him vigorously. When they are both bathed and clothed, she hands her brother over to her mother and hurries over to wake up Emeka and Blessing. It's a mile to their mission primary school.

Ngozi finishes her breakfast quickly. It's Friday and many people will pass through the depot on their way to work or to the towns or cities for the weekend. But Ngozi has more than trade on her mind, she wants to say goodbye to the man she knows as father. So she hurries, sets up her mother's store by the roadside, fills her tray with fruit and groundnuts, shapes a piece of cloth into a circular pillow, places it and the tray on her head and readies herself for the three-mile walk ahead.

Ngozi's bare feet sink into the red sand. 'Will he be there?' she asks herself as she walks along the dirt track. 'And if he is, what do I tell him? Does he know? Has Mama told him?' She strides along the path, her arms stretched upwards to grip the tray on her head. She feels the sun as it rises, its heaviness on her arms, the prickle of sweat between her shoulder blades, and the ground heat up until her feet are hot then cool, hot then cool. Each step carries her towards the answers.

Further along the path a woman stands outside a shop unlocking the padlock at the door.

'Good morning, Mama Chiedu,' calls Ngozi.

'Morning.'

A smile spreads across Ngozi's face, and her lips part to let out the words that threaten to collide in her mouth. 'Mama Chiedu, did Mr Tobenna tell you? This Sunday I go to Enugu. I don't want to go, O, but Mama is sending me. Mr Tobenna says it's the only—'

But, as usual, Mama Chiedu quickly turns away.

Ngozi's smile fades and she draws back the words perched to emerge, settles them down again, and watches Mama Chiedu's back. *Maybe she will turn round,* she thinks. But she doesn't. Ngozi continues, spirit hunched, along the path.

It's not that Mama Chiedu's response is any different from any other morning, but it seems, to Ngozi at least, that on this day, her last day, after two years of walking this route, of good mornings and hellos, that Mama Chiedu's response could have held a little more . . . maybe a little regret, maybe a little more acknowledgement.

Ngozi closes her eyes, breathes a heavy breath and wishes things were different, that her family, this village, were different, and at that moment it seems that maybe Enugu holds the answers.

A quarter of a mile along she passes Mr Tobenna's house, a two-storey building. It's as big as her hut is small, as admired as theirs is despised. Stella, her friend, stands on the first-floor balcony, all crisp and starched and fresh in her blue-and-white school uniform, her face shiny with Vaseline, her hair neatened by her mother's sweet hand.

'Ngozi!' shouts Stella, as she sees her friend pass by the compound gates.

'What?'

'Is that the way you greet me? I was only going to tell you that we are leaving early today. I have marching practice. Daddy can give you a lift to the depot.'

'O, okay, thank you,' says Ngozi.

Stella runs down the steps to join her friend and helps put the tray in the back of her father's van.

Mr Tobenna emerges two minutes later. He's a short man and with some difficulty climbs into the van to brush down the inside seats. He scratches his peppergrain hair and rubs at the sweat raining out from between the folds of his fat neck.

'Papa, can we give Ngozi a lift?'

'Yes, yes, of course. Both of you get in the back,' beams Mr Tobenna, exposing his yellow teeth. 'So are you ready for your trip on Sunday?' he asks as he secures the lock at the back of his pickup.

'I'm not sure.'

'What do you mean?'

'I mean, I'm ready, even happy to go 'cause of my schooling, but I don't want to leave Mama.'

'I know, it's hard. You're a bright girl and you need an education, and besides, you'll be more use to your mother once you have a trade. God knows that woman has worked hard ever since our schooldays.' Mr Tobenna nods his head with regret. 'But life hasn't been good to her, it just hasn't.'

'Yes, sir. Sir, will you be coming to church on Sunday?'

'Yes, of course – we have to send you off with God's blessings. But, Ngozi, when you go to Enugu, make sure you come back, you hear?'

'Yes, sir.' Ngozi gets down from the van.

'Okay, O,' laughs Mr Tobenna as he gets back in the pickup and drives off over the bumpy road.

'*Oloma* – orange! Groundnut! Banana!' shouts Ngozi under the mango tree where Mr Tobenna dropped her before heading off to his office on the other side of the depot. Ngozi looks over to where most of the action occurs, near the depot gates. Her eyes alight on sellers weaving in and out of stationary vehicles filled with passengers, buses making their way through the iron gates and tattily clothed conductors swinging from open doors. She is usually a good seller, strategic. But now she's not, now she stands quiet under the tree, eyes the crowd from a distance, looks from face to face, but cannot see him, her father.

'*Oloma!* Banana!' she shouts from the shade. '*Oloma.*'

The faint sound of Nelly Uchendu dances through the air from the radio of the yellow ten-seater bus parked near by. The driver wipes the windows, removing the dust settled there from yesterday, then starts the engine and hurries to join in the business over by the gates.

Ngozi glimpses the shape of three children in the distance, dressed in blue-and-white uniforms. They are heading towards her. She breathes in, readies herself.

'Ngozi, how are you now?' says the eldest.

Ngozi ignores him and looks away. They'd fought during the weekend, over the old military tank left behind after the Biafran war, which serves now as a plaything for local children.

'I heard your mother, the *ashawo* woman, is getting rid of you.'

Ngozi lifts her left hand, spreads her five fingers. '*Waka!*' she says, swearing at them.

'Look at you,' says the boy. 'Wretched dirty fool.'

The other two laugh.

'And yourself, look at you – your face looks like a dog's backside,' says Ngozi.

'Look at you, you're . . . you're . . . a bastard child!' he says.

'*Osu's* baby,' pipes his sister.

They all join in. '*Osu's* baby! *Osu's* baby!'

Ngozi ignores them and bends down to arrange her fruit, which she lays out in small pyramids.

'*Osu's* baby! Bastard child!' they chant, picking up small stones and beginning to throw them.

Ping, ping. Stones hit the tray. She continues, puts the bananas to one side and begins to count. A stone stings her upper arm. The anger gathers. But she grabs her arm, rubs away the pain, then places a few oranges in a small plastic bag and watches through the corner of her eye as they draw closer, the stones clenched in their left hands. *Ping.* Ouch! A stone hits her temple, the pain shoots through her, she lunges, makes a grab at one of them, but they are already running away.

'She dey come, O!' they shout as they go.

Ngozi remains under the mango tree.

They begin to make their way back to her. '*Osu's* baby! Bastard child!' they taunt.

'Leave her,' shouts an older man.

The children look at him, then back at Ngozi and poke their tongues out. They turn and dance away, jerking their bottoms up in the air as they head to catch their bus for school.

'Don't mind them,' says the old man, 'they're just troublemakers.'

But Ngozi commits to memory the taunts, the reactions, the village gossip, which come to her in little whispers, in pitying looks, in Catholic attitudes. And in reaction a hunger rises in her stomach, it rises against words that she knows have been said, are being said. It's a hunger that she cannot control, cannot yet release. It brews inside, not fully understood. And Ngozi swallows it down deep, loads her tray on to her head, and wanders over to the crowd in the distance.

'*Oloma!* Banana!' she shouts.

'How much?' asks the woman on the yellow bus.

Business is underway.

Late morning. Ten thirty, and all her goods are sold.

Ngozi stands again under the mango tree, the empty tray at her feet, an orange in her pocket, and counts her money. With the extra profit she's made from some tourists who were passing through the depot she can buy leaving presents, one for Blessing, the other for Emeka. Maybe two exercise books; might even be enough for a pencil – Blessing would like that. Ngozi folds the money into a dirty cloth and ties it under her top around her waist, then searches for him again among the dwindling crowd.

Most mornings she would see him by eight thirty, but this morning is different; he's not come yet and it's almost time to leave. She scratches her head and looks over by the broken-down buses, then over at Mr Tobenna's office, then at the gates, and still he is not to be seen. It will soon be lunch and there will be a rush at her mother's food store.

She takes the orange out of her pocket, bites, and sucks slowly, very slowly, drawing out the minutes. But still he does not appear.

It's time.

She places the empty tray on her head, adjusts herself, and is ready for the journey home, but she wants to say goodbye, she has to say goodbye, and turns to look, one last time, holds her breath, prays. And then there he is, over by the gates.

He gets quickly out of his car, kisses his wife and son, waves goodbye and climbs into the bus. Ngozi watches it pull out of the gates and disappear.

She hates him – her father, that is. She hates him with a passion that only a child who has witnessed unfairness towards a mother can hate. It's all mixed up in there: the hate, the love, the wanting of what should really be hers to have. It's not the way she'd imagined it, this glimpse of him, but like a camera she captures it.

In her mind, at night, half asleep, it replays itself more slowly. He turns to see her and there's recognition in his eyes, her departure noticed, and he places his palm on her head, kisses her softly like he did with his wife and child and says, 'Goodbye.'

Ngozi has few memories of her father, mainly because she has chosen not to remember the arguments, or the tension, or being woken with a shake and the kerosene lamp that shone in her face when he would suddenly appear and remove her from her mother's bed. But there are moments she cannot forget, cannot sweep away, that will stay with her into adulthood and then, maybe then, she will realize their significance. Ngozi closes her eyes and for one second seals his image, locks it, buries it, then walks through the gates to begin her long journey.

The gravel dirt nips at the soles of her feet and its jagged-ness shoots vivid memories through her. She remembers the day Emeka was born and her father's joy at the birth of his first son; until then he hadn't noticed her or Blessing. She remembers his visits, before Ike was born, the three of them lined up for inspec-tion, and how, like a governor on a school visit, he would pat their heads awkwardly. But most of all she remembers his very last visit and the look he left in her mother's eyes. It seems to Ngozi that hope left her mother's eyes that day. Later she over-heard conversations, heard people say his family had found him a more appropriate wife.

Ngozi feels the gravel give way to the smooth heat of tar. Her eyes follow the snake road as it disappears in the distance, deep into the bush.

Her father said to her mother once that he did not care she was *Osu*, or what his family thought, or the village – he loved her. Ngozi overheard him on one of his night visits as she fell back to sleep in the next room. There is a sadness that Ngozi can see now, even when her mother smiles or laughs. She's tried to make it go away, tried to be all the things her father should have been, but it will not go.

Ngozi hates her father in love, longs for what he should have been and how it should have been. Maybe that is why she prayed to catch sight of him, but what is there for her to say – only words that need to be spat out, that need to be matured before she's able to say them to help alleviate the pain. So it's not the words or the contact but the pure sight of him that she needed to say goodbye to. She's frightened that the little she does have, his image, will take flight when she goes, leaving only a ghost to fight.

St Mary's Catholic Church is big. On a good day it can seat nine hundred, on a bad day five hundred. It's the only Catholic church for twenty miles and serves the three neighbouring villages: Obowi, Obiada and Nnesi. The ceiling is so high that to a child like Ngozi the ten-foot cross on the roof appears to touch the sky.

Ngozi sits eleven seats from the back of the church with Mr Tobenna, Stella, her mother and siblings. Eleven seats further forward than they would normally sit, and thirty rows from Chief Justice Okolo's family who, when they are in the village, always sit in the first row. But you see, they are with Mr Tobenna today.

It's a beautiful church, with a wooden ceiling and a red carpet running down the centre aisle. Colourful bunches of plastic flowers sit on stands scattered around the front pew. Ngozi, like other members of the congregation, is proud of her church and spent an hour last night wiping the dust from between the petals. She also puts what she can, sometimes more, in the two-foot-high basins placed at the end of each aisle, during the five collections that take place in the Sunday service. In fact she sings and dances all the way up there with the rest of her family, hoping that the more she sings, the more she dances, the more they might receive God's blessings.

Today she wears her yellow nylon dress and she pulls and tugs at the midriff to loosen the tight fit. There's a tear at the bottom of the left seam, but it's the only good dress she owns. Besides, it's the only thing her father has ever brought them, her and Blessing, and her sister has insisted they wear the matching dresses. One last time.

Ngozi looks up at the ceiling, along the aisle to the front, hears the boom of the priest's voice, the thump of his fist on the pew.

'Matthew, chapter five, verse three – it says?' He holds his hand to his ear. 'I can't hear you. It says . . .'

There's a shuffling of paper as Ngozi finds it.

'It says,' she says in her clearest voice, '"Happy are those who know they are poor."'

'For the kingdom of heaven belongs to them,' choruses the congregation.

'Amen,' shouts a voice.

'With the blood of Jee-suss,' says another.

It's one of her neighbours. Ngozi watches the sweat make its way down the side of the woman's face and drip from her jaw, while the man beside her wipes his ample neck with a handkerchief. She reaches for the Mass sheet, fans herself, pulls again at her dress and looks up and longs for a touch of breeze from the overhead fans that cool the priest and choir up there in the front.

'Dear Lord, there are some among us who will be travelling today. Dr Samuel's children will be returning to Lagos where they own businesses – you see, the Lord takes care of his own,' says the priest, his Bible held tight to his chest. 'Chief Justice Okolo will be returning to Enugu with his children, the youngest of whom is studying medicine in the United States of America. Please Lord protect them. Guide them safely to their destinations. Protect them on our treacherous roads. Deliver them safely to their final destinations.'

'Amen,' the congregation choruses.

'Go in peace to love and serve the Lord.'

'Amen.'

Out in the church grounds, with Mass over, Ngozi plays with Stella while her mother and Mr Tobenna move her bundle to the back of his car. Mr Tobenna will drop them at the bus station.

'Stella, come,' says Ngozi.

'Why? What are you going to do?'

Ngozi holds a small unripened mango behind her back.

'Come, I want to tell you something.'

'I know you – you're up to something.'

'Okay, I was only going to tell you about the Bimba Boys.'

Stella steps forward. She loves the all-boy Christian group that tours the surrounding parishes. 'What about them?'

Ngozi reaches out and stuffs the mango down the front of her dress and runs.

'Ngozi!' shouts Stella as she chases after her.

As Ngozi looks over her shoulder she collides with Mama Chiedu.

'Ah!' says Mama Chiedu.

Stella turns and runs in the opposite direction.

'Sorry.'

'Sorry, what?'

'I'm really sorry, Mama Chiedu, O. I didn't think—'

'That's the problem – the young don't think.'

'Sorry, Mama Chiedu. I didn't mean to—'

'Enuff.'

'Yes, Mama Chiedu.' Ngozi turns to go.

'Ngozi?'

'Yes, Mama Chiedu.'

'Your Uncle Tobenna tells me you're leaving today?'

'Yes, Ma. We leave on the one o'clock bus.'

'If I had known yesterday, I could have given you something.'

'You didn't know?'

'No, your uncle just told me, but I suppose it's a good thing. You will need your education – God knows, no one is likely to marry you.'

Ngozi's lower jaw drops. Her heart tightens with the suddenness of these words.

'I'm only stating what you already know. The people around here are too small-minded. Look at them: they profess to be Christians and yet when it comes to marriage they remember you're *Osu*.'

Ngozi nods out of politeness and ponders how to untangle herself from Mama Chiedu.

'Take this.'

'But, Mama Chiedu—'

Mama Chiedu takes hold of Ngozi's hand. 'But nothing. I want you to take it. Every morning you've passed me and said good morning. Even after Chiedu's death when I wanted to hide away from it all. Now you're going into that world. It's a treacherous place – I know. Take it; you will need it.'

'But—'

'But what? Make an old woman happy and take the money.'

'Thank you, Mama Chiedu.'

'Take care of yourself.'

'Thank you, Mama Chiedu.'

'Now shoo,' she says.

Ngozi grasps the money and, looking back over her shoulder, scampers off to join her family. It's time to leave.

6

The Garden of Night

NGOZI SITS BY the window and watches the landscape race by. At first, lone palm trees sway tall above the dry spiky grass, but they are soon swallowed completely by the bush as it grows greener and denser.

Beeeeeeep!

'Jesus!'

'He just miss, O!'

Ngozi holds on to the window frame to steady herself, then she puts her head out the window to watch the dust from the road swirl up as a white Peugeot 505 disappears.

'Ngozi, bring your head in,' says Nneka.

'Hey, driver!' shouts the woman in front, holding an infant in her lap, as the bag above her head threatens to topple out on top of her.

Her husband jumps up quick and jams it back into place. 'Only God knows where they're hurrying to.'

Beep beep beeeeeeeeeeeeeeeeeep! The bus overtakes three cars at once.

'Driver!'

'Driver, make you slow down.'

'Me self I no ready to die, O.'

'Mr Man, make you shut-up! It no be you who make bus late,' says the conductor. 'When you dey safe in Enugu, we go travel back and me self I don't want make journey for dark.'

Understanding the conductor's concerns, the bus falls silent.

A man in the back starts to sing, quietly at first, a few seated near by join in, and then he shouts, 'In the name of Jesus!'

'Amen,' shout a few in return.

'In the name of Jesus!'

'Amen,' shout a few more.

'In the name of Jee-suss!'

'Amen,' shouts the bus.

'You have to praise the Lord.'

'Hallelujah!' sing the passengers.

'Brothers, praise the Lord.'

'Hallelujah!'

'Sisters, praise the Lord.'

'Hallelujah!'

'Ha-la, Ha-la, Ha-la, Hallelujah.'

And their hands clap, their feet stomp, their voices rise to rock the bus, to be heard in heaven, to wake up the Lord.

'Cover us with the blood of Jesus,' prays the man.

'With the blood of Jesus,' they respond

'Cover our lives with the blood of Jesus.'

'With the blood of Jesus,' says Ngozi, then looks out the window to see big lorries push back the bush, like policemen driving back a wild crowd, subduing the wilderness, after which lie wide-open spaces of yellowish red soil, which lead up into the hills. Fallen trees lie near the foot of the hills, and on the other side lie metal pipes, twelve metres long, ready to take over the landscape.

Ngozi turns to fix her dress and the ribbon in her hair. She sees her mother's frown and reaches across for her hand.

'Ngozi, I love you.'

'I love you too, Ma.'

Thump! The bus drives over a hole. Everything in the bus jumps with it.

'You know, if there was any other way, if there was a way I could keep you . . .'

'I know, Ma. Don't worry – I'll be fine, O.'

'Yes, you'll be fine. You will be fine. This isn't the way I wanted it. I didn't want you to have to work for strangers just to get an education. It would be different if you were nearer home.'

'Ma, Uncle Tobenna said the Asikas are nice people.'

'I know. I just wish I had the money to send you myself. But once you have your education, things will be better for you than it has been for me. You will need it. You know there are few men willing to marry an *Osu*.'

'I know, Ma. I understand. I will work hard, O.'

'Ngozi, promise me, if you have any problems, if you're not happy, if, if . . . if a man touches you, if he . . . if you're not happy, you will come home.'

'I promise.'

Thump!

'Don't worry, Ma. God will take care of me.'

'Yes, he will.'

An hour later, as the bus slows down before driving into the city of Enugu, Nneka turns to look out the window. On the roadside to the right, a burnt wreck of a car sits smouldering, a charred body lies beside it. Nneka quickly lifts her hand to cover her daughter's eyes but she's not quick enough. They drive further into the town. Past houses that are three, even five, storeys high. Past the football stadium. Over the rail track. Past Ogbete market which spreads out for a mile, with huts, most of them closed, cobbled together with bits of spare wood and tin sheets, seeming to sit comfortably in the mud beside the open sewers and the filth and the stench. Ngozi watches a little boy, no older than her brother Ike, squat in the mud beside the flooded sewer and suck an orange.

'Is this Enugu?' asks Ngozi.

'Yes,' replies her mother.

Ngozi turns her head to look away and shudders.

They stand in the Asikas' backyard. It's in the government reservation area, the GRA, with colonial-style buildings and nice little gardens, as English as the British could get in Africa back then in the1930s when they were first built, now home to the Igbo middle classes.

Hope, a girl of thirteen, stoops over a wide metal bowl, doing the washing. 'Ma?'

'Is this the Asikas' residence?' asks Nneka.

'Yes. Can I help you?'

'Please can you tell your mistress that Miss Nwosu is here with her daughter?'

Hope nods, wipes her hands on the front of her dress, and heads inside.

Ngozi looks over the bungalow.

There are five random holes in the wall to her right, just big enough to fit half her index finger. These were left over a decade ago, at the end of the Biafran war, when a man was marched and lined up against the wall and shot dead for a reason that Ngozi hasn't got a clue about now, but many older folk will never forget. These holes remind her of Mr Tobenna's face, his deep pores like little craters. In fact the whole house reminds her of Mr Tobenna, or no, maybe her father, or men in general. It's broad and strong like them. It radiates confidence, the ruggedness, the certainty of a fighting man's man, with a few battle scars included. But the flowers hanging from each window box, three on either side of the back door, smile broadly, and this gives the house warmth, it welcomes. Her home, the hut in which she was born, always seemed tentative, as though the spirit of the hut crept there on tiptoes, waiting for them to leave.

'Madam, dey come,' says Hope, coming back into the yard with three wooden chairs.

Mrs Asika emerges a minute later, with her daughter Nkiru following on behind.

Ngozi sees Nkiru's little rag doll in her chubby hand, and although she's bigger than Blessing, almost her own size, she estimates her age at no more than six.

'You've had a long journey,' says Mrs Asika. 'Please sit down and let me get you something to drink. What would you like?'

'Some ice water, thank you,' replies Nneka.

'Hope, please get them some ice water,' says Mrs Asika. She draws her daughter Nkiru on to her lap and strokes her hair, neatening her style as she speaks.

Ngozi watches Mrs Asika's hand stroke, lift and stroke again. It's a quick fluid motion, almost like water cascading over a paddle.

Mrs Asika's hand is straighter, not as curved, not as slow, not as gentle as her mother's. This morning she watched her mother in the mirror as she caressed and teased her hair into place. Felt the heat and weight of her mother's hand on her head as she combed through her short stubborn locks, and then the warm moist breath on her scalp as she kissed her and let her go. But sitting here, across from Mrs Asika, from this stranger, watching her hand move up and down, up and down, brings a wanting. It peeps out from behind a door in her mind and she looks sideways at her mother, reaches out, touches her hand, holds it, squeezes it, closes her eyes briefly and squeezes harder.

Nneka feels the small plea, squeezes back, then firmly untangles herself from her daughter's grip.

'Hope will show her what to do,' says Mrs Asika. 'It will be mainly household duties like cleaning, shopping, cooking – those sorts of things.'

Ngozi's mother nods. 'And where will she sleep?'

'We have a spare room to the side of the kitchen where Hope sleeps. Ngozi will sleep in there with her.'

Ngozi's mother assesses Hope momentarily and decides she won't be too bad an influence on her little girl. 'What about her schooling?'

'She will go to the school around the corner between 3 p.m. and 6 p.m. after Hope is back from morning school. In fact it's one of the best evening schools in the state. Hope is doing well and is at day school now, so we need help while she's there. But I'm hoping that if Ngozi shows promise in a year or two, once Hope has finished, she can also transfer to day school for her final-year exams.' Mrs Asika turns and smiles at Ngozi, a wide-open smile.

Ngozi is struck by its warmth, which glows like freshly made *akamu*, all puffy and smooth and steaming with heat. It soothes her.

'What about holidays?'

'We normally let Hope go home to her father's people in the village one week during the Christmas period, a week at Easter and two weeks during the summer, but we will have to arrange it with Hope so that they don't go home at the same time. For instance, Hope can take Christmas then Ngozi can go home for the New Year.'

'So she'll be home in three months, after Christmas,' says Nneka. 'But how will she get home? I mean, do I come and get her? She can't just—'

'Don't worry. I'll give her the money and the driver will make sure she gets on the bus safely. All you have to do is meet her at the other end. I understand how difficult it is for you. I am a mother too.'

And for the first time since meeting, their eyes do not flutter around each other like the dance of flies. They stop. Hold. They meet across the barriers of class, wealth, and education. They meet within this world of men's men, and within the boundaries that cage them both. The arrangements are made and when the two have finished, Ngozi walks her mother to the end of the road. It's five in the evening, a light breeze stirs, and a bird chirps noisily on the branch of a tree.

'Ngozi, be good.'

Tears fill her eyes and she hugs her mother tight; her head barely reaches her mother's chest.

'You'll be home soon. Three months isn't very far.'

'I know but—'

'Besides, they seem like good people.'

'But—'

'Look at me,' Nneka says, lifting her daughter's chin. 'It's for the best. With an education things will be better for you – for all of us. Now wipe your eyes and be strong.'

'Yes, Ma.'

'And smile.'

'Yes, Ma.'

'And remember what I said: if you have any trouble, any problem, you come home.'

'Yes, Ma.'

'You take this money and get the first bus home, you hear?'

'Yes, Ma.'

Nneka gives her daughter a long strong hug, then releases her. 'I better go; it's getting late.'

Slowly Ngozi lets her go and watches her walk gracefully down the road until she disappears from view.

*

She walks steadily back into the tension of the yard where three sets of eyes stare back at her. She skids on its slipperiness. *What if they do? What if they don't?* she thinks. And she tries to balance it, calm it, uncoil the fist at her centre. *Three and me*, she thinks, and the fist curls up again like a spring as her eyes dart from Mrs Asika to Nkiru to Hope. But then, as if they sense her unease, Hope turns around to finish the last of her washing and Nkiru skips back into the house to take the gossip of the new arrival to her father.

'I know it won't be easy, but you'll be okay with us,' says Mrs Asika.

'Yes, Ma,' replies Ngozi and looks at her feet.

'Can you write?'

'Yes, Ma.'

'Good. Tomorrow you can write home. You do know how to send a letter?'

'No, Ma.'

'Oh well, okay, I'll have to show you. Meanwhile, go with Hope and get settled in. Tomorrow she can get started on showing you some of your chores.'

She follows Hope into the house, her bundle in her left hand. A light breeze catches her as she enters through the door, but before she can understand or grasp its whisper, it's gone, almost as if this house, this man's man, was in a state of expectancy for something or someone. She walks close behind Hope. They turn right, past the dining room, through the kitchen, into a room at the end.

'You can sleep on the bed nearest the wall and put your things in the bottom two drawers in this cupboard. I'll let you unpack, then join me in the kitchen for dinner.'

Ngozi nods and looks around. There are no pictures on the walls or ornaments. The concrete floor is painted red, no rug. The room contains only what is essential: two beds, a small wardrobe and a chest of drawers. And yet it has a simple freshness that her room back in Obowi could never have. Ngozi sighs.

'You know, I was nervous when I first came too,' says Hope, 'but don't worry. Mr and Mrs Asika are nice people.'

'Are they?'

'They're fair and most times I enjoy working here. As long as you do what's expected they won't trouble you.'

'How long have you been here?'

'Three years.'

'Don't you miss your family?'

'My parents died five years ago.'

'How?'

'An explosion – pipeline. It was leaking and blew up. Several other people from my village were killed too.'

Ngozi shudders and prays her mother will get home safely.

'Anyway, I've been around for three years now and as families go, the Asikas are fine, but you might find Mr Asika too tall and too quiet. Nkiru is a chatterbox but they both love her. If you ask me, that girl is spoilt.'

'They only have one child?'

'Yes.'

'Why? I mean, with all their money?'

'It took them a long time to have Nkuri and I'm not even sure if Mrs Asika can have another. Anyway, finish unpacking and come eat. Tomorrow will be a long day.'

Ngozi wakes to the quieter crow of the town cock and feels instinctively for Blessing.

'Morning,' says Hope at the foot of her bed.

'Morning.'

'There's a lot to do. Can you collect water from the tank for their baths, then help me with breakfast. After that we have to get Nkiru ready for school and then pack food for the Madam's trip . . .'

'Where . . .' she hesitates, 'where is the Madam going?'

'To visit her sister in the North. We've got—'

'Why?'

'Her sister has had a baby. We've got to—'

'How long will she be gone?'

'You do ask a lot of questions. I don't know, two, maybe three weeks. Anyway, *jaré*, quick, quick, we have a lot to do. Once she's gone I can tell you the rest while we do the housework. Oh, and also the *Oga* will take you to enrol at the school this evening. Quick.'

Outside, Ngozi stands by the water tank and listens to the water trickle against the sides of the metal bucket. She marvels at the ease of it. At home, in Obowi, she would have a half-hour journey to collect the water from the stream. But at home she would go with Blessing and Emeka, and there would be others at the stream, splashing in the water, their childish shrieks riding the air. The coolness of the valley would massage her shoulders, wash away the day's trade, rinse away the adult grime, until she emerged clean again, a child again. And then, only then, she would breathe in its greenness, it would fill her nostrils and charge her blood until air and water soaked her through with laughter. Then the sun would dry them like a mother towel-drying her young; it cradled them in its warm heat.

'Ngozi!' shouts Hope.

She turns off the tap, struggles back inside, knocks on the Asikas' door. As she enters, the *Oga*, Mr Asika, rises from the bed and puts on his slippers.

'Thank you. Put half in the basin in the bath and the rest in the Mickey Mouse bowl behind the door,' says Mrs Asika as she untangles herself from Nkiru.

Ngozi enters the bathroom and heaves the bucket on to the side of the bath.

'When are we going to put it in?' she overhears Mrs Asika ask her husband.

'You always overreact – a few armed robberies and you want to barricade us in. I would not mind but they always happen in some godforsaken neighbourhood.'

'Humour me, Christian,' says the Madam. 'It will make me feel safer.'

'It will make you feel safer to have iron bars on the windows and doors?'

'Yes.'

'What if there's a fire?'

'I don't know. I didn't think about that.'

'Madam, I've poured half into the two small basins?'

'Pour the rest for the *Oga*. There's another basin beside the Mickey Mouse one.'

'Yes, Ma.'

'Nkiru, wake up. It's time for school, Nkiru.'

Ngozi watches as the little girl stirs and stretches, then goes back into the bathroom.

'So what are you saying about it?' says Madam Asika to her husband.

'Mummy, Mummy,' Nkuri says, tugging on her mother's wrapper, 'Mummy, I had that dream again. The one where you take me to Leventis and buy me that new lunch box with Mickey Mouse on the front.'

'Yes, darling,' says the Madam. 'Christian, I would still feel safer with the bars.'

'. . . but when we get home, I can't get out the car,' says Nkiru.

'Look, you see, even your daughter agrees with me,' says the *Oga*.

'Okay, we'll discuss it again when I get back.'

Ngozi drops the empty bucket; it rattles loudly then rolls on the bathroom floor.

'You okay in there?' asks Mrs Asika from outside the doorway. Ngozi tells her, 'Yes, Madam.'

'You don't say much, do you? Nkiru, come brush your teeth.'

Ngozi emerges from the bathroom.

'Hold on. Your dress. Don't you have one that fits better?'

Ngozi looks down at her favourite yellow dress, the one she wore to church yesterday – all her other dresses look out of place in this household so she put it on again this morning. 'Yes.'

'Come with me. Hope, where are Nkiru's old dresses?'

'In the bottom drawer in her room.'

Mrs Asika opens the drawer. 'You're slightly taller than Nkiru but much slimmer, so these might fit.' Mrs Asika pulls out the dresses. 'Try this one.'

Ngozi takes it. It fits.

It's a pink cotton dress with pink velvet around the middle. The colour is a little faded, but Ngozi's eyes glaze and begin to sparkle. She touches the velvet, spreads her fingers, glides them over its softness, smiles, looks at her reflection and turns right, then left. She thinks of the dresses worn by the children on billboards back home in Obowi, smiling down with Omo or Maggi cubes in their hands, and the rich children who looked at her with disdain from the safety of their cars while their drivers bought from her mother's store, and the teasing of the neighbourhood children. She thinks of these children, looks again at her reflection. Two tears escape each eye but she lifts her head high, smiles and says, 'Thank you.'

'What you crying for?' asks Mrs Asika.

'I don't know.'

'Dry your eyes.' Mrs Asika reaches out, strokes her face and smiles, then gives her a tissue. 'I really hope you'll be happy with us. 'Now hurry, I have a journey to make.'

*

Two small faces, those of Nkiru and Hope, press against the glass. Their eyes dart left, then right, searching out in the darkness for two white dots in the distance. Nkiru turns from the window to look back at her father who sits reading on the sofa.

'What time did Auntie say Mama will be home?'

'About seven.'

Nkiru turns back to look out the window again.

Ngozi joins the two girls. She sees a white pinhead in the distance. 'Is that her?'

'Papa, it's her, it's Mummy!' squeals Nkiru.

The car makes it way through the darkness and up the front drive, its wheels crackling on the gravel.

Hope runs outside.

'Mama, Mama!' shouts Nkiru and skips out after her. She leaps on to her mother as she opens the back door.

'How is your sister?' asks Mr Asika from behind them all.

'Fine.'

'And the baby?'

'Lovely.'

'Mummy, Ngozi's got a new school uniform. She got it on Monday.'

'That's nice, dear.'

'And Daddy bought me that Mickey Mouse lunch box.'

'We missed you,' says Mr Asika.

There is a look between them, which skims above the girls' heads.

'I missed you too,' she whispers, then turns to hug her daughter. 'How has everything been while I've been away?'

'Fine. Except your friends, the Nwagbus, the ones who live in New Haven, their car was stolen while you were away. They took it off them on their way back from a party.'

'Are they okay?'

'They're fine. I've been thinking about what you said before you went, about the bars.'

'That's nice but I'm really tired. Can we discuss it later?'

'I was only going to say that we should do it after we've finished the work on the house in the village.'

'Good. We can talk about it tomorrow,' says Mrs Asika and turns to Ngozi. 'Have you settled in here and at school?'

'Yes, Ma.'

'Good. Can you help Hope get the things out of the car?'

'Mummy, what did you get me?'

'Help Ngozi and Hope get the things out of the car, then I'll show you.'

Mrs Asika opens the boot. It's filled with bananas, oranges, plantain, pineapple and yam. The smells swirl out into the air.

'Mummy!' shouts Nkiru in excitement.

The five of them carry the load from the car and head towards the welcoming lights in the house.

'NEPA!' they cry with the neighbourhood as the lights suddenly cut out, and everywhere is left in darkness.

'Oh God, NEPA. They've taken the lights again,' says Mrs Asika. 'This country, O.'

'Hope, make up the fire outside – it will be too hot inside without the fans. And bring the chairs outside so we can enjoy the night,' says Mr Asika.

'Yes, sir.'

The family, all five of them, sit around the open fire singing old Igbo songs to the chorus of night frogs and crickets. They fan themselves, trying to abate the suffocating heat, while Ngozi sings, sings with joy, sings with them all.

M'gbogu M'gbogu mgba-titi
Obulu na ililu azu (If you eat the fish) *mgba-titi*
Igbudu dagbue-i (Then the town of Igbudu will fall on you and kill you) *mgba-titi*

Ma Obulu na iliro azu (But if you don't eat the fish) *mgba-titi*
Igbudu kwulu ka odi (Then Igbudu will not fall) *mgba-titi*

It's February, and Ngozi lies asleep with a faint smile on her face. Her dreams are filled with her new life and her New Year visit home. She returned home bearing gifts, taking a few of Nkiru's dresses, and in her sleep she hears Blessing's squeal as she put a dress on and twirled with excitement. Mostly she relives seeing the pride shine in her mother's eyes when she showed her school report. You see, Hope and her are almost like sisters, and to be Hope's sister means you cannot help but be infected by her and her ways. Every evening after the chores are done, Hope gets her books out, buries her head in them, and like the chores she taught Ngozi, Ngozi also learns how to study. Hope guides Ngozi through, helping with her English. This is their play. Hope has learnt many things in the five years since her parents' death. That things change, that as quickly as they come they can go, and that, of the many families she's worked for, the Asikas are truly good people. So she grabs at her opportunity, not like the child she is, but like one much wiser than her years. Unlike Ngozi she truly has nothing, not even the affection of a mother.

But in her sleep Ngozi is suddenly uneasy, then receives a painful poke in the ribs. She wakes and hears voices from outside.

'Shush,' says Hope.

'What?'

'Shush.'

The sleep escapes from Ngozi's eyes, the voices outside become louder, unease writhes through her like a creeping vine.

A man speaks. '*Oga! Oga*, make you dey open this door, O, it go bettar for you,' says the voice, a deep baritone voice, which hammers out the words.

Ngozi sits up.

'Shush! God, O, come, come, quick,' says Hope and slips out of the room.

Ngozi watches her disappear and sees the beams from the men's torches skip on the bedroom curtain.

'*Oga*, you no dey hear me – if we dey open this door we go kill you, O.'

Silence.

'*Oga*, I go count to ten. You go suffer if we dey open this door.'

Ngozi jumps out of bed, looks around, bolts towards the door to follow Hope.

Bang! The sound rings out in the compound.

Ngozi freezes.

Bang! Bang! Bang! The men break through the back door.

She turns back into the room, darts left, right, looks under the bed, scampers towards the door, hears their footsteps, turns back again, their voices getting closer as they enter the dining room. 'God!' she screams inside and shakes her hands as if to wave them dry. But then she sees the gap between the chest of drawers and the wall, fits herself into it, curls her small frame down into the space, squeezes her eyes shut, for if she can't see them, they can't see her. Tries to stay as still as an Oba carving, but her limbs shake as she listens to the muffled voices in the hallway. She hears a clank, a clatter, as one man searches in the kitchen next door, then a *mmurt* sound as the fridge door opens.

'You want some?' she hears the man say to another.

'Later. Peter say make we do the sitting room first, then make our way down here.'

And she hears the two men leave the kitchen.

Then in the darkness she hears a scream, Madam's scream, and a muffled whimpering coming from the direction of their bedroom. And above this she can hear the ringleader, the one with the hammer-like voice.

'Where the money?' he asks.

'*Oga*, where you dey put the money?' asks another.

'*Oga*, you no dey hear. You no hear!'

And beneath his voice Ngozi hears the high-pitched whimpering of the Madam and the low grunts from the *Oga*, as if the men are punching him.

But then there is a struggle.

Gunshots.

Silence.

Ngozi's heart pounds. She hears the men move swiftly and clumsily, and the clink, clatter, as they throw things into bags. They move from the sitting room to the dining room, to the kitchen, then she hears Hope scream as they discover her in the kitchen storeroom, and she yells like a pig about to be slaughtered as the men drag her outside.

They enter her room. Ngozi feels a red-hot heat run through her. The pain in her legs nags for relief but she feels the flashlight close to her face and freezes. 'Dear Lord, save me, dear Lord God, O, please, O.' The light moves away. Tears squeeze through the corners of her eyes. A warm liquid slips down between her thighs and forms a puddle at her feet. She hears one of the men crouch down and look under the bed, another, as he searches in the chest of drawers beside her, and another as he enters the room.

'O'boyo, wating you dey do here? You no dey see it be house girl quarters?'

The three men leave and join the rest in the living room. They continue collecting their loot until they cannot carry any more.

Ngozi hears the cock crow, sees a ray of light force its way through the gap in the curtains. She lifts her head, listens. Her hearing is like radar; it picks up sounds as faint as a leaf dropping. There is silence, but sitting on top is a faint crying sound, a constant chesty rattle, coming from inside the house; it demands an answer.

Ngozi gets up, tiptoes cautiously towards the door, out into the kitchen; it's littered with pots and smashed plates. She continues round, stepping over items, through the dining room, past broken ornaments, readies herself to run back if needed, past the clothes scattered in the hallway. There is crying which is getting louder; she enters the Madam's room. Then stands silent, not believing, not knowing, just not being able to say or do anything but stare at Nkiru lying on the floor, her head in her mother's lap, her clothes stained, her lower jaw shattered, her eyes wide open, frozen, blood on the floor, on the Madam's clothes. Mrs Asika on the floor cradling her daughter, the tears streaming in eerie silence down her face as she rocks her daughter's body backwards and forwards, backwards and forwards.

'Madam.'

No answer.

'Madam, Madam, please make you no cry. Where the *Oga*? Madam, where the *Oga*?'

No answer. Mrs Asika continues to rock her baby backwards and forwards, backwards and forwards. She mumbles.

'Madam, I go find help,' says Ngozi, as she backs out of the bedroom.

It's light outside and the neighbours are up. As she's running she collides with Mr Ike, a neighbour, with his fifteen-year-old son.

'Mr Ike, please come, come!' cries Ngozi and pulls him towards Mr and Mrs Asika's bedroom. Entering, Mr Ike sees Nkiru's small bloody body lying on the floor; he turns to his son. 'Go get help. Go get your mother; tell her to call the ambulance – no, the police.' His son turns and runs off as quickly as he can.

'Madam Asika, Madam, come,' he says, trying to pull her up and away from the body, but she won't move. 'Madam, what they look like?'

She doesn't answer, but continues rocking.

'Madam, what happen?'

No answer.

'Madam, where Mr Asika?'

Silence.

He turns to Ngozi. 'Where your *Oga*?'

'I don't know, Sir. I found them here. I was hiding in my room.'

'Madam, where Mr Asika? Where your husband?'

Mrs Asika does not answer.

7

The Morning After

'*Ewooo!!! Chukwu gini bu ifa?* What did this little girl do to anybody?' says Mrs Ike. 'Please, God! Why? *Hei!*' She clasps the top of her head.

'Where is the police?' asks Mrs Ike, standing by the window.

'She won't let me move her. The body is cold. What am I supposed to do? She just sits rocking. She won't let her go. *Hei!* God.'

'Where is this police? Two hours – two goddamn hours. Where are they?'

Ngozi stands in the middle of the doorway between the sitting room and Madam Asika's room and watches Mr and Mrs Ike. She leans against the door frame, bends her head and feels a blankness. She's half in, half out, half somewhere out there watching it all and between this halfness are the images, as solid as her own arm. She reaches out to grip her wrist, grips it tight, feels the tightness of her fingers and then the slight pain from the pressure. She breathes in, feels the air fill her lungs. Nkiru smiles and runs through the front door from school, chattering and calling for attention. Ngozi pushes herself away from the door frame, walks back into Madam Asika's room. Nkiru's bloody body lies on the floor. She touches the Madam's shoulder. 'Please.'

And there are no words.

'*Biko.*'

What is there to say?

'Please, Madam, don't cry, don't cry, O.'

Madam Asika looks up at her, her eyes searching out Ngozi's, searching as if wanting reasons, answers, something.

Ngozi reaches out, says the only thing she knows how to. 'She's with Jesus.'

And for the first time since last night, Mrs Asika looks back at her daughter's body and lets out an almighty scream.

'So how did it happen?' asks another neighbour standing in the middle of the Asikas' sitting room.

'I don't know. I heard the commotion last night but I was too frightened. We have five children of our own.'

'I know, I know. It could have been anybody's daughter. It could have been my daughter; I don't even want to think of it.'

'My husband came over as soon as it was daylight.'

'So what are we supposed to do? Do we leave her sitting there? Do we clear away the body? If we don't, it will soon smell in this heat.'

'God, where are the police? It's three hours since we started calling. If we touch anything we might ruin things.'

'Where has he gone?'

'Who?'

'Your husband?'

'He's taken my son and a few of the men to look for Mr Asika and the other house girl.'

'*Hei!* What do you mean?'

'They can't find them.'

'*Hei!* Jesus. What do you mean they can't find them?'

'They can't find them.'

'You mean it could be more than just the little girl dead.'

'I don't know. Calm down – let's just see what we can do here. Mrs Obindu, the one that lives up by there, in the big house.'

'No. I don't know her.'

'Yes, you do – the one yellow from bleaching.'

'O, yes, yes. The one with the lecherous husband.'

'Yes. She's gone home to cook and bring some food. Mrs Asika will need to eat soon.'

'So what do we do?'

'Ngozi! Ngozi!'

'Yes, Ma,' says Ngozi, hurrying out of the bedroom.

'Please, do you know how we contact the Madam's relatives, maybe her sister?'

'Yes, Ma. Madam Asika has the number in her book.'

'Please bring it.'

'Yes, Ma.' Ngozi rushes back into the Madam's room.

'They found her! They found her!' shouts Mrs Ike's son, coming into the house.

'Found who?'

'Hope, Ma. They found Hope.'

'Dear Jesus! Where?'

'In the bush, down the end.'

'Is she alive?'

'Yes, Ma, but she doesn't look good. There was blood all over her. Her clothes were all torn.'

'Dear Lord, what did those animals do?'

'Papa's taken her to the hospital.'

'One of us better go and be with her.'

'I'll go,' says the neighbour.

'What of Mr Asika?' asks Mrs Ike.

'No sign,' says her son.

'He's dead, I'm sure. I'm sure,' says the neighbour. 'That poor woman.'

It's twelve o'clock, five hours after Mr Ike called the police. Mrs Asika sits on the sofa all cried out. Mrs Ike tries to force water past her lips and Mrs Obindu, Ngozi, and four other neighbours watch through the sitting-room window as the green jeep draws up in front of the house. They watch as the five men leap out and stop to dust themselves off.

'It's the police,' announces Mrs Obindu.

'At last,' says Mrs Ike as she pushes herself up from the sofa and makes her way out of the house on to the front porch. 'What time do you call this?'

'Please, Madam,' says the sergeant, holding up his hand.

'Five hours?'

'Madam!'

'Five hours we've been waiting. Five hours. The police for this country.'

'Madam,' says the sergeant as he pushes past Mrs Ike and enters the house, 'where the body?'

'In the bedroom. I can't believe you people. This woman's daughter is dead, her husband missing, and you walk in here—'

'Please, Madam, I'm not in the mood.'

'You're not in the mood?'

'Listen, as it is I don't have enough men. On top of that, two were shot dead this morning at the patrol point – between them they had nine children. I've just come from telling their wives. God knows how they are going to manage 'cause we've not been paid for two months now. So when I say I'm not in the mood, I'm not in the mood. So please show me to the body.'

'This way.'

'What time did it happen?'

'About four o'clock this morning.'

'Witnesses?'

'There was Hope and Ngozi and the Madam of course.'

'We remanded in custody four men this morning travelling along the Enugu to Onitsha motorway who we suspect may have carried out the robbery, but we need the Madam to come to the station to identify them.'

'She's not in a good state.'

'For her sake she needs to come and identify these men sooner rather than later. I would have asked her husband but—'

'You found the husband?'

'Yes. He was lying unconscious along the highway two hours ago, but—'

'Thank Jesus.'

'I'll come,' pipes up Mrs Asika suddenly. 'I'll come. My husband, is he okay?'

'We can take you to see him once you've identified the men.'

It's seven in the evening and the Asikas' yard is filled with people. The police have departed, leaving only two to guard the house, and Nkiru's body lies in the police mortuary.

Mrs Asika is stretched out on the bed in her room listening to the voices outside. Mrs Ike and Mrs Obindu lean over her, trying to get her to eat their pepper soup. Mrs Asika's sister and relatives will soon be here. Mr Asika's family are at the hospital, except for two who stand outside in the yard with Mr Ike and Mr Obindu, trying to entertain the number of people who have come to give their condolences.

'I really don't understand what has happened to this country,' says one of the men in the yard to the others. 'In all my years I've never known armed robbery. I've always been able to leave my house open. And to kill a child . . .'

'O, friend, things da change, O,' says another.

'But to change this much?'

'I don't know about you but tomorrow I da put the bars for windows and doors,' says another.

'But we have always slept with the windows open, sometimes with the back door open to let the breeze circulate.'

'I really don't understand,' says the man again.

No, they do not understand. I realize they truly do not understand. For these city folk do not see the farmland that cannot be tilled, or the waters that cannot be fished, or the thick black molasses that covers them both, taking livelihoods, leaving hunger and desperation in their wake, corrupting their land, their minds, their ways. Nor do they see the village folk who sit in village meetings struggling to find solutions, frustrated as they watch self-important men in self-important clothes and self-important cars pass through on their way to somewhere, somewhere out there. To wheel and deal, to make decisions that directly affect them and grow fatter off the fruits of their land, while others perish among the rotten debris of what is left behind. Yes, this thick black molasses which they call oil, which they take like a medicine, take it to cure one part, while it destroys another. If only they would stop. Just for a moment. Talk. Together. For it is their land. Then they would find another solution, another way. But to them, to these men and women standing in the Asikas' yard, this seems so far removed from what has happened to this little girl. Their answer, their solution, is to install bars, one by one, caging themselves in, distancing themselves from each other, allowing the seeds of mistrust to grow, giving fertile ground for the weeds of greed and corruption to take control.

But for the Asikas this is not their immediate concern. Getting through the week, the day, the hour, the morning, the funeral, is their immediate concern. And even as time passes, after Nkiru has been buried, and the visitors have taken their leave, they are still left to face the reality of it all. Like others they install iron bars at the windows and doors. Each evening, just as the sun sets, they imprison themselves in that cage, hiding behind the bars with a muffled terror. An unexpected knock at the door sends the household into a frenzy.

'Who's there?' asks Mr Asika from behind the metal doors, trembling, a cutlass in his hand, and his heart ready to explode. 'Who's there?' he shouts more loudly.

The two young girls, Hope and Ngozi, are not so brave; they scurry and run. Ngozi reacts like a gazelle sensing danger, remaining still as a statue, then without warning scuttling to safety, often under a bed or in a kitchen cupboard. Hope does much the same, but she dies a thousand deaths while she hides there, clutching her body tight, rolled up like a ball, trying to diminish herself, hide her breasts, clamping her knees and thighs against the pain she remembers. The atmosphere is thick, sharp with fear, it holds them all hostage.

'Papa Nkiru, it be Samuel from next house. I bring soup which my wife done make for you.'

The household sighs with relief and the pounding in their hearts slows down.

They exist like that until one day Mr Asika, tired of the fear, the grief, the dreadful memory he relives every time he enters his house, of the change in his wife, in himself, comes home to announce they are moving to America. He applied for work and has received several offers. If he is going to exist in fear it is better to do it in healthier and wealthier surroundings. And like so many others before him, with the knowledge, the willingness and the skills to build, he packs up his family's belongings and within a month they are gone. Hope goes with them, of course. They adopted her – they with no child and she with no parents. Thank Chukwu he works.

8

No Hiding Place

I WATCH THE soapy water sparkle in the hot midday sun; its diamond bubbles shimmer as they swirl around the washing bowl, hypnotizing me in their vortex. Towering corn stalks sway in the breeze, all the way from the yard to the university in the distance. Wind is calling again, but I do not go to him yet for today the spirits have summoned me back, and so I stand watching her, watching Ngozi kneel on the bumpy earth floor in front of the house, tiny stones piercing her knees. She lifts her arm and shades her eyes from the sun to watch the cars in the distance crawl their way home on the campus path. She scratches her short peppergrain hair, then looks over at the small mountain of dirty clothes beside her, then to the line where Mr Obindu's white shirts hang dripping dry in the sun. She gives a deep sigh and places another shirt in the washing bowl. She gathers the ends of the shirt collar between her two small hands, takes care to scrub gently at the thin line of dirt along the neckline as she's been taught.

I watch her, watch her smooth dark skin glisten with small beads of sweat. She's a pretty thing, with those teardrop eyes and bright white teeth that show when she smiles. I do not know what draws me back to her, but each time there is something familiar about her. Sometimes it almost feels as if I'm watching myself.

There are five of them in this household: Mr Obindu; Mrs Obindu, his third wife; Nkemjika, Nkem when shortened, their other house girl; Emmanuel, their sixteen-year-old houseboy, come errand boy, come business helper and occasional driver; and of course Ngozi.

Mr Obindu, the *Oga* of the house, is a fifty-one-year-old lecturer, who studied at Oxford University in England.

He has four children from two earlier marriages. His first wife died in childbirth, but bore him twins, girls. His second is not well and is locked away in an asylum; she bore him two children, also girls. All are away either at boarding school or university; now they are older they make excuses and spend their holidays with the families of their respective mothers. This suits Mr Obindu because it was too much trouble living with five women.

Mr Obindu is best described as particular. Particular about his shirts, about his shoes, about his car, which always shines, so much so that he checks his appearance in its jet-black body every morning. As I said, he is particular, even down to the type of polish used on his beloved Mercedes: French polish, specially imported, which Emmanuel applies under his supervision twice a week. Yes, he is particular about everything, except of course his choice of wife.

Mrs Obindu, his third wife, is not educated and nor is she from the same social background as he is. This is a great source of embarrassment to him. He believes in two things: education and status. He cannot tolerate people with neither quality.

Mr Obindu met his wife on a visit to his village almost fourteen years ago, a day after her sixteenth birthday, six months after his second wife was locked away. I was not there when they met, but I felt their meeting. You see, there are choices that the living have to make, important choices, that determine their destiny, no matter how young, no matter how limited in experience, and that is life, the gift of life, and eventually either their joy or their pain.

At the time, Mr Obindu needed someone to look after his four daughters and to bear him the son he desperately wanted. He had been looking for an educated woman, preferably a doctor or lawyer, young, about twenty-five or younger, and from the right social background. Carol Obindu fitted only one of his requirements. She was a true village girl, twenty-one years his junior when they met in the local market that afternoon. It was easy for him, an educated man, a lecturer, to turn her head with pretty words that sounded like the golden droplets she imagined rained in England, and in that meeting he turned her head from the boy I had wished for her. The boy who ran her little errands, who walked miles to buy the plastic bangles she once mentioned she liked, who adored her in spite of herself. The choice of man was her choice, the destiny she chose. But then she did not, and still does not, understand that her choices manifest in time to tell the truth about her character. In turn, Mr Obindu enjoyed the worship in her eyes, the sight of her buttercup skin and the pertness of her breasts, with nipples that seemed to point upwards towards the sky. But Carol's parents were strict Christians and would not allow her to see him unaccompanied, and she being young and aware of their wrath, did not disobey. So he married her, when his passion was almost at its climax and barely containable.

The passion that once shook his body and dulled his mind died long ago, and her pert breasts no longer point to the sky; her buttercup skin is no longer vibrant but ashen from the persistent use of bleaching cream, which leaves dark patches around her knuckles, elbows and eyes. Her greatest sin, in his eyes, is not bearing him the son he desperately wanted.

'Ngozi!' shouts Mrs Obindu from the house. 'Ngozi!! What is wrong with this girl?' she asks as she gets up from her chair and stands in the doorway on to the yard. 'Ngozi!!!'

'Yes, Ma!'

'I hope you no go take whole day for clothes?'

'No, Ma.'

'Nkemjika go need you for kitchen once she dey return from market.'

'Yes, Ma.'

'So hurry up now.'

'Yes, Ma,' replies Ngozi as she pushes her hands deeper into the washing.

'If I dey leave you people, nothing go be done for house,' mutters Carol as she joins her friend at the dining table.

Carol is well built, some would say pretty, but there is a harshness around her eyes and mouth, and a sadness that has grown over the years. She sits at the dining table facing her friend, several batches of material spread out between them. Ngozi laid them out on the table earlier, taking care to match and display them in a way she hoped would provoke a sale. Mrs Obindu, Carol, has a good head for business, learnt from the times when as a child, like Ngozi, she used to sell fruit by the roadside, and even in friendship, while entertaining, she cannot help but try to make money. She recognizes a similar talent for business in Ngozi, and grudgingly uses those talents wherever she can to her own advantage.

'Hmm, you have to have eyes for back,' says Carol. 'These house girls go rob you blind.'

Her friend nods in agreement and then fingers the fabric in front of her. 'This one dey shine, O.'

'You da fit steal show,' says Carol.

'How much?'

'Two thousand *naira*.'

'Hey, too expensive, O – it no be my wedding.'

Mrs Ebo's daughter will be getting married next weekend. It's a society wedding. Most of the town's prominent families will attend. The Ebos are cousins of Mr Obindu and Carol has not been asked to help, a snub that she has duly noted. However, she will be attending with her husband.

'You know Mary Ordu?' her friend asks, sifting through the pile to her right.

'No.'

'Yes, you do: Mary Ordu from Queens School.'

'You mean Timothy Nkwo's cousin.'

'Yes.'

'The one that owns Okyida luxury buses.'

'Yes, that exact one. You know she dey trade for England. Well, her cousin Nkoli dey tell how she dey go trade one time. When she return she dey find her husband and the house girl for bed.'

'No!'

'You can't trust them. Some of them go want steal your husband before your eyes, O. I even hear that some while you dey sleep, go open door for armed robbers, let them in.'

Mrs Obindu nods her head in empathy, then bends to pick up a burgundy-and-gold satin george. 'What about this one?'

'It nice, O. I have handbag which dey go. How much?'

'Eight hundred *naira*,' says Carol. 'If you dey want, I go take you to my tailor. He dey make clothes well well.'

'Where he dey?'

'For Acharra layout.'

'Okay, O.'

'Ngozi!' shouts Mrs Obindu. 'Ngozi!! . . . Ngozi!!!'

'Yes, Ma.'

'You no dey hear? Go tell Emmanuel to bring moto for front of house.'

'Yes, Ma.' Ngozi runs out to get Emmanuel.

The two women gather some of the cloth from the table and then their handbags.

The white Peugeot 504 pulls up at the front.

'Emmanuel, make sure you deliver all that material today.

'Ngozi, tell Nkemjika that I dey want my white blouse ironed for meeting tomorrow. Make you clean the black shoes, the one which have gold strap. Pack the material which we leave on table in my trunk and sort out the ones for delivery so E'mma can go and come back quickly. Make sure you clean that bathroom before I return, O,' she says, 'and Ngozi, tell Mr Obindu that we dey for tailors.'

'Yes, Ma.'

'Why are you still standing there?' asks Carol. '*Biko* move,' she says as she lifts her hand as if to slap her.

'Yes, Ma,' exclaims Ngozi, dipping swiftly to avoid Carol's backhand, then hurries into the house. She hears two car doors open outside in the yard, walks slowly towards Mr Obindu's study. The car doors slam and she exhales a deep sigh as she hears Mrs Obindu drive away, then braces herself to face Mr Obindu. She knocks lightly on the door.

'Yes,' he answers.

She enters. '*Oga*,' she says quietly, 'Madam say make I tell you that she dey for tailors.'

He nods his head. She begins to back out of the room.

'Come, come in.'

She looks at him blankly.

'Come in. I want to talk to you.'

She steps back into the room uneasily.

'Sit down,' he says, pointing towards a leather grandfather chair. She crosses her legs awkwardly and continues to stand.

'How are you finding it here?'

'Fine, Sir.'

'I spoke to your mother the other day when I passed through Obowi on business. She seemed to be happy with you being here.'

'Yes, Sir. Please, *Oga*, how is my mother? And my sister and brothers? Are they fine?'

'Yes. I gave her some money for them. Told her you are doing a very, very good job.'

'Thank you, Sir,' she says, beaming.

'Yes. I'll be helping with the school fees for the younger ones in primary while you're here, now that the mission is closed.'

'Yes, Sir, thank you, Sir.'

'In fact I can be a very generous man to those in my employment.'

'Yes, Sir,' she says, shifting her weight to her other leg.

'You seem to be flourishing,' he says, eyeing her sprouting breasts, which form little bumps against her faded cotton dress. 'You're developing well, putting on a little weight. You've developed nicely even in the four months you've been with us.'

She wriggles under his gaze. Doesn't speak.

He smiles at her. She shifts her eyes to the floor. 'I have washing for yard, Sir. Mistress dey want me finish before she return,' she says quietly.

'Don't worry, you will,' he chuckles. 'Come here.'

Ngozi doesn't move.

'Come here,' he asserts, then follows it with a smile.

Ngozi moves forward cautiously. Something doesn't seem right about their conversation, but she cannot explain, nor does she understand, why she's so frightened.

He picks up her hand. 'You're a strong little thing, aren't you?' His hand moves slowly up her arm, past her shoulder, his piercing eyes tracking its progress, he spreads his fingers on her back, moves further down and touches her bottom fleetingly. Then he returns his gaze to smile down at her.

'Sir, Mistress dey want me finish washing,' she repeats.

He laughs. 'It's a shame you don't have time to play. You're so young. She works you so hard, doesn't she?'

'No, Sir. Oh no, Sir. But I have washing to finish before Mistress returns.'

He grazes his hand on her stomach, moves it up. He stops and starts to tickle her under her armpits.

'Please, Sir, Madam go want me finish washing,' she cries and tries to push at his hands. He laughs. Then as suddenly as it came his laughter dies, he withdraws his hands and there's an intensity in his eyes.

'Ngozi!'

They both hear her name being called.

'Ngozi!'

She runs as fast as she can out of the room into the sunlight.

'Ngozi, where have you been? You haven't even finished the washing yet. If the Mistress comes back now she go have your behind,' says Nkemjika.

Ngozi mutters an apology – she's glad to see Nkem – and gets back to her washing. Nkemjika goes into the kitchen to start preparing the evening meal.

'Nkemjika, there's no water for water tank,' she says in a panic.

'Well, go tell Emmanuel to go fetch water,' Nkem replies irritably.

She runs to the boys' quarters. 'Emmanuel, please, O, water no dey for tank. I need finish washing before Madam bust my behind,' she pleads.

'How much washing you dey have?'

She points towards the backyard, where a pile of washing lies beside a large white basin.

'I no go collect enough water for that size clothes.'

Her lip quivers and she lifts her hands and flaps them round and round her head.

'Calm down,' he says. 'If you go collect clothes then I go help you wash them for stream.'

'Thank you. Thank you.'

It's six o'clock, early Saturday morning. Ngozi awakes with a jolt and looks towards the door. She searches out the sound she heard in her sleep, sees the undisturbed chair wedged under the door handle and breathes a sigh of relief.

She's edgy these days. It's as if her nerves tread on hot tarmac, making her take little jumpy steps. The sound of Mr Obindu's footsteps, the boom of his voice, the mere sight of him even in the company of others, makes her shake, and flee. And if you were to stop her and ask her why, she could not fully explain. All she could tell you in her naive but determined way is, 'It dey for smile, it dey scare me.'

But Ngozi is clever. I watch her. I speak to her, try to warn her when he's coming. I feel her trying to listen, even though I know she cannot hear me. But she can sense me. She tries hard not to be left in the house alone with him. If she's given a message to pass on to him she gives it to Nkemjika. On the few occasions she's been left in the house with him she quickly takes her bucket to collect water, and doesn't return until she sees Nkemjika walk up the hill or Mrs Obindu's car on its way home.

But sometimes when walking through the corridor or cleaning in their bedroom while others are busy in another part of the house, she is caught by surprise. On these occasions, his hand fleetingly grazes her arm or breast. Just quickly, enough for it to be construed an accident but too often for it not to be deliberate. After these encounters she feels like taking her metal bucket outside into the boys' quarters' washing cubicle to scrub herself clean. The thought of their last encounter makes her sick. At night, like tonight, it wakes her and will not let go.

Carol, Mrs Obindu, had sent her to get her handbag from their bedroom.

Ngozi picked up the bag quickly and turned to walk out, when Mr Obindu appeared from nowhere, blocking the doorway.

'Do you want to get past?' he said, laughing.

'Please, *Oga*.'

'Go on, try.'

'Sir, Madam say she want her handbag. She go come look for me if I no return.'

'Try and get past,' he demanded. 'Try.'

'Please, Sir.'

'Try.'

The two positioned themselves like rugby players. They prepared to tackle. She moved to her left, he moved right. She moved right, he moved left. She knew with a bitter desperation that she had to get out of that room. She charged, but he was too big. He grabbed at her and his hands began to roam everywhere. He held her tight against his chest with her back to him, his arms wrapped around her waist. She felt his breath against her ear, then his cracked laughter.

'You'll have to get better. Or maybe, you want me to catch you?'

'Please, Sir. Madam go come look for me.'

His hand moved down between her legs; he pressed himself into her back. She flinched.

'You like it,' he whispered. 'Don't you? You like it. Don't worry. You know what goes on between a man and a woman, don't you?'

Ngozi flinched again, she tried to push his hands away, prayed for help. 'I go scream, O,' she bluffed. As his hand moved deeper, tears filled her eyes. 'Please, O, I go scream.'

'Ngozi!' called Carol from outside. 'Ngozi!!' she said again, wandering in search of her. 'Ngozi!!!'

He let her go. She fled out of the room and straight into Mrs Obindu.

'Waytin you dey do for room?'

Ngozi stood in front of her, speechless.

'I say waytin you dey do!'

'I, I, I—'

Mrs Obindu slapped her across the face.

The force unsteadied her.

'You dey steal for my room! Ah, you dey steal from me!'

'Calm down!' said Mr Obindu as he emerged into the corridor. 'The girl was looking for a mouse I saw in the room,' he lied.

'Oh. Why you no say?' says Carol to Ngozi. 'Why you no say so? Fix yourself and go help Nkem for kitchen.'

Ngozi replays the incident and touches the side of her face. Thankfully, today is Saturday, and she has an instinct that rings inside her like an alarm; it rings loud enough that she cannot ignore it. She listens. She knows what must be done.

In an hour they'll be gone, except Emmanuel and herself. But now it's time for her to get up and do her chores.

'Morning, Nkemjika,' Ngozi says, yawning while stretching her legs and toes as far as they'll go.

'Go get water for tank and put it for fire. They go want leave soon soon.'

She hurries away to carry out Nkemjika's request, and as each second passes it fills her with frustration, as each minute passes it seems to expand, the hour ticks away, time creeps silently, until finally they, Mr and Mrs Obindu, are ready. They emerge from the bedroom, shiny, matching, wearing traditional dress.

'Ngozi, Emmanuel, make sure you lock up well well. I don't want to return and find armed robbers have taken all my things,' says Carol.

Mr Obindu looks on in irritation, then heads towards the car that Emmanuel has brought to the front. 'Carol, please can you hurry up before I leave you?'

Mrs Obindu climbs into the car beside her husband. Nkemjika sits behind the driver's seat in the back and waves to them through the back window, as the three of them drive off into the distance. Ngozi watches the trail of dust settle behind them.

'I better go deliver the material Madam dey say I deliver,' says Emmanuel.

'Okay.'

'You go be okay for house?'

'Yes.'

'I go soon come,' says Emmanuel.

She watches as Emmanuel disappears round the corner heading towards the other car, then hurries into her room to collect the bag that the Asikas gave her, and the money that Mama Chiedu forced into her hand the day she left Obowi. It's as if she has known all along that Mama Chiedu gave her the money for something important, and as she counts it, she's grateful. Grateful that she's not spent it on frivolous things, as she's been tempted to since leaving Obowi. But every time she's wanted to search out the money to buy sweets or a new ribbon for her hair or feminine toiletries, as she's done with the money her mother gave her, she's seen Mama Chiedu shaking her head with disapproval and has packed away the desire in obedience. As for her bag, the one the Asikas gave her, the handles have long since broken so she supports it under her arm, then hurries into the kitchen, before putting it down again to grab a chair to stand on. She stretches out her hand high above her head to reach the jar on the top shelf of the food cupboard, brings it down, empties the *gari* into a plastic bag and stows it in her suitcase. She has a strong feeling she's going to need it.

Ngozi walks quickly, then slowly, quickly, then slowly, all the time looking back at the house, her bag on her head. Tries to act casual in case a neighbour or one of Mr and Mrs Obindu's friends spot her. Soon she will be home, not long to go, just a bus journey, just a walk from the station.

Not long to go. Keep your head down. Do not look in anybody's eyes – they will see into you, might see the running in your eyes. Only a short ride, only a little walk. Soon you will be home. *Dalu Chukwu.* She is safe.

'Ngozi,' squeals her mother, 'Ngozi!!!'

Nneka drops the bowl in her hand and it spins round and round in the dust as she runs to greet her daughter.

'Mama!' she shouts, gripping the bag on her head. 'Mama!'

Six months have separated them. She swings her bag off her head to the ground, and they clasp each other tight, and the others pile in, hug Ngozi, welcome her home.

'Ngozi, waytin you dey do here?' cries Nneka with delight.

'The Obindus say I can come visit,' she lies.

Emeka and Blessing take her bag and drag her by the hand up the path towards their hut.

In the late evening, when all is quiet except for the echo of crickets and owls, when the excitement of the reunion has died down, when Emeka and Ike have gone to bed, Ngozi sits in the hut with Blessing. The kerosene lamp between them invites giant shadows into the room. They reminisce and reacquaint themselves. Ngozi looks around and sees the things she did not see when she first arrived. They talk in hushed tones.

'Blessing, waytin dey happen to Mama. She dey look tired, like someone who dey recover from sickness.'

'Ngozi, she dey sick here for two months. We dey fear, think she go die. We here for house dey pray morning and night. We dey pray, O, pray, O, until praise the Lord he send your *Oga* come help us. *Hei!* You're lucky you have such *Oga*,' she says in admiration. 'Ngozi, I tell you we all here dey starve. No money dey come except that one which I dey make selling oranges for bus station. It hard these days. The money no da stretch any more.'

'Why you no send for me?'

'We send message for you but you no reply.'

'I no dey get message.'

'Well, we dey see people who go for town, tell am to deliver message.'

'I no get the message,' insists Ngozi in despair.

'Well, anyway, the good thing is she much bettar,' says Blessing. 'Did you know that your *Oga* dey pay for Emeka and me to go school?'

'Yes.'

'Ngozi, you dey lucky, O. He nice man.'

Ngozi doesn't want to listen to Blessing talking about Mr Obindu and quietly excuses herself to join her mother outside. Nneka sits on an old wooden chair looking up at the moonless sky.

'Blessing dey tell me you dey sick for long time.'

'Yes, but praise be to God I dey bettar now,' she says with a smile.

Ngozi takes a seat beside her and they sit in silence looking up at the stars, a faint breeze calming their hot skin. After a moment she says, 'Mama, I run away from the Obindus.'

Her mother sits in silence looking up.

'I don't want to go back.'

Nneka continues to stare up at the sky.

'Mama, I dey think I go help you trade for market. It go be good,' she says with forced excitement.

'Ngozi, there is no future here for you.'

'But, Mama, I could make future.'

'Look at me. I don't want you to be so poor that you don't know when the next meal dey come, or how you go survive this day for that day. Trust me things dey get worst in this country. Every day I dey go for market and every day prices dey rise. Yesterday I go for market and tomatoes dey twice the price dey yesterday. Meat we no longer can afford.'

'B-b-b-but, Ma—' she says, trying to interrupt, to plead.

'Listen to me,' says Nneka leaning forward, 'if you stay for the Obindus you go get education, maybe a trade. Mr Obindu say he go send you learn tailoring. I dey see things dey get tougher here. Education go make your life bettar.'

'But, Mama, Mr Obindu he dey scare me. Something not right with him. He dey try put his hands for my body.'

Nneka closes her eyes tight, clasps her hands, raises her head, almost in prayer. She knows, she understands what her daughter's words mean. She looks at Ngozi sideways, and knows her daughter doesn't yet truly understand her own innocent words, spoken as a child. Her fears emerge. Over a year ago she had told her, 'Ngozi, promise me, if you have any problems, if you're not happy, if, if . . . if a man touches you, if he . . . if you're not happy, you will come home.' A year seems a lifetime ago to her now. Seeing death does that. She lifts her quivering hand to smooth back her hair. What are the choices to be made? To starve? To die? To live? To survive? These are the choices of women in this man's world. She knows. She was nine when a man first touched her. But in the room where she sleeps, on the floor beside her mat lies her purse and in it there is ten *naira* – it was not even enough to buy tomatoes at the market today.

'Mama, why are you silent?'

Nneka looks towards their hut, where her other three children lie sleeping. They almost starved when she was sick. Mr Obindu saved their lives. He gave them hope of a future. The three of them are in school now, and although she barely has any coins in her purse he sends regular money. She looks at her elder daughter, Ngozi. She can see the extra weight she carries, the extra height she's gained compared with Blessing and the healthy smoothness of her skin. She's fed, clothed and educated. With the Obindus, there is a future. What would she come back here to do? To starve like them? To sell oranges in the market for money, which the next day may be barely enough to buy even tomatoes? To be an outcast in this village? No, there is no future in that. Nneka's heart breaks and she chooses.

'Ngozi, as a woman there are some things we have no choice in,' she says and gets up from her chair. 'Tomorrow you will go back.' She enters the hut and disappears without another word. She goes to sleep and to cry over the innocence her daughter will lose. *Yes*, she thinks, *there are some things a woman has no choice in*, and she cries more, remembering the man who took her own innocence. Now her daughter will have the same fate.

The next morning before leaving, Ngozi takes the *gari* out of her suitcase and leaves it in the kitchen for her mother to find later when she's gone.

When Ngozi gets back, Emmanuel is sitting in the backyard on a small stool, his body leaning over a plate with palm oil and yam. Weary from planting corn he rubs his shoulders to take away the ache.

'Where did you go?' he asks.

'Home.'

'How come you come back?'

She shrugs her shoulders and puts her bag down on the ground.

'It be you who steal *gari* which dey for jar.'

She nods her head. 'Madam go kill me soon as she finds out.'

'Don't worry, I put the *gari* back.'

She looks at him in surprise. 'Why?'

He shrugs. 'I don't want to see you die when she finds out,' he replies.

'I will pay you back.'

He shrugs his shoulders again. Ngozi sits down beside him.

'You better go and start on your chores. They will be back tomorrow,' says Emmanuel.

Ngozi nods her head, picks up her bag and goes into the house.

Exactly five weeks, four days and five hours from the day of her return, Mr Obindu murdered her. Later that night, as the crickets sang their night song and all else was quiet, he crept along the dark corridor. There was no Mrs Obindu to ask him where he was going, or Nkemjika to interrupt: she had accompanied Mrs Obindu to the village to see her parents. He knocked softly on Ngozi's door.

'Are you okay in there?'

'Yes, Sir.'

'I thought I heard a noise. Can't be too careful nowadays.'

'I'm fine, Sir.'

He turned the handle but found it would not move. 'Open this door.'

'I'm fine, Sir.'

'Goddammit, open this door!'

'Really, Sir, I am fine.'

'Open this goddamn door before I tell the Madam of your insubordination.'

'Please, Sir, please.'

As I said, he murdered her that night, not in the external sense, but in a way that cannot be seen, deep inside, in the part that fuelled her spirit, the part that kept her fearless, that embraced her innocence and exuberance, the part that kept her belief in her invincibility, that valued her.

Enugu, 1986

Mr Obindu sits reading the newspaper in his brown leather chair. He watches his wife from the corner of his eye as she applies cream to her body. He observes the way her dimpled thighs rub together, the wobble of her sagging breasts and the stupid expression she wears on her face, before she ties the wrapper under her armpit and flounces over. She leans over him and kisses his cheek.

Mr Obindu shrugs her off and lifts his paper higher to form a barrier.

Carol gazes at the back of the newspaper and then withdraws to continue dressing.

You see, everything about Carol disgusts him – in fact he despises her, maybe even hates her. She is his last resort when he cannot find anyone else to satisfy his needs, but tonight is not one of those nights; tonight is the night before Christmas Eve and Carol is preparing to go to her society function. Mr Obindu fidgets with his newspaper. He's impatient to be with his mistress – his student, a nineteen-year-old girl whose body is still young, pert and fresh. In his eyes, a woman is past her desirable age once she's over twenty-five. He thinks about marrying a new wife, about his nineteen-year-old mistress, looks over at his present one – she's getting on, almost thirty-five. Carol, Mrs Obindu, sits at the dressing table applying a mild bleaching cream to her face and arms.

'You're fat,' he says finally, putting his paper down on his lap.

Her hand stops mid-air, then she pulls her wrapper up over her breasts, securing it under her armpit again, and asks, 'You dey go somewhere tonight?'

'I might be,' he replies.

'It dey long time since we dey spend evening together.'

'Really.'

'Yes,' she says, her eyes looking down at his shoes. 'I dey think it good for us to spend time together.'

'Really,' he repeats. 'What about your society function?'

'I think I dey stay here with you.'

He remains silent.

'Please, why you dey treat me so?'

'So . . .?'

'So coldly.'

Silence. With his arms resting on the arms of his chair, he stares at her.

'Talk to me!' she bursts out suddenly. 'Talk to me.'

'What do you want me to say?'

'That you dey want spend time with me.'

He lifts his newspaper and continues to read.

'LOOK AT ME!' she screams and walks over to grab his newspaper, tears it.

They stare at each other. She pleads with her eyes.

Then she opens her wrapper and stands naked in front of him. 'Look for my body,' she says quietly, and bends down to kiss him, moving her lips over his mouth. 'Make we go sleep for bed,' she says, reaching out to touch his crotch, hoping for some recognition. After all, she is a woman who needs to be desired.

He looks at her as if she were a doll. 'I'm going out. Don't wait up for me,' he says. He gets up, lightly pushes her aside, picks up the money he left on the dressing table and heads for the door.

Carol stands, watching him go. Her eyes radiate hurt.

Reaching the door, Mr Obindu stops, turns round, 'Oh, by the way, you better put your clothes on and cover up – you might catch a cold,' he says, and closes the door behind him.

Ngozi is in the lounge giving it the final touches before Christmas. She overhears them and is relieved when the *Oga* walks past her and leaves the house. She hopes the Madam will also go, then her evening will be complete. She takes the washing bowl outside to pour away the dirty water.

She is sixteen now, a child–woman. Her cheekbones are high, her skin still smooth and deep and red, like the miracle berry, and she still has those eyes, those teardrop eyes. She was a pretty child, but she'll be a beautiful woman if she ever discovers her beauty. Her hair has grown; she keeps it simple, plaited in two cornrows, and her body is strong and womanly like her mother's.

'E'mma?' This is what she calls Emmanuel. She and Emmanuel have become close friends as well as work colleagues, a closeness that started the night she came back to the Obindus' and he saved her by replacing the *gari* in the kitchen jar. 'E'mma,' she repeats when he doesn't respond, 'waytin you dey do out here just dey look for ground?'

He smiles weakly. 'I dey think about my family,' he says wistfully, kicking the dirt. 'By now Nkemjika dey for her home enjoying.'

'When last you dey for your village?' she asks.

'This July gone, six months ago, when my brother died.'

She throws the dirty water on to the ground and collects more water from the drum to water the plants inside, and thinks of things to say to comfort him. Failing to find words, she reaches out and rubs his shoulder warmly.

'Emmanuel, Ngozi,' calls Mrs Obindu as she emerges from the house, 'I dey go. I no return till tomorrow. Make sure you lock up house well well before you dey sleep. Emmanuel, give me keys for moto.'

'But, Ma, you don't want me to drive you?' he asks, giving her the keys.

'No, I go drive myself,' she replies. She doesn't want him to know exactly where she's going in case he tells Mr Obindu. After all, the sole purpose of this is to make her husband jealous.

'Ngozi, I hope you haven't finished for sitting room, since I see that you bring broom out here for yard. The rugs still need sweeping.'

'Yes, Ma.'

Nothing Ngozi does satisfies Mrs Obindu. She either has not cleaned enough or cleaned too much, cooked too much or not cooked enough, slept too much or not slept enough.

'Tomorrow we dey expect visitors for house. Make you no come out wearing that torn dress because you dey want embarrass me.'

'Yes, Ma.'

Mrs Obindu turns to Emmanuel and says more softly, 'Make sure you lock house well,' then turns again and says more sternly, 'Ngozi, you dey hear me, make sure you dey lock house well well.'

'Yes, Ma,' they reply in unison.

They watch her disappear around the side of the house where the car is parked and listen as she drives off.

'I dey hear them for room dey argue again,' she says to Emmanuel.

'I no understand why she no leave that old man. He dey treat her like dirt. You know he dey bring his mistress here sometimes when you all for village dey visit her parents.'

'No.'

She wants to tell him that their *Oga* also slept with her when the rest of them were out or late at night when Mrs Obindu travelled. But the words are buried within her; she wants to dig them out. But is there any point? Would it make any difference, except to out her shame? So she buries them deeper and thanks God that at least, so far, she's been spared from getting pregnant.

Mr Obindu has not touched Ngozi in four months now – he's a man of new things and she's no longer new, so maybe he's moved on, and like the quiet hurricane he is, leaving his devastation behind for Ngozi to pick up the pieces, for her to piece together fragments of herself. When he's old and frail, someone just like Ngozi, for there will be many Ngozis, will sit across from him and demand an explanation. She will scream and cry for an answer, for understanding: 'Why?' But he will look straight back at her, look her in the eyes like she's mad, and mumble his way through his pitiful words and his denial, for he will have rewritten history in his own mind. And her voice will push past him, echoing up the generations to tap Mr Obindu's orphaned father on the shoulder. To question Father Peter, the English missionary, who came spreading the word of the Church way back then in 1890. His pink cheeks rosy from the booze that helped him get through the heat and fever of, as he described it, 'This dark and godforsaken land.' His body shaking either from the booze, or the heat, or the fever, as he made his way through the dusty Onitsha town, saving darky souls, holding prayer meetings for the children in the room at the back of the church. On, further up the generations to Father Peter's father. And on, and on, till it echoes back down, back down the generations to land again at his, Mr Obindu's feet. 'Why?'

Emmanuel kicks the dirt. 'The new one which he have,' says Emmanuel, 'I swear that one younger than his youngest daughter. How he dey do am I no know.'

'You dey talk like you admire am.'

'No, O. I just dey say I no understand how such an old man dey get young women to sleep with am.'

'Money,' replies Ngozi. *Or force*, she thinks.

They clear up outside and move into the house, locking the doors behind them.

'Since *Oga* and Madam not for house, let us watch TV,' says Ngozi excitedly. She makes a feast in the kitchen and they sit down in the big comfortable chairs reserved only for the *Oga* and Madam. They watch the big box and the rerun of an old Western, which has been on several times before. They are drawn into the story and talk animatedly, the action builds up, the heroine is in trouble, the villain about to be uncovered. Then without warning or apology, the film is replaced with a local programme, a dialogue between two politicians. Emmanuel and Ngozi lean back disappointed in their chairs. They contemplate the unfairness of it. A silence is created between them, as each retreats into their own thoughts. Emmanuel thinks about his brother's death; he needs to talk.

'You know what dey hurt,' he says as he forces his words out into the silence. 'I was suppose to go home that weekend he died; instead I stay here dey help Mrs Obindu.'

Ngozi feels the tension in his body and sees the glaze in his eyes. She puts her arm around him to comfort him. He turns towards her, his body shakes and she holds him tight. She hears his shallow breathing as he tries to control the tears and she holds him until she can't feel him shaking any more.

'Thank you,' he says.

'For what?'

'For listening.'

She nods. 'E'mma, you would have done the same for me, O.'

'Yes, I know, but I think . . . I mean, I have watched . . . You're a caring person. You're not like the little girl I first knew. I have watched you and I think—' His mouth is suddenly searching out hers.

Ngozi is startled at first, she freezes, but she's learnt not to resist, so she lets his lips roam her mouth, lets his tongue enter. His kiss grows deeper, he shifts her gently to the floor, moves on top of her, she lies beneath him waiting, waiting for him to use her and remove himself from her body. She lies still. Emmanuel feels her stiffen and whispers 'I love you' in her ear. She doesn't believe him, but it's nice to hear the words. That someone, that Emmanuel, could love her – that she could possibly be worth loving. He bends to unbutton her blouse to expose her bra, kisses her shoulder, her breast and the very faint birthmark on her stomach, lifts himself, draws her body into his, holds her, stroking her shoulders and breathes his dreams into the mosquito night. It's this that makes her stay, that makes her fully turn towards him, to be held, touched, and as their hands meet, their fingers entwine. Emmanuel's words are like food that feeds her soul, food that enables her to grow. And when he's finished he doesn't lift himself from her and leave, instead he turns her into his arms, and she listens to his heartbeat beneath her ear as he falls asleep.

And so they, Emmanuel and Ngozi, begin. Stealing glances as they attend to their chores, and on occasion when she's finding it difficult to lift or to carry, or complete her tasks, he's right there beside her to help, without asking, like he senses her and responds. Sometimes he brings gifts, little things, like the *udala* fruit, because she told him once when they lay together in the boys' quarters after making love that it reminded her of her mother and home, or little beaded jewellery which he buys in the local market just because he wants to see her smile.

And just when Ngozi is beginning to believe that maybe Mr Obindu has truly moved on, as she lies there daring to daydream of a future with E'mma, when Mrs Obindu has travelled to visit her elderly parents in the village, Mr Obindu comes to her. There are no soft words or gentle touches. Only the painful grasping of breasts and private parts, the intolerable noise of his grunting, the smell of his body odour, the irritation of his sweat on her body. And as she lies beneath him, powerless, feels the sharp pain as he unceremoniously lifts her legs to stab away inside her, she begins to cry. When he's finished he wipes his penis, pulls up his pants and quietly leaves the room. She watches him go. Then turns her body away from the door, and sobs.

But now it's night-time and she's awake again; she feels something, her pain. She's been dead for such a long time, but E'mma loving her has awakened her to her pain. And there are times when you need to feel the pain – it tells you you're alive; it can be good, it can be your best friend.

A month later pain gives her back her fight.

Ngozi is outside in the yard. She bends over the washing basin and scrubs away at the dirt on one of Mrs Obindu's dresses. Suddenly a thick hand pounds down hard on her back. She feels the thump, the pain, travel through her body, turns and looks up in shock, to stare straight at Mrs Obindu. Mrs Obindu stands shouting over her. She pounds down on Ngozi again, knocks her off balance; the pain of it brings tears to her eyes, and Ngozi falls on top of the pile of washing and knocks over the washing basin.

'I know it be you, I know it!' Carol screams over her.

Ngozi looks at her, confused. She tries to untangle herself from the dirty clothes, tries to pick herself up from the ground, but then she feels the sharp sting of a whip against her back and the tingle spreads. Her hands try to reach the source, to soothe it away.

'No, Ma, I beg,' she shouts. 'Please. Please Ma, God, O. Make you have mercy, O.'

'It no be you who put hand for pot, come spoil my soup?'

'No, Ma.'

'You see, you dey lie. God save us from you people!'

Ngozi looks at her mistress's face; it is bitter with frustration, hard like steel, tight from years of living with a judgemental husband and there is no peace in her eyes. Mrs Obindu hears her plea but hits her again with the whip. Somewhere at the back of Mrs Obindu's subconscious she knows what is going on, what her husband is doing to Ngozi, but refuses to acknowledge it. Instead she takes the anger out on this child–woman.

'Please, Ma, please, O,' Ngozi screams as the cow tail descends on her again.

'You think you go come to my house, come with your dirty village ways, come put hand for pot, come spoil my soup.'

'No, Ma,' she sobs through the stinging. 'I no go do it again,' she lies.

'So, you dey tell truth now. Hey, what I dey suffer with you girls, only God knows,' Mrs Obindu says in sympathy with herself. 'Make you dey leave my sight before I kill you with anger.'

Ngozi collects herself, leaving the yard as fast as she can without aggravating the jagged twinges of sharp lemon pain that radiate from her back. She goes to her room and cries herself to sleep.

Ngozi awakes to the sound of E'mma's voice. Her head is splitting and her wounds still sting.

'Ngozi, how you dey?' Emmanuel is kneeling beside her, stroking her head. 'I dey hear all the commotion dey happen for house – sound like Mistress want kill you.'

'What you dey do here? You want put me for trouble if Mistress dey find you here?'

'No worry, I see am leave the house, then I come see for you. How you dey?'

Ngozi doesn't answer. He sits down next to her; she lays her head against his leg. Emmanuel continues to stroke her head gently.

'E'mma, I no go make it in this house, O,' she cries. 'Every day she dey find something come trouble me. I want kill myself or kill am. E'mma, I want end it now.' He holds her tightly. 'E'mma, please, O, help me, O. I want leave this place. Please, please. I beg, O. I want die. I can't live here. I go do something.'

Wind calls for me.

I watch the two on the bed, wish I could stay longer, try to speak to them, but Wind is demanding my attention. He grabs my hand, pulls at me. There are more pressing matters elsewhere. If only we could help them.

9

The Beginning – The Passage

THEY SEPARATED US, unchaining some of the young girls, making them sit in a huddle on deck, leaving the rest of us still shackled. I followed the others down into the hold, one by one we entered; the devils stood around us clutching guns and whips lining the path down to that hell. I heard the sound of their whips against flesh, the sound as they hit the decks, the shouting of foreign commands, and the crying and whimpering of those around me. And as I entered, dragged along by the others, I looked up to the sky, looked up for my God, but he was nowhere to be found. As I went down further into that hell I caught his eyes, Wind's eyes, and without words I begged him to save me, begged him to rescue me. I clung to his eyes until the movement of those in front of me pulled me forwards. There were human beings just above me, with barely enough room to crawl, packed in shoulder to shoulder. I couldn't sit up for the wooden planks over my head, I could not turn left or right for the people chained beside me. Instead I looked to my right into the face of the older man beside me; he was speechless with terror, I felt his hot breath on my cheek, then to my left, a young woman with her child clinging on as she wept and mumbled. I gripped her hand tight, tried to comfort them as best as I could, thought of my baby Uzo who I was forced to leave in the shrine, wondered if he'd been found. And then I turned my face upward and cried out like the rest of them for Chukwu to save me, and in the midst of my crying I felt a wetness on my skin from the shelf above, and it dawned on me that it was the urine of the person above me. I tried to stand up, to wipe it, but banged my head on the wooden planks, then I realized that we were all to toilet right where we were. Then the hold door closed, the little light there was disappeared, taking with it the small circulation of air as the real hell of that journey began.

These days, Wind and I roam the London docks, looking for our daughter with the half-moon on the side of her face, who smelt of sweet ginger and spice from the cloth they wrapped her in. Wind holds me, I untangle myself and circle him, teasing, then stop to watch the group of young people carrying backpacks. One stands beside an imposing bronze statue, and holds open a book, from which he reads to the rest of the group. His voice is carried away by the breeze. I look down at the plaque beside the statue, a prominent merchant and sugar plantation owner, one of the founders of these docks. I look up at the stern face. It's strange to look up into the face of a man who caused your death, infected your life with his disease. I shiver, and listen.

'He was born in 1746. Robert . . .'

I often wonder if – no I don't, I believe that history was truly invented for the rich and the learned. I look back at the group gathered around the statue, their faces expectant. They are young. They will never know they stand on the very spot where I drew my last breaths. Their history has erased us.

Neither I, nor Wind, nor my baby girl exist for them. Nor the ones whose bodies were thrown like sticks into the sea. Then I had shivered with fever, from the damp and sickness, unable to breathe for the stench, squirming as rats ran over my body, with sores on my joints where the shackles rubbed away at the skin, unable to roll to the left or to the right for the bodies. I thought I would die, that they would come for me, throw my body overboard like wood, but then, as my spirit willed to pass from this world, I saw a faint light in the distance coming from an open hatch. I saw Wind crouch, moving among the bodies, searching, and with all the strength I could muster I lifted my arm and groaned for him to find me, then Wind was beside me, he lifted me, I was on his back, and he carried me, my head bumping against his back, crawling among the bodies, out into the air.

If you look closely, if you should ever care, you will find my truth hidden, filed away for the business of business, of insurance, and the taxes of this land, listed in the voyage records, counted, merely as an item among the inventory of rum and sugar.

But Wind is different, his truth can be found, if anyone should care to look, hidden in birth records, court records, tried as a common thief. They put a hangman's noose around his neck, and he kicked his legs as he struggled for air, as he bounced from that rope. Oh, my love, my love. I had already gone from the world, and so I watched on crying, patiently waiting for his spirit to join mine.

We, Wind and I, have roamed these docks and their snake river looking for our child. Sometimes it seems we will never find her, and on those occasions, he is my strength and I am his. We have seen so many lives snaking just like this river. Still, we continue, watching the changes, flowing through time. We flowed through the times when this dock was buzzing with the daily business of loading and unloading of goods, loud with chatter, through its night business, alive with drink and the fumbling of hands under petticoats. The sheer volume of goods made my head spin. And we floated into the night when the skies turned crimson, barraged with fire, with explosions fanning out like feverish rainbows, as German planes flew high in the sky. I thought it was the end. That these old docks would burn to the ground. But they didn't. Instead they came to hammer them back to life, rebuilding them, until the tallest buildings the area had ever seen began to grow, and dominate the East End skyline, the business of money, not cargo, setting it alive.

But mostly I remember the morning I thought I saw her. Wind and I saw the large white dilapidated ship steam its way from the Channel and dock at the mouth of this snake river on that misty morning. The ship made the other boats seem so small. It was exhilarating to watch the crowds at the quayside with their cameras, ready to capture the spectacle. I knew there was something different about this boat. Maybe it was all the cheering and jollity coming from the ship itself, but it was also in the air, and so we ran towards it like children.

Wind noticed first and he stopped me. 'They're like us!'

I beamed at him, nodding. 'A boat full of people just like us.'

And we floated on board among them, drunk with the excitement. I've seen many boats on which people like me travel, but never like this – these people were not in chains, nor were they there in search of a better life somewhere, instead they came standing like men. I saw a reporter trying to interview a slim man with a trilby hat. He was singing joyfully. I listened and smiled. Wind grabbed my hand, I giggled, and we danced.

Lon-don is the place for me
Lon-don this lovely city
You can go to France or America, India, Asia or Australia
But you must come back to London City.

And as we danced, he twirled me and I smelt her, the ginger and spice. He twirled me again and I saw the half-moon on the side of her face. I stopped.

'She is here. Our baby is here!' I screamed to him, and I searched and searched, tearing up and down that boat. 'My baby is here!'

But we could not find her before they all disembarked, scattering in different directions.

PART III

Michael

10

Happy Birthday

Brixton, 1986

I T'S TWO THIRTY in the morning and Michael turns the stools over, places them on top of the bar, looks over at yet another blonde who sits waiting for him, and smiles at her, then puts up a finger to signal wait a minute, and heads towards Tom's office.

These five years have been good to Michael. He is as tall and broad as his sixteen-year-old self could have hoped for, although not as much as his adult self would like. Some mornings I see him facing the mirror at his local gym, his arms pumping up and down, admiring his physique, secretly spying on the other young men behind him, before returning to his own reflection to smile and continue pumping. He's worked hard for the broadness in his shoulders, but his height – well, this is a gift from his birth mother, the only gift she ever gave him. His hair – well, that too has grown; his twisted locks sit comfortably on his shoulders in a hairstyle he would never have been allowed if Ms Lorez were still alive.

He's good-looking, some would say sexy. But others remark on how much he resembles his father these days. I think it's the cheek-bones and the reddish tint to his milk-chocolate complexion. Or maybe it's in his swagger – yes, there is a swagger in his step, a quiet overconfidence, just like his father's. In the early days, before he pumped himself out, self-doubt battled in him. So he watched Devon, copied him, as he used, so long ago now, to copy his father, Mr Watson, and then his brother Simon, until one day, he was able to take the training wheels off. And over these few years, a combination of his renewed friendship with Devon, a buried respect for the Mr Watson he saw cross a courtyard on his way to work, a wanting of the brother he tried to be like as a boy, and the gym – from all of these his studied swagger emerged, stayed and settled within him.

His steps are usually sure, but on nights like tonight, I sense a tension in him. Earlier this evening, as he made his way to work, Michael folded what appeared to be a letter and placed it in his back pocket. He passed the children's swings near the building where, one time, long ago and almost forgotten, his father, not known for making the cleverest of decisions, jumped out the first-floor window naked, escaping from the father of that sixteen-year-old he ran off with. His father, Mr Watson, scared the children, making them run away screaming, and the commotion brought out the whole neighbourhood, who watched in amusement as the girl's father chased him down the road. Michael walked on, brow furrowed, deep in thought. But more than the letter nestled in his pocket; as he journeyed on I saw his steps become shaky as he caught small reminders along the way: the faint smell of ginger as he passed the Indian store; the sight of yellow daffodils on a woman's dress, which peeked out from under her coat; the headlines of the recent riots on the news stands just outside the Tube station. The demons seemed to sit heavy on his shoulder – 'Jump, wog, jump' – and like other nights, just like tonight, he looks for a drug to escape into, and his chosen drug is women.

Outside Tom's office, Michael raises his hand to knock on the door, but then he hears Devon and Tom inside.

'What they say?' says Devon to Tom.

'It's coming in two weeks. I want you to make sure everything goes smoothly. I don't trust those guys. I want you to head up the office over there. I've got another guy to deal with day-to-day things.'

'How much?'

'Worth about quarter of a mill. Get this one right and we're made. These guys have some good connections so don't screw it up.'

Michael fingers the letter in his back pocket, then knocks firmly on the door.

'Come in,' says Tom.

'Just want to let you know that it's all cleaned up. Peter's still counting the money.'

'Great. Thanks, Michael.'

'Devon, you going home soon?' asks Michael.

'Yeah.'

'Could you give us a lift to Clapham Junction?'

'Picked up another one?' asks Tom. 'I don't know how you guys do it. Too much stamina, that's what I say.'

'Yeah, give us a minute and I'll be out,' says Devon.

Michael leaves the room. Devon follows a minute later.

'How much do they know?' asks Tom's right-hand man, glancing at the door that Devon has just closed behind him.

'Not much,' says Tom.

Tom's right-hand man nods his head.

'So keep it that way. The less anybody knows, the better.'

'As you say, boss.'

'So what were you and Tom talking about?' Michael asks as Devon manoeuvres the Ford Fiesta round a corner. The blonde sits quietly in the back. Michael turns to smile at her, touches her knee, then twists back to turn up the music a little more.

'A bit of this and that – you know, business.'

'What kind?' he asks quietly.

'Don't be stupid, you know what kind.'

Michael taps on the dashboard for a second, looks back at the blonde mouthing along to the music as she stares out the window, then turns back to Devon, leans in and asks, 'So what do you have to do and how much?'

'Tom says half a grand. If it goes through, the stakes go up. You want in?'

Michael is silent for a few seconds. 'I'll think about it. When you want an answer?'

'By Saturday. I'll have to okay it with Tom first though.'

'Yeah.'

'Slow down. My street's the second on the right,' says the blonde in the back.

Devon turns into the street, lowers the music.

Michael gets out and opens the door for her, leans into her once she's standing and gives her a long kiss, which begins to chase away the uneasiness within him.

'Thanks for the lift,' says Michael as he bends to say goodbye.

'Oh, Michael, I forgot – happy birthday, mate,' says Devon.

Michael laughs.

'By the way, you said Saturday, right? At the Baileys'?'

'Yeah, Auntie Eliza said I could invite you.'

'Do I bring anything?'

'No, just yourself,' chuckles Michael, then steps back from the car, waves goodbye, and breaks into a jog, catching up with the blonde who is halfway up the stairs to her flat.

It's almost light outside and Michael makes his way across the silent courtyard. The same courtyard that his neighbours Mr Clark, Mr Wright, and the others left of that generation, and at one time, briefly, his father, crossed, day after day, week after week, year after year. To factories, transport systems and businesses, somewhere out there, leaving so early they crept out the house so as not to wake the little ones. Those little ones are not so little any more. Many are much older than Michael. In their day, when they, Mr Clark and the others, were young, not much older than my little boy–man, they arrived carrying bold dreams in their suitcases. And as they disembarked from the ships, the planes, they shivered down the stairs, pulling up the collars of their jackets against the chill, and headed for Brixton, clutching the letter that Auntie Beryl, or Sister Sybil, had sent about this strange place called England, headed to the labour exchange. To sleep two in a bed, day shift, night shift, focusing on their dream, on the family that waited to be brought over, and despite the 'No coloureds' signs in windows, the difficulty of finding a place to lay their head, some succeeded. Some made it on to the estate, and some made it off the estate. Bought the rundown houses in the surrounding streets, a piece of England to call their own. Until Brixton was filled with big families who knew each other, partnered with each other, guarded each other, against the harshness they found, somewhere out there. Against the 'Go back to where you belong.' Against the skinheads and football hooligans. Against the police who held them under siege in their little village of Brixton. But I digress.

Michael ascends the stairs to his flat, passes the bathroom window, hears Marcia singing soprano.

'Mor-nin'.'

He slams the front door, thumps on the bathroom wall. 'We've got neighbours.'

'Mor-nin',' she sings again, to the buildings she can see through the small high window.

Michael smiles, smells the aroma of bread and chicken, hangs up his jacket and heads for the kitchen.

It's small. It misses the fresh little touches Ms Lorez would have given if she were alive. But her presence is still felt in the little plates she collected from the secondhand shop under the arches in Brixton Market, in the flowers she stencilled on the kitchen cabinets that peel and fade with age and in the old net curtains that still hang over the sink, through which you can see the high-rises in the distance.

Michael takes the food out of the oven and sits down at the small table to eat.

'Happy birthday,' sings Marcia as she emerges from the bathroom into the kitchen, then stops. 'You could have waited.'

'I'm sorry, Sis,' says Michael, looking up at her with his mouth full. 'I'm hungry.'

'It was meant to be a surprise.'

'Well, it is. Thank you.'

Marcia raises her eyebrows.

'It's really delicious,' he says and smiles.

She takes a seat beside him. Looks him up and down. 'Hey, promise you'll be back on time tonight.'

'What for?' he says.

'Just promise.'

'Okay,' he says as he chews on another piece of chicken. 'I promise.'

'So how does it feel to be twenty-one?' she asks.

'The same as it did being twenty.'

Marcia looks again at her brother, and sees the puffiness under his eyes. 'How was work?' she asks, and shifts in her seat. 'Oh, by the way, Sharon phoned last night.'

He wrinkles his nose. 'Same as usual. Did you do your homework last night or watch TV?'

'Of course I did my homework.'

'Bring it.'

'Michael, I'm sixteen. I don't—'

'I said bring it.'

She gets up reluctantly and goes to fetch her books.

Michael saw Mr Clark's granddaughter the other day with her pregnant belly, trying to manoeuvre the buggy with her two-year-old up the stairs. This makes Michael protective of Marcia – it's not the future he wants for his sister. So in reaction, he continues Ms Lorez's tradition of looking over her books. Inside he's not sure how it acts as contraception against that reality, but he saw Ms Lorez do it so many times he believes it must hold an answer.

He remembers Thursday evenings when Ms Lorez was alive and it fills him with warmth; he hears the canned laughter from *The Morecambe & Wise Show* quietly rattle out into the sitting room from the old black-and-white TV with the missing knobs, Ms Lorez and Marcia huddled at the table in the corner.

'What you goin' to be, child?' Ms Lorez would ask.

'I don't know.'

'I thought you wanted to be a doctor?'

'I know, but my teacher Mrs Strand said I should set my sights more realistically. Maybe do a secretarial course.'

'Never you mind Mrs Strand,' Ms Lorez said, the healer blood in her reacting. 'If you want to be a doctor, then you're goin' to be a doctor, you hear me?'

'But—'

'But nothing. Being a doctor about hard work. You goin' work hard. Mi na spend all this here money fi nothing less, you hear me. So what you goin' do?'

'Work hard, Mummy.'

'Mi didn't hear you. What you goin' do?'

'Work hard.'

'Dat's my girl.'

Ms Lorez held down three jobs so Marcia could go to the private Catholic school, Celestial Virgins. One at the hospital during the day, one cleaning early mornings and another at the old people's home on Saturdays. She used to say the choices the government gave her were no-hope schools. She said she knew Marcia wasn't the brightest, but she wasn't the dumbest, and with the right start she could get somewhere and not learn too many bad ways like she would in the no-hope schools. And when Ms Lorez died, he saw Marcia drive herself, work like she would find the answers in her books, like Ms Lorez was in those books. So one Sunday evening, when they were still at Uncle Fred's, to find some normality between them he asked her to show him her blue book, just like Ms Lorez did, and when she handed over her blue book with all those As, he just knew he couldn't take her out of the school. He couldn't do it to her, he couldn't do it to Ms Lorez. It had been the one constant thing in Marcia's life. It was hard for Michael to find a way to make it happen, but with Marcia helping by getting a scholarship one year, and finding a few charities to apply to, and the money from Ms Lorez's insurance, he'd found the rest. But lately, he's been finding it difficult to keep up.

'What's taking you so long?' calls Michael from the kitchen.

'I'm coming,' she says, her books in her hand. He takes them from her and reads in silence.

Michael spent most of his time trying to break out of school, to escape from its confines, the restrictions that suffocated him, to be more than he saw in his teacher's eyes. Ms Lorez didn't approve of course, and they spent most of their time arguing, that winter before she died.

'You tink you're a man now?'

'No, I just want to earn money.'

'Money, dat's all you young men tink bout. Please stay a likkle longer.'

His will collided with hers like a moth into a window; hers always appearing as if it wasn't there until he tried to go through. In the end he had no choice but to take up his CSEs at evening school, anything to stop her from going on. When she died it seemed pointless continuing, especially with Marcia to take care of, but his interest is ignited every time he opens Marcia's books – maybe it's the freedom of it, or the fact he opens her books on his terms.

Michael checks her school diary for homework, her books to confirm she's done it and then her grades.

'Can't you speed up a bit?' she asks, growing impatient.

He looks up from one of her books. 'In my own time.'

Marcia leans back in her chair. She observes her brother as he reads over her work.

Michael isn't a proper Rasta, just a fashion one. The locks are neat, recently trimmed at the local barbers on Acre Lane. His work clothes, black shirt and a pair of black trousers, are the closest he gets to dressing up.

Marcia loves her brother with such a force it frightens him, it's the kind of love that is hard to live up to, the kind that grabs you, fills you with panic, 'cause you know one day it's bound to shatter. Michael sees it in her eyes. It weighs on him.

I remember watching what happened not long after Ms Lorez's death, when the social workers came for Marcia.

'You're not taking my sister,' said Michael.

'But, Michael, you're too young to be able to care for yourself and your sister.'

'I'm not letting you in. My sister stays here, that's it.'

Marcia had been beside him as he stood at the door talking to them, one eye pressed to the keyhole, then he'd turned to her. 'Marcia, call Uncle Fred and Auntie Eliza over here. Now!'

She stayed at Auntie Eliza's that night. The next day Michael went out and got them legal help. Auntie Eliza and Uncle Fred helped with the bill.

'Where were you last night, Michael?' she asks when he finally gives her books back.

'Mind your own business,' he says, then looks at his sister and relents. 'At work.'

'But you finish at three on a Thursday night and you should have been home by three thirty, four latest.'

'Bwoy, you're nosy aren't you?'

'Well, where were you?'

'Marcia, just go to school. I'm tired, okay?'

'Not until you tell me where you were. I was worried about you.'

'If you must know they wanted me to stay behind and clear up some stuff behind the bar,' he says, his gaze avoiding hers.

'You could have called.'

He spent the night with the blonde from the club, but that isn't the sort of thing he can tell his baby sister. He doesn't want her thinking it's all right for a woman to sleep around, not his sister.

'Well, I'm sorry. I'll call next time,' he says, seeing her face. 'It's almost half past – you'd better hurry and get to school. You'll be late.'

He watches his sister collect her things and rush out the door, then turns on the radio, tuning into a pirate station. He sings along to Chaka Khan's latest, starts to sort out his finances, stops halfway. Then with a furrowed brow he brings out the letter he folded away in his back pocket yesterday, places it beside his diary on the table, looks down, touches it, but changes his mind, then suddenly picks it up and unfolds it. The figure seven hundred and fifty pounds flashes back at him. He breathes in, wipes his hand over his face, rubs his chin, then puts the letter back on the table and pulls back his locks.

Last week Sister Frances called him.

'Mr Watson?'

'Yes.'

'This is Sister Frances from the Celestial Virgins Upper School.'

'Hello, Sister.'

'Mr Watson, I'm sorry to bring this up but we've been looking at the status of Marcia's school fees and have noticed that they've not been paid these last two terms, plus you still owe some from last year. Can you tell me when you'll be paying these outstanding fees?'

'I'm working on it at present.'

'I'm sorry, Mr Watson, we need something more concrete than that. We really don't want to have to do this, but I'm afraid to inform you that if we do not receive the fees by the end of the month we cannot allow your sister to attend the school or sit her final-year exams.'

'That isn't fair.'

'I know, Mr Watson, but we have three hundred other girls to look after and if you aren't paying the fees it's affecting them. I'll be sending a letter to you by the end of the week.'

That was last week and now here is the letter.

And yet they are almost there, Marcia is almost done, only one more term left, but seven hundred and fifty pounds – where is he going to get the money from?

Over the last year he's avoided Sister Frances's attempts to talk to him at the school, paid as much as he could as he's gone along in the hope he could drag it out, but here it is. There's no more avoiding it, time has run out, end of the month they'll exclude her, and her final exams start in May. *Almost there*, he thinks, sees Ms Lorez's disappointment, starts to feel his own failure but rejects it, bites his little fingernail and wonders about Devon's job. It sounded easy enough, would solve the problem, but there's an unease inside him. As I said, his chosen drug of escape is women, so instead, in order to escape from the real problem, he picks up his diary, sifts through the pages as he wonders which girlfriend he owes a call. He has too many things to remember, so he keeps a diary where he writes in code which one he's due to see and which one he owes a call.

He's interrupted when the phone rings.

'Hello.'

'Don't hello me. Where the hell were you last night?'

'And a good morning to you too, Sharon.'

'Where were you? You bastard.'

'Don't ask such a stupid question. I was at work. Why you bugging so?'

'No, you weren't. You liar.'

'What am I suppose to have done now?'

'I saw you leave the club with some woman. You fucking bastard.'

'What, you're checking up on me now?'

'No, no,' she stammers. 'I phoned Marcia last night and she said you were at the club so I went round to see your birthday in with you, and there you bloody were, leaving with some woman.'

He hates nagging women, especially ones that check up on him.

'Listen, I don't know what your problem is – calm down. You're getting paranoid,' he says. *Take control, think quick, think. I left the club with Devon last night.*

'You mean you saw me leave the club with Devon and a woman last night,' he says.

'But, but—'

'But what? You saw me leave the club with Devon and his woman and now you're phoning me up to bug me.'

'You're lying,' she says.

'Listen, if you don't believe me, phone Devon and ask him.'

'I will.'

'Go on then.'

'But.'

'I don't know what your problem is – you're always accusing me of something. How can I be in a relationship with a woman who doesn't trust me?' he says, his voice rising.

'I'm sorry, but—'

'This really isn't working, Sharon. I think it's best if we—'

'I'm sorry, Michael, I'm really sorry. I suppose it's my experiences that make me jumpy. I'm sorry.'

'Well, you can't keep judging me by your past relationships. If you keep bugging about something, what you worry about the most, you're gonna make it happen.'

'I know. I'm sorry.'

'It's okay. We're still meeting later?' He makes a mental note to buy her something. Nothing expensive, but romantic – she'll like that.

'Yes. I suppose it's not too late for me to say happy birthday,' she says, her voice softer.

'Not at all.'

'I was thinking about you all day yesterday,' Sharon says.

He hears the smile in her voice. 'I've been thinking about you too, baby. How you been since Monday?'

'I've been aching all over,' she says.

'Really. Do you want me to help you with that ache?'

Sharon laughs. 'I'm not going to work today. You want to come over and celebrate?' she says.

'Just try and stop me. I've got a few things to finish over here. I'll be over after noon.'

'I'll see you laters then. Make sure you hurry over, baby,' she says and puts the phone down.

He wonders if he has enough condoms and bends over to make a note in his diary to get some from the chemist around the corner. Ms Lorez warned him once about tricky girls who get pregnant to trap a boy and for the price of a council flat. But this is not the reason why he's diligent about his condoms, nor because it's 1986 and AIDS is a death sentence, for Michael is not exactly the most careful or diligent of young men to make notes in diaries about such things. After all, he's a lad, a twenty-one-year-old lad, who has all the hormones and desires, and the opportunities most lads his age don't have, and a little advice from Ms Lorez given some five years ago isn't going to stop the force of that tide. So the true reason, like most things in Michael, is hidden, camouflaged behind simple actions and decisions, so airy it seems dumb. You see, you have to peel back the layers to get to it, so many layers, and somewhere among these layers Michael is sure, as sure as he is that tomorrow will come, that the sky is blue, that he is all man, not a queer like Ronny at number 25. He's one hundred per cent sure he wants to be a father, wants to hang out with his kid, wants to be there for him, maybe like Simon was there for him, buffering him from the full depth of their father's bad choices, a little substitute dad, instructing him along the way.

'Mans don't do dat,' or, 'You can't be crying like dat, Michael. Mans dem don't cry like dat, man.'

Michael knows what his son will look like, and surprisingly he's not a mini Michael, but a mini Simon and Mr Watson. Maybe it has to do with the relationships he wishes to recapture and redefine. Either way the condoms are bought not in reaction to AIDS or tricky women, but subconsciously in not wanting to pass on that mental trauma that afflicted his brother, and trying to control, the only way he knows how, the spread of it, and in reaction against Mr Watson, his father, and the devastation he left behind.

His father, Mr Watson, walked out on them when Michael was seven and his birth mother, Jackie Watson, had already left when he was four. Both left behind a fragility, a fear of abandonment, which rests inside him, which he can't or does not want to acknowledge.

It's inside under deposits of skin and muscle, and the weight of air he breathes in to expand his chest, and which he's worked hard at to keep from caving in on him.

And so Michael passes his wardrobe on his way to lie down between clean navy sheets, which Marcia changed the previous night. He backtracks to catch his image in the full-length mirror. 'Hold it, man. Hold it,' he says, imagining himself as a male model on a shoot and takes a stance with folded arms. His image recharges him. 'You've got it, you've got it, I got it,' he sings to his reflection as he breaks out into a dance, his head and shoulders gyrating in the opposite direction to his arms. He stops, takes off his shirt, flexes his muscles and admires his physique. He imagines submissive women, clad in bikinis, dancing at his feet, touching him, wanting him. *Yeah, they're coming along nicely*, he thinks as he inspects his muscles. The bed looms enticingly and he jumps up in the air at an angle, like a basketball player aiming for a dunk shot. He bounces two, almost three times on landing and sinks his body between the sheets. His mind drifts to erotic fantasies of Sharon but these are invaded by thoughts of school fees, Devon's offer earlier, Ms Lorez, Simon, Mr Watson and the need for condoms.

'Allison! Phone me about the homework,' shouts Marcia after her friend, who's in pursuit of her bus, then turns to enter the market and hurries to the bakery.

It's Friday.

Mum died on a Friday, she thinks, but quickly chases the thought away. Instead she fills her head with her checklist: *Pick up cake. Done. Present. Done. Cooked his favourite. Almost done.*

She exits the market, past the noisy Christians singing on the pavement to her right, flinches and covers her ears as she walks by the preacher shouting through a megaphone, his face contorted with the effort. She continues walking a while until she reaches the traffic lights just outside the station. She waits for the lights to change, breathes in the cold sunshine, looks left, then right, checking for a safe gap in the traffic. She wrinkles her nose as the earthy scent of raw meat from Murray's Meat Market hits her nostrils. She turns round to look at the red-and-white shop front.

There is longing in her expression – that shop holds memories, of Saturday-morning shopping with her mother, of meeting and greeting aunts and uncles, her mother standing there relaying the latest gossip to them. She used to shift from foot to foot, her muscles aching as she put the shopping down, full of weighty foods – yam, green banana, plaintain – while the adults talked on, oblivious to her plight.

On occasion Marcia's face would light up as an aunt would gently pinch her cheek and say, 'Look at you, child – where you growing to?' Smiling down at her, pleased to see she was doing well.

'And she good at school – good girl, don't give too much trouble,' Ms Lorez would beam back, just before exchanging warm hugs.

A final gentle pat from the auntie, 'Good girl,' before they moved on to speak to the next acquaintance, her mother proudly introducing her before getting into a little more gossip.

She longs to hear that pride in her mother's voice again, wishes for the familiarity, warmth and innocence of those exchanges.

Beep beep beeeeep!

A driver blows his horn as a pedestrian throws himself in front of his moving car. The driver waves his hand and shouts out of his window at the pedestrian. Marcia looks over at the lights. They are still red.

'Hi.' Justine, Auntie Eliza's daughter, joins Marcia at the traffic lights.

'Oh, hi. Where you coming from?'

Justine is Auntie Eliza's last-born. She's two years older than Marcia, but Marcia has always felt much younger.

'Doctors. Had to pick up Michael Junior's prescription.'

She has a three-year-old son, named after Marcia's brother Michael.

'He's not sick, is he?' asks Marcia.

'No, just needed to get a replacement inhaler. How's my main man, Michael?'

Marcia tells her about Michael's birthday.

'Mum was saying something about you guys coming round on Saturday.'

'Yeah, I spoke to her yesterday,' replies Marcia.

'By the way, tell Michael, Junior's been asking for him.'

The pedestrian lights change from red to green and the girls cross with the crowd.

'Those Christians are definitely in full force today,' says Justine, observing them across the road.

The group carry a banner over their heads; some shake tambourines, others hand out leaflets. Their preacher is still clasping the megaphone to his mouth. 'Jesus is Lord!' he yells.

If he strains any more, thinks Marcia, *he'll shit himself.*

'What you laughing at?' asks Justine.

'Nothing.'

Marcia looks at the followers. They drink in the preacher's words. She stands contemplating the dreariness of the women, the few men among them, their clothes and shoes . . . Marcia stops, backtracks. There he is, standing tall, solemn, renewed.

The small artery on the side of her temple starts to pulse, the blood pumps hard. She stands, stares at him.

The guilt invades her, runs through corridors, opening doors that had been locked and bolted, pulls out the things she had neatly folded and packed away, throwing them high, scattering them, leaving a mess as it rushes through. Dear God. He's here, across the road, only a few yards between them. And the world goes on, people walk past, rush past, they do not see her, they do not see him, but she sees him, she definitely sees him.

They'd been in the kitchen cooking that day, Ms Lorez and Marcia.

'You grate the carrot this way,' Ms Lorez said.

'But I don't want to make juice. I want you to show me how to make ackee and salt fish.'

'Lord Jesus, why you carry on so?'

'Please, please, can we make ackee and salt fish?'

'Only after we make the carrot juice, and you finish cleaning up.'

'But I've tidied up the sitting room.'

'Marcia, you no 'ave eyes. You no see the state of this kitchen floor. You and your brother, I don't know which one's worst.'

'Okay. Okay. I'll sweep and wash the kitchen floor,' she said with her hands up in the air.

'And take the rubbish out,' added her mother.

'And take the rubbish out.'

Ms Lorez retired to her bedroom after they made the juice, to sort out the pile of washing in black dustbin bags sitting on her bed, which they had washed at the laundromat earlier that morning.

'Mum, I'm taking the rubbish out,' Marcia called after she had finished tidying the kitchen.

'Make sure you take your keys and close the door,' Ms Lorez called back.

Marcia left the door ajar, then went to the chute to throw away the rubbish. It was full, so she went downstairs to the big bins. When she returned, the front door was wide open. She paused, looked down the hallway, heard the voices coming from her mother's room.

'Mum,' she called out as she walked down the hallway. The voices grew louder, angrier, as she drew closer. Then she heard her mother scream. She ran towards the bedroom and pushed the door wide open.

There he was, Simon, standing over her. The big butcher's knife in his hand. Laundry scattered everywhere. Her mother slumped half on the bed, half on the floor.

Simon looked sideways at Marcia, his eyes wild, then turned back, lifted his hand high above his head, plunged the knife down. Her mother screamed. Marcia screamed, ran to grab the knife from him, heard the thud as the knife entered into her mother's body, saw him pull it out, saw the blood shoot out. The blood. Oh God, the blood.

'NO!' screamed Marcia, grabbing at his arm.

But Simon pushed her off with his free hand, kept her at bay; with the other hand he lifted the knife high above his head again.

Marcia leapt as high as she could, grabbing at it.

With one blow, he shoved her across the room. She felt pain as she landed against the wall, banging her head, slid to the floor, saw him swing his arm up, saw him stab and stab at Ms Lorez as she lay on the floor.

'MUM!' cried Marcia as she got up again, but Simon pushed her hard. This time she landed in the middle of the floor, felt the sharp pain in her spine, tried to get up but her legs gave way.

'The maggots are alive. I have set her free!' he yelled.

Marcia bent over on the floor, crawled and struggled to get to her feet. 'Mum!' she sobbed. 'Mum!' She got up and jumped at him; he threw her to the ground again. He made the sign of the cross.

'She is free,' he said, panting now. Then he threw the knife to the floor and ran out of the bedroom.

Ms Lorez lay on the floor, breathing heavily. The laundry everywhere. Blood everywhere.

'Help!' screamed Marcia as she leaned over her mother trying to pull her up. She couldn't. She ran out into the hallway, her sweatshirt and jeans drenched in blood. 'Help! Please, somebody help me!' She banged on the neighbours' doors, smearing blood as she banged, but no one came out. She ran back inside, picked up the phone, dialled 999.

'Please, I need an ambulance,' she sobbed down the line. 'Please don't let her die. Please.'

She put the phone down, went back out into the corridor, but no one was there. She called Michael, and sat back down at her mother's side, gently caressing her head, sobbing.

She remembers that day vividly. For a long time she tried to block it out, but seeing him now in that moment was as if a water filter had removed all the impurities, the cloudiness, which fogged her memory, making that day gleam. For a year afterwards, Ms Lorez's death filled her sleep, and she was frightened to be alone in her own bedroom, to walk past the room that used to be her mother's, to open doors, to close doors; she had to check again and again that it was locked behind her.

And at night she would wake in a sweat, the guilt riding her. 'I should have closed the front door. I should have closed it . . .' she said, while Michael or Auntie Eliza rocked her back to sleep.

Uncle Fred and Auntie Eliza are the only ones who know the full story. They thought it best, as Michael and Marcia had not wanted to talk about it, not even to their children. Instead they told those who asked that a madman had stabbed Ms Lorez to death, not that the madman was Simon, Marcia's brother.

'Hey, Marcia, that guy over there, don't he look like Michael? In fact he looks like the guy in the picture in your album the other day?' says Justine.

Marcia doesn't know how to acknowledge this man who turned her life upside down, with whom she shares a father, with whom she shares the same nightmare. But there he is, free. *How?* she wonders. *When?*

She heard that the judge had found him not responsible for their mother's murder on account of mental illness. Michael had told her she was safe 'cause Simon was locked up in hospital. She had thought that meant that he'd be locked away for a long time, possibly for ever.

'Marcia?' asks Justine. 'Don't you think?'

She looks quickly at Justine, then back across at him. How can she deny him, her own blood?

'No,' she replies. 'He doesn't.'

Justine doesn't know Simon. Ms Eliza and Ms Lorez were childhood friends, but they'd lost contact over the years, only rekindling their friendship a year before Ms Lorez's death. By then Simon was almost out of their lives.

'No, he doesn't look anything like him,' she says again, and quickly turns to get away.

'Are you sure? Because that guy sure looks like the one in the photograph in your album,' says Justine, trailing after her.

Marcia looks back at Simon; a battle rages within her. She checks to see if he's seen her, to confirm he's not following them.

Simon stands among the rest of the Christians, engrossed in the preacher's words.

'Don't be silly, Justine. I'd know my own brother, wouldn't I?' The town hall clock strikes three.

'Why you so pissed? All I said is he looks like your brother – chill out, girl. You know, you take things too seriously.'

They don't talk again until they reach the foot of Brixton Hill, outside St Matthew's Church.

'I'll see you laters then,' Justine says, distracted by the sight of her baby's father across the road in a black Ford Fiesta. The car vibrates to the boom of its music and he nods to the beat, perching his black glasses on top of his head. He owes her three months' child maintenance. Justine wants it. Marcia doesn't wait to see the confrontation; her mind is cloudy with her own questions. Michael has always insisted there's no reason to feel guilt. He said that before

Ms Lorez died Simon smoked too much, took too much speed and was wild like a mustang; they let go before he broke them.

Once, as Michael held her wet body after one of her nightmares, he said to her, 'I should have killed him before he got to her.' She, Marcia, felt his arms tighten around her, the ice spread from his heart to the rest of his body and in that moment, a brief moment, she wondered if she knew him.

She knows Michael is hurting. She caught him once crying over a picture of them all. Mr Watson holding a chubby Marcia, Ms Lorez, Simon and Michael standing beside their father. All smiling back at the camera, like some sort of seventies Cosby family. He told her he was crying over their mother, but she knows it's the three of them he misses.

Michael and Simon are full brothers, same mother and same father, Simon being the senior. Mr Watson, needing a mother for his children, married Ms Lorez six months after they met, then a few years later, after being caught with the sixteen-year-old, he went the same way his first wife went – never returned from going off to work, went off with that same girl.

Marcia takes the short route home. She runs up the road, past St Matthew's Church, through the estate, enters the flat, locks the door, checking and rechecking the locks, then calms herself. 'Today is Michael's day,' she says to herself.

On Saturday they'll be at Auntie Eliza's house to celebrate, but today is his day, his day alone. She calls out, 'Michael?' He doesn't answer; he isn't in. *He'll be home later*, she thinks, goes back to the door to check the locks again. Then busies herself preparing, fixing a sign reading 'Happy Birthday' over the sitting-room window. Anything to stop the thinking, nagging, nipping gently at her insides. She hangs streamers and balloons around the room and returns to the kitchen to finish cooking Michael's favourite dish: oxtail, kidney bean and yam soup. When all is done she sits on the settee and waits for his return, switches on the television to stop the itching thoughts.

Channel 4's seven o'clock news ends. Michael is not home yet.

Marcia gets up, looks out the window. *He'll be home soon*, she thinks. He usually calls if he's going to be late; he promised he wasn't going anywhere. She walks over to the TV and turns it over to watch *Coronation Street*, but jumps up again to look out the window.

The phone rings.

'Hello.'

'Marcia, honey, it's Auntie Eliza.'

'Hello, Auntie,' says Marcia. 'Michael's not home yet.'

'That's okay, honey, wish him a happy birthday for me. I might not get a chance later on this evening – I'm on night duty. Are you and Michael coming over tomorrow? Leroy told me he told you guys but I just want to make sure. I know what Michael's like – he'd forget his own head if it wasn't on his shoulders. Make sure you remind him now. I'll be cooking up a storm and I'll be upset if he doesn't turn up now. It's not every day that it's your twenty-first.'

'Yes, Auntie.'

'How are you, child?'

'I'm fine,' says Marcia, but she wants to speak, to speak about Simon, wonders what use it would bring. Instead she says, 'I've got my exams coming up in four months' time, but I'm on top of everything.'

'I know you are. You're a good girl – keep working. Don't let them men out there turn your head from your books, you hear me? God will provide if you just keep working. Put it in your prayers: you'll reach that medical school where you want to go. Trust in the Lord.'

'Yes, Auntie.'

'I'll see you on tomorrow, so you make sure and keep reminding Michael about it and I'll see you all about three, okay?'

'Yes, Auntie.'

She puts the phone down and looks at the clock on the mantelpiece – it's twenty to nine. Michael has still not returned.

When Michael finally phones, it's half past ten. She takes a fork from the set table in the kitchen, bursts each balloon with a bitter *bang*! Tears down the birthday sign over the window and eats the kidney beans and yams, pushing them into her mouth, not chewing, just shoving them in to hold back the crying that needs to be let out.

It isn't the first time Michael hasn't kept his promise. She knows he's with a woman and it hurts to know her brother chooses to be with someone else, particularly tonight. It hurts because today she found out that he, Simon, is out; because somewhere deep within her she prepared this surprise meal not only for her brother but her mother, who died on a Friday like this before she got a chance to say happy birthday.

11

Saturday

IT'S EASY TO see on entering the Baileys' home that it's happy. It isn't in the children's chatter that ripples through the hallway, nor in the family picture that greets you, quietly perched on the small table beside the phone. It's in the soul, as if the heart of this house cries out, 'Welcome, my friend, welcome!' See the dent in the wall near the front door, the worn burgundy carpet, smell the food that mingles with the scent of drying clothes, hear the years of childish laughter and parental reproaches ingrained in the walls and stored away in their plaster.

'Come in, child,' Eliza booms joyously. 'What you standing out there for? I won't bite you. Michael, sharpened that knife yet?'

Junior hovers at the end of the corridor outside the kitchen, looking in. Eliza stands at the stove, stirring the stew. Her plump form shakes with laughter as she watches her grandson.

Marcia sits at the table with Auntie Eliza's two daughters, Sonia and Justine, and Stanford's wife, Jean. The four peel carrots, the last addition to the menu of beef stew, dumplings, curry goat, yam, green banana, fried plantain, rice and pumpkin soup.

'There anything else left to do?' asks Marcia.

'No, nothing, child,' says Eliza with a smile, reaching out to touch Marcia's cheek. As usual Marcia arrived two hours earlier than anyone else, and Eliza was glad to have the help.

She's a sweet girl, Eliza thinks. *Nice girl for one of my sons. Her and Mark are about the right age, but he's too wild – maybe Leroy. Yeah, Leroy.*

The women's banter is free as they share the latest gossip in the newspapers. But Marcia sits at the table, quiet, staring down at the carrot in her hand as she peels, too frightened of saying the wrong thing, too anxious to look up, hiding her bad, the one that caused her mother's death, that denied her brother, wondering what to do if Simon turns up at the flat. On the outside, she wears a calm persona, but inside there is the damage, inside she straps herself into her straitjacket, its thick buckled straps made of her desire to be perfect, to not let the world see the shame, the fear, the truth.

'Did you see the story in the evening papers yesterday about the Royals? Oh, what a scandal,' Justine says, 'and with all that money and position. I'm telling you, no class.'

'You see, money don't bring you happiness or common sense,' says Eliza, directing her comment at her daughter.

Justine ignores her. 'The funny thing is that people like them – you know, that Hooray Henry set; they think they're so much better than everyone.'

'The shame of it all,' says Jean.

'Did you see the pictures?' says Justine with a top-secret look.

'Hmm. Wow, what a mess,' says Jean.

'Black people don't do them kind of nastiness,' says Sonia. 'Can you imagine if you did that to a black man?'

Justine's son, Michael Junior, stands at his mother's side, pretending to play with the hem of her dress, his young mind curious as he strains to hear the 'big' people talk.

Eliza opens her mouth to say more about the affairs and goings-on among the rich and famous, but notices her grandson. 'Where's Uncle Mark, Junior?'

The three-year-old shrugs his shoulders.

'Go look for him and tell him Grandma wants him to set the table.' The little boy runs off in search of his favourite uncle.

'Eliza, dinner cooked yet?' Fred asks, as he stands at the door twirling his car keys, having come in from the garage where he was tinkering with something or other. He nods at the rest in the room.

'Fifteen, twenty minutes,' she replies without looking back.

'Since it na cook then let me go quickly check on that toilet I install last week at that woman Beverly's place.' Fred works for the local council as one of the office caretakers, and takes on private work in his spare time. 'She call me yesterday and Ken say he want borrow mi drill.'

Eliza hears something in his voice – she knows when he's up to something – but she says instead, 'Make sure you make it back here for dinner.'

Fred waves back at Eliza, acknowledging her request, and closes the door behind him.

Michael Junior returns and tugs at Eliza's skirt. 'Granma, Granma, Uncle Mark said he set table and I helped him put mats out.'

'Thank you. You're a good boy, aren't you? Give Grandma a kiss.'

He plants a wet kiss on her cheek.

'Here, blow your nose,' says Eliza. 'Where's your Uncle Mark at now, Junior?'

'He's playing Do-Min-Os with Uncle Michael, Uncle Devon and Celia in the front room.' Celia is Ms Eliza's eldest grandchild, Stanford's daughter.

'Go join them till we finish making dinner, okay?'

'Yes, Granma.' The little boy runs out as fast as his legs can carry him to join the others in the living room.

'You see, me win again!' Stanford shouts with excitement as he slams down his last domino on an uncovered section of the dining-room table. His daughter and domino partner Celia sits beside him, beaming at the others.

'I almost had it, you know,' says Michael, who now has Michael Junior sitting on his leg. Junior crumples and begins to cry.

'Shush, what you crying for? Don't be a baby! Men don't cry,' says Michael.

'You lot better move – Mum's gonna come now and ask why you've messed up her table,' says Mark.

'I tell you what, we'll play charades,' says Stanford to the two children. Junior stops crying at once and sidles towards his uncle as they move chairs to the sitting room.

Sonia's twins do not notice the others joining them. They're watching *Scooby-Doo*.

Michael flounces down on the settee with Michael Junior and feels a pen in his back pocket. Devon joins them.

'Junior, you wanna sit here for a while?'

Junior nods his head so Michael places him on the settee beside him. He dives into his pocket, retrieves the pen and feels the folded school letter. *If we cut back this month I could get one hundred together*, he thinks, but it still leaves him over six hundred to find.

'Devon,' whispers Michael, 'that job you talked about – what do you have to do?'

'This and that, not much.'

'Like?'

'Basically, Tom's set up this courier company, and he just wants a few people to deal with the more important cases.'

'And?'

'They're a bit dodgy, but all you have to do is take things from A to B.'

'How dodgy?'

'Not too dodgy. Besides, if the police catch on, then all you have to say is you don't know nothing, you're just a courier.'

'How much?'

'It depends. The one I'm doing this evening is for a thousand – this one's special – but it'll vary from one hundred upwards. It's not regular though. But there's one coming up this Tuesday; I reckon Tom'll pay about four hundred. If you're interested, then I'll let Tom know.'

I only have to do it once, just the once, to help pay off Marcia's fees, he thinks. 'I just have to pick up a parcel and take it from A to B. That's it?'

'Yep.'

'Count me in.'

'Are you two playing this game or gossiping there?' asks Stanford, coming over.

Fred Bailey arrives at Beverly's and feels a slight twinge in the base of his back as he gets out of the car. *I'm getting old*, he thinks, and presses the doorbell.

Beverly is a single professional woman in her late thirties who hires him to do her DIY. She lives two streets away from his friend Ken. Fred enjoys the gentle teasing and banter that he shares with Beverly while he works and has a little fantasy that if he were a little fitter, a little richer or maybe even a little less married, there might have been something between them.

'Who is it?' Beverly asks in a high voice. She's cultivated an almost perfect upper-middle-class English accent.

'Fred.'

'To what do I owe the pleasure of your company?' she says with a smile as she opens the door.

Her immaculate appearance makes his seem even shabbier. She's wearing a lilac cashmere cardigan, a white T-shirt and navy blue leggings. Her straightened hair is neatly tied back in a ponytail. She has cinnamon lipstick on, which goes with the freckles on her cheeks, inherited from her Scottish ancestor, a slave master. The Scottish heritage is a fact that she secretly likes to point out to everyone, while pretending annoyance.

'I was passing through – my friend just live so. Thought I'd check and see if your toilet still a work,' he says.

'I'm glad you're here. It's still making that strange noise every time I flush.' She opens the door wider and lets him in.

He follows her up the stairs to the toilet, flushes it.

'Do you know what's wrong with it?' she asks.

'I think so. Give me a minute. I've got mi tools inna the car.'

As he gets his tools, her phone rings.

Outside as he opens the boot of his car, he remembers her young body, her firm muscular bottom as he followed her up the stairs. He wishes he were young again, feels old age setting in, sees it approaching every time he looks at his children, all five of them, and even worse when he looks at his grandchildren. Time is going too fast; he wants to grab hold of the fragments he has left. He's always been attracted to middle-class women – it's their proud stance, their noses that point up to the sky and their way of talking that suggest good breeding. Beverly reminds him of the middle-class women he looked at from afar as a youth in Jamaica, but they were so highbrow they'd walk past him and dismiss him like he was a tattered dishcloth. Her closeness stirs up old feelings of wanting something he couldn't attain in youth. It makes a small part of him believe that maybe he could obtain it through her.

He goes back to the house with his toolbag. Beverly sits at the bottom of the stairs, legs crossed, a fluffy bedroom slipper hanging off her bare manicured foot, talking animatedly on the phone. He opens his bag to pull out a few tools, and listens in to her side of the conversation.

'I knooow,' he hears her say. 'Exactly. I went to Bath and it was so lovely. I would like so much to live there; the people are so civilized. Not like in London. Especially not like Brixton – it's such a chaotic place. Too many of us here, you know,' she whispers, 'tends to spoil an area. I avoid it if I can.'

His ears prick up and he strains harder to listen. *What's the damn fool woman talking about?* he thinks. *Of course Bath's lovely – they used the likes of you and me come build the damn place.*

'Oh yes, I know I won't be able to get black food. But I can't eat it – it's too spicy for me. I prefer a nice Sunday lunch: a bit of salmon, some asparagus, or pâté with a light salad and vinaigrette.'

No wonder the woman look so pale, she na eat! he thinks.

Her cat sidles up beside her and purrs as it rubs its head against her legs. 'Oh, I couldn't possibly do that. Oh, you are a devil. Mmm, mmm.' She strokes her cat and giggles. 'Jerry's so good to me.'

Jerry is her sickly-looking lover that he's seen on occasion. *The man don't even look like he could get it up*, thinks Fred.

Her voice quietens as she relays juicy information to her friend. 'He's such a good man. A man of the eighties. A good lover. Let me tell you,' she says in a whisper.

Fred's ears strain all the harder.

'He folds my clothes before we make love. Isn't that sweet?'

Folds clothes! Folds clothes? Damn fool man. When Eliza and me ready now, last thing on our minds is fold clothes. Fold clothes. When I want my woman and my woman want me, all we want do is be close. About fold clothes, if I ever did stop to say to Eliza in the middle of making love and say, 'But, Liza, I want fold clothes,' she go bust my head, man. Bust it up good! He kisses his teeth in his head.

It isn't her words, or her fancy manner that Fred reacts to but her tone. There's something in her voice, something disconnected, something missing, and for the first time he stops to examine Beverly and compares her to his wife. She lacks the generosity of spirit of his Eliza, and although she's younger, she's not as youthful and carefree as his Eliza. He looks at her, actually *looks* at Beverly. Instead of wanting her for her assumed high-class manners, he pities her. She's constrained within walls she cannot see, walls that she thinks separate her from her race, but only entrap her in their falseness. He believes in success, pushes his own children hard, but Beverly has lost something, lost herself, lost the spice of life, the ingredient it takes to add flavour to a bland dish, the little extra that makes life more than just a need to satisfy a hunger, but the need to fully enjoy its meal. She lacks that something he hears in Eliza's voice or any of the women he knows who can spice up a story, make it appetizing to the ear, make you salivate for more. It's a fact: Beverly is boring.

He finishes working on the toilet. He eyes her properly as he comes down the stairs and for the first time sees the sharpness in her face, the tight way she holds her body. *A man could cut himself on her.* This realization leaves him with a feeling so strong for his wife that if she were there at that precise moment he would grab her and not let go. *Fred, you're an old fool,* he thinks, shifting his tools to his other hand. *An old fool.* He laughs at himself, indicates to Beverly that the toilet is fixed, waves her goodbye.

Ten minutes later, he's home. He goes straight to the kitchen and gives his wife a long lingering hug. 'Thank you,' he says and plants a kiss on her cheek, pats her big behind, then walks into the sitting room to sit with his children and grandchildren. The five women stare after him with open mouths.

'What was that all about?' asks Justine.

'I swear that man gets crazier by the day,' replies Eliza and turns to continue ladling out the food.

'Dinner's ready,' shouts Justine, taking a dish through to the lounge.

They all gather around the table. Fred blesses the food steaming in the bowls laid out before them and they sit down noisily, pass the dishes around and eat.

When they've finished, Justine takes Marcia upstairs to her room to put Michael Junior and the twins to bed. Fred takes Leroy into the garage to help fix the old car. Mark disappears somewhere. Eliza, Sonia and Jean tidy the kitchen and gossip, but this time the gossip is about people they know. Stanford, Michael and Devon retire to the sitting room to watch the boxing.

'You know, Sharon rang me this morning,' says Devon under his breath to Michael.

'What did you tell her?' he murmurs back.

'I got your back.'

'Thanks, mate. I owe you one.'

'What you guys whispering about?' asks Stanford.

'He's got woman trouble, mate,' replies Devon.

'What kind?' asks Stanford.

'Trust me,' replies Devon, 'you don't wanna know.'

'What, some sister's giving you the runaround?' asks Stanford.

'Sister! Na, man, he don't deal with them – too much trouble,' jokes Devon.

'What do you mean?' asks Stanford.

'I mean, Michael don't date black women.'

'Devon, shut your mouth, will you?' says Michael. 'Of course I date black women.'

'When last did you date a black woman, Michael – what, you were fourteen, fifteen?' asks Devon. 'At that age it ain't dating.'

'But wait,' says Stanford, 'come now. Michael, you mean to tell me you ain't dated a black woman since you were fourteen?'

'I . . . I've dated. Besides, I'm telling you, black women are too much trouble. Got too many hang-ups. Too aggressive, man.'

Now, as said before, most things in Michael are hidden behind simple actions and decisions. After all, it's a simple decision to make – boy meets girl, boy likes girl, girl dates boy. But when the boy keeps meeting the same kind of girl, the same blonde-haired, blue-eyed kind of girl, is it really that simple? So you have to peel back the layers in Michael to find the truth, and the truth is that somewhere, at some place, at some time, he began to feel a powerlessness in himself and maybe, just maybe, I'm not saying it is, but it might have started that night the police cornered him in the cell: *Jump, wog, jump.* Or maybe it started when his teacher Ms Fribbens told him to sit in the corner 'cause he was an aggressive little boy, when all he was trying to do was defend himself from little Tracy Spencer with the blonde hair and blue eyes. Or maybe it began on those Saturday mornings when he sat watching *Tarzan* movies, where seemingly senseless African men brandished spears, waiting to be saved. Or maybe it goes further back, to his birth mother, to his father. Maybe even further back than that, through the generations. Unknowingly being passed down a baton of scars, because their job was to survive, to hand on the baton in the hope of a better tomorrow, for the next generation to make it better than it was, a baton all the way down from his great-great-grandmother who lay down in the bowels of a slave ship wishing for death, fighting for life.

'Listen, if you're complaining about black women,' continues Stanford, 'then you're also talking about black men – we are their fathers. All I'm saying is, what you running away from?'

'I ain't running from nothing. Besides, I don't have a problem. I like who I like – it's as simple as that. It's just a preference,' says Michael. 'The world is full of variety and mine for the taking.'

'Then why aren't you taking it?' asks Stanford. 'Tell me this: you don't like black women, what happens when you have a daughter, Michael? Even if her mother is white, she is going to be black – what sort of pride in herself are you going to teach her?'

'You're just being a hypocrite. I like who I like. You've got white friends.'

'Yes, I have white friends, and you know Adrian – he's my best friend. I would trust him with my life. But that isn't the point. The point is that if you're saying to me you don't like black women, don't date black women who are a reflection of you – and that includes your sister Marcia and your mother, God rest her soul, Ms Lorez – you're running from something, and it ain't going to make it better.'

'Cha, man, leave me alone. I just happen to fancy who I fancy. Don't see nothing wrong with that.'

And this feeling of powerlessness, of not being quite right, not being good enough, raises its head just like it does every time eyes follow him in a shop. Every time he hears the clunk of a car door as he walks by. Every time he sees the nervous movement of a head and the grabbing of a bag. Every time a black man is killed in the street, on the news, on the television, in the cinema. It sends the same message: his life does not matter; he does not matter. *Jump, wog, jump,'* they said that night Rizzlar was killed in his cell. And these feelings sit below the surface – he carries them like invisible shackles, and he reacts against the weight. You see, being desired by a blue-eyed Tracy Spencer, controlling her, gives him back a little sense of power.

'There's nothing wrong with me. I can't help who I fall in love with.'

'But that's not the point. When you keep falling for the same—'

Justine and Marcia enter the room. 'What you guys talking about so seriously?' says Justine.

'Nothing,' says Stanford as he sits back in his chair.

'Stanford, remember you said you'd teach me that new dance from Jamaica,' says Justine.

'Not now, I'm tired.'

'Please, please, pleeeeeeease,' she says, pulling at his arm.

They move the armchairs to one side of the room, and Stanford begins to teach Justine and Marcia the new dance. Devon sits back, laughing at them. Michael sits quietly, watching. He taps his hands on the table and smiles, but it doesn't reach his eyes.

And just like the young black men who take a knife and stab each other and their future, this sense of powerlessness, of not being worthy, this reaction against it, leads to the murder of himself, at his own hands.

At night, when the dishes are washed, the grandchildren are in bed and the children have gone out, Fred lifts the lid to the outside bin and places the rubbish inside, while Eliza perches on a chair in her bedroom and stretches out her hand to the top of her wardrobe. She feels the white box hidden behind two small suitcases. They bought the cases together in Kingston before setting sail for England, one week after they were married. The British government called on them to rebuild the mother country after the war, and so they came. She wrote a little love letter inside the lid of one case for him to see once he unpacked, but that was almost thirty years ago when they were young and foolish. Eliza gently feels the side of the case and remembers the day Fred came striding across the dance floor to ask her to dance – the stars shone that night, the twenty-second of January 1948. But Fred had been an angry young man, distrustful of others in the way poverty can teach you, and he had no trade, no direction, and two children with different women by the time Eliza met him. So she struggled against her feelings. She had ambitions for herself and her newborn son, Stanford. In time, she won, and Fred learnt his need for her was more than physical, more than emotional, more than his life offered without her. It was then that Fred found himself a trade and direction, and then Fred and Eliza began. Unlike many of their contemporaries they've prospered for a poor couple from the fishing village of St Catherine, raised five children together – Stanford, Sonia, Leroy, Justine and Mark. They were blessed, and Eliza often steals glances at her husband and ponders on the day Christ came into their lives.

Eliza brings the white box down from the wardrobe and opens it. It contains a lace nightdress, purchased three weeks previously from a fancy shop in France while on a day trip organized by the church. She unwraps the nightdress from the delicate tissue paper, takes scented toiletries from the top drawer of her dresser, and enters the bathroom where she's running herself a luxurious bath.

The fat on her plump body wobbles as she sinks naked into the white foam. The warm water washes away the tension of the day. She closes her eyes and lies tranquil, feeling the soft water lap against her skin.

'Eliza, how long you gonna hog up the bathroom?' shouts Fred. He stands outside the door. He wants to get to bed, church is earlier than usual, and the pastor has asked him to help move some chairs.

'When I'm good and ready. Do I ever complain when you hog the toilet and smell up the house?'

He kisses his teeth. He's too tired to wait, shakes his head, can't understand why after thirty-eight years of marriage she still locks the bathroom door. He wanders back into the bedroom, puts on his pyjama bottoms, turns off the lights and climbs into bed.

Eliza takes the scented cream from the side cabinet, oils her ample figure and surveys her body in the bathroom mirror. Her breasts are large, with thick stretch marks due to the rigours of childbirth; they hang like two motionless pendulums forming an upside-down V partition on the chest; the nipple ends sit comfortably on her protruding stomach. She touches them and tries to lift them back into the position they were in, in her youth, but on letting go they fall back to where they were. Her eyes move down to her waist which has several indentations from the folds of fat that sit around her midsection before spreading out into hips and thighs, and back in again. She's aged, she thinks to herself; her figure's not what it used to be. It's been a long time since they were together physically as husband and wife, four months exactly. Their lives have been busy, filled with their children's problems, looking after grandchildren and work. The longing for him grows within her. Slowly she pulls the lace nightdress over her head, luxuriating in the fineness of it, then adjusts it around her body. Taking the comb from the side of the sink she pulls it through her hair, applies some lipstick, takes a last look in the mirror and is ready.

Fred's mouth is half open as he drifts off to sleep. Through his drowsiness, he hears the faint sound of music and awakes confused. He looks over to the window. Eliza stands by the old 45 record player, silhouetted by the glow of a single street lamp from outside their window. The sound of his favourite Ella tune floats in the air.

'Come now, man, you na want dance?'

Fred wrinkles his brow, looks over at the clock on the bedside table. 'Eliza, it's twelve thirty. We have church tomorrow.'

'Come now, just a likkle dance,' she replies softly, holding her upturned hand to him.

'What do you? You lost your mind?' he says as he turns his back on her, punches his pillow, gives a grunt and a little mutter before settling back down to sleep.

Eliza begins to hum to the tune.

He senses her coming closer, then feels the indentation of the bed as she sits sideways.

'Fred, how comes you na want dance with me no more?' She rubs her breasts against his turned back.

He feels her hardened nipples against him and smells the scent of her perfume. He turns towards her, feigning annoyance, and as he turns Eliza stands up from the bed and takes his hand.

'Come now, come dance with me a likkle while.'

She tugs at him and he gets out of the bed, still grumbling under his breath. 'Woman, why you can't leave me be?' He tries to keep his face serious as she wraps her arms around him, tries not to look at her as their bodies start to sway to the music but the impulse is too much and when he looks at her glowing face, that is his undoing – he breaks into a big smile and they both laugh. His arms encircle her, and he holds her tight as they sway.

'Remember how we used to dance like this when we only had Stanford, before the other little ones came along?' asks Eliza.

'Yes, I remember. Do you remember that shebeen I used to take you down by Vauxhall way with Marcus and Delores?' Fred asks wistfully.

'Yes, I remember.'

He gives his wife a little 'dip', and they both laugh at their unsteadiness.

He becomes serious. 'I love you more than I ever thought possible, Elizabeth Flora Bailey. There's been times in our marriage when I thought we weren't going to make it. Times when I was ready to walk out that door, but we've come through. When I think of those times when we both almost gave up, it scares me to think that I could have never be here loving you the way I do and receiving the love you give.'

Eliza kisses him gently, holding on to the folds of fat around his waist, stretching to meet his lips and overcoming the obstacle of his belly.

They kiss for a long time, then retreat beneath the sheets to take their time to explore each other more fully.

Exhausted from expressing their feelings towards each other, they fall asleep pillow-talking as daylight raises its head again outside.

At church the next day, Fred praises the Lord with all his heart, grinning from ear to ear. When people ask him what happened to his stiff back, he doesn't tell them that Eliza tried to kill him with loving last night. Instead he says with a slight laugh on his lips, 'It's old age, man, it's old age.'

12

Just Got Paid

MICHAEL CHAINS THE bicycle to the railing and stands to look up at Waterloo station. The ticket for the left luggage is attached to the clipboard held firmly in his hand. His palms are sweaty, so he switches the board from his left hand to his right and adjusts his sweatshirt with 'Tommy's Fast Efficient Couriers' printed on the front.

It's half past ten, some time after the end of the morning rush hour, but people still mill around inside the hall; their chatter seems to hum and twitch like the gossip of seagulls; a whistle screams over their conversations. Michael makes his way to the far end, past the sandwich shops and the entrances to platforms five to twenty. At the counter he hands over the ticket. The assistant returns with a navy carryall, clutching it tightly due to its five kilos of weight. Cycling swiftly through the traffic, Michael delivers the bag to an address in Kilburn. An old lady answers.

'You Paddy's mother?' he asks, using the words Tom told him to say.

'Yes, Irene, but Paddy will be home next week Tuesday,' she answers.

Getting the right reply, Michael hands over the package. The old lady signs off on the clipboard, then hands him a letter.

'Give this to Devon,' she says.

Back at the courier office Michael finds Devon sitting in the rear room, his feet on the desk. 'So you run this outfit.'

'Yep.'

'How come? What you know about running a business?'

'Nothing – Tom's got this guy training me up. He says he trusts me and he rather have someone he trusts in here. Besides, once he's trained me up, I can show you the ropes; it'll free me up a bit. Anyway, how'd it go?'

'It was easy. Too easy. What's in the packages?'

'I told you it's dodgy but not too dodgy. It's best you don't know in case the police start sniffing around.'

'It's not drugs, is it? I don't wanna be involved in that.'

'Would I do that to you?' says Devon. 'Me and you, we go back a long way. We're mates – no, we're brothers. I know what you're like on things like that. Don't worry, I wouldn't send you out like that. A bit of dirty money that needs washing, that's all. Here's your pay.'

Michael holds out his palm.

'One hundred, two hundred, three hundred . . .'

That's Marcia's fees almost taken care of, Michael thinks. *Only four months left.* 'That was easy, real easy,' says Michael. *Too easy.*

'Tom says there's another one in two weeks. You in?'

Michael hesitates. 'All I have to do is take it from A to B like the last one?'

'Yep.'

'And no drugs?'

'Michael, trust me.'

'Count me in, then.'

Time passes fast when days are consumed by routine, day blends into day, some good, some bad. Years can pass that way. But there are moments that seem to raise themselves above the routine to reveal underlying truths, and sometimes they explode, so there is no choice but to be shaken, to be changed by it. And so it is with Michael and Devon, and Marcia and Michael, and Michael and himself.

Marcia sits at her desk studying for her first-year medical exams. After the hard work, the sleepless nights, the panic attacks, the pure hell of her wanting something so badly she couldn't sleep, she couldn't eat, she got the two As and a B she needed. Her mother, Ms Lorez, was right: it was hard work that paid off in the end. But the truth is it was in the blood, that desire, that wanting to heal, handed down from an ancestor who foraged in the bush, searching for plants to heal, who sat upon a ship in sheer despair heading to the new world, that baton of survival successfully passed on.

Marcia looks out the window. She can see the other estates surrounding them, but her thoughts are not on what she can see from her bedroom window, nor on her books, nor her lectures from yesterday, but on Simon, her brother. It's years since she first saw him among the Christians, years since she first started spotting him out and about in her Brixton neighbourhood. But yesterday, he, Simon, stopped her in the street.

'Hey, Marcia,' he called.

She turned to see him, and in that moment when his voice rang in her ears, as she knew it one day would, she did not know what to do. So she froze, while people in the street pushed on past.

'Marcia,' he pleaded.

She backed away, holding her rucksack tightly to her chest.

'Marcia, I'm sorry,' he said, as he pushed forward a small bundle. 'Please. Look,' he said, 'you have a niece who wants to meet you. My daughter.'

She peered distantly at the small baby in his arms, saw the doll-like hands, the waving fingers, the wide face, the little mouth. The baby's eyes flickered at her, then closed, as she sucked her thumb with vigour.

'She looks like you when you were a baby, Marce. Just like you. Carry her.' He held the baby out towards his sister. 'Do you remember how I used to carry you?'

Marcia looked from baby to father, at its fragile face, at the adult who held her. Remembered the knife, the butcher's blade, the dull sound of it piercing through her mother's flesh, and moved to try and take the child from his arms. She glimpsed the faint birthmark, a half-moon, on the side of her face, above the hairline, not yet hidden by hair, and her eyes lingered on the baby's full lips before they parted in a yawn. *She looks like Michael*, she thought, then looked up at her brother's eyes, recalled how he used to carry her high on his shoulders, replayed the laughter of her big strong brother, not the monster holding the knife high above his head. His closeness suffocated her, she tried to breathe, gulped in air, then she turned and ran, ran up the hill, through their estate, ran on home, up to her bedroom, locked herself in. She flung herself on her bed and began to bawl. Later, frightened for the child's safety she called the police, demanding they do something for the child's sake. They came back saying they understood her concerns but there was nothing they could do on account of him being fully discharged; he was being seen regularly and posed no danger. They put her in touch with a nurse at the hospital who calmed her down.

That was yesterday, and now she thinks of happier times when Simon used to take her to the swings to play and buy her ice cream when he wasn't supposed to. It was their little secret. Simon had been the one to walk her to school, and on cold frosty mornings when it was too chilly for her, he would carry her on his back and they would sing to forget the sharp pinch on their ears, noses and hands. He was the one she talked to; he made her problems seem important. Michael was always busy with friends. Yesterday she'd wanted to reach out to him and hold her little niece in her arms but the vision of him stabbing her mother had churned in her head.

Her emotions are jumbled like a ball of tangled wool. She needs to talk, to open the door and let it out. But there is no one to talk to. Marcia opens her mouth to scream, but no sound comes forth. She picks up the phone but shame and guilt spread through her. The words spring out but she pushes them back in like a jack-in-the-box and forces the lid firmly over them. She places the phone receiver back in the cradle.

She wishes to turn back the clock, another chance to close the door, to be rid of the guilt, for her and Simon to be the way they used to be. The truth is that somewhere deep inside her, somewhere she's not aware of, she is scared. Her brothers and her father have taught her to be scared. She's afraid of Michael, she doesn't fully understand him, of the way he treats women, of the amount of money he seems to have nowadays. She's afraid of Simon, of his savagery, of the savagery of life handed down with the invisible baton, of the guilt inside. Afraid to speak about it, to drag it out, of all the things it will bring, of her father, of abandonment. Plain afraid of men. She's jealous of Justine, envies her free spirit and the safety her parents Eliza and Fred have given her. She wants to be free like her, to be secure, not frightened of the future, but this is what life has taught her: that with every step, there's a landmine awaiting her tread to trigger it. You see, her safety, her protection disappeared a long time ago. First her father, then her mother. This stops her from exploring relationships like other young people her age; she was forced to skip this stage. So the only way she knows how to deal with life is to be goody Marcia, to be in control, to do the right thing in the hope of a better tomorrow, to be the adult she was forced to become at eleven. Just like her mother and her mother's mother and on, and on, and on.

'They're just a bunch of poofters. They can't even kick the fucking ball properly!' shouts Devon at the TV screen, gesticulating at the screen. 'Kick the bloody ball to Hoddle, you arsehole.'

Michael sits on the settee beside Leroy, Uncle Fred's son. They both root for Crystal Palace. 'I told you they couldn't hack it. Tottenham are just a bunch of wimps,' says Michael.

'Yeah, your team just got lucky – now if Ian Wright was in our team we'd have wiped the floor with you. Crystal Palace has no strategy, no technique – they don't play football, they just know how to kick the ball long distances and score on fouls.'

Michael smiles. 'Devon, you're sad,' he says, shifting forward to crack open a beer.

Ms Lorez's ghost sits on the mantelpiece, smiling awkwardly from a golden frame; she sits uncomfortably, watching the changes that have occurred over the last two years. There are new things which fight to replace her presence. The rug and gold-coloured curtains are recent additions bought with the money Michael gets from his courier job. The colours clash, and the place looks more like a showroom for a rappers' video than a home.

The game finishes. Crystal Palace wins.

'High five,' says Michael.

Leroy raises his hand to hit palm against palm.

Devon sulks and retires to the kitchen to get a snack and returns to the sitting room with a sandwich and three cans of beer. He gives his friends one each. Leroy takes a sip and turns over to watch *EastEnders*.

'You know, Hattie would be good-looking if she wasn't so dark,' says Michael.

'Yeah, she's dark like an African,' says Devon.

'Wasn't your ex-girlfriend Saddie African?' asks Leroy.

'No, no, man, she wasn't African. Her mother is white.'

'But her father is African. Doesn't that make her African?' says Leroy.

'Listen, Leroy, I have nothing against the pisspot people, but Saddie was no African.'

'Besides,' says Michael, backing up Devon, 'Saddie is too pretty to be African. Those women are ugly – ugly and with a capital U. I wouldn't go out with one even if you paid me.'

Leroy gives them a pitiful look.

'Leroy man, chill,' says Devon.

'Anyway, let me interrupt with a more important topic – Devon, what time is the pickup?' asks Michael.

'Nine,' answers Devon.

'You guys, I don't know what you're both into, but this doesn't sound right to me.'

'Well then, keep out of it,' says Devon. 'Nine o'clock sharp.'

'Nine sharp.'

'I think I'll go and talk to Marcia. I'll get more intelligent conversation out of her.'

'Oooh,' chorus Michael and Devon as they throw a cushion after him.

Michael alights from the bike and looks at his watch. It's nine o'clock in the morning. He enters through the sliding doors and walks up to the reception of Pagnus House, just off Bond Street. A security guard sits behind the counter.

'I'm here to pick up a package from Katrina at the Hyphen model agency.'

The security guard points towards a brown parcel with red ribbon sitting on the counter.

'Can you sign?'

The guard raises his eyebrows.

'It just says that I've picked up the package from here.'

The guard signs.

An hour later Michael stands outside a warehouse in Camden. The building is a converted stable; over the door in bold italic writing is a sign: *Le Mirage*. He's been ringing the bell for the last ten minutes. He calls Devon on the walkie-talkie.

'There isn't anybody here.'

'What do you mean?'

'I mean, no one's answering the bloody bell.'

'Are you sure?'

'Of course I'm bloody . . . Hold on, someone's just walked past. Excuse me, sir, excuse me! I don't suppose you know where the lot in there are?'

'I'm afraid you're not going to find anyone in there at this time: it's a nightclub. They don't usually open up till eight or nine in the evening.'

'Thanks,' he says to the passer-by. 'Devon, he says it's a club and they don't open till nine this evening.'

'Don't tell me we've screwed up on the time. Stay there. Let me make some calls.'

Michael leans up against the blue wooden door and kicks his toes in between the cobblestones.

'Michael, you there?'

'Yes, mate.'

'Tom says there's been a mistake – the times have got muddled up. Bring the package back to base. We can sort it out tonight.'

That evening, Michael gets out of the car with the package under his left arm, and with the other feels for his cigarettes in his shirt and tracksuit trouser pockets.

Devon is walking up the street with one of Tommy's bouncers.

'Oi, Devon, hold up.'

'What?'

'Hold up.'

'What now?'

'Ciggies. Gotta buy some ciggies. I left them behind in the office.'

'You're joking?'

'No. I've gotta buy some ciggies.'

'Michael, just give me the package.'

'No, it won't take long – the shop's right over there.'

'Just give me the damn package. I've had a bad day and I'm not in the mood.'

Michael hesitates – he wants to get paid for delivering the package, but decides he trusts Devon to give him his money, and hands it over.

'Where you say it's at?'

'Go under the bridge and then it's the mews on your right. You can't miss it – it's called *Le Mirage*.'

'We'll see you in there.'

There's a queue at the newsagent's so it takes him eight minutes to get a pack of ten, so when he arrives at *Le Mirage* he sees Devon already entering the club at the front of the queue.

'All right?' he says, winking at an attractive blonde in a short silver dress as he walks by. Her arms are folded and she's shivering from the cold. Her boyfriend looks the other way, pretending not to notice the interaction. Michael walks further up the line. The crowd is more fashionable than he's used to; they look like yuppies.

'You got a light, mate?' he asks a young white guy as he nears the front. The boy takes an apprehensive step backwards, and Michael laughs inside. He's seen that look many times before; he predicted that look before he even asked the question.

The boy digs into his pocket to bring out a lighter. 'Here,' he says.

'Thanks. Listen, I don't suppose you know what this club is like? What type of music they play?'

'It's usually acid with a bit of house mixed in, but tonight might be different – there's a new DJ called DJ CJ.'

'How much to get in?'

'A fiver before ten.'

171

Michael checks his watch. It's almost quarter to nine.

'Thanks, mate,' he says, and continues walking up to the front to talk to one of the bouncers. Clocks a few pretty girls as he makes his way.

As Michael approaches, a man in a tight bomber jacket raises an eyebrow at him.

'My mate Devon just went in. He's here to see your boss.'

'And?'

'I wanna go in and join him.'

'What's my boss's name?'

'I don't know.'

'Then you're not getting in here for free then, are yah?'

'I don't wanna get in for free. I'm here on business.'

'Then you won't mind paying.'

Michael eyes him up for a moment, then decides it's not worth the argument, pays the entrance fee at the counter and passes into the club.

In the smoky interior, the music vibrating, he asks a man behind the bar for directions to his boss's office, but the music is too loud for him to hear. He decides to wait by the entrance to catch Devon on his way out.

Billy Ocean's new record comes on; he starts to bob his head to the music and scans the room. He focuses on a group of women, watches them jiggle their behinds, and their breasts bounce to the music. Michael must be Michael and women make him lose direction, so he buys a drink, takes a sip, places it on one of the tables to his side, and heads for the curvy girl among them with the long blonde hair. He moves up against her back. She turns, smiles and carries on dancing.

'What's your name?' he asks her after several minutes of swaying to the music.

'Tracy. And yours?'

'Mikey,' he replies. 'You here alone?'

'No, I'm with friends,' she replies and points at two girls dancing beside her, one Asian and the other black.

She looks independent enough, he thinks.

'Are you here alone?' she asks.

'Well, I came with some friends but I seem to have lost them,' he replies. 'Would you like a drink?'

She nods and they both head towards the bar, gently pushing their way through the crowd.

'I don't remember there being so many people when me and my girlfriends first came in – does it usually get so crowded?'

'I don't know. It's my first time here.' He gives her his I'm-a-naive-young-boy look, and assesses its effect on her.

'So you're a *Le Mirage* virgin,' she says.

He grins and looks away boyishly, peers at her through the corner of his eye, mirrors her, answering her questions, saying what he thinks she wants to hear, smiles when he needs to, nods in the appropriate places, in the appropriate way, looks away shyly, until the girl becomes intoxicated by her own reflection. The music slows down and he asks her to dance. A soft, passionate voice filters through the bebop sound; it mellows the tone of the night. He manoeuvres her against the column that stands to the side of the dance floor and they dance like this, not talking, enjoying the feel of each other.

Across in the club manager's office, Devon hands over the package to the owner.

'What happened to you this morning?' asks Charlie, the boss.

'I sent one of my men to deliver – there was no one here.'

Charlie turns to one of his guys. 'Give me a knife.'

'I phoned Tom. He said we got the wrong time – you meant nine this evening.'

'No, it was for eleven this morning. We thought you done a runner. We've been looking for Tom all day.' The owner slices a knife through the top of the package and opens it. 'What's this?'

'What do you mean?'

'I mean, what the fuck is this?'

Devon leans forward to see inside the open parcel. 'It's shredded paper and three packets of sugar,' he says. 'What's suppose to be in there?'

'You tryna be funny? You trying to be fucking funny?' Charlie launches across the table to grab him by the collar. He pulls him in close. Devon can smell his bad breath.

'I . . . I . . . I don't know. Tom never says what's in the packages. I'm just the delivery boy.'

'There's supposed to be three and half kilos' worth of heroin in there. Where is it?'

'Heroin? No, Tom never said nothing about any drugs. He said dirty money, diamonds, and occasionally maybe a little bit of weed. He said you lot were trying to wash your money. I don't know anything about drugs.'

'Shut it. Where's Tom?'

'I don't know.'

'Harry, help him remember?' The owner pushes him away.

Tom's bouncer moves in but they hold him back. Harry grabs hold of Devon's jacket collar and punches him twice in the stomach, *pfff*, *pfff*, and then in the face. Devon's eyes shut in pain but he holds still. Blood seeps from the corner of his closed lips.

'Now, I said, where's Tom?' shouts Charlie.

'Honest, I don't know,' whispers Devon.

'I don't think he learnt from that,' says one of Harry's colleagues.

Harry moves in while another bouncer holds Devon ready. Harry draws his arm back and hurls another punch at Devon's stomach, then straight in the face, twice. Blood begins to stream from his nose. Devon hangs his head, tongue slightly out.

'Now, I'm going to be kind and ask you one more time. Where's Tom and where's my stuff?'

'I . . . don't . . . know.'

'Harry . . .' orders Charlie.

Michael follows the blonde up the stairs out into the early morning chill for some fresh air and a quick smoke. He breathes in the cool air, pulls her close. There are a few others milling around, deep in conversation. He looks across the road and in the distance he sees some commotion with a group of men; he thinks he recognizes Devon. He untangles himself from the blonde and edges closer to the kerb to get a better look.

'Devon!' he shouts.

Michael faintly hears Devon say, 'Let go,' and one of the men mutter back.

'Devon, you okay, mate?' shouts Michael over the growl of a passing lorry as he begins to cross the road. He makes out Devon grabbing for something in one of the men's pockets, sees them struggle, pushing back and forth, then the man punches Devon in the stomach. Devon gasps and doubles over. Michael hears a girl behind him scream. The men scatter.

'Get them!' shouts Devon hoarsely as Michael jogs up to him. 'Get after them,' he says, waving him on.

Michael starts to sprint past his friend. The men are quick and have already dispersed. He hesitates and tries to catch his breath, hears the wail of a police siren, then carries on after the man who attacked Devon. Two hundred yards down the road, he manages to catch up with him, grabs hold of his shoulders and spins him around.

The man flashes a bloody knife at him. 'Come on, wog! I fancy knifing you too.'

Michael lets go and backs away as the man slashes at the air; the steel seems to sparkle under the street lights. He dodges it, feels the presence of someone behind him.

'Give this message to Tom. We'll be back. We want our stuff and we'll be back to get it. I'll get you both another day.' The man looks around, then runs off into the night.

'You all right, Michael?'

He turns to find Tom's bouncer beside him.

'What was that about?' asks Michael.

'We didn't deliver what he thought we were delivering.'

'What was that?'

'Three kilos of heroin.'

Michael's eyes widen. '*What?*'

'I take it you didn't know either.'

He shakes his head. 'Just wait till I get hold of him,' he shouts before he dashes back to find his friend.

He spots Devon. 'What the hell . . .?' Devon is kneeling on the ground, clutching his stomach. His beige cord jacket is drenched in blood.

Devon looks up at him. It's in his chestnut eyes – they bulge with pain.

'Somebody call an ambulance!' screams Michael, his voice breaking. He sees the beads of sweat at his mate's temple, the blood beginning to pool on the pavement. 'Somebody call a fucking ambulance!' he shouts again to the small crowd gathering round. He gets down on his knees, holds his friend close, cradles his head on his lap.

Devon's eyelids flicker then close. His head falls to the side.

'Call a fucking ambulance!' he screams again at the crowd, then looks down to see the muscles in his friend's face relax, almost into a smile. He holds him tighter, whispers and sobs into his ear, 'Hold on, mate, don't go, don't go!'

Like in a movie, in a minute he'll hear 'cut' and all action will cease, Devon will get up from this cold London ground and laugh, laugh like always, because this must be one of his practical jokes.

Michael looks at his friend's feet, notices the dried leaves teasing his shoes and the early morning damp beginning to cling to the toecaps. He looks again at his friend's face. It is now totally slack, almost at peace. Michael knows – he's seen death before.

'Dear God, not again,' he wails. He folds his body over his friend.

'We better go, mate,' says Tom's bouncer, pulling on his arm. He grabs at Michael's collar, pulls hard. Michael gets to his knees then stands up.

'Charlie'll be after us now,' says Tom's bouncer breathing heavily as they hurry along.

'But I've not done anything. I didn't know what was in the package.'

'Yeah, but they don't know that. If I was you I wouldn't go back to your flat.'

'But my sister's there.'

The bouncer shrugs his shoulders. Michael sees a red phone box further up the road, jogs towards it, grabs the receiver and slams some coins into the slot.

'Marcia, listen to what I'm saying. Get out of that flat now. Don't wait to take anything. Just go.'

'But, Michael, why—'

'I said get out now, I'll explain later. Go to Uncle Fred's. I'll phone you over there.'

'But, Michael—'

'I said get out now!'

Michael leans his head against the cool glass, catches his reflection, the terror in his eyes.

'I've not done anything. I should've stayed where I was, taken my chances with the police,' he tells the bouncer.

'And what? Get charged for drug dealing?' he says.

'But I didn't know – how could he do that to me? He was my best mate.'

'He didn't know neither. Anyways, I think we stand a better chance if we separate. They'll be looking for both of us; we don't wanna make it easy for them. Here's my number – if you hear of anything, phone me. I'm gonna look for Tom.' The bouncer strolls off up the road. Michael watches him as he rounds the corner out of sight.

He gets back into the phone box and calls the club.

'Mr T's,' answers a man.

'David, you seen Tom?'

'Not since this morning. He left saying he was going to pick up something from home. But all hell broke loose this evening. The police were round, asking questions about Devon and the courier company, raiding the joint. Before that we had the gang from North London looking for Tom. What's going on?'

'I'll tell you later. If you see Tom, tell him I'm in trouble and I need help.'

'I will. Do you need anything?'

'A change of clothes would be great and Tom's address if you have it.'

'I'll see what I can do. I'll leave it in the bins by the lane down the alley. You know the place.'

'Thanks.'

Michael rings the doorbell and knocks impatiently on the door. He's been ringing the bell for the last minute. There's a light on upstairs, but no one answers. He knocks again.

It's a big detached house, out in the Kent countryside. He found Tom's address in Devon's address book – David had left it for him with the change of clothes, streets away from Tom's club, 'Mr T's'. This is Michael's first time here – you see, in all the years he's known Tom he has never been invited. To be truthful, Michael doesn't have much interaction with Tom except through Devon, but Devon often talked about the grandeur of the house, especially after attending a party or two out in the Kent countryside on a Saturday evening.

Michael rings the bell again, looks again at the light in the room upstairs, wonders whether he should give up, but then where would he go? Charlie and the gang are after him for the missing gear, and as for the police it might be too big a risk, so Tom is his best option. He walks around the side of the house to the back garden in search of life. A full moon shines a pool of light on to the lawn, which is lined with flower pots. The garden's big enough to play five-a-side football. His attention is drawn to a faint glow downstairs in what he assumes to be the kitchen, so he walks round to peer through the glass door. Inside, he spots gleaming surfaces and smart cupboards. Tom's wife, Kate, sits at the table. Her shoulders shudder up and down. She's obviously crying. Michael has met her once or twice before. He knocks gently. 'Mrs Jenkins. Kate.'

She doesn't look up.

He knocks harder. 'Mrs Jenkins, it's Michael – Devon's friend.'

Kate looks up, wrinkles her eyes and nose at him, and walks over to the back door. 'What you doing here?' she asks, wiping beneath her eyes with a manicured nail.

'I'm really sorry. I wouldn't have come but I desperately need to speak to Tom. Is he in?'

She gives a short laugh. 'No, he's not.'

'I'm sorry, but I didn't have anywhere else to go. I need Tom's help. Devon's dead.'

Her face shows horror and she abruptly opens the door.

Michael notices a scrunched-up ball of paper in her right hand. 'Devon's dead?'

'Yes. Didn't you hear the doorbell?'

'The doorbell? Oh yes, but I thought you'd just go away if I ignored it. What d'you mean, Devon's dead?'

'He was murdered – stabbed to death a few hours ago.'

'How? What happened? Here, sit down.' She gestures to a chair.

'I'm really sorry, but do you know where Tom is?' Michael persists.

Kate is silent and then gives out a bitter laugh, an if-I-don't-laugh-I'll-cry kind of laugh.

'You see, I'm in trouble and I really need his help.'

She laughs again and hands him the scrunched-up paper, then sits herself back at the kitchen table with her head in her hands.

Michael unfolds it carefully and reads:

Dear Kate

As you know, we've not been getting on too well lately and I'm sure you know this was coming. This wasn't an easy decision to make or thing to do, but your sister and me have fallen in love. We didn't mean for it to happen but it did. We've gone abroad. Don't come looking for us.

Your loving husband
Tom

Michael is speechless. He looks at Kate, his eyes wide and questioning. 'So does that mean he's not coming back then?'

Kate looks up with tear-filled eyes. 'You know, I think you might be fucking right,' she says sarcastically.

'So what am I gonna do? I've got men who want to kill me.'

'I don't know. I don't have a clue.'

'But what *am* I going to do? Devon's dead and they're after me, and the police—'

'Oh my God,' says Kate, as if the news has just sunk in. 'I only saw him yesterday. He came round to talk to Tom about rearranging times. He was full of it. Laughing and joking about taking a holiday.'

'What times?'

'I don't know. I overheard Tom say something about rearranging a shipment or a collection time. He wanted Devon to collect something at eight instead of nine. It didn't make much sense to me because once Devon left, he phoned someone else and arranged to have it collected at ten from your offices.'

'I don't believe this,' says Michael slowly. 'Do you know, I mean, did you see what Tom had delivered?'

'No, but Jason, one of his guys, brought a brown package with red ribbon round later on and left. Why you asking?'

'I don't believe it,' says Michael slowly.

'What don't you believe?'

'I think Tom's run off with these guys' gear and—'

'And what?' says Charlie, the owner of *Le Mirage*, as he walks in through the back door with two tall, broad-shouldered men dressed in black close behind.

In an instant, Michael has pushed the chair back with a screech and is diving for the door leading to the hallway but they catch him easily and shove him back on to the kitchen chair beside Kate.

'Hello, Kate.'

'What you doing here?' she responds drily, as though she'd expected them to turn up.

'Looking for Tom.'

'Join the club.'

'This is no laughing matter, Kate. He's taken something that belongs to me and I want it back.' He steps towards Kate and is about to touch her neck when Kate throws off his arm.

Undeterred, Charlie puts a hand on her shoulder and whispers in her ear, 'Now, Kate, I want my fucking gear.' His grip tightens around her shoulder and then around her neck. Kate tries to wrench his hand off, but Charlie slaps her so hard her eyes fill with tears.

Michael starts out of his chair. 'Hey, there's no need—' One of the guys has suddenly pulled a gun and is holding it to his head.

'Now, Kate, where is Tom?'

'Honest, I don't know.' She's sobbing quietly now and finding it hard to breathe.

'Now, I want a fucking answer or else someone's going to get hurt around here.'

'I wish I knew 'cause I want to kill him myself,' she mumbles.

'Yeah, right – you don't expect me to believe you?' Charlie says, clicking his fingers. One of his men pulls Michael down on to the floor and on to his knees, presses the gun into his temple.

'If you don't give me an answer in the next twenty seconds, we'll waste him.'

'Honest, Charlie, I don't know where he is,' she hisses. 'Look,' she says, pointing to the letter on the kitchen table.

He reads it and throws it back on the table. 'You have two kids, don't you?'

Kate doesn't answer.

'Well, I want what belongs to me and I want it now. So, until he brings back what's owing to me, I'm going to borrow something of his. By the way, where are they?'

'I don't know.'

'What do you mean, you don't know?'

'I don't know. I've not seen them all day.'

'Don't give me that shit.'

'I've not seen them.' Kate's eyes are closed and her voice is low.

'What d'you mean? What, they're floating around in space, are they? They're invisible kids, are they?'

'Yes. No.'

'Well, where are they? I want to know now.' He pulls a gun out from his belt and points it straight at Michael, who is whimpering now, kneeling, head bent with the force of the other man's gun at his temple. A cat suddenly pokes its head through the cat flap. By the time it has drawn its entire body through the flap in one swift action, Charlie has shot it.

'Molly!' shrieks Kate. The cat lies in a pool of blood.

Charlie points the gun back at Michael and starts to count.

'Eight, seven, six, five . . .'

'All right, they're at their nan's,' murmurs Kate.

Charlie puts the gun down. 'Then let's go,' he says. He pulls Kate up from the chair by the arm, then turns to his two men. 'You stay. If they're not there I'll give you a call and you do the business.' He juts his chin at Michael.

Charlie marches Kate out of the kitchen and into the hallway.

Michael's whole body is trembling. He thinks he's wet himself. After a while he hears some commotion outside, someone has collapsed, a quiet thud like the sound of a gun being fired with a silencer, then heavy boots coming back towards the door. Michael screws his eyes shut, his head still bent into his chest.

There's a bang as the kitchen door is kicked open. Four armed police pour in, pointing rifles. 'Put your guns down now! Now!' One of Charlie's guys lifts his arm to shoot. The police fire at him; the other man drops his gun. Michael topples sideways to the floor. The policemen approach, their firearms pointed at him. One of them speaks: 'I'm arresting you on suspicion of murder and the trafficking of drugs. Anything you say will be taken down in . . .'

Michael lies motionless on the kitchen floor while the police handcuff him, and the feel of the cold metal brings back old memories. They drag him to his feet and march him out to the vehicles waiting outside. Through watery eyes he spots Kate sitting in the back of a police car at the far end of the drive. They push his head down, bundle him into a separate car and drive off.

13

The Wait

MICHAEL IS LYING down on a hard bench. He hears a clank as another heavy door slams shut and the singing of the drunk in the next cell. They want to charge him with the murder of Devon, his best friend. He had laughed first, and then cried. Now he sits up on the hard bench, leans forward, and his locks fall to cover his face. He's in trouble, in trouble like he never knew he could be, as deep in it as a sewer worker, and that's not even taking the drugs charge into consideration. He's agitated with it, vulnerable, his eyes all wide with it, his head about to explode. He counts to ten and breathes, tries to control his panic. He hears the rattling of a key in the cell door and looks up. The door swings open and in walks a white man with a briefcase.

'Your sister wants to know if you're all right,' says the man.

'And you are?' asks Michael.

'Your solicitor: Daniel Jones-Galbraith. Stanford Bailey hired me. They're waiting outside.'

Michael nods his head, pulls back his locks and there's a long silence while he tries to think what to say.

The solicitor clears his throat. 'I understand, Mr Watson, that they've charged you with drugs trafficking but are still compiling evidence for the murder charge. Apparently there are several witnesses who say you did it. They saw you just before your friend dropped to the ground. Can you tell me what happened?'

Michael begins to tell him about the package yesterday morning and the club and finding Devon bleeding from the stomach, and then what happened in the kitchen at the house in Kent. The solicitor calmly takes it all down.

'There doesn't seem to be much evidence,' Daniel says. 'The police won't have much of a case, but we've tried to get you out on bail and it's set too high for you to afford. I'm afraid you're going to have to hang in here a little longer. There'll be a charge hearing on the tenth. I'll find out more and see you back here on Monday morning.'

The solicitor taps on the door.

'Don't worry, it'll all be fine,' he says. The door opens and he disappears.

The court case starts today. Michael is dressed in a black suit and white shirt, his locks tied back. He's never worn a suit before, but then he's never been to court before. With his cuffed hands, he pulls at the unfamiliar sensation of the tie around his neck, takes a quick look back at the prison building behind him as he walks towards the police van, breathes in, then out, and watches the cold mist escape from his nostrils. The guard opens the door of the van. He climbs in and takes a seat opposite a little window in the top left-hand corner. The door slams behind him and the guard bangs on it twice. The engine starts up and the van moves off. Michael catches glimpses of red brick, then blue sky and the green of the tree tops as they drive through the streets of South London. *This is it*, he thinks. *The beginning of the end.* You see, he has an uneasy feeling about all this, uneasy like a sensitive stomach at sea. They've dropped the murder charge, as they said they didn't have a witness for that. As for the drug-trafficking charge, what evidence do they have?

Michael stands in the witness box.

'So what did you think you were couriering, Mr Watson?' asks the prosecuting barrister.

'I was never told.'

'Now do you expect us to believe that you were getting paid as much as five hundred pounds per package and yet it never occurred to you to ask exactly what it was you were transporting, Mr Watson?'

'Yes – I mean, I did ask Devon but he promised it wasn't anything bad.'

'When you say Devon, you're referring to Mr Harris, the deceased?'

'Yes.'

Marcia and Stanford watch from the gallery. She's still shaken from having to identify Devon's body. Devon's brother was nowhere to be found, Michael was in custody and the club was closed, leaving only her left to do what his next of kin or any of the numerous guys that Devon and Michael used to hang out with should have done. But it seemed to her that everyone appeared to scatter as soon as trouble came, like worker ants on feeling the tremor of a stamping foot. Hearing the lawyer refer to him, Devon, as the deceased sends a shiver down her spine.

'And this Mr Harris, was he not a regular at a club called Mr T's in Lewisham?'

'Yes.'

'In fact you and he used to be more than just regulars, didn't you, Mr Watson? You used to work there?'

'Yes, I did.'

'And was your employer a Mr Tom Jenkins?'

'Yes.'

'Mr Tom Jenkins, a well-known South London gangster.'

'I didn't know—'

'Quite a notorious character.'

Michael tries to interject. The barrister continues.

'The police raided two of his businesses previously under suspicion of drugs being sold on the premises. And yet you expect us, Mr Watson, to believe that you had no idea what it was you were carrying?'

'Objection, my Lord. What happens to Mr Jenkins' businesses bears no relation to my client or this case, as he was an employee of Mr Jenkins, not a partner, and at the time of the alleged offence he was employed by the deceased, not by Mr Jenkins,' says Michael's lawyer.

'I am at present trying to prove the links between them, my Lord.'

'Proceed.'

'Is this not you?' The prosecutor hands a picture over to Michael. Michael takes it. 'Yes, it is.'

The lawyer takes back the picture and hands it to the head juror to pass among the jury. 'Let the jury take note of the date and time in the left-hand corner of the picture. Now, Mr Watson, you agree that is you in the picture?'

'Yes.'

'What are you wearing and what are you carrying in your hand?'

'A sweatshirt with "Tommy's Fast Efficient Couriers" written across the chest. I'm carrying a blue holdall.'

'Members of the jury should be aware that the police were carrying out surveillance both of the courier company and the premises in the picture over some months. And although the deceased ran it, its owner was a Mr Tom Jenkins, a man well known for his brutality, and Mr Watson's previous employer. An hour after this picture was taken, an hour after the defendant, Mr Watson, delivered that package, the premises were raided and that exact holdall was found with five kilos of heroin in it. Now, Mr Watson, do you really expect us to believe that you had no idea what was in the packages?'

'I really didn't. Honest, I didn't,' Michael says, looking at the jury. 'Honest, I didn't know.' He pleads with them but most look away, except for the foreman who stares back, stares back with the force of a judge's hammer. *Guilty* shouting back at him. *Guilty*.

'That will be all, Mr Watson.'

He sits still, waiting for it – it lines the air, it's in people's faces as the police tell their side of the story. No evidence, no drugs found on him, no fingerprints linking him to it, no solid facts. He just happened to be the wrong colour, the wrong sex, the wrong class, with the wrong education, and that made him guilty before the trial even started, before evidence was even heard, before they knew that he was in the wrong place, at the wrong time, mixing with the wrong crowd.

The next day, Michael is found guilty.

Michael takes it in, inhales it like Vicks VapoRub. It clears his mind, awakens him, takes him out of the trance he's been walking in all these years since his mother's murder, and he understands, he understands Ms Lorez. He understands her objections to Devon and the other kids, the choices she made for him, the future she could see, that he hadn't, that she feared, that he hadn't.

Five days later, '. . . I sentence the defendant to three years' imprisonment . . .'

Michael hears the three years. He's properly awake now, alert with it – the words 'guilty' and 'three years' have awakened him from his stupor. And he wonders about prison, the cold, hard reality of it, and the years he is to spend there.

PART IV

Ngozi

14

The Lizard Tongue

Lagos, 1988

L AGOS IS ALIVE: it bustles with noise and dirt. People jostle and
fight their way through the streets. Roads with large craters,
gutters brimming over with sewage, and hills of rotting garbage slow
people down as they struggle to make their way to work. Street
merchants, taxi drivers and disfigured beggars tout for business
along the motorways, adding to the chaos of the morning traffic
jam. The car horns can be heard for miles around as drivers beep in
frustration, while the start of the morning heat begins to create big
patches of perspiration on people's shirts. Yes, Lagos is alive. It comes
at you in surround sound, it blazes, it breathes, it bursts with life.

Ngozi makes her way through the commotion to the bank where
she works as an assistant at the reception desk. She's been in Lagos
now for over two years.

After the morning when she was beaten by Mrs Obindu, she had
only three choices: to take her own life, to kill someone else – the
Obindus – or to run away. Ngozi tried the first but wasn't successful, and had begun to plan the second but chickened out.

I watched their conversation unfold.

'E'mma, come run with me,' whispered Ngozi into the room darkened by the drawn curtains.

'Ngozi, I no sure,' answered Emmanuel. Once again he had tiptoed into Ngozi's room to help dress the wounds on her back.

'But, E'mma, I thought you say you love me.'

'Yes, but where we go run, O?' he said. 'Sit still. Let me put the dressing on.'

'To the city, to Lagos.'

'What we go do there? How we go eat?'

'I don't know. But, E'mma, don't you dey want more, just dey serve all your life?'

'Yes, but Lagos?'

'E'mma, we go find work there – we go find more there than here.'

'I no sure, O. You know, Ngozi, I love you, but—'

'But what?'

'Sit still. Nothing. Let me dey think about it.'

So Emmanuel thought about it. He had plans, had always had plans, just different plans – he was quietly ambitious, you see, and he'd figured out a long time ago that he had more opportunities at the Obindus' than anywhere else. He was learning all about the textile business, working on Mrs Obindu's customers, gaining their loyalty and when the time was right, his plan was to set up his own business to compete with his old employer. But E'mma loved Ngozi so he gently cleaned the cuts on her back, tended to them till they were healed, quietly listened to her pleas. You see, he wanted to make her happy, wanted her, and Ngozi, in her own way, in the only way that she could, cared for him back, but she knew there was something better out there for her, better than Mr Obindu, than Mrs Obindu, better than killing herself and if it came down to it, better than E'mma. But it didn't come down to it, so on the fifth night after her beating, E'mma came to her with a plan.

'Tomorrow I go take Mr and Mrs Obindu for church. When I drop dem, I go leave am there, come carry you. You go get bus go for Lagos. My cousin who dey for Lagos go meet you. I go speak to him, tell 'em that you be my wife. You understand?'

Ngozi, eyes bright with excitement, nodded her head and hugged him tight.

'After I drop you for station, I go return for church. Mr and Mrs Obindu no go know. You understand?'

Ngozi nodded her head again, a faint smile on her face.

'You know, Ngozi, I love you. You understand what I dey say? You go be my wife?'

Ngozi hesitated, looked at the man in front of her, then nodded her head again. Slowly.

'Good,' said E'mma, 'then I go sort out work, my cousin go help, then I go join you for Lagos. Then we go marry. I love you,' he said again as he packed up the dressings.

Ngozi watched him as he left the room, her brow wrinkled with worry.

The next day when Mr and Mrs Obindu were at church, he took her to the bus station and kissed her as he put her on the bus.

'I go soon join you, O,' he said, placing all the money he had in the world into her hands – the money he had saved so far for his business. 'As soon as I sort out work, we will be together.' The bus driver beeped for them to hurry up. 'Don't worry, my cousin will be at the bus station in Lagos waiting for you. I love you, O, we will be married soon,' he said. 'Don't worry,' he mouthed at her as she boarded the bus, 'I love you.' She watched him waving as the bus pulled away.

That was the last time she ever saw poor E'mma.

On the journey down from Enugu she sat next to an elderly trades-woman, with small bright turquoise studs in her ears, travelling to Lagos on business.

'I love the colour of your earrings,' said Ngozi.

'Thank you,' smiled the woman.

Ngozi's scared eyes touched her, reminded her of the three daughters she had left at home.

Ngozi sensed her warmth, her motherliness, and so began to tell her about her trip, about her fiancé, about E'mma's cousin meeting her at the station, and the lady in turn told her about her husband and daughters.

Once arrived in Lagos, Ngozi clambered out of the bus, her neck craned to see if she could spot Emmanuel's cousin. She collected her luggage from the hold, took her place under the shade of the makeshift bus shelter, sat on top of her suitcase and waited.

'Are you sure you will be all right, my child?'

'Yes. He go collect me soon.'

'Okay. I'm over at the offices over there, making arrangements for my shipments if you need me. Just ask for Mrs Okonkwo.'

'Yes, Ma,' smiled Ngozi, 'but E'mma promised he'll be here.'

'Okay, O.'

And so Ngozi sat on top of her suitcase in the shade watching the busy-ness of the people in the station, searching out a figure that could be E'mma's cousin, and waited, and waited, and waited.

She looked up at the sky. In less than an hour it would be dark, and suddenly she was afraid of this big city, wondered what she was to do, where she was going to sleep.

'You okay, child?' asked Mrs Okonkwo as she passed back through several hours later to check to see if she was still there.

'I don't know. My fiancé's cousin he still no dey come,' said Ngozi, looking upwards at the darkness coming.

Mrs Okonkwo saw the fear in her face. 'Do you have the address?'

'No, O, the trip was planned fast and I forgot to ask for the address.'

'Then why don't you come with me? It will be night soon. We can leave a message with the bus station office and you can come back tomorrow.'

Ngozi looked up again at the sky, glanced outside the station gates, back at the lady and nodded her head. She got up wearily and followed Mrs Okonkwo, dragging her suitcase along behind her. She came back to the bus station the next day, and the next, but never found E'mma's cousin. The truth is that if she had waited just another five minutes the first day she arrived she would have met E'mma's cousin and her life would have been different, but that's life, that is how it happens, how we can change paths without knowing, without understanding the significance of a decision.

E'mma will throughout his life often think back to his first love and wonder what happened to Ngozi, wonder whether she's alive or dead, wonder why she never arrived at the bus station. He'll name his eldest child Ngozi – it will never leave him, even though he'll become successful, more successful than the Obindus, will travel far and wide, to India, to China, to Holland, to South Africa. Even when he finds another love to make him happy, even as he bounces his baby girl on his knee, this not knowing will never leave him. So in small moments, in the middle of saying goodbye to a loved one, he will pray to see them again and wonder with sadness about what happened to his first love, the one with the teardrop eyes.

For one week Mrs Okonkwo took Ngozi under her wing, advised her about city life, helped her find cheap accommodation and guided her through the bewildering chaos, but she had to leave, promising to return in a month. Once again life intervened and Ngozi never saw her again. Life sends its angels along the way – they enter, unknowingly change it in some significant way, and exit, having done the job they were sent to do.

Many years later Ngozi will find out that her angel never saw her cherished family again. She died in a car crash returning home, her body left by the side of the road, bloated in death, till her family came looking and found her there, unrecognizable except for her dress, her pillaged suitcases which lay near by, and a small bright turquoise stud carelessly dropped in the dirt, in someone's haste to get away. You see, on that motorway that links Enugu to Lagos, the Igbos to Lagos, the Igbos to the coast, and the hinterland to the ports, there are few traffic rules; in my time there were no rules at all. Many people have died along this route. Today, burnt-out car wrecks bedeck the landscape, warning drivers to slow down, but they don't. Young men think they are invincible, you see, and old men hang on to bad habits. Life is cheap along this route.

In my day, when I was alive, that route was a dirt track, heavy with the bush, the sting of the heat and the loud echo of the animals that lived by it. There were no cars. We made that painful journey by foot, our bodies heavy with the weight of the shackles on our wrists and around our necks, our minds terrified of what lay ahead. I saw a few lucky ones die around me – God knows why I did not. Our deaths did not matter to our captors. Our families could not come looking for us, but they mourned. I know my mother, my father, my husband, they all mourned my fate.

But this story is not about what happened to me. As I was saying, Mrs Okonkwo died along the route, and her death left her three daughters alone to fend for themselves. Their father could not cope after his wife's death – she was the main breadwinner – and soon their loving home fell apart. Each child was sent to a different relative, to begin a new chapter. Another layer. Another baton. In my time there were so many orphans created, so many men taken, families, villages ripped apart. In my village the women had to become strong, had to take up what was left, many taking to the fields, adopting the children left behind, forced to protect the men who were left, and so our culture developed, forced to counteract the effect of our losses. But that is how it is, and the journey has been long and many continue on it, despite the uncertainty, despite the harshness of it, despite knowing that all can be ripped away at any moment, that hunger can arrive as soon as evening. A simple decision to go out into the world to feed your family can end in darkness.

I went to collect yam from the field to feed my family – a simple decision, and yet my world and our world was changed because of it, but despite life, despite death, this condition has created different people from the ones I knew when I was alive. But still they, we, survive, because those who were left have always had to step in. It's hard to explain, but amid the hurt and the hardships, the sweetest most painful living can be found, born out of the uncertainty of tomorrow. And yet still I see them smile and laugh as though yesterday was nothing. But let me get back to Ngozi.

Ngozi used the money E'mma had given her to rent a bed in a poor part of Apapa, where drug addicts, thieves and poor God-fearing folk lived side by side. The room was dark and dingy, the bed filthy and the other occupants, female of course, coughed and spluttered through the night. And when the moon was bright, its blue-white light seemed to spread serene magic among her roommates and not a noise, not a sound could be heard from them. On these nights, after eight, she would hear prostitutes at work on their clients outside, and wish herself to sleep, a desire deep inside to fight through. When she looked down the alleyway the morning after such a night, the ground would seem littered with condoms. She often wondered how they could afford to buy so many. But it was somewhere to lay her head and it was relatively safe: the landlady kept an eye on her at the request of her angel with the small turquoise studs who had briefly adopted her.

Each new day, she pounded the dusty unpaved streets, wrestled her determination, under the hot sun, amid the noise and commotion of the city, and looked for work, any kind of work. Going from restaurant to restaurant, house to house, office to office, asking and sometimes pleading for employment. After a month, she was defeated. But while she was fighting to find work, the government implemented a structural adjustment programme, as guided by the World Bank and IMF. Everyone in the city was edgy, apprehensive, as they watched prices begin to rise quickly. The atmosphere made her anxious. The next morning, she gathered her belongings to return to her family in the village. But at the bus station, she discovered she did not have enough to get home. And so Ngozi sat on the dry earth beside her suitcase in the middle of the station, totally defeated. Now as we've seen, sometimes life sends angels, because at the other side of the bus station, Stella, Mr and Mrs Tobenna's daughter, was just climbing down from a bus from Obowi. She cast her eyes over to where Ngozi sat dejected on the ground, and recognized something familiar about the figure. Her curiosity aroused, she headed over to get a closer look.

A tear escaped Ngozi's eye and fell in slow motion down her cheek on to the ground, shattering into what seemed like tiny marbles.

'Ngozi?'

Stella's face came into view like a mirage. It spoke.

'What you dey do here?' she heard Stella ask and Ngozi reached out to touch the watery illusion – it was solid, it was Stella, and the tears in her eyes poured down her cheek. Her friend's face was like a kerosene lamp in the night, like the sun after a rainstorm, like an answer to a prayer. Stella saw the desperation in her friend's face, dusted her off and took her home.

That was almost two years ago. Now Ngozi makes her way through the Lagos traffic on the ten-seater minibus. Pushes her way past the other passengers to the front exit, gets off at her stop. Rushes up the side steps to the staff entrance of the bank and through security, throwing a warm smile at her colleagues as she makes her way to her seat beside the main receptionists at the front desk.

Ngozi is one of three receptionists' assistants, a job that Stella's friend Ifeoma had helped her find, with the assistance of a sugar daddy Ifeoma was seeing at the time. Ngozi is proud of her job: this is a step up in her world and so she's always punctual and courteous, and works well with her colleagues, particularly Mrs Ebo, her boss, whom she adores. She watches and copies her every move.

'Good morning, Mrs Ebo,' she says.

'Morning, Ngozi,' says Mrs Ebo, who is the senior receptionist. 'Did you take Mr Johnson's typing down to the typing department last night?'

'Yes, Ma,' replies Ngozi.

Ifeoma had told her that it was a good job in which to meet wealthy men – she herself had met many before settling on the one who kept her and gave her the position she currently enjoys in the bank. So Ngozi always makes sure she looks her best at all times, even invests half her wages in sewing the most fashionable outfits she finds in the pages of the latest gossip magazines, like Ifeoma had advised. Ngozi is not pretty in a Western sense. She may not resemble the beauties in African American or Black European magazines but she's really striking, particularly now that Stella and Ifeoma have taught her how best to dress to suit her figure and use make-up to enhance her features, and now she's grown into herself she's like a sculpture. Heads turn when she walks by, not because they want to observe a pretty woman, because there are many pretty women around here, but because they are compelled to take notice, to take another look – they are forced to by her features, the classic quality of them, like a carving. Her high cheekbones blend with two limpid teardrop eyes, her skin is smooth and dark like sweet molasses, her lips full like a juicy mango, her hips wide as her waist is slim, and when she walks now, she moves like a gazelle. If she had been born in another time, men would have climbed mountains, slain lions and gone to war for her, but in this time, in this Nigeria that she knows, among the men she's interested in, the rich, they desire lighter skin, longer hair, thinner hips in women better known as 'Shining Beauties', like they see in the magazines.

So when Mr Ben MacDonald, a white Scottish man, an oil worker, arrives at the reception desk that morning, she can't understand why he's talking to Mrs Ebo but can't take his eyes off her.

'Yes, Mr MacDonald, we can sort out the exchange for you,' says Mrs Ebo. 'Ngozi, please take Mr MacDonald over to the exchange department.'

'Yes, Ma.'

Ngozi gets up from behind the reception desk apprehensively, his stare making her uncomfortable. 'Please follow me, Mr MacDonald,' she says in her shaky new English.

'No, please call me Ben.'

Ngozi smiles and signals for him to accompany her.

'So you're called Gozi,' he says as he follows her, wiping his brow with a handkerchief. Mr MacDonald is an older gentleman, in his late forties.

'Yes, sir,' she replies.

'You know, you're stunning.'

Ngozi looks back at him, a little taken aback. 'O, thank you,' she says and continues her way towards the exchange department. 'Here we are, Mr MacDonald. My colleagues will take care of you.'

'Thank you. Is it Ozi or Gozi?'

'Ngozi.'

'Thank you, Gozi. Do you know Lagos well?' he asks.

'Yes, to a degree.'

'Well, I'm new in town and I was wondering—'

'Hello, sir, Mrs Ebo phoned ahead and said Ngozi was bringing you over,' the bank cashier says, shaking Mr MacDonald's hand. He turns to Ngozi: 'Thank you.'

It's now an hour later and Samuel Okafor arrives at the reception desk.

'Hello, beautiful,' he says.

'Hello, Mr Okafor.'

Samuel Okafor is the son of a very wealthy businessman whose business is not always, shall I say, legitimate, and the nephew to Governor Okafor. He's a playboy and very well known around town, particularly to Mrs Ebo, who has grown familiar with the whole family through their dealings with the bank over the years. He's heavily into computers, and studied computer science at Harvard over in the States. He recently needed help with obtaining a million *naira* as quickly as possible for a business transaction, and Ngozi located the right names for him and directed him to the right people in the bank. He said to her, trying to be helpful in return, 'You know, you should look into getting into computers – after all, it's the future, especially when you see what is happening in the States. One day there will be lots of money to be made here.' At the time Ngozi had not fully got what he was talking about, but had nodded her head in fake understanding.

'Samuel, please can you leave my staff alone,' says Mrs Ebo. 'Now, what can I help you with?'

'Ah-ah, Mrs Ebo, I've not come to trouble you or your staff, O. I just came to say thank you to Ngozi for all her help the other day.'

'Well, I'm sure that Ngozi appreciates your thank you,' Mrs Ebo says protectively. 'Now, is there anything else I can assist you with?'

'No, Mrs Ebo. You and your team are doing a great job. But I understand it's Ngozi's break at midday and I can see she's about to grab her bag and go, so I hope you don't mind if I take her to lunch to say thank you properly?'

Mrs Ebo looks at Ngozi and wants to say something to put her off the playboy in front of her, but she also doesn't want to be rude because she knows his family are good customers of the bank. She exchanges a warning glance with Ngozi – she'll talk to her later about Samuel's reputation. 'Please have her back here in forty-five minutes, there are some errands she has to run for me.'

'On the dot, Mrs Ebo.'

Ngozi comes home from work in a rush and busies herself with preparing for her date.

'Na, you *biko*. The girl di too fine,' says Stella with a thumbs up, as Ngozi does a twirl for them.

'Na, you and Maryam Babangida go fight tonight,' says Ifeoma. They both sit behind her on the bed, clapping their hands with joy.

'Go sit down, *jare*,' Ngozi says, smiling at her friends, while parading up and down, bottom swinging in the air like a pendulum.

They burst out laughing, falling over one another.

Ngozi looks at herself in the cracked full-length mirror propped up against a flaking wall, once sky blue, but now, in some places, red-black with dust and dirt. She's ready. She peers at herself in the mirror but doesn't fully appreciate her reflection. She doesn't see how the clothes she wears pale in comparison to her beauty, but instead stands admiring the george satin that she feels makes her a little better-looking.

'When he go collect you?' asks Stella.

'Soon. I told him when he come he send someone for front of shop come call me.' This is her third date with Samuel Okafor.

'Remember what I tell you, make sure he give you plenti monnie before you dey sleep with am. You no go see toilet paper which he dey use clean yash once you dey spread leg give am,' says Ifeoma.

Ngozi nods her head. She's grown close to Stella's friend Ifeoma over these few years and in many ways she looks up to her. There's a silent recognition between them, an understanding when they speak about their childhoods or the families they've left behind, that goes over Stella's head. You see, although the expense of city life appears on the surface to have equalized them, for Stella also works as a receptionist for a big corporation, the truth is that for Stella this life is an adventure, an interlude before returning to the security of her family and settling down with a good match, but for Ifeoma and Ngozi this is real life. Their families rely on them and whatever they can send home, but despite their differences from Stella they both love her deeply, for Stella is Stella, unique in this world of snobbery and status.

Ngozi thinks about the letter she received from home this morning from Blessing, asking for money to help pay the rent and outstanding school fees. She thinks of her life at the Obindus' and it fills her with dread. She shivers, looks over at Ifeoma through the mirror.

Ngozi is grateful to Ifeoma for her job. She's watched her play with wealthy men over the last two years, steadily upgrading to the one she has now. Next week she's moving out to her own apartment, she holds a good position in the bank as a secretary, always dresses immaculately, but best of all always has money to send home, thanks to her wealthy but very married boyfriend. At present, to get the things Ngozi needs, to find her way back to school, her only option is to meet rich men. She doesn't have the contacts or the opportunities. She thinks of her village, of their Catholic attitudes, of her sister, and wonders if she'll be able to go through with it, but there is no choice.

Mrs Ebo has warned her against Samuel, said he was nothing more than a good-time boy. Ifeoma has also warned her not to settle for him. 'In truth, O, Samuel is only good for meeting bettar contacts, he's too much, O, but if you want to try?' she said, shrugging her shoulders. 'You would be bettar with someone older, like his papa. The older ones are more likely to give you what you want without asking for too much in return.'

Ngozi turns to Stella and Ifeoma with her back to the mirror.

'If he dey ask,' Ifeoma continues, 'who you dey live with, tell am na you and your elder sisters dey live for house, that way if he dey want see you more he go want pay rent.'

Ngozi nods.

'Oh, by the way, Mrs Ebo dey tell me that there be some white man dey come for bank today come look for you.'

'White man?' quizzes Stella.

'That's Mr MacDonald. I'm trying to avoid him before people come think I be *ashawo*.'

'So which man dey take you out tonight?' asks Stella.

'Samuel Okafor.'

'Samuel Okafor, Governor Okafor's relative?'

'Yes.'

'Na, you *biko*,' says Stella with another thumbs up.

'Ma, there be man for front of shop say he come for you,' says the little boy as he knocks on the door to their room.

'Thank you. Go tell am I dey come.'

'Yes, Ma.' The boy hurries away.

Ngozi slows down her preparations, and takes her time talking to her friends, just as Ifeoma advises.

The metallic Mercedes outside the shop attracts the attention of the local children. They pace around the V-boot like expectant hyenas anticipating a kill. They don't touch the vehicle for fear of retribution from the owner, but continue to pace, hoping for a chance, manoeuvring round the smelly gutters to get a three-hundred-and-sixty-degree view of the car, dreaming of the day when they'll escape from their poverty and own such a machine. Samuel waits beside his car, watching the awed faces of the children, secretly despising the wretchedness of the people around him. When his date finally emerges from the shop, he sighs with relief.

'Ngozi, you dey look fine, O,' says Samuel as he holds open the passenger door. He watches her position herself in the front seat, closes the door, then walks around to the other side, and drives off to a party in Victoria Island.

Army personnel stand on guard at the entrance to the Governor's mansion.

'Make you show me invitation,' says a soldier.

'Ah-ah, Tunde, you don't know me?'

'*Hay, Orga*, I didn't see you. Since when you dey get V-boot? Where your BMW?'

'It dey for garage. How your body, Tunde?'

'My body fine, Sir. Your uncle and father say when you dey come make you see dem for study, there be man they want say introduce.'

Samuel nods his head and smiles in acknowledgement as he drives through the gates, then calls out, 'Tunde, make you park car for back garage,' as they vacate the motor. Tunde jogs towards them to collect the keys.

Imported European cars fill the compound, and the house girl inside Ngozi wants to scream in disbelief. She's read about these people or caught glimpses of them on television or in magazines, and now she's about to be among them. She wants to jump with excitement but does not. Instead she suppresses the urge to skip and run her finger along everything in sight, and tries to give the impression of a person totally accustomed to it all.

Ngozi waits while Samuel gives the car keys to Tunde, listening to the sounds of the late evening. Crickets make a merry tune which sails on the breeze, blending with the melodies of Sir Shina Peters' rhythmic drums, as both surrender, both intertwine, creating a beautiful song in the dusk. Day bids farewell to its cousin night and the sounds of nature and man live in perfect harmony. She breathes in and holds her head high before entering the house, while Samuel guides her gently by the elbow. The room is abuzz with the sound of live high-life music. Men and women dance and shake, and the bright colours of their dress appear like water rapids reflecting the colours of the rainbow. White handkerchiefs wipe away sweat from brows, while the men, in rivers of cotton, stick money to the damp faces of their wives dancing in the centre of the room.

Samuel guides her past a buffet table with trays of chicken, beef, *jollof* rice, white rice salads, stew and much more, and on towards the library. Ngozi looks back in longing and plans to return later when no one is looking, to snaffle food into her handbag to take back to Stella.

'Uncle, Papa, Tunde say you want to see me?' says Samuel as he pokes his head round the door of the library, signalling to Ngozi to remain outside.

'Hey, come in. I want you to meet Mr Akinyele, the owner of Olunde Services.'

Samuel ventures further into the library, leaving the door slightly ajar. Ngozi hears someone in the room grunt.

'Mr Akinyele tell me how he have building work for the new Enugu state. I go leave you with him and your uncle, make you get acquainted.'

Samuel's father exits the library, closing the door behind him.

'Can I help you?' he asks Ngozi.

'I'm just waiting for Samuel,' she replies, her hands crossed demurely in front of her.

Mr Okafor looks at her. She's not a 'Shining Beauty', but she has an innocence, a strikingness, about her face that he likes. His eyes travel down her body.

'Samuel will be a long time. Why don't you come with me? He'll join you later after his meeting. Would you like something to eat?'

She nods, then follows him.

'So you're one of my son's friends?' he asks.

'Yes, sir.'

'How long have you known him?'

'Two weeks,' she replies.

'Not long then.'

As they stand beside the buffet table, she quickly works out her best strategy. He's an older man, rich, used to women offering their services to him. She searches her mind for any information Samuel might have indirectly given her about his father, little things that might give her an idea of how to kindle and keep his interest. The band stops briefly and people crowd around the buffet table, pushing them closer together. She's sure Mr Okafor can almost feel her breath on his skin. He tenses. Her eyes are hidden, downcast, as though she's too shy to look at him directly. She appears young and unspoilt to the older man. His curiosity is aroused.

'What is your father's name?'

'Nwosu, from Obowi.'

It's a common family name.

'Is my son your boyfriend or are you married?' he asks.

'You are very forward, Mr Okafor.'

Mr Okafor doesn't apologize. He's direct, he doesn't know how to be subtle, and it's very rare that he finds a woman interesting nowadays, so he doesn't believe in dressing up his intentions in pretty words.

'No, we're friends and I'm not married.'

He smiles at her. His eyes search the room for his wife.

'You mean to tell me a girl as pretty as you is not married yet?'

Ngozi bends her head, laughs nervously as if she's embarrassed.

'You must have a boyfriend.'

'No,' she says, then looks in the direction of the library, pretending to wonder if his son's meeting is over. Mr Okafor is provoked and his interest increases. There's now a competitive edge around her and he likes competition, especially against a younger man, even his own son.

'So what does a young girl like you do if you don't have a boyfriend?' he asks.

Her large eyes widen and dance back at him, and she lowers her voice. 'That is my business, O.'

To Mr Okafor, she's now a mixture of virginal sensuality and womanly confidence. *Which one is she?* he asks himself.

He looks down at her bosom, to where the blouse exposes flesh. His hands are sweaty. He licks his lips quickly like a lizard and brings out a business card and a bundle of money from his pocket, puts the card on top of the money, takes a firm hold of her wrist and places the cash gently in her hand.

'When you feel like letting me know what you do, I'll be interested,' he says, then draws her closer and whispers in her ear, 'There's more where that came from.' He flicks his tongue at her earlobe and walks off to find his wife.

He's confident he'll see her again. In a country where there is so much poverty and no social security, you see, he believes money can buy almost anything.

Ngozi continues to wait for Samuel. She's in shock, the money still in her hand. *How much did he give me?* she thinks as she stares down at it. *It's too much to count.* She quickly comes to her senses and stuffs the money away in her bag. It's in this state that Samuel finally finds her ten minutes later, standing alone by the wall.

'Sorry, I had to meet a man for business,' he says.

'It's okay.'

'Do you want to dance?'

They dance till late. Samuel is frightened to accompany her home himself at such a late hour – her neighbourhood has a bad reputation for housing armed robbers and drug addicts – so he arranges a driver for her. While she's in the car Ngozi discreetly counts the money Mr Okafor gave her: two thousand *naira*. She's never received so much money in her life. She contemplates the wad in her bag, fingers the green paper until a tear begins to slide down her cheek as she thinks of the money she'll be able to send back to her sister and mother in the village.

Ngozi undresses in the dark, gets into bed. The night air is hot and she glances over at Stella who lies still in her bed.

'You awake?' she asks into the darkness.

'No.'

Stella turns in her bed. She's unable to sleep due to the heat – it's suffocating. Once again NEPA has cut the electricity so the fans can't be used to ease the flame in the air, nor can they avoid the stench from the gutters outside when they breathe. Both women lie on their backs, with only a light wrapper to cover their nakedness.

'Do you remember what it dey like before, when we were children?' Ngozi asks desperately.

'Waytin you mean?'

'I mean, before this here chaos dey call life,' she says, then shakes her head against the bed. 'Nigeria, O. Remember how we dey play when we young? I dey poor in those days but I was still happy. Those days were sweet, sweet like ripe pineapple, O.'

Time passes between them. No words are spoken. Instead they listen to a baby's hollow cry drifting from across the compound; its faint wail echoes and rebounds off the courtyard walls. Overlapping this sound are wild dogs howling, singing love songs on top of hills of rotting rubbish that spill out on to the road, while underneath hums the familiar night-time chirping, blending with everything else to give the Lagos night its own unique tone. But still Apapa sounds deserted in the hot night. It echoes Ngozi's mood. It says nothing – there is nothing and her future spirals downwards in front of her.

'Stella, *sabi*, you enjoy yourself over there in England when you go for holiday?' asks Ngozi.

'Yes, the people there dey live life, O,' says Stella.

Ngozi is solemn. 'There's nothing you go want for that country you no go get. I no dey understand people wey say they no have money for that country. When you see dem for TV, everyone dey smile.'

Stella begins cautiously. 'Ngozi, life over there isn't as easy as you think. When you walk on street the people don't smile, O. If life was so good, tell me why they don't smile? It's like their spirit done run away. If I had money there's nowhere else like Nigeria with all its troubles, there's nowhere else I would rather live. This is my home.'

'Yes, I dey hear,' says Ngozi, but she doesn't hear – to her, across the ocean is the promised land. As if to stop the negative force of her friend's words, she suddenly raises her voice, crying, 'I want more!' with such force that it overwhelms, possesses her. 'I dey want more, before my life dey pass me by.'

Stella laughs nervously. Sensing Ngozi's mood, she thinks it best not to say any more.

'Mr Okafor go help me.'

'Are you sure?'

'Yes, I go get him to pay my school fees.'

'Na, you *biko*, how you dey get am to pay,' her friend laughs. 'Anyway, na, you and Maryam Babangida,' she says with respect.

They chat a little while longer, but sleep soon captures Stella in its arms and silence falls.

Three days she waits. Three days, thirteen hours and thirty-five minutes to be precise, but this time she's more than prepared for Mr Okafor. Ngozi chooses her dress carefully in order to show off her figure, just enough to tease him, to make promises to his fantasy, but not enough for him to think or mistake that the promise is made in reality. She's not looking for a one-off – she needs to make a stronger connection – so she rehearses every line, every look with Ifeoma, plans the meeting in her head, paying attention to detail.

Smoothing her dress down, she knocks on the outer door, enters and heads straight to the receptionist. There are four other women waiting in the reception area, each with a story, but none of them have been granted an audience with him, so they wait in hope. Ngozi takes courage when his secretary signals for her to go in. She knocks.

'Come in, come in, my dear,' says Mr Okafor.

Ngozi walks into the room, moving steadily towards his desk, sits down, crosses her legs. The silk dress she wears, Stella's dress, falls away to reveal her legs. Mr Okafor's eyes dart to her thigh and back up to her eyes. He laughs. She has his full attention.

'So, my dear, how have you been?'

'I've been fine, O,' she replies. Putting her hand on the desk and bending forward to pick up a miniature statue, her dress falls forward, exposing the upper curve of her bosom. Mr Okafor laughs again and bends forward to stroke her hand. Ngozi withdraws it quickly before he can touch her.

'I thought I would visit you after the other day.'

'I'm glad you came, O. I've been thinking very seriously about you.'

'Not too seriously, O?' says Ngozi.

'Hmm, very seriously.' His pink tongue plays against his lower lip.

She looks at his fat paunch and podgy hands, and for the first time notices an odour. It is strong, heavy like the smell of cooked meat. It is Mr Okafor. She breathes in but finds it difficult to sift out his scent and inhale plain air. Instead she's immersed in his aroma and it makes her nauseous.

Ngozi's eyes wander around the office. It's spacious. Piles of paper clutter his desk. A half-open filing cabinet stands to the left. A settee lounges to the right. Pictures cram the white walls which are yellowing with dust. In one photograph Mr Okafor shakes hands with the previous governor. Next to it is a picture of Mr Okafor with a smiling European whose hair is white like the Santa Claus on a Coca-Cola bottle. In another Mr Okafor is in traditional dress, showering money on native dancers. All the pictures in the room carry the same theme: Mr Okafor. He clears his throat. Her attention turns back to her host.

'I want to thank you for the monnie. I bought a dress your son wanted to get me. You know we women like our independence,' she says.

Mr Okafor shifts in his chair. Her statement about his son has clearly irritated him. *Hmm, that small boy*, he thinks. *I can do better.*

'Anyway,' she continues, 'this is a short visit. I was just passing.' She hopes her visit is not too short – it has to be long enough to whet his appetite, but short enough to increase his craving. Ifeoma has taught her well, you see. She gets up from the chair.

'You can't be leaving so soon.'

'Yes, I was just passing through.'

'It's not fair, O – you've only just come.'

'I have things to do.'

'Well, make them include me. Stay for lunch. Come, let us go to Awolowo Road and eat for restaurant.'

Ngozi has never been to the exclusive eating places in Ikoyi, and salivates at the possibility. She finds it difficult to control herself, to stick to Ifeoma's rules. 'Point three, it is not good to show a man that you are impressed. Gratitude, yes. Impressed, no.' And she so wants to reel this man in.

'You dey tempt me, O, but I really have things I have to do.'

'One of these days I go make you tell me these things you dey do.'

212

'And one of these days I might tell you,' she jokes.

'It sounds like a threat,' he says.

'No, seriously, O, I have to meet your son; he's waiting for me.'

'What for?' he says with a slight sneer.

'We are friends. I'm helping him at the bank.'

'You bettar be telling the truth, O,' he warns.

'Ask your son?'

He won't, of course – he doesn't want his son to know he's after the same woman. He sits back in his chair, watches as she leaves the room, and shakes his head. His curiosity is aroused and he's looking forward to her next visit.

Ngozi returns to his office three days later. This time she brings okra soup with pounded yam for lunch, and when she lifts the lid the aroma is sweet – that alone sends Mr Okafor to paradise. He breathes it in to get its full effect, then eats like a hungry man, until satisfaction dozes in his stomach. She leaves afterwards with one thousand *naira* in her pocket. It's a good life, good employment, a thousand *naira* for keeping an old man company, but as always there is eventually a price – it comes sooner or later, but it comes.

'Ngozi, Mr MacDonald is here again,' says Mrs Ebo as she watches him walk towards the reception desk.

'Yes, Mrs Ebo,' answers Ngozi as she also turns to watch Mr MacDonald make his way over.

I sit on a low wall beside the desk, watching the white-haired man stride towards them. He carries a little weight but is still strong-looking, and he's slightly rosy around the cheeks from too many nights drinking with his colleagues at the expat bar. But his features, they are familiar, maybe a little chubbier, a little smoother, cleaner, not so . . . so etched with the hardness or madness that cruelty brings, but still familiar. In my lifetime, before these glass-fronted buildings and tarmacked roads sprouted into existence, this was a small but lush grassland with dirt-track roads that we were forced to walk along. And I remember the first peek of a grey building in the distance; it seemed to wave at me through the grass, and I falsely hoped for some relief from the fever and the weight pressing down around my neck, arms and ankles. I felt the hot sand of the track road between my toes as they marched us further along the coast. The ocean and its sandy friend glimpsed in the distance to my left between the palm trees, its light breeze offered me some comfort. The skies were blue above and further on in the distance, out in the ocean, barely visible, I saw something that seemed to sit on the waters. It was strange, but everything was strange: the customs, the languages spoken around me. Little did I know then – I was but a mere girl, whose world was her husband's village, her village, who was reared and fed on their love. And so, as we drew nearer to the grey building that waved at me in the distance it seemed to grow and grow and grow. I had never seen a building so big, so vast. They marched us through two large wooden doors that appeared almost as tall as the palm trees outside, through a dark hallway, out into a courtyard, and that was my first glimpse of him – the man, the one that Mr MacDonald reminds me of. He stood above us on a balcony, a gun in his hand, bellowing to the others below. They stripped us further. I stood fully naked, a hand forcing my mouth open to look inside. My jaw was pulled to the right, then back again to the left. Lifting my heavy arms up, bound by the shackles, forcing my head down, searching for something in my hair. All the while the man stood above. I heard a raised voice behind me, what sounded like a struggle, then a gunshot. I looked back, as much as the shackles would allow, and saw one of my fellow countrymen on the floor. I knew he was dead from the flow of blood on the ground. I looked up at the man, Mr MacDonald, or the man who looked like him. There was no penitence in him, no recognition of what had just happened, except for a laugh and the barking of more orders to his colleagues below, who led us quickly through to what I now know were the dungeons. I have seen many Mr MacDonalds come and go in this land, each new wave, each new trade brings them, and this time it is oil. And so I sit watching this Mr MacDonald, wondering what this one will bring.

'How can I help you this morning?' Mrs Ebo asks Mr MacDonald.

'Morning, Mrs E-bo. I must say you look lovely today. I was wondering if Gozi would mind helping me with my exchange again?'

Mrs Ebo looks at him. She wants to say something. The words are almost formed but she thinks better of it, and instead she says, 'Ngozi, please help Mr MacDonald.'

Ngozi gets up from her chair, smiles and signals for him to follow. She's happy to help – after all, this is Mr MacDonald's fourth visit and on each occasion he's been a very generous tipper although she's not allowed to accept tips, but around here everyone does, including on occasion Mrs Ebo.

'Gozi, I still haven't had a chance to see Lagos,' says Mr MacDonald as they walk along. 'I understand there are a few things to see but I have a little problem: no one to show me around.'

'That is a shame, O.'

'Yes, a real shame. I was wondering if you had a little spare time,' he says, 'you know, to be my tour guide.'

Ngozi hesitates, looks at him walking beside her. She likes Mr MacDonald. He's always been nice in the few interactions they've had, but does she want to be seen in public with him? That is a different matter. In her village where she was brought up, only prostitutes and loose women hang around white men. She looks at Mr MacDonald again. He seems nice, she thinks, he tips gener-ously, and besides, she doesn't have to stand close to him. If she keeps her distance people might not think they're together, not in that way anyway. There's no harm in showing him around.

'I'm free on Saturday,' she says. 'I can show you around Lagos then.'

'Saturday is fine. It works for me. Shall I pick you up?'

Ngozi quickly shakes her head. She's proud and imagines him looking down on where she lives.

'I'll come to pick you up from your hotel.'

'Okay then.'

'Saturday.'

Mr MacDonald emerges through the hotel doors. Ngozi spots him and heads over.

'Good morning, Mr MacDonald. Come with me – I've arranged a taxi for the day. It will be cheaper and make things easier. I thought we could start at the National Museum, then on to Tarkwa Beach.'

Mr MacDonald follows Ngozi and climbs into the waiting taxi. She gives the driver instructions and then leans back in her seat beside him. She smiles awkwardly at the white man next to her, and wonders whether it was a good idea to sit in the back with him.

'Gozi, I'm so glad you agreed to show me around.'

She smiles.

'You know, you're a very beautiful woman. Do you have a boyfriend or a husband?'

She smiles to herself. 'Unfortunately not, Mr MacDonald, but—'

'You know, you can call me Ben,' he says, smiling back at her. 'And I don't bite, I'm really a teddy bear, and I really do want to see what Lagos has to offer.'

She looks up at him and there is such genuineness around his eyes that she cannot help but smile back. Her shoulders relax. He stretches out and covers her hand with his. 'I have a feeling today is going to be a very good day,' he says as the taxi pulls away.

As she shows him around the museum, his conversation is easy. He's not like the other men she has known. There is no struggle between their worlds, and as she points at artefacts and reads the information beneath, she wonders about this Mr MacDonald, wonders about his world and how easy it must be, and there is a dance between them. In his presence she is Ngozi; she doesn't feel the hierarchy she'd have felt between her and the wealthy men like him from her own land. She likes this feeling of not being less than, less because she has no father's name to truly speak of, less because her family are but poor village folk, less because . . . there are so many becauses. And in the midst of showing him things and laughing, she stops, looks at their reflection in the glass cabinet housing the artefacts, and realizes that maybe, just maybe, she doesn't care what others might think of her and this white man.

They sit at a beach restaurant eating a late lunch. The cool breeze brushes over them, and he reaches out again to cover her hand on the table. She half smiles, but doesn't remove her hand.

'So, Gozi, tell me more about yourself, your life.'

'What do you want to know, O?'

'How many brothers and sisters do you have? Have you always lived in Lagos? How long have you worked at the bank?'

'No, O. I come from a small village called Obowi. I have two brothers and a sister. And I have worked at the bank for just over a year. And you? How come you are here in Lagos?'

'My company sent me. I work on rotation so I'm here for six to eight weeks at a time and I go home for two weeks.'

'You work in oil?'

'Yes.'

'And what of your life in England?'

'I don't live in England. I live in Scotland.'

'Scotland. Is that different from England?'

'Yes. So tell me about your village.'

217

And so Ngozi began to tell him about her village and a little about her childhood. He listened, took it all in, and the poverty in her tale unsettled him, and when she dropped him off at the hotel he felt compelled to pay her much more than Ngozi would have got in her monthly wage at the bank. Once again she sat in the back of the taxi and began to believe that maybe she could have the things she had always wanted, and that maybe, just maybe it wasn't so bad hanging out with Mr MacDonald.

Ngozi has so far avoided Mr Okafor's attempts at finding her alone; she only meets him at his office. Although she likes the money Mr Okafor gives her, she's having second thoughts. The more she sees him, the more he makes her nauseous. It isn't only his smell but his habits. He sometimes clears his throat of phlegm and spits it out the window, or scratches his armpits then sniffs his fingers, and most of the time the sweat pours off him like water running down the slopes of a contaminated sewer. She's begun to cringe any time he comes near her or accidentally touches her.

But the money is good. She's received a letter from home – Blessing is doing well at school, and she's been able to send the family a lot more money than usual to cover extras. Besides, there is no other employment she knows of where she can get so much for spending an hour talking to an old man, and between the money she's been getting from him and from Mr MacDonald she now has some savings that might just get her back to school – only for one term, but it's a start. So she returns time and time again, promising herself that as soon as he shows signs or starts making advances she will handle it and not return.

On her seventh visit as she walks into his office, she notices two things. First is the overpowering smell of Mr Okafor's body odour – NEPA has cut the electricity supply yet again, so the air conditioning and fans usually at work are idle. Second is the determination on Mr Okafor's face and the tension in his outstretched arms.

'Come in, my dear. Sit down. I'll be back in a minute.'

Ngozi takes a seat and hears him talk to a few people in the reception area, then he returns and stands with his back to the door.

'Mr Okafor, are you all right?' asks Ngozi.

'Shush,' he says and puts his ear to the door to listen for a while.

'Is everything okay?' she says, then gets up from the chair.

It's then that he locks the door and puts the key in his pocket.

They look at each other, Ngozi in disbelief, Mr Okafor with a grin.

'Why you do that, O?' asks Ngozi.

'Come now, stop playing games. You know what I want.'

She looks at the window but there is no other way out except through the office door. 'I go scream,' she threatens.

'No one go hear. I just sent them to lunch.'

He walks towards her; she backs away to the other side of his desk. He moves left, she moves left. He moves right, she moves right. Then he lunges across the desk and chases her around it until he's dizzy.

'Ngozi, why you dey play so. Look, if you dey cooperate, I go give you more monnie.' His smile is stretched across his face like a clown. He reaches in his *dashiki* tunic and brings out a wad of multicoloured *naira* bills as thick as a brick, fanning it in her face as if asking her to take in its smell.

Ngozi reaches out to grab the notes.

He takes her wrist, pulls her around the desk with surprising strength for a man of his girth to stand in front of him. 'You'll have to get smarter,' he advises and leans her against the desk.

She holds herself rigid.

'Give me what I want and I go give you what you want,' he whispers in her ear. His hand reaches up and kneads her breast like dough, then moves down between her thighs.

She flinches as a terrible nausea fills her throat.

'You like it,' he whispers again in her ear. His bad breath fans her skin. 'You want me – you know you want me. Just spread leg, give me.'

Ngozi sees Mr Obindu. Mr Okafor is Mr Obindu. Mr Obindu is Mr Okafor. There is no beginning, no end. She sees Mr Obindu on top of her, his hand over her mouth squeezing out her muffled sounds, tearing her as he forces himself inside, and the fight in her takes over. Ngozi yanks her wrist away, kicks her knee into his groin, and in a sideways move flings herself across the desk. He pulls at her, and she bites, bites hard, her teeth locking down on his meaty flesh.

Mr Okafor lets out a loud yell and lets go.

'Mr Okafor, are you okay in there?' shouts his secretary as she knocks sharply on the door. 'Mr Okafor, are you okay? Let me call the police.'

'No, don't!'

But his secretary is gone.

'Give me the key, give me the key, O!' shouts Ngozi. 'You think you can treat me anyhow?'

'No,' he replies, then throws the key at Ngozi.

Ngozi catches it and unlocks the door. She runs out of the office, out of the building, before the police can arrive. She's afraid, unsure what Mr Okafor will tell the police, because he is as rich as she is poor. She imagines herself in handcuffs and the unpleasantness of a Nigerian prison cell. Suddenly she feels alone in this big city, needs to be safe, thinks of Mr MacDonald – his maleness and whiteness in her mind might offer some protection. His hotel is not far, and she finds herself running towards the only man she knows in Lagos, towards his hotel.

'Please, O, is Mr MacDonald in?' she asks shakily at the front desk.

She watches the receptionist pick up the phone and speak to him. 'Who are you?' she asks Ngozi, holding the receiver close to her ear.

'Ngozi.'

'Ngozi, sir. Okay, I will let her know.' She turns to Ngozi. 'He'll be down in a minute.'

Ngozi fidgets as she waits for him to come down, then she sees him striding across the floor towards her. Suddenly she's relieved, runs to him, buries her head into his shoulder and cries.

'What is this all about?' asks Mr MacDonald.

'I'm sorry, Mr MacDonald, but there was no one I could turn to. I'm really sorry,' she says and buries her head in his shoulder again, leaving a wet patch on his pale yellow polo shirt.

Her tears are plentiful – more than simply for Mr Okafor. It's the first time she's really cried since leaving the Obindus and arriving in Lagos.

'Come, come, my dear, what on earth has happened?' His voice penetrates her fog.

'I'm really sorry, Mr MacDonald, really sorry, O, but a man I know just attacked me – he tried to force me to have sex, O. I didn't know where else to run. I don't have family here except for my best friend but she's at work, and I am afraid, O.'

'Shush, shush. I think we need to report this to the police.'

'Police? No, O – no police. This is Nigeria, O! The man who attacked me is a wealthy man – no police.'

'Okay, calm down. No police.'

'Thank you, Mr MacDonald.'

'What are you going to do?'

'I don't know. Maybe it's best if I go home.'

'Okay, let me take you home.'

Mr MacDonald steps out into the traffic outside the hotel, hails a taxi and they both get in. He puts his arm around Ngozi, comforting her as they travel. The landscape through the window begins to change – the buildings getting lower, dirtier, the people more dishevelled, the air dustier. He begins to wonder whether it was a good idea to offer to take her home, but it is done, so he sits in the cab feeling progressively more anxious. Without warning the taxi driver swerves off the main road and down a bumpy side street. Mr MacDonald looks out of the window, sees rows of two-storey buildings defeated by the dust, a hill of rubbish to his left, watches the children squealing and playing on top of it as the taxi passes by, thinks he can detect the faint foul smell of the sewers.

'You live here?'

'Yes. Just a little further, down to the right. Please stop in front of the shop, O,' says Ngozi to the taxi driver.

Mr MacDonald looks around at the crumbling buildings, the wretched clothes of the children playing in the street. He sits in the taxi looking ahead, doesn't attempt to get out.

'Will you be okay?' he asks Ngozi as she starts to get out of the taxi, and pulls on her arm to draw her back to him.

'Yes, thank you,' she says, looking straight back at him. 'My flatmates will take care of me. I would invite you in but we share the one room.'

'Don't worry,' he says, reaching over and kissing her softly on her cheek. 'We will speak.'

Ngozi climbs out of the taxi and slams the door. She watches it drive away, notices the look in his eyes as he waves at her – almost one of horror – before the taxi disappears into the distance. She looks around her neighbourhood and for the first time since she moved to Lagos feels ashamed. She pats down her skirt, wonders if she will ever see Mr MacDonald again and what she will do if Mr Okafor calls the police on her, then turns to hurry up to her room to ask Stella for her advice.

This morning Ngozi is in the middle of sorting out messages and letters addressed to people who work in the bank.

'Mr MacDonald is here again,' says Mrs Ebo, giving Ngozi a look.

Ngozi glances up to see Mr MacDonald walking across the cool bank lobby towards the reception desk. She fixes the pins in her hair and smiles broadly at him.

'Morning, Mrs Ebo. Morning, Gozi. I thought I would come and check on you.'

Ngozi gets up from her desk to greet Mr MacDonald. Mrs Ebo hovers close behind. 'I thought I might not see you again,' she says quietly to him.

He laughs. 'You can't get rid of me that easily.'

Ngozi smiles into his eyes. It's been a long time since a man cared enough to find out if she was okay, and she likes it, misses it. She thinks for a brief fraction of a second of E'mma, then refocuses on Mr MacDonald.

'Are you free for lunch?'

'Yes, yes. Mrs Ebo, is it okay if I go to lunch now?'

'Yes, my dear.'

Ngozi collects her bag quickly.

Mrs Ebo watches as the two of them disappear, a concerned look on her face. *It will not end well*, she thinks, and shakes her head. She's tried talking to Ngozi but she's not listening. *It will not end well*, she thinks again and gets back to her paperwork.

The restaurant is full. Ngozi looks around in awe – she suggested this restaurant because she knew it was somewhere that the bosses in the bank went to but didn't really think Mr MacDonald would take her there. She leans into him.

'You okay?'

'Yes, O. Of course.'

Mr MacDonald kisses her on the forehead and takes her hand as a young woman shows them to their seats. 'The other day, where I dropped you off, how long have you lived there?'

'Over a year. It's bettar than where we used to live.'

'Really?'

'And you, O. How long you dey for Nigeria?'

'I don't know. Like I said, I work on rotation, so I'm here for about six weeks and then go home for two. Do you enjoy working at the reception desk in the bank?'

'Yes, but to be honest, O, I would rather go back to school, but I can't afford it.'

'Really. What do you want to study?'

'I don't know, O, maybe Business.'

'Business,' he says with a laugh.

Ngozi stares at him with a puzzled look.

'Nothing. Don't mind me.'

'A friend of mine said I should get into computers, but I don't know.'

'So tell me how come a beautiful girl like you doesn't have a boyfriend?'

Ngozi shrugs her shoulders.

'And you, *ka*?'

'Me?' he laughs. 'We're talking about you.'

'But what make you leave Scotland, come for Nigeria – what you want for Nigeria that you can't get for Scotland?'

'My company sent me here for a few years and—'

The waitress returns and takes their order.

'So there's no boyfriend or husband?' asks Mr MacDonald, as if confirming something.

'No, O.'

'Good. While I'm here I need someone to show me around, hang out with, show me the real Nigeria, 'cause you people really seem to enjoy living in this chaos,' he says. 'Don't worry, I'll be very generous in compensating you for your time.'

Ngozi feels a little uncomfortable.

He continues. 'I don't really know that many people here apart from my colleagues. Look, I promise if you show me around, I'll spread the good word.'

Ngozi looks at Mr MacDonald.

'Deal?' he says with a smile.

She hesitates, then smiles back. 'Deal,' she says.

They both lift their glasses and clink on it.

I watch them holding each other over at the departure gate. It's Mr MacDonald's last day in Nigeria, the end of his rotation, but he'll be back in two weeks. His six weeks have gone quickly and I would have missed them but for an errand that I hurried back here for. As usual this airport is busy, far too busy for my liking, but those two over there, they're in a world of their own.

'You'll come back?' asks Ngozi.

'Don't worry, I will,' he laughs. 'In two weeks.'

'Two weeks?' she repeats.

'Yes.' He bends to kiss her.

'Not here. We don't kiss in public, O.'

'Okay.'

'I'll miss you,' she says.

'I'll miss you too.'

'Two weeks?'

'Yes.'

'What am I supposed to do while you're away?'

'I told you, look for an apartment for us to live in. It has to be in the areas I told you about, otherwise my company won't agree. The agent has your number so she'll be in touch.'

'Two weeks?'

'Yes. Trust me. You have the money I gave you?'

'Yes.'

'Sir, you're obstructing the rest of the customers,' says the airline official.

'Sorry,' he says, then turns quickly to Ngozi, grabs her, hugs her, pats her behind, then lets her go, picks up his hand luggage and heads smiling through the departure gates. 'Two weeks!' he calls back at her.

She watches him disappear through the gates, feeling a little awkward and wondering if anyone saw him pat her behind.

But there's nothing she can do but let him go and hope he'll be true to his word. Last night they made love for the first time and she gave a little part of herself, something she didn't think she was capable of, something she thought Mr Obindu had robbed her of long ago. She did, and still does in her small way, love E'mma but their lovemaking was too close to the abuse of Mr Obindu for her to be able to feel her own desires. And now, standing here, watching Ben disappear, she wonders whether she did the right thing, but after six weeks of being with him and getting to know him, she could not have made any other decision. So she watches him disappear and wonders whether she's been foolish. 'Two weeks?' she asks the air he leaves behind.

15

Playing House

So it began: two weeks apart, six weeks together, two weeks apart, then back to start again. Playing house, just the two of them, playing parts that deep inside they've always longed to play. Ngozi as wifey: preparing his meals, soothing his brow, satisfying his aches, taking care of him, taking care of herself, nails done, hair done. The outside world left somewhere out there to tend to itself. No questions asked. 'Cause to ask the questions, she might interrupt this dream, this game they both partake in – to ask the questions could take her back to that world of uncertainty, of struggling and worrying about how to get by to help the family she loves. In this world, her dreams are fulfilled, she's back in school, practising her English and her numbers, and there's more than enough to send back to Blessing, her mother, her brothers who she speaks to over the phone now, once a week. They're happy, all six of them. Ngozi is truly the madam. Her new home is pretty, like all the rest in this suburb. Mr MacDonald has taught her many things, and like the others she has house help, a driver and a cook. At a quick glance she looks like the rest of the women in this neighbourhood, but they know she is different, for they are respectable women, and so I overhear them talking among themselves about the white man and his mistress who live at the end of the road, at parties and gatherings that Ngozi is never invited to.

Well, as for Mr MacDonald, as I've said, I have seen many Mr MacDonalds come and go in this land. In my lifetime my Mr MacDonald left death, destruction and, yes, life. Life forcibly created, born into this world to be fatherless, mothers sold on into the new world, and his sweet little toffee ones left behind, left to suckle off this ravaged land, and once again the land gave, it quietly brought forth what they needed, to feed them and quietly absorb their tears – and still it absorbs their tears. And as for him? He returned home to sit on gentrified boards, leaving legacies for other people's children of churches, libraries and parks, settling into his comfortable parlour chair, a pipe hanging from his pursed lips, hands outstretched to warm himself by the fire, draped in the clothes of good old sweet Grandpapa. 'Good old sweet, sweet Senair.' Over there in his mansion in Glasgow's merchant city.

But this Mr MacDonald, is he the same? There's something different about him – maybe it's in his eyes, or in the way he joked with the men who carried his luggage the first day I saw him arrive, or the look of horror at the local poverty the first day he took Ngozi home. I sensed he wanted to help, and yet? And yet? Well, maybe, it's the drug called exchange which turns his head. Here he lives a life richer than he ever could back home in the Glaswegian tenement block where he was brought up. Or maybe . . . it's Ngozi. Maybe it wouldn't be so easy to have such a beautiful young girl tend to all his needs back home where he comes from. Or maybe it's this world, which sees his whiteness and bows with a 'Yes, sir. No, sir. Anything else, sir?' So they, Ngozi and Mr MacDonald, keep playing, playing at house, enjoying the parts they've chosen, but like everything at some point it has to be interrupted. It happens, slowly and quietly at first, somewhere in one of his two-week absences. At some point Ngozi starts to ask herself the questions.

Where does he go? What does he do? Who does he see? And so the questions begin, getting louder with each new rotation. And neighbours' outside conversations make their way through her fog. 'You know they send that English man that *Amaka* dey see straight back to England.'

'No.'

'Yes.'

'What about the child she dey carry?'

What about the child?

Ngozi overhears the conversations, the stories, but nothing really matters. It really doesn't matter when there are more immediate worries to take care of, and it really doesn't matter until the day she's leaning over the bathroom sink at Stella's house, fighting the nausea, wondering if she has anything left in her to give, Stella holding her hair back.

'What you dey eat this morning?'

'Just a little *akamu* and *akara*. Maybe it was the *akara*,' lies Ngozi as she looks at her drawn face in the bathroom mirror. Her Ben, her Mr MacDonald, is due back tomorrow. She back-calculates her dates, and suddenly the fog lifts and everything is as clear as day. What is she to do? she asks herself.

'Why don't you lie down in the bed? Come.'

Ngozi lies down on the bed and the tide of nausea begins to recede. 'As I was telling you, Chiedu and his family went to see my family yesterday in Obowi,' says Stella.

Ngozi turns her head on her pillow to look over at her friend, and smiles weakly, an envy inside her. She wishes it was her, but in this world there is no Chiedu for her. Stella is from a different class to her, from a good family – her father Mr Tobenna is a good man.

'I spoke to Papa, and he said he like them.'

Ngozi nods and wonders if her Ben, Mr MacDonald, will ever ask her to marry him.

'They really like each other. He said that Chiedu's father went to the same small school as him.'

Ngozi sees Stella's mouth move, the words coming out, but she puts a hand to her stomach and wonders what is to become of them. Should she keep her baby or should she get rid of it before Ben finds out, not interrupt their dream, at least till she's managed to finish school?

'They agreed, so the wine carrying will be in August,' laughs Stella. 'Can you believe it?'

Ngozi suddenly feels a surge of panic. 'I want out now!' she says desperately, as if her life depends on it.

Stella stops her chat.

'Stella, I really want out of this country.'

'Ngozi, what?'

'I want out. I'll never really be anybody here.'

'What you talking about?'

A hunger to escape curls up in knots in her stomach, pulling at her insides. 'Stella, you know for me there will never be any wine carrying, there will never be anyone to marry me here.'

'Ngozi, what are you talking about? What about Ben?'

'What about Ben?'

'He loves you.'

'Does he? Does he? Then where does he go every six weeks? Tell me, Stella. Where does he disappear to?'

'I don't know.'

'You know I love you, O, but you and me, we've been friends all these years, but we really don't come from the same world.'

'What?'

'Stella, you, your dad, O, your mother, you're good people, but we don't come from the same world.'

'Ngozi, what you dey talk about? We both come from Obowi.'

'We come from the same village but you're not *Osu*, Stella, you're not *Osu*.'

'What does that matter?'

'Stella, it matters.'

'Ngozi, you're talking rubbish – most people are Christians now. These things don't matter any more.'

'Don't they, Stella? Maybe to you, but to most families they still matter. I'm tired of it all, O. I'm tired of always being looked down on. I'm tired of being reminded of my station.'

'But, Ngozi, who is reminding you?'

'Stella, I just want out of this country. I want to go somewhere where these things don't matter. I dey stay here, just dey let my life pass me by, O.'

'Ngozi, things abroad aren't as easy as you might think.'

'Really?'

'Really.'

'Then let me go find out for myself.'

'Okay, O.'

They stare at each other. Stella breaks into a smile first.

'I'm sorry. So tell me about the wine carrying,' says Ngozi and forces a smile back.

Ngozi lies awake, staring up at the ceiling. Her Ben, Mr MacDonald, is due back tomorrow and she wonders what the next day will bring. Is this the end, the end of acting out the dream? Reality truly has set in and she touches her stomach. Could she take this child home to her village? Bring it up there? Lagos would no longer be practical. But if she went to the village, how would she survive, with what money, with what future? She turns on to her side. Could she get rid of it before he knows, continue the dream? Would he accept it? Could he marry her? Would he? She breathes deeply. She wants so much more, has always wanted more than this. She wants so much more that it hurts, and deep inside. For the first time she is forced to acknowledge that she truly has no trust in her Ben, loves him but does not trust him. His silence when he's away, not a phone call, nothing – she knows nothing about his other life when he's away. Before it did not matter, but now with this child she is forced to face the whispers at the back of her mind. She turns in the bed again, reaches for the place where her Ben lies when he's here. She loves him, but prepares to face the possible truth.

And suddenly she feels the fight in her, feels it surge, and this fight is now not only for herself. 'I am strong. I am strong,' she says out into the night air. There's a resolve in her, a decision made – their best chance is somewhere over there, over there in the promised land, in England, or perhaps Scotland. She won't allow him to leave her, abandon them here. Over there, all she needs is a chance, all she needs is a chance and she can make a life for herself and her baby. She can get a job and with the foreign exchange she could do so much more for herself and her family. Her mind made up, she turns and goes back to sleep.

It's Saturday. She waits in the international arrivals hall just as she's done so many times before, watching the faces of the people as they come through. She envies the families, the greetings of sons, of daughters. She touches her stomach and wonders – will she ever know their lives, feel their belonging, the warmth, the protection? Ever since she can remember, she's always had to fight alone, but this fight is not only for her survival, it's now for them both. She sees him, his white face among a sea of black. He stands out and she steels herself, but something inside her begins to crumble. 'I am strong,' she says to herself, then gathers the pieces together, walks towards her Ben, her Mr MacDonald, the best smile she can muster on her face. 'Welcome back,' she says as he gathers her in his arms, lifts her and twirls her around. She laughs – maybe it will be okay, maybe everything will be fine, maybe her Ben will be different.

'I've missed you,' he says.

'I missed you too, O.'

He smiles. 'Quick, let's get home,' he says and hurries her out into the chaos of the arrivals traffic outside. She has a taxi waiting for them.

She laughs as they rush along. 'So how was your trip, O?'

'Fine,' he says.

'What did you do?'

'You know, this and that.'

'What is this and that, O?'

'You know, this and that.'

'And your family, O?'

'What's with all the questions?'

'Questions? I only asked about your family.'

'Look, I'm tired. I've just had an exhausting flight and I'm back at work tomorrow, so I'm not in the mood.'

Ngozi nods her head and obeys. They continue the journey home to the apartment in silence.

She runs his bath, puts out his nightwear to change into. The house help comes into the bathroom carrying hot water to add to the bath.

'The food dey warm for stove, Madam.'

'Thank you, O. When it dey finish, bring it for room.'

'Yes, Ma.'

She hears him in the bedroom and returns to turn down the bed just the way he likes it. Goes over to soothe his head.

'I missed you,' he says.

'I missed you too.'

He sits on the side of the bed, draws her close to him. 'You've put on a little weight while I've been away. You'd better be careful or I might trade you in!' he jokes.

She smiles weakly. 'I've run your bath, O.'

He pats her behind. 'We have unfinished business,' he whispers in her ear as he slips into the bathroom.

She watches him go and starts to unpack his suitcase. As usual everything is newly washed and ironed, neatly packed away, everything has a home, and she wonders who it could have been that packed it for him. She knows it wasn't Ben, he's not that careful. She smells his shirts and they smell of care, of attention, and suddenly she cannot live in this dream, and she sits on the bed holding his shirt, wondering what she's going to do. She's tired of thinking, of trying to sort out what she's going to do, wondering how she's going to find the money to keep her baby, wondering what is going to become of them if she goes back to the village, but whichever way it is to be, she needs to know. She needs to know if he's with her or if she has to do this alone, and if she's alone how she can do it. This is Nigeria – no government help, no family help, a single woman by herself. She doesn't want to live her mother's life, but maybe she has no choice but to let this child go in order to survive, maybe there is no choice but to terminate.

Mr MacDonald comes out of the bathroom towel-drying his hair. He sees her sitting on the bed clutching his white shirt.

'What are you doing, just sitting there so silently?'

'Ben, who packed your suitcase?'

'I did, of course.'

'Ben, please tell me the truth. Who packed your suitcase?'

'What's wrong with you today? All these questions.'

Ngozi begins to weep. 'Please, please, Ben, I'm pregnant. Now, who packed your suitcase?'

Ben's face has turned even whiter than it usually is. 'But you're on the pill. We talked about this. I told you – I told you not to get pregnant.' His voice rises.

'I am. I'm just as shocked as you, O. You think I wanted to ruin what we had here?'

'I told you – I thought you understood.'

'Understood what?'

'I thought you understood what we have here. That this was just while I was here.'

'I didn't plan this, O.'

'You stupid girl.'

'Ben, are you married?'

'You stupid, stupid girl.'

'Are you married?'

'You've ruined everything.'

'Are you married?'

'Yes, goddammit, I am. You can't keep it. You've got to get rid of the thing.'

And there is her answer. The truth plain and simple to hear. But what to do with this truth? Ngozi is silent as she takes it in. The man she thought she had isn't the man standing in front of her, and worst of all is how the life she's carrying inside her, the child that they both made, that he could describe their child as 'the thing'. And so she takes in the answer, breathes in the answer, is finally fully sober with the answer.

'I see, O,' she says, gets off the bed and continues to unpack his clothes.

'What do you mean, you see?'

'I see.'

'You see what?'

'I see. Your food, it's getting cold, O. Shall I call the house help to bring it in?'

*

Mr MacDonald is at work. She busies herself with jobs around the house, tidying the bedroom, laying out a clean polo shirt and linen shorts for the evening, completing the finishing touches to his dinner. She is finally clear in her head what she wants and what she must do, and she wants her baby. But how she's going to make it work she doesn't know. How she's going to feed them both in this Nigeria, without Mr MacDonald, without a family she can rely on financially, she has no idea.

'You're back, O,' says Ngozi, as she watches him come through the door and toss his briefcase on to the floor in the hall.

'Yes.'

'I've laid out your clothes and your food is prepared; the house help will serve it once you are ready.'

His eyes alight on a suitcase by the door.

'What's with the suitcase?'

'I think you told me everything I needed to know last night, O.'

'Where are you going?'

'To Stella's.'

'Don't be so damn stupid.'

'What do you expect me to do? If I had known you were married, do you think I would have moved in with you? As poor as I might be, O, as poor as my family may be, I have pride and it was not in my plan to repeat my mother's mistakes, but here I am.'

'Where did you think I went when I was away?'

'I don't know, O. I trusted you. I thought you were different to our men here, but I now see that you are the same, just in paler packaging.'

'Anyway, put the damn suitcase away, we have a baby to discuss.'

'What is there to discuss, O? You already told me to murder my own child.'

'Don't be so . . . And how are you going to feed this child?'

'I don't know.'

'When I met you, you were barely making ends meet. I really don't know how you think you're going to manage.'

Ngozi is silent.

'Where are you going to live?'

'I don't know, but is that really your problem, O?'

'What the hell do you think of me?'

'I don't know – I don't really know you, O. Isn't your plan to leave, disappear to England like the rest of you do, back to your wife?'

'What kind of man do you think I am?'

'I don't know. I thought I did, but then again I didn't know you had a wife, O.'

'Go and sit down.'

'But—'

'But what? We have to discuss this.'

Ngozi leaves her suitcase in the hallway and goes into the sitting room.

'Sit.'

She sits.

'Now hear me out. I'm over twice your age. I've lived a little. Now, as much as you might fantasize about this child I know it would be much easier if you were to get rid of it. I'm not always going to be here to help. My company will transfer me back to the UK at the end of this year.'

'Mr MacDonald, how many children do you have?'

'What's with the Mr MacDonald?'

'How many children do you have?'

'Three.'

'How old are they?'

'Fourteen, sixteen and twenty-one.'

'Your oldest is only one year younger than me.'

He's silent, then says, 'Yes.'

Ngozi begins to sob silently.

'Ngozi, stop crying – there is an easy solution.'

She carries on crying. 'You want me to murder my own child? That I cannot do. My mother did not murder me despite all the difficulty, the poverty and the worry she went through, so how can I murder my own? It is not in me to do such a thing.' She gets up from the sofa, walks over to her suitcase in the doorway.

'Joseph!' she shouts.

'Don't be ridiculous, how are you going to look after a child by yourself in this country?'

'I don't know, but I've not asked you for anything, have I?'

'No, you haven't.'

'Joseph, please take my suitcase downstairs and hail me a taxi.'

'Yes, Ma.' Joseph picks up her suitcase and heads out of the apartment, his quiet footsteps pattering down the hallway.

Ngozi follows and closes the door quietly behind her.

Ben, Mr MacDonald, stands in the small local shop housing matches, cigarettes, sweets and crates of empty recycled Coca-Cola and Fanta bottles. He waits patiently for Ngozi. The shopkeeper sent a small child five minutes ago to knock on her door in the internal compound. He sees Ngozi push her way through the beaded curtain in the doorway.

'What are you doing here, O?'

'Don't be silly. You dropped a bombshell on me and walked out. Did you expect me to just let you go?'

Ngozi looks down at her feet.

'Look, is there anywhere we can have a private conversation?'

Ngozi looks over at the shopkeeper, then thinks better of it. 'We can walk.'

He follows her outside to walk along the dusty roadside; passers-by come past, giving the white man a stare.

'*Onye ocha!*' says one man as he walks past.

'Come, we can go in there.'

They enter a makeshift eating place, order drinks and sit in a quiet corner.

'Why did you leave?'

'There was nothing more to say, O.'

'Nothing more to say? What are we going to do about it?'

'We?'

'Yes, we.'

'I thought you told me what you want me to do?'

'Well, it makes sense?'

'To you.'

'To anybody. Look, I'm not about to leave my wife, and my assignment could finish at any time.'

Ngozi looks down into her drink.

'Besides, you're still a child yourself—'

'Now you know I am a child?'

'What about your studies?'

'My first-year exams will be done in three months, and I'm due end of August.'

'And after that? How can you look after a child yourself as well as study?'

'You can help?'

'Be serious. Look, I might as well tell you now I've applied for a transfer home. Do you hear me? That means I won't be around for much longer.'

Ngozi stares at him and fights back her tears. Her mother never brought her up to take a life. Despite everything, her mother had all four of them and she was in a worse position than she is – how could she get rid of this life inside her? 'But—'

'There are no buts,' says Mr MacDonald. 'Look, it's the best thing to do. I'll take care of it all.'

Ngozi looks up at him again, her eyes brimming with tears.

'Don't make a scene. Look, focus on your studies. Finish your degree.'

'With what money?'

'Don't worry, I'll take care of that before I leave. Just be a good girl and sort out the other thing and I'll sort out your school fees.'

Ngozi stares back at him, wondering if she ever knew Ben, 'cause he definitely did not know her.

'Be a good girl and wipe your tears.'

Ngozi bends her head. I catch a glimpse of her eyes, those teardrop eyes, and I see her might flicker in them, like the night she fought to be born into her dirt hut. I look over at Mr MacDonald to see if he's seen it too.

'Don't worry, I'll sort you out before I go. It'll all be all right. I've enjoyed spending time with you. You're a good girl, I know.'

Ngozi looks at him in silence. His empty words ring in her ears.

'Look, I have to go now but once it's all sorted, I'll pay the hospital and the school fees. You know how to get in touch.' He gets up, places some money on the table. 'I'll see you around.' Then he walks out. 'Taxi!' he calls.

There's another flicker in her eyes, easily as intense as the night she was born, the night she fought to stay alive, and for some reason I almost feel sorry for Mr MacDonald.

'Stella, he cannot keep me down.'

'Ngozi, I'm sure he was trying to do things for the best.'

'I might be poor but I am no fool. He thinks I am a poor, ignorant fool he can play with – well, he has truly wakened me.'

'Ngozi, you're overreacting.'

'I am going to have this child.'

'But, Ngozi, he's right – you have no choice.'

'Stella, I have a choice. I might not like the consequences of it, but I have a choice.'

'And what do you think you'll achieve going over there?'

'I don't know. But at least I'll have the satisfaction of staring him in the face and letting him know I am nobody's fool. He cannot just treat me like this and then discard me.'

'Don't you think it would be bettar to stay here, finish your studies – after all, he's paid for it, and then—'

'Finish my studies here? Then what? Nigeria is full of graduates who cannot find jobs. Besides, now I've finished my exams this is the best time for me to go.'

'But what makes you think things will be any bettar there?'

'I don't know but I've got to try.'

'But—'

'Look, I have only myself to rely on. There is no man who is going to ride in here and rescue me. I don't expect him to suddenly turn around and be who I thought he was, but at least my child's chances will be bettar than mine. And besides, I need to fight to make my own way in this world, and even if I manage to work for only a little while over there, the exchange will help when I get back.'

'Ngozi, I'll be surprised if they let you on the flight – you're too far gone.'

'We will see tomorrow. Did you bring the documents for me?'

'The visa and your invitation letter are in here. I explained to my friend your situation. She's happy to help you for the few weeks you'll be there.'

'Stella, thank you – I appreciate it.'

'Don't worry, just come back safely.'

Bright and early Ngozi gets out of the taxi and takes a deep breath. She looks at the entrance doors to the airport, walks tentatively up to the airline check-in desk, her eyes darting nervously around, her hands shaking. This is what she's always wanted, to be on her way to the UK. She touches her stomach and wonders what Ben's reaction will be when he opens the door to her and her pregnant belly. She wonders what she'll do if his wife and children are home. She doesn't want to involve them, but how else can she do this? Her child deserves better than she can ever provide, so she contemplates – maybe she should meet him somewhere?

Some time ago, on one of his rotations, when the questions began, she came across some mail addressed to him in the UK when unpacking his suitcase. She doesn't know why but at the time she copied this address and kept it, and as she looks in her handbag for her ticket and passport to hand over at the check-in, she's grateful that she had enough sense to do so. Her hands tremble as her luggage trundles along the conveyor belt. At the gate, the door to the plane appears in front of her like the opening to the great Awhum cave; it seems to grow, and as she moves closer to boarding, blood begins to pump in her ears. She's expecting someone to pull her aside. Finally, she's through the door and greeted by smiling stewardesses, who do not attempt to stop her from leaving. She holds on tight to her armrest as the plane tilts and takes off.

Wind and I watch as it flies by, and wonder in its wake.

16

The Beginning – The Journey

H<small>E BROUGHT ME</small> out on to the deck, laid me down and I breathed in deep. I filled my lungs with the fresh sea breeze after suffocating in the hold. I took in more breaths, each one shallower than the last. I felt the air cool my feverish skin, the sores at my wrists and ankles. The throbbing at my temple began to subside, the disorientation and nausea ebbed away. I placed my hand over his; the unevenness of the skin beneath mine surprised me. I looked down to see thick, deep, criss-cross scars on the back of his hand, and looked up to question. Wind looked down at my hand over his, then straight into my eyes, and I thanked him without words. He nodded, then turned away.

'This one is still alive, sir.'

'Good, good. Get my medicine chest. I'll see to her in a minute.'

It was early morning and quiet on deck, except for the distant whimpering sound of the girls they had separated from us. Last night I had heard the faint sound of music and male laughter as they played with them, but later, much later, came their screams.

'Continue checking for more.'

'Yes, sir.'

Wind left me and disappeared into the hold again. He brought out the corpse of the young woman who had lain beside me, her child still clinging to her, no more than three years old, all eyes. He took the child gently from her body, and the child began to cry as Wind handed him to me. I took him, held him, rocked him like he was mine, like he was Uzo. Wondered where my child was. Had Eze found him at the shrine? The little boy's crying would not cease, so I kept swaying with him until his crying softened to a sob, and looked on as Wind went down into the hold again and again, bringing out another and another.

Each morning, just before the sun rose, they would check for the dead. Each morning he brought me and the orphaned child out first for some relief from the torment of the hold. Each morning I put my hand on his, gently stroked the scars on the backs of his hands. Each time he looked into my eyes and I thanked him as he gave us food which I suspected he had squirrelled away. Each morning he looked at me, as if wanting to apologize, as if wanting to tell me something, to make me understand, before looking away sadly, and every morning, just before sunrise, I heard the splash of the dead as they threw the bodies overboard as though they were nothing more than sticks.

On occasion, I heard the rumbling of plots to take control of the ship among a few of my countrymen, but they were too few and we did not all speak the same language to properly coordinate such a plan. Nevertheless, desperate, they did eventually try to overpower the guards but went down fighting. Two of them realized that their struggle was to no avail and hurled themselves overboard into the vast sea.

Nearing the end of the voyage, the weather began to change, a heavy storm brewed, the ship pitched and rolled violently, and I lay beneath the deck, even more nauseous than usual, with the boy by my side, listening to the groans and shrieks of fellow captives.

Unlike other mornings, that day the hatch did not open. There was no relief from the suffocating heat, the sickness and foul smells. Night followed day and still no one came. I lost consciousness.

Later, sometime in the middle of the night, I awoke to someone unchaining me, looked up to see Wind at my feet again. He placed a silencing finger on his lips, motioned for me to follow. I hesitated, remembering the young girls who had been kept back, could not decide which fate was worse, but made up my mind to follow with the child on my shoulder. Wind managed to put both of us on his back and carried us out of the hatch, up on to the deck.

There was a chill in the air outside, silent except for the lapping of the sea against the sides of the ship. Above us shone the moon. He placed us down on the deck, brought us food. I ate, fed the half-sleeping boy, and we sat in silence listening to the water. There were no words between us. Now I could give him a closer look. He was tall, strong, but as well as the marks on his hands, there were more on his chest and a distinct scar in the shape of a half-moon at his temple. I reached out quickly to feel it beneath my finger. I wanted to ask him so many questions. I wanted to know who his people were. Why was he on this godforsaken ship? What or who had caused the scars? Where was this ship even going? What was to happen to us? Were we to die? But we did not speak each other's language. Then, as if he'd heard the questions in my head, he spoke.

'Sailor. Freed slave,' he said, pointing to his chest.

I did not understand. Then suddenly he sprang up and pointed out across the waters, motioned for me to come and see.

'Jamaica,' he said as he pointed, looking first at me and then out to sea, a light in his eyes.

I looked out to sea, to where he was pointing. In the distance I could just make out the dark outline of land. And then I felt my tears begin to flow.

Wind put his arm around me and I rested my head on his chest and cried even more. He placed his large palm softly over the back of my neck.

I had not thought I would survive this journey, and the truth is that if Wind had not fetched us almost every day, had not given us relief almost every day, we – I and the boy – would have perished like his mother.

But what did that land mean? Was it their land, the place where they were to finally eat us?

Jamaica waved to us in the distance.

I didn't think I would ever see Wind again, that he would ever be a part of our lives, and as they led us off the ship, my eyes held his, his held mine. As if he wanted to say something, to shout out something, but he didn't and instead stood motionless on the prow of the ship, watching us. He willed me on, to be strong, as they led us into the unknown.

PART V

Michael

17

The Crossroads

Brixton, 1990

ICHAEL SITS AT the window of the fast-food restaurant. It's early afternoon. His leg shakes with nerves as he searches through the glass for his sister. His locks are pulled back and his body is less pumped, but he looks more of a man now. It's in the face, in the lean edges of his body, in the way he observes, in the way he carries himself – less bounce, more economical. Life has definitely left its imprint these past three years.

He picks up his drink, then puts it down, picks it up again. There's a sense of bewilderment and, yes, wariness about him. He struggles to adjust, to make sense of this new outside world.

In prison that first night, he'd walked in a daze down the broad corridor, his bed pack clutched tight to his chest like a shield. The rattling of the prison warden's keys in his ears, the shouts from prisoners lying hidden in their cells, he felt in a trance. And when he entered the cell, then heard the clank of the door behind him, the rattling keys growing fainter as the guards walked away, the starkness of it hit him with the force of a tsunami. The shock, the disbelief – here he was, actually locked up. If he had not been a man, my little boy–man, he would have stood there and cried.

That is how he did his time, half in a daze, half as if walking on eggshells, as if he couldn't trust life any more. Except for the nights when he lay awake, tossing and turning, the feel of the rough prison blanket irritating his skin, as he angrily punched the pillow beneath him trying to get comfortable, trying to figure out how he actually got there. But three years of lying awake, tossing and turning, of trying to work things out in his head, have not been enough to yield answers, to help him make the big decisions. But it's easier to believe in your actuality than in your dreams. Easier to listen to your cellmate's tales of hard luck than to fight and create your own second chance, easier to believe there are no other choices, except down, down there in their small worlds. But he has something they don't have – he has Ms Lorez's love in his veins. Her words built his young mind, lifted his chin, supported his thoughts and ideas. It's now up to him to decide what sort of man he wants to be. And the question is, which path will he take? It's time to decide. He's reached that crossroads.

Michael turns away from the café window, stretches out his limbs, wipes his wet lips with the back of his hand. He hears a chime from the town hall clock, looks at his watch. Marcia is thirty minutes late.

It's the third anniversary of Devon's death and three months since Michael's release. He gives a faint smile as he recalls Uncle Fred leaning against his battered old Cortina in the cold November frost, the white mist steaming from his nostrils. Michael heard the prison doors boom closed behind him, and there he was, out in the world again, trying to decide which way to head. And there he was, Uncle Fred in the near distance, waiting. Michael hadn't been expecting him, and the sight of him caused him to breathe in with such unexpected relief and his eyes to prick with tears. To board a bus that cold frosty morning would have filled him with a loneliness he did not want to deal with. He walked towards his old uncle carrying his few possessions in a clear plastic bag. Uncle Fred pushed himself off his beloved car and lifted his arms to embrace him in a bear hug.

'It's done, son,' he murmured into my boy–man's neck. 'It's done.'

'It is,' he said, breathing in the smell of his uncle, of family dinners and gatherings missed, of Auntie Eliza, of home. He could not let go.

'Gotta look forward now.'

He nodded, still holding on.

'No point looking back. No point.'

Michael nodded again.

'You ready? Everyone is waiting for you at home.'

He broke into a smile. 'Thank you.'

The police never did find Devon's killer. Devon was murdered and the world went on, and this thought sends a shiver down Michael's back – it could so easily have been him. In the early days everything and everywhere reminded him of his friend and the times they spent together as boys, playing, joking and planning their futures. Then they believed they could conquer the world. The grief is getting easier to handle, but still, when he's alone with nothing to occupy his mind, or asleep, he sometimes thinks he hears Devon.

'I got ya, didn't I – I had you going real good, mate, didn't I?'

Life has taught Michael many lessons these past three years. When he was first arrested it was as if a bomb was set off – friends and girl-friends quickly scattered, leaving only the Baileys in the aftermath. Sharon tried: she visited once. I suppose even she had her limits, and being associated with a drug dealer was hers. Good old Uncle Fred picked up as many of the pieces as he could. And as Michael sat there on his first visitors' day, in that godforsaken prison hall, the other inmates nattering away around him, anxiously looking towards the door, shame, defiance and shock all wrestled within him. And when he caught sight of Uncle Fred walking towards him, he could not help but break down. He stood to welcome him like a man, but his shoulders shook. Uncle Fred grabbed hold of him and held him tight, and then the tears came.

'I can't believe I was so stupid,' he cried.

'I know, son.'

'I didn't know. I really didn't know.'

'It's okay. I know. I know you.'

So someone believed him. He held on tight for fear of falling. And so his long journey began.

Marcia, Auntie Eliza, Leroy and on occasion Stanford came to visit. And on the days when he was really low, when he sat needing someone to care for him, to hold up his spirit, to ease the memories of Devon lying in pain on that damp Camden street, of the judge's sentence, 'Guilty', of the disappointed glare from Ms Lorez, Uncle Fred would appear, as if he sensed his need.

In prison there wasn't much to do except read. He spent many an hour in the prison library, trying to escape his reality, and when he wasn't reading, he thought. Sometimes he would think so much his head would ache, sometimes he felt he would drown in it all. He thought about life, he thought about death.

Devon's passing was like a mirror, and when he looked in it he didn't like what he saw. Death at times makes you see more clearly what you can't see in life. His life, the one he had with Devon, meant nothing to anybody. Devon left nothing. The world went on and his life passed almost as if he had never existed.

Still deep in thought and sitting in the café, Michael picks up a newspaper left behind on the next table. He scans it. March against the poll tax set to go ahead. UN warns Rwanda is on the brink of civil war. Black youth killed in racist attack in South East London. Black pupils failing at school. AIDS to increase tenfold in Africa.

Rebel England cricketers defy ban in segregated South Africa. He puts the paper down and his spirit paces, trying to find a way out of the box. Three months of walking the streets in search of a job weighs heavily on him. He recalls eyes closing down like shutters whenever he's tried to explain where he's been for three years. This morning he all but pleaded with the foreman on a construction site for a chance. He shakes his head as the words and statistics from the paper march in his brain, trample over his desire to make something of himself. Who will give him work with a record of drug trafficking? His thoughts march in his brain, they stride like foot soldiers, they wage war. Left, right, left, right. They bombard him with negative images, negative thoughts, and it takes its toll on his armour of hope. The battle for a better future, for more than the here and now, is being lost. But can this war be won? For many before him have fallen, many have surrendered, broken by the fight.

'Give me a coffee,' he overhears a tramp asking the waitress. He turns to watch. The tramp is jumpy, his eyes are wide with hunger and a little insanity. Michael thinks of his brother Simon and wonders, well, just wonders, and then quickly banishes the thought away.

A white girl walks past the window pushing a buggy with a mixed-race child with wild and curly hair; her sweet face smiles as she waves her toy keys.

It would be nice to have a daughter with pretty fair skin like her, he thinks.

Believe it or not, he wants a child, to leave some legacy, to leave a part of him on earth. Devon didn't do that and Michael wishes he had, that there was a little Devon for him to watch grow.

It starts to drizzle outside and people begin to run for shelter. Marcia is still nowhere to be seen.

His old vicar comes in and joins the queue now forming at the counter. He buried Ms Lorez ten years ago. Ten years. Like yesterday. The vicar cranes his neck to see the menu on the wall.

He's not changed, thinks Michael, and gets up to throw his uneaten food in the bin.

'Sorry I'm late,' Marcia says as she rushes breathlessly in. 'Last-minute patient, motorbike accident. You know, you really need to get yourself a pager – I could have warned you.' She tries to pull her hair back into some sort of order. 'Shall we go? I rearranged the viewing for one thirty; we've got five minutes.'

Michael follows her outside into the drizzle and traffic. 'Where's your car?'

'I left it behind. Alan gave me a lift. Besides, by the time we get to the car we'll already be there.'

'How is Alan?' he asks, wanting to know what was going on between them.

'Oh, he's fine. He's got a new girlfriend.'

'That's good. I was beginning to think he might be AC/DC.'

'Who, Alan? Nah,' she says, 'he's just picky about who he goes out with. Unlike someone else I know.'

Michael pretends he doesn't hear or understand. 'Anyway, where's this flat?'

'It's round the corner by Trinity Gardens.'

'My, my, you're going up in the world, aren't you?' says Michael.

'Yeah, I know,' she teases.

'You're gonna get the best reception staying there.'

'Best reception of what?' says Marcia.

'Of the new station. Choice. They're supposed to be somewhere round here?'

Marcia looks at her brother in confusion.

'Honestly, you must be the only one who doesn't know. Do you actually live in Brixton?'

'What, just because I don't know where bloody Choice is?'

They pass the outside of the building where the radio station is based. Michael pauses, looks up at the small plaque, squares his shoulders.

'Michael, we don't have much time.'

'It's black-owned, isn't it?'

'Yes, I think so – and?'

'Just asking.'

'Well, hurry up – we're late.'

'Well, shoot me,' he says, then makes a funny face at his sister, suddenly feeling in better spirits, catching up to pull her closer in a headlock.

Marcia laughs, glad for this happy exchange. She'd wanted to wait before moving out, till she finished her studies, saved a little money, maybe to buy a little flat, but since Michael's release, things between them have been strained. His mood swings are beginning to affect her. And it's like he can't let go, wants to take things back to where they were before he went in. But you can't go back, can't retract three years of living as an independent woman, of making your own decisions. She's not the little Marcia he left behind. She too has been affected by his absence. Life has taught her its lessons as well so she's been force-ripened into adulthood, wiser than many girls her own age about danger and uncertainty, but this makes her careful, too careful, leaving her under-developed in so many ways. But the little girl inside still needs her brother's sanction. So when her friends Alan and Pakash show them around the three-bedroom Victorian conversion, nervously joking with Michael, who doesn't smile, she watches his reactions, looks for signs of his approval as they move from room to room, wills him to like it, and breathes out when he finally breaks into a smile on their way out.

'So what do you think?' she asks while heading back to their estate.

'It's okay,' he says. 'I don't know why you want to move out anyway.'

'I need my own space and you do too,' she says looking at him as they approach the high street, 'and honest, Michael, they're just friends.'

Michael puts his arm around his sister and bullies her into a hug, and as his sister turns to break away, just as they pass the bus stop, he sees a little girl pull away from her grown-up and hurry towards them. Her little arms open wide. 'Auntie Mar-sia,' she says, beaming. 'Auntie Mar-sia.'

He sees a man run after her – Simon. He catches her as she reaches Marcia's side, her little pudding hands reaching up towards her auntie. Simon scoops the little girl up into his arms. There they stand. The three of them, looking at each other. Simon with apprehension. Marcia in fear. Michael in disbelief. His eyes dart around – he stares at the little girl, at Simon, at the little girl, at his sister, sends Marcia a horrified glare of incredulity. He sees Ms Lorez lying, eyes flickering in pain, dying in her hospital bed.

His fists clench. He tries to stay in control, to control the desire to knock Simon down, knock the life out of him with a big fat fist into his face, but the child is there, in the way, arms tight around her father's neck. So he turns, from him, from her, from what they should have been, from it all. Turns quickly and walks away. Marcia half follows, but glances back at Simon, silently pleading for understanding, before turning fully to chase after Michael.

Marcia struggles to keep up. 'Slow down,' she pleads. But he's too angry to respond. She follows him up the high street, across the estate and through their front door. 'Michael!'

'I don't want to hear.'

'Please, Michael, listen to me. Listen to me! I've being meeting Simon for about a year now.'

He looks at her and the word 'traitor' flashes in his eyes.

'I had to, Michael. I just had to. Please try and understand.'

'Understand WHAT?' he shouts.

'I had to. Something in me had to. I love him, Michael. You've got to understand he's my brother too. I love him . . . almost as much as I love you.'

'He killed her.'

Marcia tries to explain but he interrupts her.

'How could you, Marcia?'

'I . . . I first bumped into him over three years ago,' she says. Michael is pacing up and down the sitting room. He puts his hands over his ears, screws his eyes closed, but she continues. 'I saw him with his little baby, Michael, her—'

'He killed her in cold blood.'

'—her hands were so small and delicate, Michael.'

'Murdered her like she was a dog.'

'I thought if he could care for such a fragile thing, some of the old Simon must still be left in him.'

'Don't you remember how she looked on that hospital bed, struggling to breathe? Don't you remember her body, cut up with knife wounds, Marcia?'

'I saw everything, Michael.'

'THEN HOW COULD YOU?' he shouts as he turns and walks out the room.

'I love—' she starts to say as Michael slams the door and the windows rattle. '. . . him,' she says to the door. Then she drops to the floor, holds her head in her hands and bursts into tears.

When they first started speaking she was too frightened to trust Simon, was scared that the monster would reappear. So she'd gone to the hospital where he'd been held, asking questions, needing answers. They said he'd suffered from a psychosis brought on by a bad trip or medication, and he promised he hadn't touched either since the nightmare of that day. She was still frightened he might turn, but the more she let him in, the more she remembered why she'd loved him, why he'd always been her hero. Somewhere in all the mess, during those first short meetings in a little café, seated by the door for a quick escape, in those small exchanges, she began to find the gentler, caring Simon she'd known as a child, not the monster of that day.

Michael goes for a walk, tries to dissipate the angry energy that is churning and burning up inside him. He gets to the top of the road and looks back at the estate. It looms tall and majestic like a prison. Prisons can sometimes have that look – aloof, detached, cold but regal.

It's an old estate built during the fifties after the war, so it's not as tall as the other blocks of flats in the area, but it's tall enough, seven floors above the ground; they live on the second. When he was younger he used to escape to the rooftop to look out over the city – that was before Ms Lorez died and he had to grow up, become father and, where possible, mother to Marcia. He remembers looking out at the expanse, at the jagged roofscape, how it had made him feel like a god. He turns, needing to feel that importance, that control, retraces his steps back to their block and leaps up the stairs two at a time.

Marcia stands by the window. She watches him turn and disappear back into the building. She waits in silence, listening for his key in the lock.

Michael has climbed to the rooftop. He looks out, sees building upon building. In the distance, looming above them all, he can see the top of the NatWest Tower. Much further to the right, he thinks he sees the new Docklands skyscraper. There's a freedom, an elation at the sight. He grips the concrete edge as he looks out over London. At his feet lies broken glass, and hidden, trapped in cracks, are rusting Coke cans, dirty crisp packets and tatty supermarket bags, but he doesn't notice these things. He feels the freedom, a weightlessness – he could almost float, like the carrier bag which drifts softly past his ear into the expanse before him, floating high, then dipping low, swaying up, tilting down. He wants to float away, so he closes his eyes and feels the cold wind blow against his skin. An image of Ms Lorez lying on her deathbed interrupts his peace. He breathes in, tries to float again. Devon's blood-soaked body. He breathes in harder. 'We find the defendant guilty.' He grips the ledge more tightly. The thoughts of black, white, nag at him, of black statistics marching on him, the hidden narrative in TV programmes, films, newspapers bite at him. 'You ain't shit!' they shout back. And Simon – yes, Simon. He feels the fear, does the sums, adds, subtracts, adds again. Mother plus father equals same genes. Equals? Same madness? His mind conjures up Simon beside him. He backs away from the edge, jumps in the air to dislodge the image, shakes his head to get rid of it. Devon's blood-soaked body lying on the cold autumn ground flashes over and over in his head. Ms Lorez lying in her coffin. Then himself, a lonely old man rocking on a bed in an empty room. These images take him down and he kneels beside the broken glass. 'I can't take NO MORE!' he shrieks into the wind.

'Who am I?' he asks the air. Silence. He questions again: 'Who the fuck am I?'

This is his crossroads. Which path will he take? Will he be lost? Opt in? Opt out? Or will it finally break him?

'Where am I coming from and where am I going? What do I want?' he asks the air.

No answers are given.

He touches his face, breathes in the polluted air, gets up from his knees and grips the concrete ledge to peer over. He sees the ground, seven floors down, and begins to feel giddy.

'If I jump, I'll be free.' Temptation pulls him closer. He grips the ledge more tightly. 'If I get up now I'll jump. If I move I'll jump.'

He stands still. His grip tightens, the veins in his hand stand out. 'Calm down, it ain't happening,' he says to himself, but the urge is strong. He moves closer to the edge.

'MICHAEL!'

He turns, sees his sister running towards him. He steps away from the edge, collapses on the floor and starts to sob.

'Michael.' Her voice is calm as she reaches out to him, hugs him. 'Its okay, Michael,' she says, stroking his back. 'I promise I won't see him again,' but her words are hollow. Inside, she knows his tears are for more than just Simon. She holds him close, hears her brother reach down into his gullet and rip out a deep wrenching cry – it seems to grab the bottom of his stomach, pull it right out through his throat and out of his mouth and it shakes, it shakes them both.

'Don't worry. Whatever it is, we'll be all right,' she says after a while.

'Marcia,' he cries, and grips her even tighter. 'Marcia.'

'It's okay, Michael. It's okay.'

She holds his body as he cries like . . . like . . . like she's never seen before – it scares her. She steels herself. The tables are turned. And he grips so tight she finds it difficult to breathe, but she keeps on holding him till he can't cry any more.

'You okay?' she asks after a long while.

Michael nods.

'Can you tell me what all that was about?'

Michael isn't even sure what it was about, let alone how to explain it to her; he just knows he feels better for it. He turns to his sister. 'I don't know. It's everything. It's nothing.'

'What do you mean?'

'I mean, it was seeing Simon today and it being three years exactly since Devon's death and me looking at myself and wondering about me. I mean, am I going to die like Devon? Is that all there is? Am I just going to live and then die and then nothing, like I didn't exist? It was bad enough before I went to jail, but now with a record, who's going to hire me, who's going to want me? I've been out three months and I can't find a job. I might as well go back to—'

There is silence between them.

'Marcia, what did we do wrong?' he asks moments later.

She understands his question. 'I don't know.'

'It seems as if every time we try and lift our heads, something happens to drag us down. I mean, it keeps happening, I mean, just when I thought we were going to be the black Brady Bunch, Dad ups and leaves, and when we're just settling and getting used to it all, then Simon loses it, and as if that wasn't bad enough he had to go and kill her and—'

'I know,' she says and rubs his back again.

'And this constant battle, and always being under suspicion, and having to prove myself all the time, constantly having to believe in myself, and having it torn down, and having to rebuild it time and time again, and always having to second-guess, and always doubting. I sometimes wonder if it's worth fighting against, and I should just give up and become what they want me to become. Do you think we're cursed? Do you think black people are cursed?'

'No, I don't.'

'Then how come if anything bad is gonna happen, it'll happen to us tenfold? How come if people are gonna die, you can bet people of colour are gonna die from it tenfold, or suffer from it tenfold, or live through it tenfold?'

'I don't know, Michael. I wish I had the answers. I wish I could magic up some great explanation for it all. I'm just trying to get through this one day at a time before I get up there. All I do know, Michael, is that things are changing.'

'How the fuck can you say that, Marcia? Have you looked around lately? If we're not killing each other, then other people are doing it for us,' he says.

'Michael, it doesn't look like things are changing because we're living it. But over time, just as when we look back to our great-grandparents' time, we've moved a whole galaxy forward. We're just entering a different phase in the fight: it's mental, it's more hidden than before. We've got to fight to empower ourselves, to believe in ourselves and not believe the hype, as Public Enemy says.'

'Maybe you're right.'

'I've got to believe I'm right, Michael, otherwise I'll just give up now. Every time I switch on the television there's always something negative to concentrate on. Every time I talk to people, be they black or white, there's always something negative to chew on. It's almost as if the TV, the media, the stories I hear around me, the people we see and know around this estate are trying to rob me of my belief, trying to stop me from succeeding. Taking away my will to fight and carry on, but I won't let them, Michael, I just won't let them.'

Michael nods his head.

'Just think back to a hundred years ago, just over a hundred years, Michael. In our great-grandfathers' and -grandmothers' time, we would have been out there cutting sugar cane for some slave master on some plantation, being whipped. For Christ's sake, we might not have even known each other or Mum – they might have sold us at birth. Or even forty years ago, would I have had the opportunity to go to the school I went to? Mum didn't. Look how far we've come as a family. I'm going to become a doctor because of you and Mummy. There are thousands, millions out there like me, Michael, succeeding, doing well, because of people like you and Mummy. Now it's time for you to believe in yourself.'

'It's not easy when you have a record, and on top of that you're a black man.'

'And so what? I believe in you and that's not going to stop us.'

'It's so easy for you, isn't it?'

'No, but I'm young and life hasn't worn me down like it did Mum and Dad. And you're too young for it to get to you yet.'

'What are you, some old woman in disguise?'

Marcia smiles. 'No, but seriously, what is it you want that you can't have?'

'I don't know.'

'Then what was all that about an hour ago?'

'I . . . I . . . I – You promise you won't laugh?'

'I promise.'

'I want to be something, that's all.'

'And what will make you that something?'

'I don't know, maybe owning something of my own. Building my own business. Something I can look back on and say, I built that. I created that. Something I can leave behind and make any child I have proud of me.'

'What sort of business, Michael?'

'I don't know, maybe my own bar or nightclub or something like that, but who's going to lend me the money?'

'I am.'

'Don't be silly.'

'I'm not. Okay, I might not be able to afford it now but when I'm a GP I'll be able to back you. Meanwhile, I've saved a little which I was going to use on my deposit and my first two months' rent. Why don't you take that and I can carry on living here? Start something small, invest in it, maybe get yourself a little market stall and slowly build up from there.'

'Don't be silly – I can't take your money.'

'Okay, think of me as your partner, as an investor. It'll be our business. A family business. After all you've done for me these years, it's my turn.'

Michael looks at her, uncertain.

'Well, it's better than having no job and being on the dole. It's worth a try.'

'I'll think about it,' he says, then gives her a weak smile and a feather punch on her cheek. 'You know, Sis, you're wiser than your years. You're right, but I'll still think about it. And you're right about keeping your head down and your hope alive. Maybe I'll look into it, go and check out the market stalls. Find out how much a slot will cost. See what's possible.'

She smiles back at him.

He turns towards the ledge, looks out at the sun falling lower over the city and puts his arm around his sister. 'Do you think Ms Lorez can see us from up there?'

'If I know Mum, she's busy running about saying, "Where me pickni dem?"' She's remembering the occasion their mother came to the school to pick them up and they hid, because they wanted to stay longer for the afterschool club. Marcia had just started in the infants and Michael was in his last year of the juniors.

Michael laughs at the memory, then his face clouds over. He remembers what they, the five of them, Mr Watson, Ms Lorez, Simon, Marcia and he used to be like. There were many happy times then.

'Michael,' says Marcia after several minutes.

'Yes, Sis.'

'It's me and you, isn't it – you and me against that world, ain't it?'

'Yes, Sis,' he says with his arm curled around her, both of them looking out across London. 'Yes, Sis, it's you and me against the world.'

Stanford comes through the front door into the house in a mad dash. The door slams loudly behind him. 'Did you hear?' he shouts from the hallway, poking his head into the kitchen where his mother is in the throes of making Sunday dinner.

'Hear what?' she says.

'Mandela?' he shouts back, now heading towards the parlour.

His mother follows behind, drying her hands.

'Give me the remote!' he shouts at the kids, and then lunges for it. Uncle Fred and Michael look up from their game of dominoes at the dining table.

'What? What's happened?' demands Eliza.

'They're releasing him.'

'What you talking about?'

'Yes, what you talking about, son?'

'They're about to release Mandela!'

'I don't believe you,' says Eliza.

Stanford looks at his watch. 'What time is it?'

'Almost three.'

He finds the channel. All eyes turn to the television. The Baileys watch with open mouths. Michael holds his breath. They watch as all of a sudden a convoy of cars stops at the gates. Then there he is, Nelson Mandela, Winnie by his side, saluting the crowd.

'I don't believe it!' shrieks Eliza. 'I never thought they would let him out.'

Uncle Fred goes to his wife and hugs her. 'Twenty-eight years,' he says. 'Twenty-eight long years they had him locked up.'

Michael looks on in silence. He drinks it in.

'Me and Johnny were arguing about it while we were upgrading the computers at the Polytechnic. I said they would never release him. I can't believe Johnny was actually right,' says Stanford.

'I never thought it would happen in my lifetime,' says Uncle Fred in a shaky voice, wiping away a tear.

Michael watches this grey-haired man walk out of prison with dignity, into freedom, saluting the crowd, and there is a strength in the way he carries himself, a determination on his face. Michael absorbs it. *Twenty-eight years in prison, and I did three, and I wasn't fighting for a whole nation. Just look at him – he doesn't look broken at all. Twenty-eight years?* he thinks to himself. 'Anything is possible, isn't it?' he asks Uncle Fred.

'Yes, son. I didn't think I would live to see this. Anything is possible,' says Uncle Fred.

'So what did they say?' Marcia asks Michael as they sit in her car just outside Brixton Market.

He leans his head quietly against the headrest, breathing in short spurts.

'What did they say?'

He turns to look at her, then breaks into a broad smile. 'They said there's a stall available for a week on Friday.'

Marcia screams with joy, reaches over to hug her brother. 'Oh, thank God,' she says and hugs him again.

'I've got to tell Alan,' she adds. 'He was up with me on the phone half the night.'

'I thought he had a girlfriend?' he asks.

'Yeah, we're just good friends. Anyway, I feel like celebrating. What do you fancy?'

'Indian or some real backyard cooking at Take Two,' he says.

'Okay, pizza coming up,' she says jokingly and heads off to find dinner, leaving him in the car. The book she's currently reading, *The Ancient Kingdoms of Africa: Songhai Empire, Mali Empire and the Kingdom of Ghana*, sits on the dashboard.

Michael picks it up, flips it around, then bounces it up and down in his hand. The last time he read a book was in prison, and he only started so he would have something to do with his time. But now, in the outside world, he actually realizes he misses it. He opens the cover and starts to read the introduction.

'Can I borrow this?' he asks when Marcia returns with their curry takeaway.

'Sure.'

Michael reads Marcia's book and then many others like it. Within the mountain of books that pile up on the floor of his bedroom, he begins to search for answers; he's hungry for them. He begins to wear Afrocentric garments, grows his locks longer, wears wooden beads around his neck. 'My Nubian sister', 'My Nubian queen' and 'It's spiritual, man' become his favourite catchphrases, like some seventies hippie who's got lost in Brixton. And it's not the words or the way he dresses, because that's okay so long as it comes from the heart. In Michael's case though, it does not reach the heart and comes off as fake. He throws himself into his ethnic roots. It's become a religion to him and like any religion where one doesn't truly believe, it cannot save, so he becomes like a promiscuous Christian, or an alcoholic Muslim, or a blaspheming Jew. But, it must be admitted, after reading all these books, he does begin to find answers to some of his history, and come to understand that he did have a story before slavery. But he still can't find an answer to the most important question of all: 'Who am I?' He keeps on searching, keeps on asking, keeps on trying on new ways, new personas. And at one point, he even flirts with the Nation of Islam, accosting the boys selling the papers on the corner by the town hall, but the closer he gets, the more the suit doesn't quite fit. But they've opened him up to the idea of a higher power, and so he begins to look more deeply, to ask more widely, and eventually to pray.

Michael is working in his new job selling records when it happens. He's in the middle of the market surrounded by stalls, and people upon people, when the answer comes. He couldn't tell you if it's in the music, or the sea of black faces, or simply a feeling, but the answer rises up, spreading like molten lava, it conducts its way through him, until he's consumed. It's as simple as breath itself, and a chain breaks inside him, it collapses and relinquishes its hold on him. He's searched for the answers in all those books, in people, in everything and everywhere, except in himself. The answer has been there all the time. He looks around the market and sees fathers and children buying wares together, men sane and not so sane, strong men, tired men, hope-lost men. But he believes in himself and in the higher power guiding him. His vision becomes clearer, brighter, as though cataracts have been removed. He looks around and sees women, beautiful women, their skin smooth and brown, their wide smiles, big bottoms, small bottoms, gaps in teeth, broad happy mouths. He sees their beauty, and begins to see his own beauty too. The answer settles itself in him, makes itself comfortable and at home.

Since this unexplained moment at the market, when alone, he often whispers into the mirror, 'I deeply love who I am, where I'm from, the history of me, and the people that made me.' And in finding the answer he sees what he didn't see before: the beauty in his broad nose, black skin, big lips, gappy teeth, tightly curled hair and the women who reflect him. You know, those big-bottomed, wide-hipped, curly-haired, broad-nosed, big-lipped, strong-willed, not-going-to-take-any-shit, get-on-with-it women. 'Cause these are his features, the features his daughter will have, features passed down by his ancestors, given to him by God, the reasons for centuries of survival. He whispers, 'Who is Michael Watson?' and an inner voice replies, *I am!*

Suddenly the hair on his head has become a lie. Not his. Not him. It's the masquerade he hid behind when he'd still not met himself. He walks into the barbers to rid himself of its falsity. As each long lock falls to the ground, he's relieved of the weight of years spent living a lie, until Michael, the stepson of Ms Lorez, the brother of Marcia, stares back at him in the mirror, dark eyes smiling. 'Hello,' he says in greeting, 'welcome to a brand-new life.' He reaches up and touches the birthmark now revealed at his temple, just below his hairline, and which now glistens in the reflected light.

With his hair now cut off, the urge to talk to his mother pulls at him. He waits for the sun to rise, then makes a journey to the cemetery, kneels at her graveside, clears away the greenery that covers the ground. 'Mum, I've not been around in a long time, 'cause I've not been myself for a long time. I love you, Mum, love you so deeply it hurts. I used to think I hated myself when you just died like that, blamed myself for not being there to prevent it, but now I know there's nothing I could have done. It wasn't my fault, wasn't anybody's fault, but life. I was scared for a long while, felt like a coward, did a lot of things to get rid of that chicken feeling. Somehow I got all muddled up inside, all that responsibility scared me, even more with Marcia always looking at me like I had all the answers. Well, I'm here to thank you, Mum, for being there for me, for taking care of us when our birth mum ran out on us and even after Dad left. I love you, Mum, so deeply I couldn't tell you how much. I wish God had made you my mother in blood as well, but that's just life again. Most of all, Mum, I wanted to tell you that Michael's back and I'm finally the man you taught me to be.'

After visiting the graveyard, the next day in the market among the yams, green bananas, okra and African spices, the love pours out of him. Now, it doesn't mean he walks around like those flower-power people, it just means he accepts who he is and gives love, although it's tough love at times. And it doesn't mean he will never question himself again, 'cause he's human and human beings are forever changing and developing with each new experience. What it does mean is that he questions, but this time he listens to his inner voice. The dark moments no longer seem so dark. He has faith and hope to pull him through.

18

The Search

'YOU BACK AGAIN?' George says as Michael stands on his doorstep for the third time in a month. George is the boss, one of the original Brixton Frontline boys, one of the few that made good.

'You said I should keep checking in,' says Michael.

'Yeah, but mi didn't mean every day, son.'

'Well, things could have changed since yesterday?'

George laughs. 'True that. Mi think you a work at di market?'

'Yeah. Got my own little stall selling records. Fridays.'

'So what you a do here?'

'Well, business isn't easy and I need to pay the bills. Besides, it isn't so simple for someone like me to get a job.'

George, the boss, nods his head in understanding. A few weeks back when Michael was totally desperate, he'd begged him with such misery that only someone like George, who'd lived a life like George, could truly understand. Michael, sensing there was something he could trust about the older man in front of him, had opened up, told him, dejection hovering in his words, that he'd been inside, that he needed a job. George had listened, understood Michael's desperation and the words he left unsaid. He'd understood that Michael's anguish wasn't so much about what had already passed, but was more about the future, the fear of going back, of not being able to escape from that cycle. George had felt pity, but at heart he's also a businessman, so he'd told him to come back in the hope that the young man would find something else in the meantime. Michael had disappeared for a while, until recently.

'What happened to your hair?'

'Cut it.'

George looks back into the house and then again at Michael. 'Well, mi tell you what – mi need stuff shifting, sand, bricks, cement, dat sort of stuff, help smooth things with the brickie, help speed up the work. Nah easy work.'

'I know.'

'Your hands don't seem like dem built fi it.'

Michael looks at his hands, then back at George. 'It's work, isn't it?'

'Yeah.'

'So where's the stuff you need shifting?'

'Come with mi. Let me introduce you.'

Michael follows George into the muddy yard where they're building an extension to the house so they can split the place up into flats. They walk past the digger towards where the brickie bends over aligning his string.

Michael gets straight down to work, helps as fast as he can, makes things easy for the brickie, and the brickie takes to him; they have a laugh and it makes the work go faster. The brickie asks for Michael for the next day, and the next, and the day after that. George looks on, smiles, nods his head in approval. There's something about Michael he likes: maybe it's the enthusiastic way in which he works, or how he seems to fit in, but I suspect it goes deeper than that – there's a recognition and he's willing him to do well. When Michael's done with the brickie, George asks him to come back and help the roofer, and after that the plumber, the plasterer, the decorator, and each time he watches Michael, giving little suggestions, and Michael to his credit listens. He studies what the brickie, the roofer, the plasterer, the plumber do, learns a little at a time, pieces his future together, even finds a few evening courses recommended by George.

And now as Michael makes his way up Brixton High Street beside George, after buying lunch at the takeaway on the corner opposite the town hall, he seems to notice for the first time the changes in the area.

'There've been so many changes,' he says, then pauses. 'Since . . . since I went . . . you know.'

'Yes, mi do. Trust me, there's a lot more to come.'

'I remember when that fast-food joint was Times Furniture store. My mother saved hard to buy her first posh sofa from there.'

George chuckles. 'I remember those days too, son.'

'She was so proud of it – didn't want us to ruin it so she left the plastic on and every time we sat on it, it made these squeaky sounds,' he laughs.

'When mi did grow up we were too poor to buy from dat store, but things ave changed. Now mi wife a buy furniture from di best of di best, and when mi see the bill, all me want do is fi cry.'

Michael stops, looks in the estate agent's window, then speaks loudly over the sound of a passing bus. 'This is new.'

George peers more closely into the agent's window. 'Been open about a year. Mi only see yuppies go in here so – never seen any black folk.'

Michael looks at the sales particulars in the window, recoils from the price. 'Nearly £100k for a three-bedroom house. In this area?'

'Yep,' says George knowingly.

'You know they're going to open up a Body Shop just down the road.'

'Yep.'

'Do you think the last riots made a difference? Maybe the government is finally investing – things are going to get better for us all?'

George laughs. 'No, son. That's not what's happening. Come. Look over deh – what you see?'

'KFC.'

'No. In front. What you see?'

'Yardies.'

'And what dem doing?'

'Selling drugs.'

'Now look over deh, in front of the library. What you see?'

'Alkies.'

'Now, I've lived in this here Brixton most of my life. I even spent a likkle time as a youth on the Frontline before me see sense, and I never seen things like this. Wi sold a little weed, but never drugs; as for the alkies, never seen them out like this. So ask yourself why?'

'I don't know, modern times?'

'Modern times,' says George with a chuckle. 'I suppose it could be or it could be dem a run down the area through di front door and buy up through di back. The only problem is the black folk in this here area don't want to listen: they fi quick to run, say they want get away from the ghetto. Well, they fi find themselves where they go run to.'

'So you wouldn't leave if someone was offering you £100k for your house?'

'Listen, if you ave an aunt or uncle thinking of selling, tell dem to hold on, it ain't time yet. This here area going get like Clapham and Battersea one day.'

'Really?'

'Yes, really,' says George. 'Anyway, hurry up, lunch almost done.'

Michael speeds up, follows George back into the converted flats.

'Wi soon finish up here,' says George.

'I know,' says Michael, wondering what he is going to do next.

'Mi did think say you come help out pon fi next project inna Stockwell.'

'Yes,' beams Michael, 'of course.'

George smiles back at Michael. 'Wi go make a man out of you yet,' he says, and a lifetime friendship is formed.

Michael follows Uncle Fred into the garage to help him work on his car.

'You know the Joneses down the way,' says Uncle Fred.

'Yes.'

'They're thinking of selling up and moving out to Thornton Heath.'

'Really?'

'Well, you seen how the area is changing. He said he want build a little place back in Jamaica for his retirement.'

'That's the third family we know moving out.'

'Yeah. At this rate the only black folk left will be the ones on the estates.'

'Do you know how much he wants to sell it for?'

'I think he put it on the market for say 100, 120.'

'Where did you say they live?'

'By Salam Road,' says Uncle Fred. 'Why? What you thinking?'

'Not much. You know, I just remembered, I was supposed to meet up with Marcia.'

Michael waves goodbye and makes his way back to the flat.

'Marcia, you know the Joneses? You used to go to school with the brother.'

'Yes.'

'Uncle Fred was telling me they want to sell up one day and retire to Jamaica.'

'Really?'

'I was thinking, you know, that offer about going into business? Does it still stand?'

'Yes.'

'Well, I was thinking maybe we could buy it, do it up, rent it out or sell it.'

'How you going to do that? With what money?'

'Well, I was thinking with your credit and deposit you could get the mortgage and I could do the work.'

And so Michael bought that house, broke it up into flats, sold them, bought another, did the same, sold it, then with two more did the same, then three more but this time kept one and rented it out, repeated it again and again. That is how Michael began to make money and over time forged a good future for himself.

But like most men who have nothing, he thought that money would bring him that inner peace, that complete satisfaction, but it didn't. There was still a restlessness, a calling inside. So he searched for that answer and accidentally one day, as he walked past his old youth centre, heard a rowdy meeting being held inside. He walked in, sat at the back, watched and listened as a group of forty, maybe fifty, men and women, including a few children running up and down, tried to make sense of the death of a son in police custody, tried to figure out how best to get justice for him, get their voices heard. And as he sat and watched, he thought of Rizzlar, felt the guilt that still lived in him, of not being able to do anything, of not speaking out, of the powerlessness that was his silent companion. So he stayed, got involved, and finally found a home.

PART VI

Ngozi

19

Not As Expected

London, 1993

DROPLETS OF RAIN cascade down the window, windscreen wipers dance to their own beat, as the bus stops to let on a few early morning passengers, cars speed by, splashing water on to the kerb.

Ngozi sits at the top of the bus, watching the dark morning sky slowly turn to daylight. It's two years since her plane landed on English soil. She's thinner than I remember and her protruding stomach is no longer there. The baggage of nervous anxiety carried with her on that flight is now safely packed away and her visitor's visa is now turned into a student one. She's relatively settled, as settled as one can be in a foreign land surrounded by an alien culture. But what does that mean, 'settled'? Does it indicate her happiness in this new land, the paradise filled with angels and gold that she came looking for, or does it mean that she's found the freedom and choice that she desperately expected? Only Ngozi can answer, only she knows the true depths of what she's searching for in this metropolis. Yes, 'settled' is the best way to describe the external her, but inside, deep inside, although these last two years have quietened her, she's still the same Ngozi that I saw yell and fight her way into this world.

Back there in Nigeria, this old empire had been the answer, her definition of heaven, the only way of creating a future for her unborn child. Now it's not so clear. It's muddled, jumbled and agitated like the movement of air and electricity. It's not as simple as she had thought; it is never black and white. I suppose that's why God created colour.

Ngozi looks around at the few people on the top deck of the bus. *Stella was right, O*, she thinks. *People don't smile.*

A middle-aged man gets up from his seat in front and walks past her towards the stairs to the exit. He's well dressed, but his eyes are dull, almost vacant, his shoulders hunched, almost defeated. She thinks she recognizes him but isn't sure. He looks a little like the old man who greeted her the night she arrived in Heathrow Underground Station with a 'Fuck off, black cunt' as she stood facing the confusing Tube map on the wall, trying to figure out how best to get to Stella's friend's place. All the while she was shifting her weight from foot to foot, rubbing the ache at the base of her spine, distracted by the white mist in front of her that swirled and curled from her nostrils. She had turned to see who had spoken to her, and watched him walk further along the platform. She pulled up the lapels of the coat Stella had lent her around her face in search of warmth, and began to shiver with this unfamiliar cold that was slowly seeping into her bones. At that moment she had not fully understood his words. She had thought – well, she had seen gangster movies back home, heard stories of unruly Jamaicans and thought maybe he had associated her with those other black people. A few moments later, further down the platform, she had seen him with two young black men, well dressed, who appeared to be abusing this same old white gentleman. She assumed they were Jamaicans with no respect for their elders, and coming from where she came from that was unforgivable, so despite the fact that he had been so rude to her earlier she had wandered over, eager to intervene on the old man's behalf. The two young men walked away, looking daggers at her. Then the old man walked up to her and spat in her face.

'Go home. Go back to Africa where you belong, you bloody parasite. That's all you coloureds do – always got your fucking hands out begging. Lazy, that's what you lot are. Now you wanna come over here and live off the likes of us taxpayers. I fought in the war, you know.'

She recoiled from him in shock. She tried to find words but could not, and instead she took out a tissue, wiped the spit away, then walked off while the old man carried on ranting. And that was her welcome to paradise.

If only she had known about her great-uncle Ifeanyi who died cutting his way through the forest of Burma in the Second World War for his colonial masters, the sweat glistening off his bare black arms, making a path in a war he didn't fully understand, although he made that path anyway. His friends, school friends, new friends, by his side. His gun secured upon his shoulder. If only she had known about the moment he died, looking into the eyes of the so-called enemy, that fraction of a second that could have saved his life. Eye to eye they stared at each other, African soldier to Japanese. That hesitation. That recognition of human being to human being. Before reason stepped in. The shouts around them bringing them back to the why. Both lifted their rifles. Both fell. And he lay upon that thick forest grass looking up at trees and sky, hearing the gunfire around him, feeling the blood slowly soak his shirt, and then the heaviness of his eyelids, and as they closed, he must have wondered if he would ever see his love back home in Obowi. If she had known about the day they came to her village way back then during the First World War, recruiting young men with oh-so-sweet promises, only for them to disappear like ghosts into their colonial masters' war, never to return. Or the homecoming of her second cousins and their friends and the screams of joy that could be heard from mothers who thought they would never see them again, and the wails of despair for those who didn't make it. Maybe if she had known then she would have found words, something appropriate to say in response, but she did not. And so they both walked away, ignorant of their own history, leaving her great-uncle Ifeanyi to be among the forgotten ones. Maybe coming from their continent made their sacrifice seem less important. Instead, Ngozi had walked away indignant, wondering why it was such a bad thing for her to want more and to have left her home in search of it.

For if it wasn't for the old man's great-great-uncle Thomas, who set sail upon a ship fleeing England, fleeing poverty, in search of a better life, who never once looked back at the white cliffs, felt the freedom of the sea rage through his hair, stood at the bow as it rode the waves to Africa. The lower decks loaded with brass pans, guns and blood cloth, only to steal, rape, torture and murder his way to a fortune. If it wasn't for the old man's great-great-grandfather, who sat on a ship's deck, hands chained, oh-so-grateful for escaping the gallows, thanking his Lord and Saviour, wondering what lay ahead in this new land called Australia. To look upon what he called the 'poor naked darkies', swig on his fermented juice, jump on a horse to hunt, rape, massacre the Aborigine people, and use their babies for sport. Burying them alive with only their screaming and crying heads above the ground, and with his friends laugh and joke as they kicked their heads off like footballs. For if it wasn't for them and many like them, the world would not be the way it is. America, Australia, New Zealand, Africa would not exist as they do. England would not be the way it is. And the stories and fate of the Native Americans, of the Aborigines, of the Maori, of the African peoples, of so many, would be different. At least Ngozi did not steal me away, shackle me to a ship upon the water and leave me on a cold warehouse floor to gasp for life and air, my newborn child ripped from my arms, in search of it. At least she's not killing anyone in search of it. Her sin, if it is a sin, is purely to want and work for a better life.

It has been two years now and Ngozi longs for home. Yes, home. But her mission has only just begun. Her ambitions quietly surge her forward. Its energy is plentiful. But her dreams are different now: they are no longer of escape, but of return. The child she arrived fighting for has long been taken away. But success will be her revenge. And will she find it? For many have come before her and been imprisoned by their dreams, not able to go back, not able to go forward. Will she make it through this maze of rules and procedures and systems that she's not been born into, or will these systems shackle her and gobble her up?

She looks at her watch. It's five fifteen in the morning, plenty of time for her to make it to her cleaning job, the first job of the day. There are two others, one at her local fried chicken shop and another cleaning engagement at night. In between her three jobs she fits in studying for her access course for a degree in business and computer science. And in between that, with the little free time she has left, she makes up business plans and hopes for the day when she'll have the time and money to implement one of them. And in between that she finds ways of sending money back home to Blessing to look after the family and build what she can back there for when she returns. They send letters, keep her updated on life in Obowi.

Ngozi is possessed, fuelled by the fear of failure and the dream of success. For it's only through success that she can make any sense of it all. She touches her stomach. Thinks of her child. Remembers her first week in Britain, walking along the cold grey road, not long after disembarking from the London to Glasgow bus, heading towards Ben's house. She had looked at the neat front lawns with finely shaped hedges, the front doors of the identical blond sandstone brick houses all in a row, searched out the right door number and there it was. A solid black door. She fixed her clothing, walked up the path, knocked, waited and wondered whether it was the best idea. Maybe she should have phoned ahead, maybe she shouldn't have made the journey at all. And then it was too late. The door opened.

A petite woman answered. 'Hello.'

Ngozi stood staring at her.

'Can I help you?'

'Yes, O. Is . . . is Ben in?'

'Ben?'

'Yes, Ben.'

'And who are you?'

'Ngozi,' she said, looking back at her. This woman was younger, smaller and prettier than she was expecting. Ngozi looked down at her shoes, then up again. Despite the step up from the porch into the house they were almost at the same eye level. She noticed the woman's dishevelled hair, the tiredness under her eyes and the way her stripy jumper didn't match the flowery cotton blouse underneath. She looked harassed, as though she didn't have time to worry about coordinating her outfit, like a busy mother. Ngozi had thought through the different scenarios as she travelled up to Glasgow. She'd talked it through with Stella's friend and it was clear that she needed to fight for her baby's future, and raising it poor in Nigeria without Ben's support was not a life she wanted for her child. So she'd made this trip, boarded the bus with fight in her belly. But standing there in front of Ben's house, in front of his wife, the words she'd rehearsed would not come, so instead she said, 'I'm a friend. From Nigeria.' Then she felt a slight tinge at the base of her back. She grimaced and rubbed it.

'Are you all right there?'

'Yes, O. Just a little pain.'

Ben's wife looked down the road and back again at Ngozi. 'You said a friend?'

'Yes,' said Ngozi and half smiled at her.

'You might as well come in and take the load off your feet. How far gone are you?'

'Five months.' Ngozi followed her down the corridor to the sitting room. It was pretty tidy, with one corner full of children's toys. She motioned for Ngozi to sit down.

'I'm afraid he's in Aberdeen, won't be back till Friday.'

'Oh.'

'You've come a long way?'

'Yes, O. I notice you have children's toys. I thought Ben's – sorry, Mr MacDonald's – children were all grown?'

'From his first marriage, yes, but we have two daughters, five and two.'

Just then, the two-year-old barrelled into the room with a doll in her hand.

'She's cute, O.' Ngozi did the maths. This child would have been born just after she'd met Ben. She felt a rush of angry heat rise up in her. She watched as the little girl climbed on to her mother's lap.

'You've had a long journey?'

'Yes, O. Came from London.'

'Can I get you something to drink? Cup of tea?' Ben's wife asked while neatening her daughter's hair.

'No, O,' she replied, watching the quick fluid motion of Ben's wife's hand stroke, lift and stroke again. There was a sense of déjà vu, as if she'd sat watching this happen before. She thought of Mrs Asika, her first employer, and her mother, and suddenly everything wasn't so clear. She looked at this woman stroking her daughter's hair and there was Mrs Asika, back there in Enugu, and there was little Nkiru, and her own mother in Obowi, and her mother's mother. She looked up at the family pictures arranged haphazardly on the mantelpiece. In one Ben was seated, his wife beside him, their daughters on their laps. They looked so happy as a family. The sort of family she'd wished for as a child, and suddenly she did not have the heart to tell this woman. But did she have a choice? *Maybe it's best if I just speak to Ben directly. Maybe he'll see sense. Maybe we can work it out*, she thought. And so she sat in that parlour opposite Ben's wife and prayed for an answer, guidance, some resolution.

'Glasgow's a long way to come just to see Ben? It might have been better for you to phone before coming, especially with your being pregnant.'

'I'm up here visiting other friends as well,' she lied. 'I thought I'd just pop in to say hello since he was so kind to me and my family in Nigeria.'

His wife smiled. 'That's Ben – he has such a generous nature. I'll let him know when he phones this evening.'

'I bettar be going.'

'Can I call you a cab?'

'No, O. I'm fine.'

Ngozi got up from the sofa and followed the woman into the hall. And as she went out the front door she felt something trickle down her leg to her ankle. She stood on the doorstep, looked down, lifted her skirt slightly, to see a thin line of blood, then turned back to look at Ben's wife. 'Please—'

'I'd better call an ambulance.'

That seems almost a lifetime ago now as Ngozi makes her way cautiously down the stairs of the double-decker bus and alights at the bus stop, crosses the road to join her work colleague at the side of the polytechnic building.

'Morning, Issha,' she calls from behind.

'O, I didn't see you there.'

They go in the cleaners' entrance and begin climbing the stairs.

Ngozi has formed a close friendship with Issha, a plump Yoruba woman, married with four adorable children. In another life they could have been sisters.

They show their passes to security, head towards the cleaning cupboard, take out their trolleys, press for the lift, then move on to the computer rooms to start the clean.

'I no dey see Sandra these days, where she dey?' asks Ngozi as she bends to wipe and polish a desk.

'You no dey hear? The police come carry am for deportation,' replies Issha, moving a chair to empty a bin.

'You no dey say. How they find am?'

'Be her sister dey tell am, so Sunday say. He say na her and the sister's husband dey sex together,' says Issha.

'No!'

'Yes, O. Sunday and them dey live for same place. I told you that girl be type to spread legs like open door. I see the way she dey make eyes at men left, right and centre.'

'Issha, no be the girl's fault. Sunday dey tell me the sister's husband have plenty money, and the sister and he no dey sleep together. He say that the husband dey see different women. If that be so then Sandra dey thing she get some of it before the authorities send her back.'

'Look, Ngozi, I no dey care what the girl dey think, it no right to sleep with your sister's husband. The girl be *ashawo*. She dey use her private parts make money.'

'Issha, it no dey do with right – desperate times call for desperate measures.'

'Listen, the girl was not desperate. Please, let's not talk about her – I don't want to argue.'

'Anyway, Issha, how your pickin?'

'They fine. Shola dey panic for GCSE exams – teacher go tell am results for mocks today. As for the twins they watch too much football. Their father go return on Saturday so we go see how much they go watch.' Her husband frequently travels to their homeland to check on the house he's building for their return home one day.

'And little Fola?'

'Hmm, just dey cause havoc for house.'

Ngozi smiles. Her own daughter, had she lived, would have been almost two like Fola. She smiles faintly and looks away so the pain cannot be seen in her eyes. But she can't forget lying on the A&E bed, the doctor looking at the ultrasound monitor, trying to find a heartbeat, Ngozi willing her to find a heartbeat, but nothing. Then the true reality of it, having to give birth to her dead baby, holding her little foetus in her hands. She named her Annabelle. When she had been in Ben's home she had prayed to God for an answer, but not this answer, not this answer. And as she lay in the hospital ward the morning after, trying to come to terms with it, floating in and out of sleep, suddenly there he was, the man she had once called her Ben, whom she had hoped would be her future, there he was, whispering in her ear, thick fingers gripping her wrist so tight it hurt.

'You fucking bitch, I told you to get rid of it. Well, it's done now, so don't come anywhere near me, or my wife, or my home. You hear me, you little piece of shit?'

He kept a grip on her wrist, twisted it so hard, that she thought it was going to snap. Tears brimmed in her eyes.

'You hear me?'

She nodded, felt him push her wrist away, get up to smile at the woman in the bed next to hers, and turn on his heel and walk away. She watched his back as he walked out, and the only words to ring in her ears were 'you little piece of shit'. This was the man she had thought she loved, was different from her small-minded Catholic village, from the Obindus, from Mr Okafor, from so many. She watched him walk out of her life and vowed, vowed to show him, show them all, to wipe away that look of superiority, to be more than he or they could ever be.

'Anyway, *jarry*, tell me how your love life?' asks Issha, bringing her back to now and handing her a clean duster.

'Why every time you ask me?'

'Because I look forward to the day when you go say that you dey see one fine body.'

Ngozi rolls her eyes in exasperation.

'You know it's not right for a young woman your age to work! Work! Work! You go look round one day, O, and your youth dey gone. All you dey do is study and work, study and work. Look how long I know you and I never hear you say you dey go for party or meet friends. You're not a Church girl so I don't understand that kind of living.'

'Look who dey talk – I don't dey see you visit friends.'

'Listen, you and me are not the same age. I have four children and a husband. If you carry on the way you dey go, then you'll end up alone,' Issha says. Then more gently, 'You know, Sunday dey tell me how he like you.'

'Please, Issha, if I want a man I go find am myself. I don't need you to fix me up. I just have more important things to focus on, O.'

'Okay, O, I've told you what I have to say – it's your life,' replies Issha.

The women continue moving chairs and emptying bins. There is silence. Two hours later they are finishing off in the lecture hall when Sunday joins them.

'Ha, you two dey do good work, O. Look how everything dey shine,' he says.

Sunday is the supervisor for the company the polytechnic outsources their cleaning to. Their boss, Jim, an Irishman, has four supervisors in total: one Irish, two English and Sunday. However, he leaves most of the difficult communication or what he calls the tricky bits, like the firing, up to Sunday. I heard him say once that it was best to leave Sunday to deal with those sorts of things since they all come from the same parts, and that he would employ more English workers, but they don't stay around as long, and besides they cost more. He's been looking into hiring more of the

Portuguese migrants he's come across lately, but said, 'They don't speak good enough English, not that the lot around here are much better.' Then he laughed.

Sunday is an Igbo boy, the son of an Owerri trader, a village close to Obowi. He's considered a good catch as men go. A graduate from the University of Lagos, a doctor by profession, he stands at just over six foot – broad, muscular, lean, not handsome, but passable. To add to that, he's also in the Church, a good Christian, not only in name but some would say in spirit as well, although from my observations he does suffer from verbal diarrhoea.

Like many Nigerians of his generation, he was forced to leave a country he loves, to find some way of not wasting away in a nation where too many graduates find it hard to feed themselves, let alone get a job. He is, at present, studying to take his doctors' exams which should allow him to practise in the UK, but meanwhile he has to survive and has too many extended family members relying on the money he saves from his two jobs, which he sends home every four months.

Sunday was attracted to Ngozi at first sight. Her quiet demean-our and the way in which she always contains herself has made his feelings grow. Sometimes he catches himself fantasizing about her, and in these fantasies they are lovers, mates for life. In his dreams he's her first and only love; in his dreams she wipes his brow after a hard day's work, dutifully feeds him like a good wife would, gently caresses the ache from his muscles and whispers encouraging and loving words, forever supportive, forever beautiful. The problem is that now he's no longer satisfied with just his fantasy: he wants what he perceives to be the real thing. She has without knowing burrowed under his skin until he cannot pretend any more. He believes that he just needs to let her know – after all, a good woman like her would know what a good catch he is.

'Issha, how your pickin?' asks Sunday.

'They are all fine, O. Hey, look at the time! I bettar hurry before I miss my train – I've got to take the twins to school. Ngozi, please, O, can you put my things away?'

Ngozi looks up from wiping a desk and nods.

Issha presses for the lift and disappears with a wave as the doors close, leaving Ngozi and Sunday to put away the cleaning equipment.

'Ngozi, are you going towards Brixton today?' asks Sunday. They often travel home together on the same bus – he lives at the Oval and she in Stockwell – but this morning she has a class first thing.

'Yes, but I just have to drop off something for someone.'

'Okay, will you be long?'

'No, five to ten minutes.'

'Then wait for me at the bus stop. I just need to lock up. I won't be long.'

Ngozi makes her way through the corridors towards the computer help desk. It's still quiet. Seven thirty in the morning. A few of the lecturers and staff are beginning to make their way through the turnstiles at the entrance. She enters the waiting area, rings the bell at the counter, peers through the half-closed shutter. Stanford Bailey and a colleague sit at their desks at the back. She bangs on the shutter, waves when they look her way. Stanford gets up from his seat and heads out to greet her.

'I know it's a little early, O, but I just had to come and thank you.'

'For what?'

'I got on, O. I've started the course.'

'Congratulations.'

'I wouldn't have had the courage to do it if it wasn't for you, O.'

'I'm really proud of you.'

'Please take this,' Ngozi hands him a gift bag.

'Champagne . . . Chocolates?'

'It isn't much, but I am really grateful.'

*

291

That first week back from Glasgow after losing her baby, Ngozi is battered, but there's no time to dwell, no time to mourn, just over five months left, she calculates as she sits on the bed looking at the stamp in her passport. There's so much she has to do before going home. For home is not easy, and there's her family, and there are no guarantees of what truly awaits her on her return, and now Stella's to be married there's no going back to her old life in Lagos. There's only one focus: the exchange. Three pounds an hour she's been told – thirty pounds a day she's calculated. She'd have had to work a whole week to see that kind of money in her old job. In two months she can earn enough to keep a roof over her head for a year. Five months would set her up, at least for a little while, buy her enough time to figure things out once she's home. Stella's friend has said that she might be able to find work over on the big industrial estate without too many questions being asked.

The next morning she wakes to the alarm, springs up early, three a.m., just as Stella's friend has told her. She closes the front door quietly. The cold cracks the sleep from her eyes. She walks down the empty roads, the yellow street lights glowing above her, round several corners, just as she's been directed, and there it is, the entrance to the industrial estate, three barriers wide. She approaches the barrier on the left, shuffles down the side of the security cabin, taps on the window.

'Don't know, love. I can let you in,' he says, 'but you'll have to check with each of them yourself,' he adds, pointing to the vast number of units behind him.

And so she does. Finds a job in one of the units. The eleventh place she checks that morning. A big warehouse processing and packing peeled and cut potatoes for large offices and school canteens, cash in hand, no questions asked. It's £2 an hour. Not what she was expecting, but still a lot more than she could earn back home, and she's still at Stella's friend's place, although she's beginning to ask how long Ngozi's intending to stay. The job itself isn't difficult and the people are pleasant enough. Sometimes she helps sort through the potatoes, other times she's moving large containers from one point to another, and at the end of the day she helps with the cleaning. She learns a good deal mopping that warehouse floor and washing down the large cutting machines. She catches the beginnings and ends of conversations as she busies herself wiping away dirt and potato residue; learns quickly not to ask too many questions, as the ones who do seem to disappear. She does think it odd that there are no English workers apart from the supervisors, but to be honest, her focus is on earning as much as she can before going home and I really do think the miscarriage somehow silences her tongue. She keeps her head down and does what she needs to do, works as many hours as they'll give her, sometimes ten, other times as much as thirteen, collects her money and comes back to do it all again the next day.

It's during one of her short morning breaks that she first meets Issha, six weeks into the warehouse job. Ngozi's sat eating her breakfast on the small makeshift wall of wooden pallets between the warehouse and the unit next door. Issha smiles at her as she passes to sit on the pallets furthest away. It's seven o'clock in the morning and daylight's struggling through. Ngozi snaps open her plastic food container, and the smell emerges and wafts over to Issha.

'Hmm, *akara*?' Issha asks.

'Yes,' Ngozi says laughing.

'My mother use to make the best *akara* in our town,' says Issha. 'People use to come from miles around to buy her *akara*.'

'My mother too, the best in our village,' laughs Ngozi. 'In fact her cooking was second to none.'

They smile at each other across the pallets before Issha turns to look towards the offices next door.

'They're not open yet, O,' says Ngozi. 'They open around seven thirty. That's when I see the lights come on.'

'I know,' says Issha. 'I thought it was seven but on the door it says seven thirty.'

Ngozi nods, her mouth full, then looks down to pick the next piece from her container.

'How is the work over there?' asks Issha, tilting her head in the direction of the warehouse.

'OK, O, but the hours are long,' says Ngozi. 'What do they do over by yours?'

'Cleaning. Big offices, schools, banks, that sort of thing. I just need to get a few things sorted this morning, otherwise I'm out and about.'

'How much do they pay per hour?'

'Roughly three to four pounds, depending on the job.'

'Are they looking for people?'

'They are always looking for people,' says Issha, getting up and gathering her belongings as someone parks, gets out of a car and starts to open the unit door. 'I better go.'

'Nice meeting you!' Ngozi shouts after her. 'Maybe one day I'll let you taste my mother's recipe.'

Issha laughs and waves back at her, but somewhere midway between the wooden pallets and the front door of the neighbouring unit, she hesitates, stops, looks back, then turns and walks swiftly back to where Ngozi's sat eating.

'It's not really my business and I don't really know your situation, but there is something about you . . . Anyway, *shah*, maybe you remind me of my younger sisters . . . Anyway, it might not even be relevant, but the girls in the office they often talk about that warehouse – they say every so often it gets raided by immigration? As I said, it's not really my business and it might—'

'Oh,' says Ngozi, not sure what to do with the information. 'I—'

'Thank you. Thank you for telling me.'

'I bettar go. Make sure you take care,' says Issha as she walks away clutching her belongings and looking back at her nervously.

Ngozi watches her walk off and wonders what to do. She's comfortable with the warehouse job – it's long hours and she knows she's not being paid what she'd get if she was allowed to work legally, but so long as she can keep living at Stella's friend's place she can make it work. Besides, time is not on her side – she's got less than three months left. But to be found working could mean deportation, and she's not ready to leave; she's not yet earned enough to pay for a year's rent back home. Maybe it's God's way of telling her to move on, she thinks. Maybe God's telling her something. Maybe she should listen.

The next morning she arrives at the industrial estate an hour early, knocks on the doors of all the units with lights on; each boss shakes his head.

'Sorry, love, we need men. This isn't women's work,' says a big buster of a man pointing a gloved finger at the men loading his vans.

She starts her shift late that morning. It's taken a little longer going around the other units than she'd anticipated and so it's later than usual when she takes her break. She's sitting on the wooden pallets, snaps open her plastic container of food and glances over at the unit next door, and there it is, fully lit. As she takes a bite of her *akara* I see the question, the tiny, piercing spark of light. The should-she or should-she-not battle in her brain, while Issha's warning repeats in her head. She tentatively picks up her plastic container and walks over to the unit, knocks on the door. No answer. Knocks again. No answer. She puts her hand on the door handle, presses down, it opens and she walks in. In the room are four desks, and behind the desks are reinforced-glass windows leading into a warehouse. At one of the desks is a woman on the phone.

'I'm sorry, Mr Williams. I don't know why they've not turned up. They could still be on their way.' The woman raises her eyebrow at Ngozi. 'Please, Mr Williams, let me get off the phone, sort this out and call you back.' She puts the phone down. 'Can I help you?'

'I was wondering if you had any work.'

'You look familiar. Where do I know you from?'

'I work next door, O. I do the cleaning. I usually smile at you in the mornings when you're rushing to open up.'

'Yes.' She nods. 'That's it. You're usually by the pallets on a break.'

'Yes.'

'Can you hold on?'

'Yes, no problem, O.'

The woman picks up the phone and begins to call a number of people, most of whom don't answer, and when they do, they appear to be on another job they can't get away from. Finally she gets through to someone who seems to respond positively.

'When can you start?' asks the woman as she puts the phone down.

'Who, me?'

'Yes, you.'

'How much do you pay?'

'£3.50 an hour.'

'Any time,' replies Ngozi.

'Can you start now?'

Ngozi hesitates; she's on her break. If she leaves now, how will she explain it to the warehouse next door? So far, it's been guaranteed work, and on top of that, what about the money due to her for the hours already worked this morning? But there's something in the woman's expression that says to her if she doesn't say yes, right there and then, she might never have the opportunity again, and at almost twice the rate it's a chance worth taking and she can sort out the warehouse issue later. Besides, a voice inside has been nagging away since her conversation with Issha the day before.

'Yes, I can.'

The woman writes down an address on a piece of paper and hands it to Ngozi. 'A lady called Issha will be waiting there for you. Just follow her instructions and when you're done, come back to the office and we can sort out the pay. Here, take the office number and tell Issha to call me when you guys are done.'

Ngozi takes the paper. 'How do I get there?'

'Just take the number 35 bus from outside the gates and it'll take you straight there.'

Ngozi slips back into the warehouse, grabs her belongings, mumbles something about an emergency to a colleague, and walks out feeling guilty.

Later that morning, she's not there when the immigration police draw up in vans and block the exits from the warehouse. A few workers escape by scrambling through the toilet windows high up in the walls. The police check documents, ask questions, round up at least six of her colleagues. When she hears the news, Ngozi thanks God for Issha's warning, for listening, and that's the start of their sisterly friendship.

Sometimes I think she's a blessed child, other times I am not so sure, but I do know this world has a plan for her, and she's been wise, although sometimes foolish, but when it has mattered over these past years, she's listened, learnt, and paid attention to her inner voice. It has guided her well. I see the day their company wins the contract at this polytechnic, see the first time Issha and Ngozi, with their colleagues, walk up the stairs chattering among themselves excitedly as they pass through security, happy about their induction day, the large corridor before them empty of any students. But like the freshers, due to follow in two weeks, they walk down the corridor green, taking in every detail. For this was a step up from the public toilets that Issha and Ngozi have been cleaning for the last seven months. Here is a place of education, a place of respectability. Unlikely to find used condoms from unknown johns, or heroin syringes with traces of dried blood at the tip, or abuse from lowlifes who think they're somehow better because at least they don't clean public toilets. Or, as they once did, the body of a young woman slipped down between the toilet and the cubicle wall, syringe still hanging from a vein in her arm.

When Issha and Ngozi were little girls, education was the question, the answer and the solution. And so it is that Ngozi believes that the mere fact of her being here will rub off, that by working here it'll unlock the doors she so desperately wants to open. And so for the first time since arriving in England, she walks around doing her job with a smile on her face, open to people, to learning, to whatever this place can possibly throw her way, asking questions of anyone she thinks might answer. And that is how she comes across Stanford Bailey in the computer centre early one morning, maybe six or seven o'clock. He sits at one of the many computer desks, typing in code, trying to solve some problem. First, she gently wipes the surfaces of the desks around him, carefully lifting each keyboard to dust underneath, empties the bins and moves furniture, and still he shifts around and sits at the computers, eyes down, typing away, not noticing her.

'Do you mind, O?'

Silence.

'Sir? Mr? Do you mind, I need to hoover?'

'Hmm?'

'I need to hoover.'

'Sorry, am I in your way?'

'No, O. I can work around you. It's just the noise – I didn't want to disturb you, but I have to hoover.'

'Yes, of course.'

Ngozi starts up the machine, and he continues to sit, eyes locked on his mysterious task.

She finishes, looks over at his fingers tapping away, sees white writing moving fast across the blue screen. 'Sir? Mr? What you dey do?'

Stanford looks up, a little irritated. 'New software. Trying to make it work.'

'Software?'

'Yes.'

'What type of software? It looks complicated.'

'It is and it isn't. It just takes time working through the coding and fixing the errors.'

'O.' Ngozi puts down the hoover and goes to stand behind him. 'I wish I could do that, O.'

'Hmmm,' says Stanford, looking back at her, then back at the screen.

'I said I wish I understood it, could do that.'

'Hmmm.'

Ngozi gets the message, picks up the hoover and lead, and leaves the room to join Issha in the lecture hall.

The next morning when Ngozi arrives in the computer centre clutching her cleaning materials Stanford is sitting in the room again.

'What happened? You've not been home?'

'Yes,' Stanford says laughing, 'I have. I'm beginning to make headway now – should be out of your way by tomorrow.'

'I'm happy for you, O. It looks so complicated. So how you get into this computer thing?'

'Computer science, in school.'

'It looks difficult.'

'Like everything it takes patience.'

'Back home everything is still done by hand, O. But I suppose if I went back with computers there could be money to be made. A friend told me once I should get into it.'

'Where is home?'

'Nigeria.'

'Do you miss it?'

Ngozi laughs. 'Now that is a question! Yes and no. I miss my family. I miss the fruit. There is nothing sweeter than a mango from our own tree – the fruit over here is just not the same. I miss my village, the pace of everything. But I don't miss the uncertainty, not having money and not finding a job. I don't have the connections.'

'When do you think you'll go back?'

'I'm not sure. I am going home, but first I have to figure out what skill I can take with me to keep food on my table. How much does it pay?'

'What, computers?'

'Yes, O.'

'It depends, but it's well paid and at the moment they can't get enough people. It's growing so fast but there aren't enough people with the right skills.'

'So computers might be a good skill to have.'

'Yes, I would say so.'

'How do I do that, O? I don't even know how to switch the damn thing on, and all the courses cost money. Everything is so expensive.'

Stanford looks at her, the hoover by her side, imagines her back home in Africa, imagines how difficult it would be for her, thinks of his hero Mandela and says, 'Why don't you meet me here first thing in the morning? We could do ten to fifteen minutes, teach you the basics, see if you even like dealing in computers.'

'Are you sure about that?'

'Yes, of course. By the way I'm Stanford. Stanford Bailey.' He holds out his hand and smiles.

And that is how Ngozi begins to learn about computers.

Ngozi stands at the bus stop waiting for Sunday. She looks inside her bag, rechecking her books for today's lessons, flicks through her floppy disk case to confirm she's picked up the right ones, then looks up to notice what's going on around her. It's getting busy with people marching towards local offices and others rushing to catch connecting buses and trains into the city. She takes a look at her watch, wondering whether to get the next bus. Sunday seems to be taking his time.

'You got a light?'

She turns to see a young man, early twenties, shirt hanging untidily over his jeans. 'No,' she says and continues to squint down the road in the hope of seeing the red shape of a double-decker bus hove into view.

'You know, you're well kris. *Psst, psst.* Miss! Miss!'

'Ngozi, is this man bothering you?' says Sunday, finally turning up.

'It's okay, O,' she says, reaching out to touch his forearm, 'he was just asking for a light.'

The young man walks past her, gives her a smile as he passes, revealing one gold front tooth. Then limps off to get on the number 50 bus, which has just pulled up.

'I don't like these Ogede people. They are nothing but trouble – no upbringing, no ambition, all they know is that weed they smoke,' says Sunday.

'Sunday, please.'

'Please?'

'Yes, please,' she says, then quickly moves towards the kerb, arm outstretched to stop the number 133. They climb the stairs to the top deck and take a seat towards the back.

Ngozi looks out the window down towards the pavement which is stained with chewing gum and gathering litter. She sees the terraced shops and the tops of people's heads as the bus pulls away. Breathing in, she thinks of Issha's advice, and for once acknowledges her loneliness. There is no Stella here to talk to, or her sister if she wishes to seek advice, or friends to laugh with and wash away the daily struggle of bills and the sheer unending boredom of it all. She looks over at Sunday sitting beside her, arms folded and legs open. Sunday likes her, she knows this. He looks at her like a glutton looks at cheesecake. For the first time since meeting him, since being in England and losing her baby, she turns and looks at Sunday as a woman looks at a man. He's not bad-looking, not handsome but passable. There's a quiet strength to him which she likes, a simplicity in the way he thinks and approaches things, a masculinity to his physique, a broadness in his shoulders and in his hands, which implies . . . Well, never mind what it implies. The truth is, she looks at him for the first time and likes what she sees, but the problem lies in his conversation. Even now, as she sits beside him trying to calm her mind before the day truly begins, with classes and study and assignments, he just won't stop talking. She looks at the side of his face, at his large ears, and at his mouth which won't stop moving, looks back out the window at the people milling about below, then back at him and he's still talk- ing. She grips her bag, imagines hitting him with it, but – and this is a big but – his hands, his shoulders, his lips awaken her. She had thought these urges had died in the hospital along with Annabelle, but here they are again, knocking to be let out. This morning she awoke tense, needing the feel of a pair of masculine arms around her, all solid, broad, hot, the smell of salty earthy lemons filling her nostrils. She imagines him on top of her, large hands cupping her breasts, moving inside her. She catches her breath in shock at her thoughts, sees his lips move, before realizing he's actually asking her a question.

'So waytin you dey do when you no dey study or work?'

'Pardon?'

'I said waytin you dey do when you no dey study or work?'

'O, nothing. I just dey watch TV.'

There's a pause.

'Well . . . would you like to come with me to go see the new Eddie Murphy film? Waytin they call em?'

'You mean *Boomerang*?'

'Yes, *Boomerang*. This Friday?'

Ngozi looks down, fiddles with the clasp on her bag, shifts uncomfortably in her seat.

'Do you want to come?'

Her inner voice screams *No!*, but she hears the word 'Yes' come out of her mouth. 'I mean no. Yes . . . Why not? Yes. Thank you,' she replies.

Sunday breathes out.

The bus approaches the stop for her college. Ngozi quickly gathers her bag of books and presses the bell.

'I'll meet you by the library on Friday.'

Ngozi nods as she squeezes past his long legs.

'Six thirty,' he calls after her as she disappears down the stairs.

Issha was excited when Ngozi told her.

'But I don't even like him,' she said to Issha over the phone. 'He talks too much.'

'Ngozi, give him a chance. He's a good catch. Trust me.'

So here she is on a Friday night, tired from trying to work on her assignments in the library, working three jobs, wondering why she even agreed to a date when she has more important things to think about and do, but most of all she was not in the mood to dress up and entertain a man. Quite honestly, she's had a bellyful of men to last her a lifetime. So she stands in the hallway of her old Edwardian building, converted into bedsits, with the payphone receiver in her hand, listening thankfully to Sunday's answering machine.

'Leave a message after the beep.'

'Sunday, I'm really sorry, O, but I can't make it. Something has come up. I'll talk to you on Monday at work.' Then she runs up to her room on the first floor, changes into her dressing gown, switches on the television and begins to stuff biscuits into her mouth.

Twenty minutes later: 'Is she in?' She hears the male voice at the door downstairs.

'Shit, O, it's Sunday!'

She hears his heavy footsteps make their way up the stairs. She jumps up, runs to her wardrobe, biscuit still in mouth.

'Ngozi,' says Sunday, tapping at the door.

Quickly she grabs her dress hanging on the door and pulls it on. 'Ngozi.'

'Sunday?' she questions, opening the door slightly. 'How you know my address?'

'Issha gave it to me. She said it best I pick you up?'

'Didn't you get my message?'

'What message?'

'On your answering machine.'

'I've not come from home. Is everything okay?'

'Never mind, O, it doesn't matter now. Give me ten minutes and I'll be with you.' She closes the door, changes out of the dress into her newest top and least scruffy skirt while he waits on the landing.

They go to the ABC to see the film. Two hours later they're sitting in the pizza restaurant facing each other. Ngozi looks past Sunday to the two couples getting up from the table behind him, leaving behind scrunched-up paper napkins, empty plates and drained glasses. She wonders about them, their lives.

Sunday clears his throat. 'Ngozi. Ngozi!'

'I'm sorry, I was dreaming, O.'

'I said, how you dey find film?'

'Fine.'

In truth she found it silly, in parts boring – so boring she counted how long she could hold her breath: forty-seven seconds. Then counted the fluff on her top: twenty bits of fluff. For good measure, how many people she could see in the darkened cinema: one hundred and two. But Sunday sat beside her exploding with laughter, he hit down hard with it, curled up then uncurled with it and Ngozi watched on, not getting it.

'And when Eddie Murphy come in for that shop!' says Sunday, revisiting the highlights.

Ngozi sees Sunday's lips move, thinks of the assignments left undone on her side table, and wonders whether, if she gets up early enough, she might be able to finish one before starting work tomorrow. She notices Sunday asking a question, nods her head in the hope it'll cover up the fact she's not listening. Frankly, she thinks, she'd have more fun listening to stew bubble. A few minutes later she's saved by the arrival of the pizzas. Sunday pushes a large slice into his mouth which keeps him quiet for a while.

What am I doing here? she asks herself. *Just get up and tell him you're not interested, O.*

But just as the courage comes, Sunday reaches across the table and puts his hand over hers. She feels the fine invisible hairs on the back of her hand, his touch jolts through her, it travels down into her stomach, down further, awakening her once again. The truth is, if she'd been another type of girl, brought up in a different way, she'd have reached across the table, pulled him towards her and satisfied her need. Simple. But she's not that type of girl, from that type of world, so instead she sits across from him, bites her lip, trying to understand these sudden urges, magnifying it into something bigger than it really is.

Sunday watches her across the table. He sees the way her eyes don't or won't meet his. He sees her bite her lip with what he perceives to be nervousness. She reminds him of his mother. His precious mother he left behind at home, who sacrificed everything to send him to medical school. Always made sure he was dressed in crisp white shirts, running water or not, electricity or not. He, the eldest of five, the only boy among girls, was their prince, their world, the only one who could truly carry on their family line.

Sunday feels the softness of Ngozi's hand beneath his, likes the feel of his hand engulfing hers. He hears himself babbling but cannot shut up.

'You're a quiet woman, very decent,' he says.

Ngozi chokes on her soft drink. Decent – this is not a word that Ngozi has ever associated with herself, nor has she known anyone to describe her in that way, and after her life in Obowi, Mr Obindu, Mr Okafor, Ben and the death of her baby Annabelle, it's not a word she would have ever used in connection with herself. After all, a decent person does not allow herself to be used like a thing. A decent person would have a father who loved her. A decent person would still have her baby – God would have allowed a decent person that at least. She says the word out loud, 'Decent.' She likes the sound of it. She looks across the table at Sunday and she likes the reflection of it.

'You're not like the girls over here, wild. You're contained, hard-working, qualities that I consider to be good in a woman,' he says. 'I am a serious man and I have been studying you from afar, and I have chosen you out of all the women I have seen to become my girlfriend.'

Chosen me. How dare you? Otolu babow gie, she swears to herself, and as if to slap him she announces boldly, 'I'm *Osu*.'

There's a silence.

'And?'

'I . . . I . . . I just thought I'd tell you,' she says, momentarily taken aback.

'Anyway, as I was saying, I have chosen—'

Ngozi stares at his chin from across the table. She's used to a reaction, to flight, to cooling off.

'Sunday, did you hear what I said? I said, I'm *Osu*.'

'And so? I'm a Christian, such things don't bother me, and besides that we are living in modern times – we are not in our parents' generation.'

Ngozi looks at him, unable to fully close her mouth. Sunday is not as typical as she had previously thought.

'I'm a serious man. I don't like playing games,' he says.

I suppose he's not too bad, O, she thinks, trying to persuade herself.

'It will be good for us to see each other. As I work hard during the week, Saturdays and Sundays will be best.'

Unable to respond in any other way, Ngozi nods.

'You are available?'

She nods again.

They start to see each other on a regular basis. They go to Thorpe Park, to the cinema, visit friends, take long walks around her neighbourhood, picnic in Brockwell Park or simply sit, chat and eat ice cream at the bandstand on Clapham Common.

The sex comes two months later. It is good. Ngozi is satisfied, but it's his crying that confuses her. That first night, she awkwardly patted his back as he lay on top of her, curling his head into her shoulder, resting all his weight on her. She found it difficult to breathe and shifted his weight as much as she could towards her side, and still he sobbed into her shoulder, having given into his base needs, to temptation.

The living together came two months after that. It's practical. Ngozi is glad for the extra money available to send home to Blessing, and put towards the costs of her course. She gets used to his constant folding, his obsession of having all his shoes and shirts neatly lined up, his several bottles of cologne which seem to dominate the space on top of the chest of drawers, which they just barely squeezed into the one room, and of course, sometimes, the crying after sex. And for a while, nothing eventful happens. Sunday continues working his job and stays on his course to allow him to practise medicine in the UK. Ngozi continues with her jobs and her business and computer course. But that's how it goes. You get up and do your nine to five, sometimes even five to nine, watch a little TV and then go to bed. Up again the next day to start it all again. More than four years can pass in that way, before you even realize things have changed, or that you have changed.

'People's club of Nigeria, O, *ndi ezi bo omume*,' the male voice croons through the loudspeakers – it's an old and familiar song, which pulsates through the school gymnasium, packed to the rafters with elders, parents, children and a few teenagers from the club that has rented the school premises for an event. Ngozi watches from her table as the Owerri women prepare to take centre stage with other invited guests. She hears the two people closest to her taking notes for their planned festivities, due to take place later in the summer.

On the next table two women sit ordering their children to get more *jollof* rice, more peppered beef, more *moi-moi*, more drink, which they either stuff in their mouths or in their handbags.

Ngozi smiles, watches the children run around trying to please their mothers; she sees her child self, the one who stood by the roadside selling oranges, and marvels at how she got here. Having had enough of her part-time jobs, she took a risk almost two years ago and set up a cleaning business with Issha, who needed more flexibility to be with her kids. Issha's husband helped with the initial capital, and sharing bills with Sunday afforded Ngozi the luxury of that risk. They, Issha and herself, now have three contracts: one with a secondary school, another with a small engineering company and the last with a branch of a major high-street bank. But that is not the reason why Ngozi sits smiling, marvelling like she does, for this morning she took a trip to the bank, asked for a statement for her business account, and not really thinking, looked at her statement as she walked away from the counter and stopped in shock. Three hundred and ninety thousand pounds were sitting in her business account. She looked up and around, looked back down at the statement, then returned to the counter.

'Sorry. Excuse me, O,' she said to the lady behind the glass partition, 'you've made a mistake.'

'Mistake?'

'Yes, you've given me the wrong statement,' she said, sliding the paper back under the glass.

The lady checked the statement and gave it back. 'No, that's your statement.'

'Can't be, O?'

'It is.'

'I'm telling you, it isn't.'

'But it is.'

'Can I speak to someone – a manager? This needs clearing up,' Ngozi said, her voice rising. She was frightened of some accusation of fraud.

The bank manager escorted her quietly into a backroom, closed the door silently and sat her down.

As stated, Issha and Ngozi had opened a cleaning business and split the jobs between them. Issha, being more hands-on and better with people, dealt mainly with the staff and customer side of things. Ngozi, being more into computers, dealt with security checks, especially after they won the contract with the bank, also inventory, logistics and payroll. So Ngozi being Ngozi had developed a software program to make her life easier, to tackle most of the major issues such as reordering stock more quickly and efficiently, to allow her more time for her studies. She learnt a lot through that cleaning business – learnt what she was good at and what she wasn't good at. She watched Issha deal with the staff and how they warmed to her, allowed her to take control. She wished she had the skills to manage and persuade people just like her. And when she finally graduated five months ago and couldn't find a corporate job as she'd wanted, she went back to that old software she'd created after reading an article in the paper about the future of software and the new dot-com era. She dusted it off, redesigned the user interface and set about selling it.

She sold it first to her old cleaning company, who were bigger than when she first joined them; it was easier as she knew who was who within the company. She sat in that waiting room, rubbing her palms together, checking and rechecking her presentation.

'They'll see you now,' the receptionist said.

She smiled, straightened her skirt, pulled at her jacket to ensure everything was in the right place. Picked up the presentation, her notes, her business cards and a copy of the software for demonstration, and entered the room, ready to sell, calling on her eleven-year-old self, the one who knew how best to sell oranges by the roadside, who knew how to compete and win among rivals.

She was sick in the toilets afterwards, and decided there had to be a better way to do it, but nevertheless she had won her first contract. She read, called, questioned and asked her way to Mr Bridges, the first person she employed to sell her software. Though she had no money, he warmed to her – something inside told him this was a good horse to back – and so he took the job, selling on commission only. And that was what had led up to the moment when she looked at a balance of almost four hundred thousand pounds. As she sat there opposite the manager who was reading through the statement, working out where all the money had come from, it became evident. She backed out of the room apologizing, and went home to make a call.

'Mr Bridges, there is almost four hundred thousand pounds in my account, O.'

'Is that all?'

'What do you mean, is that all?'

'I reckon you should have more than that coming in soon. Your software is selling really well.'

'But I don't understand. At the price you're selling it, you would need to have sold hundreds, maybe thousands of copies to make that kind of money.'

'Well, that's what I tried to get hold of you to talk about. Your original price point was too low. I started selling the software at the price you gave me, but one guy laughed me out of his office saying it couldn't be any good as similar software was selling for ten times the amount. So when I looked into it, he was right. You didn't get back to me so I made a decision, went in at half the price of your competitors, and it's been selling like hot cakes since then. By the way, I have a list of requests for a few minor changes. I also promised them backup and support for a yearly subscription in line with your competitors.'

'But, Mr Bridges, I wasn't expecting it to take off like this. It's only me behind the business: there is no backup and support.'

'Well, you'd better start building a team then, and fast.'

The evening is progressing and the Owerri women have long finished their dance. It's now time for speeches, and so some – those who can without causing offence – find their way towards the school grounds outside. They gather near the car park beside the netball courts to discuss more important matters, matters that cannot wait, lest they are forgotten.

'So, Sunday, when are you getting married?' asks his auntie. 'Now that your studies are finished and you can practise fully as a doctor, you must find someone.'

'But, Auntie, I've already found someone.'

'Ta, let me not even hear what you just said again.'

'I thought you liked Ngozi.'

'Look, Sunday, I'm telling you this for your own good. You can't marry her, ho-ha! It will bring disgrace on the family. How can you marry a house girl, and worse still an *Osu*? That is what is wrong with you young people today – you come over here and follow everything these people do. Your poor father will die of a heart attack. How can you forget who your family are, who your father is? Ah-ah! It's bad enough that you bring her here where everybody can see you and gossip, but to tell me you want to marry her . . . My son, your head is not correct. Say you marry this girl, what happens when you eventually go home? Any children you have will become *Osu* like her. Please don't think as a Westerner without a culture, you are Igbo.

'You know, I am leaving tomorrow. I've told you several times about this girl – a medical doctor from a very good family, twenty-four, very pretty. Just say the word and I can arrange for you to meet her. She's over here for a small time, staying with her auntie and uncle. A very good girl. Take the phone number and ring her. Tell her that Auntie Bessie gave you her number. I've told her about you – she is very interested in meeting you.'

'Auntie, I don't want—'

'Shut up and take the number,' his auntie says, pressing the number into his hand, before turning her attention to other matters. The speeches inside have finished and the dance floor is open. 'Hey, wait, O, they are playing my tune. Come, make we go dance.'

He follows her back into the hall where she dances and wiggles her hips, raising her arms all the way. His eyes fall on Ngozi. She's just a few yards away, dancing with a group of women. She gives him a smile and waves at him. He waves back and begins dancing beside his auntie. Sunday looks at Ngozi across the room and over the heads of the other people. He really does love her, but he wonders if his love is strong enough to withstand family pressures. When they first got together, it seemed easy. He had thought that since his family were Christians, he'd be able to persuade them that such things didn't matter any more – after all, Igbo men are marrying Caribbean, American and white women, and nobody knows their backgrounds nor do they seem to care. These things are accepted nowadays. He had thought he'd be able to marry Ngozi too, but her being *Osu* was proving too big an obstacle to overcome. He hears his auntie's words: 'It will bring disgrace on the family. How can you marry a house girl, and worse still an *Osu*?' He remembers his mother's disapproving silence over the phone every time he brings Ngozi's name up in conversation, and his cousin's words of advice: 'It is not the done thing.'

He plans to return home in the not-too-distant future but he and Ngozi would never survive over there – the family pressures would be too much. He touches the phone number in his pocket and wonders if he should call this girl. She sounds nice; his auntie said she was pretty, young, a doctor like himself, all the things his family would be proud of, but she's not Ngozi. Sunday excuses himself from his auntie and makes his way to the other side of the hall to dance at Ngozi's side.

'How are the preparations going?' he asks.

'Fine, O,' she says. 'Sunday, I went to the bank today—'

'How long did you say you'll be gone for again?' He's referring to a trip to Silicon Valley that Ngozi has just arranged.

'Two weeks.'

'I'll miss you, but I'm sure you'll have a great time.'

Ngozi smiles. 'Stella is very excited. She can't wait to show me around.'

Her friend Stella, who married her sweetheart Chiedu, is now living in Silicon Valley with her husband, a lecturer at Stanford University; they're expecting their first child. Ngozi is due to fly out to see her and attend a short programming course.

'Stella will take good care of you,' says Sunday. 'What day are you leaving again?'

'Saturday.'

'This Saturday?'

'Yes.'

'I wish I was coming with you.'

'So do I, O, but you have your interview on Monday.'

'Yes, maybe next time.'

'Yes, next time,' says Ngozi. 'Sunday, you look worried. Is it the interview?' She strokes his creased brow.

'Me? No, I'm fine.'

'I'm sure you'll do very well. I'll phone once I get there.'

'Please don't worry. Just go and enjoy, but don't talk to any strangers,' he jokes.

Ngozi laughs. 'I won't.'

'What were you going to say – that you went somewhere today?'

Ngozi looks at him, starts to find the words but changes her mind. *Best to tell him after his interview*, she thinks. 'Nothing. Let's just enjoy our last night.'

They dance till late, but something inside Ngozi is uneasy. She can't shake the feeling and it confuses her. She doesn't fully understand it, but inside her spirit whispers, quietly nags away, warning that nothing will ever be the same again.

20

The Beginning – Jamaica

THAT MORNING, ON our first day in Jamaica, after they led us
from the ship and I could no longer see him, I turned my
head, looked ahead, like Wind was in the past. I did not think our
paths would ever cross again. I thought I was to die, to be eaten
by the devils. I did not imagine that the journey on the slave ship
was the beginning of our story, not the end, that the world I left
behind in my village would become a mere dream, a life lived by
someone else. And I envied the innocence of that girl, that me,
who heard the sound of the *oja* flute soaring like an excited free
bird, who kicked up the dust as the bells at her ankles rang in her
ears and danced with a freedom and joy I would never know
again. I did not, or could not, have imagined the life on the plantation into which I was sold, where even the horses on which the
white overseers rode back and forth, gun on shoulder, would be
treated more humanely. They tried to season me, beat me and the
others into submission, made us speak only in their tongue,
stripped us of our names, chaining us at night and feeding us like
hogs, before letting us free to harvest the fields. From dawn to
dusk I heard the wind rustle through the grass of the sugar cane
as we bent ourselves crooked under the hot sun, the light

glistening off the backs of the shirtless men as we chopped the cane with machetes, tossing it aside to be collected, the drivers flogging anyone who dared to rest. More died along the journey, from hunger, from disease, from depression. And yet I survived.

And, yes, I ran. The first chance I got, in the late evening when the light was not so good, when they were not looking. I ran, through the field of cane. It smacked and cut me, my feet bled, but I ran among the vermin of the field, through the night, with only the moon and my *chi* to guide me towards the mountains, towards the maroons who it was rumoured could help a runaway slave.

We fell in love, Wind and I. It was a surprise to me, as big a surprise as when he walked back into my life bringing supplies for the maroons during the slave revolts. We carried the supplies on our heads up into the mountains. We fell in love amid the chaos of war, and the running from the British soldiers who flooded the Island, trying to contain the uprising.

He was weary the first night we slept together, weary of the slave ship, of the senseless deaths, of the fight for freedom, of the life of a negro. I was frightened of our tomorrows, of the fight yet to come, of the death that would surely meet me, and so I chose to love him, to spread my legs and love him with all I had in me. It was a choice I freely made – the only choice I made freely since being kidnapped from my land. I listened to his breathing, stroked his scars, kissing away the pain, lifted myself to meet him. I felt his trembles, his crying and loved him more. In the morning I raised myself from him and prepared myself for the fight, for death.

She was made in love, up in the mountains, made in the courage to fight for freedom and cast away our chains, and like the love that grew between Wind and me, she also was a surprise, and she grew and flourished despite everything, until she could no longer be ignored, until she became our hope.

Wind wanted me to go, said he would hide me and the boy away on the passage. He said that in England there were no plantations, and if one could get there, freedom would follow. He said that the streets were hard with barely any work for a negro, but a life of cold poverty was surely better than the feverish life of an Island slave.

'Can't you see there is nowhere left to run?' Wind begged. 'Years ago, they shipped the maroons of Trelawnay to Nova Scotia. They chained and lined them up in the port. They will surely do the same to you.'

'Yes, but Haiti still burns – they say it will be free. And Jamaica too, eventually.'

'The war is over on this Island. They've taken it back.'

I felt the baby kick, touched my stomach.

'Come with me to England. Please.'

I turned away.

'Why do you not listen?'

'She must be born free.'

'Do you not think I want that too? The child is mine also. When we were making her, I did not think you would live to see tomorrow, but here she is – our miracle.'

Wind was born in England, the land he wanted to take us to. He said that his mother was a slave from the Islands, but she had simply disappeared into those streets, never to be found again. He said that although the English enforced slavery in the colonies, they could not do so in England, where it was illegal. He said he had always wanted a family of his own and a place to call home.

'But on that godforsaken slave ship. I still wake screaming from the nightmare—'

'There will be no slaves on board this time, and it has been washed and drained and loaded only with sugar, rum and spices from the Island.'

'And if they find me on the ship?'

'And if they find you here? You will surely hang.'

I looked across the Island, saw the lights from the camps of the British troops. The maroons had lost the uprising of 1796, and although I did not want to face the truth, it looked like we were losing this one, too.

'You and the baby are all I have in this world.'

Well, Chukwu must have been on Wind's side, because a week later, the day before his ship was due to set sail, the British troops raided us, and I was forced to flee, along with the boy I'd rescued. So I fled towards the only one I could flee to: Wind. He kissed me tenderly in the shadows, the orphan boy by my side. I would not leave him, so he had no choice but to take the two of us on board the slave ship bound for London.

PART VII

Their Story

21

The Meeting

San Francisco, 1998

NGOZI CLOSES HER books and applauds the lecturer along with the rest of the class. She's taken in so much information this past week that her head is spinning with it all. She looks around the room at her fellow students. They're young, male and pink-cheeked, except of course for the two Asian men in the far corner. These young men fill this valley with their presence, with their awkwardness. Back in London, Ngozi had thought there'd be more women and people of colour; she'd thought America would be more diverse, with more opportunities for people who looked like her. But these young men she's met on this short visit are nice enough. Most seem to come alive, buzz, spark once alone and talking about their passion. Each one seems to talk faster than the others as they stand in the bar in the evenings in downtown Palo Alto, beer in hand, chattering over the music, telling her how they're either going to change the world or are already changing it.

'The World Wide Web is where it's at,' had said the young man, pushing his glasses further up the bridge of his nose, his lanky fair fringe grown out to the point where it was almost covering his eyes.

'How's that, O?' she'd said, nodding as he spoke.

'It's the new land rush,' he'd said, fishing for a card in his back pocket. She'd looked at it closely. His name was printed in black with the words 'Internet Engineer' directly beneath.

'We're in the midst of something never seen before,' he'd said. 'It's like the new frontier, the new gold rush, and there isn't anywhere else on the planet I would rather be at this time.'

'So it's big?'

'Yeah,' he'd said, laughing, 'it's big – it's going to take over this world and you need to be here, man.'

'But how do you make money out of it?'

'Look, the investors are throwing money at any half-decent thing. It's easy. You just need to come up with a reasonable idea that captures their imagination, and *puff!*, you're in. You really need to get on board 'cause anybody that doesn't is gonna get left behind.' He then caught the eye of someone he knew and raised his hand in a wave. 'Harry . . . Harry! Over here. Come meet Gozi.'

And as she now picks up the books from her desk, the rest of the class already crowding outside the lecture room saying their goodbyes, Ngozi wonders whether she should take the risk, pack up and move out here to Silicon Valley. There's an energy about these people that feeds her, feeds her ambitions. But what about her software business – what about Sunday? Looking around, she wonders if she'd truly fit in.

'Bye, Gozi,' says one of the young men, Bobby, recently moved out from Alabama.

Ngozi gives him a wave.

'Make sure you keep in touch now.'

'I will, O,' she says, heading towards the exit to collect her things from Stella's, ready for her trip into San Francisco by train for the last few days of her visit.

*

Michael has just arrived from the airport. He climbs out of a yellow cab and heaves his luggage out from the back. It's a little cool but not cold enough for a coat, so he slings it over his arm, watches the people walk by on the pavement before making his way to the hotel entrance and through the revolving doors to reception.

'You just can't get any better shopping than down by Union Square,' says the porter as he places his bags down in the room. 'It's beautiful, just beautiful. Is it London, England, you said you're from? I just love the accent.'

Michael smiles, tips the porter and walks over to the window for a look at the city. The Bay Bridge looms in the distance. He breathes in San Francisco, and ponders why it looks and feels so different from the America he knows from TV back in England. He flicks through his meeting information pack covering the deaths of black men in custody, mentally noting the start and finishing times for tomorrow, then puts his clothes away and skips downstairs to the lobby. At the information desk he asks where to buy the best towels – Marcia's asked him to get some. According to his sister, America is the best place to get such things. Then he heads out on to the bustling street, armed with a map, towards the BART subway system.

Ngozi stands in the busy lingerie department admiring rails of lacy, frilly underwear. She fingers and strokes the soft silks and ornate laces, contemplates her recent lectures and the new people she's met. She makes a note to self to keep in touch with Bobby and the others. She turns over the price tag of a pink silk bra – two hundred and fifty dollars – and recoils in shock. Then stops herself and marvels at the fact that she could, if she wanted, afford it. That she, the little girl, the one who'd stood selling fruit at the bus station back home in Nigeria, the one who'd had no choice but to leave home in search of an education, now stands in an American lingerie department able to buy as many garments as she wants. She breathes in deep at the enormity of it, takes in the dream and pinches herself. But it's no dream and she feels the pain, fear follows, and the what-ifs, and the is-she-able, is-she-capable thoughts overwhelm her. She quickly puts the luxury bra down and hurries out of lingerie into the homeware department next door, only to bump into someone in her haste.

'I'm sorry,' says Michael, almost tripping over her.

Ngozi looks up into a pair of brown eyes and all she can think to say is, 'You're British, O?'

Michael nods. 'Sorry, didn't see you.'

'You really need to be looking where you're going,' says Ngozi as she straightens herself.

As she speaks, he catches the smoothness of her chocolate skin. *African*, he thinks, then notices the way she attempts to stare him down, even though she's much shorter. He laughs silently, straightens his back, stares down into her eyes, but there's something about them, her teardrop eyes, that captures him. 'I swear,' he says, 'and this isn't a line, but you look . . . kind of familiar.'

Ngozi breaks into a smile. 'I was thinking the same, O, as I was speaking.'

'Do you live in London? South?'

'Yes, O, Stockwell. You?'

'Brixton,' he answers.

They laugh.

Definitely African, he thinks. Images of the comedian Lenny Henry shouting '*Katanga! Katanga!*' run wild in his head, adverts of starving children with flies buzzing around them join Lenny to sit quietly on his shoulder.

Ngozi smiles again.

She's got a nice smile, he thinks. But there's something striking about her, and he can't take his eyes off her. Her features are unusual, like those of a carved Ife head, and each time he looks at her he notices something new, but yet at the same time she is so familiar. His eyes move downwards to assess the rest of her, but her body is covered with a thick loose cardigan.

'I can't think where we might have met,' says Michael.

'Neither can I, O. Maybe we've seen each other around,' she says.

'So what are you doing in San Francisco?'

'I came for a week's course in the Valley not far from here,' she says, casting an eye over his clothing. *Casual. Must be an Ogede.* Images of *The Bill* or the multitude of other TV programmes where Caribbean men feature as drug dealers or thieves run wild in her mind. 'And you?'

'Conference-cum-information exchange, -cum-sightseeing,' he says.

'Snap. I've taken a few days to look around the city myself,' says Ngozi.

They laugh again.

'I'm Michael Watson,' he says, holding out his hand to her.

'I'm Ngozi. Ngozi Nwosu.'

'Goze Wosu.'

'N-go-zi N-wo-su,' she pronounces slowly.

'Ngozi Wosu.'

She repeats her name again for him.

'Ngozi N-wo-su' He finally gets it. 'I gather you're African from that name. What part are you from?'

'Nigeria,' she answers. 'And where were your parents originally from?'

'Jamaica.'

They smile at each other again, glad to have guessed right.

'I just had a thought. What are you doing after you've finished here?' he says.

'Nothing really, I'm just milling around at the moment. Why?'

'I wondered if you'd like to take a break, have a coffee.'

Ngozi quietly looks him up and down.

Michael continues to smile back at her.

'Why not?' she says. 'I would love to.'

They saunter out of the department store to a coffee shop over the road.

'So how are you finding the city?' he asks once they sit down.

'Fine, O,' she says, stirring sugar into her coffee. 'It's my first time here. I took the bus around this morning. I don't know what I was expecting but it's so compact. I even got off at a stop and tried walking up the hill but it's steep, O. I had to give up in the end.'

'It's my first time too,' he says. 'I think I was expecting a bigger, richer version of London but it's not. I know I've only been here a day but I got a semi-taxi tour this morning on my way in from the airport.'

'You know what surprises me? I was expecting to see more African Americans.'

'Yes, I was expecting to see more as well.'

'It's even worse in Silicon Valley,' she says and takes a sip from her coffee. 'I was talking to the man on the bus and he said that the African Americans here live in the Fillmore district or East Palo Alto, but they're being pushed out 'cause of the tech industry pushing property prices up.'

'Sounds familiar,' he says. 'The same thing's happening in Brixton – not the tech bit of course, but the prices pushing people out, changing the area. My Uncle Fred and Auntie Eliza are thinking of selling up and moving, maybe to Thornton Heath or Croydon.'

'Tell them not to, O.'

'I have.'

'It's funny, O – on the one hand there's this global tech boom going on in the Valley, changing the world, but right across from it all the young black men are killing themselves.'

'It's really sad,' he says, shifting in his seat to get more comfortable.

'Yes, O. But whose fault is it?' says Ngozi. 'I mean, I was speaking to some young men last week about it. If they don't want to sort themselves out, take up the opportunities—'

'Look, it's never that simple.'

'Not that simple? Just stop killing yourselves – it's that simple.'

Michael sits up, his mouth agape, closes it, takes a deep breath. 'Look, you have to understand the background here. These people came mostly from the South escaping poverty, lynchings and the Jim Crow laws. They came here in search of jobs and a better way of life. They get here, try their best to build their own communities, despite the laws against them in housing, in education, in so many ways. They find a way to build their own schools but again the laws conspire against them, shut down most of what they build. Then when things are supposed to start getting better, in come the seventies and eighties flooding their communities with drugs—'

Ngozi is taken aback. 'I didn't mean—'

But Michael is on a roll. 'I know you didn't mean, but these things are historical, it's always historical, people don't consciously choose a life of misery. It's like coming in at the end of a movie and asking why doesn't the guy on the floor just get up and walk out the cage when you've missed everything that went before, and the true point of what you're seeing is that despite all the guy's been through, he's still alive, down on the floor, devastated, wounded, but still alive.'

'I'm sorry, O. I didn't—'

He nods his head and continues. 'People do it all the time, not just with black people. Talk to an average Australian about the Aborigines or a Canadian about the First Nations people. It's such a familiar tale.'

'I didn't mean to offend.'

He's speaking more loudly now. 'Well, sometimes people have to look beyond their own noses; sometimes people need to not talk about things they really don't have a clue about. If you don't know the history or care to know, then keep quiet.'

'I'm sorry, I was just talking about what I've been told and what I see.'

'Yes, and most of those people who told you don't really know or care enough to properly find out the truth for themselves. The problem with human beings is that most only care to know once it affects them.'

'So does that mean they should wallow in it,' asks Ngozi, sitting up in her chair, 'not strive to get themselves out of it? If I had—'

'No, that's not what I'm saying. What I am saying is that we, and I mean the African diaspora, really need to cut each other some slack. Understand that there's a whole lot of healing that needs to be done, before we can truly move forward. Don't listen to people who shoot their mouths off when they don't even know their own history and haven't even got their own shit together.'

'But meanwhile the rest of the world marches on, leaving us behind, O. We don't have the luxury,' Ngozi says, leaning forward in her chair. 'Do you know that during the California Gold Rush many black slaves were able to buy their freedom and the freedom of many of their family members by coming to California?'

'No, I didn't.'

'I suppose I was thinking that maybe this tech gold rush could be their opportunity now. Get the tech companies and Stanford to fund and improve the schooling in their communities, and then they have a ready supply of people on their doorstep to help bridge the staffing shortage. It's a win-win situation.'

'It's never that simple,' says Michael with a 'Believe me, I know' look in his eye.

'Isn't it? Why not?' she says, exhausted by the conversation, slightly in awe, but still in need of a simple answer.

'Maybe 'cause the players never really change. Because it's fundamentally the same people from the plantations to Wall Street to San Francisco to the City of London, all just playing a slightly different game – the game of money, control and power. Because people are people and if it doesn't directly affect them, it's not an issue they care to pay attention to. There are many reasons.'

'That's why I think we don't have time to wallow and we need to get on board the gold rush.'

'And we have. But because in the past we have not healed, have not acknowledged our pain and resolved the issues within, we only look for ways to escape from ourselves, to move out, move on, instead of staying and building our own communities.'

'Do you think things will ever change?' she asks.

'In what way?'

'Will we ever be in a position to decide our own fate?'

'I don't know. If you'd asked me that four years ago I would've said no, but that's because of the state of mind I was in. Today, yes, I do think things will change. As my little sister said to me once, it only looks like things aren't changing because we're in it. It's always two steps forward, one step back. We've just got to keep marching forward despite it all.'

'Do you think America will ever have a black president?'

'Definitely not in my lifetime,' he laughs. 'And if they did they'd assassinate him the very next day.'

'You're right, O,' she says.

'Too many rednecks in this country,' he says, sitting back in his chair. 'I'm sorry for getting all riled up just now, it's just that I'm over here for meetings to look at the deaths of black men in custody.'

'Really?'

'Yes. Following the Rodney King case when he was beaten up by LAPD police a few years back, we formed an alliance, and I'm over here for the case of a Mr Williams, who died in custody a few months back under suspicious circumstances.'

'I'm sorry to hear that, O.'

'When I was a kid, sixteen years old, I had a friend, a local guy – his name was Rizzlar. We were arrested at the same time. I was in the cell next door. I heard them. I know the police killed him. I just know it, but it would have been my word against theirs, the word of a boy. It's never left me, the memory of what they did to him. His cries. Sometimes I think if there'd been a camera in there, it would have made a difference – footage of what happened so people could see it for themselves. Maybe then Rizzlar would have got justice.'

They sit silently for a while.

Ngozi looks at Michael and he's far away, deep in thought, and suddenly she's ashamed of her earlier assumptions.

'A penny for your thoughts, O,' she says.

'They don't come that cheap,' he laughs.

She smiles. 'You know, you look like a man with a story to tell, O.'

'I'd say the same thing about you,' he says. A frown creases his brow. 'I was just thinking that I don't actually have any African friends. Acquaintances, yes. Don't mean to offend.' He pauses. 'I've read books on Africa, learnt a lot about the history, even watched enough TV programmes, but always filtered through someone else's eyes, mostly by people born in the diaspora. I'd like to get to know the real Africa, the Nigeria that you know,' he adds earnestly.

'And I'd like to learn more about you too, about your journey, O.'

They continue to sit, finishing off the last of their coffee and cake. Ngozi breaks the comfortable silence first. She watches a man saunter past the window and says without thinking, 'The thing that gets me the most about African Americans here is how much some of them look like they could be my relative. If I didn't know better I could have sworn that man was my brother Emeka.'

'Really?' Michael turns to try and catch a glimpse of the man.

'I had it in my head that African Americans looked different from Africans or Caribbeans, like on television: all fair-skinned and more European-looking. But the more I see and meet black people from around the world, the more I realize the similarities but also our differences. I like that. I like how the spirit of Africa has been adapted to describe their individual experience, but is still fundamentally African. You know, all of a sudden I wish I wasn't so ignorant about us. I used to think that Jamaicans had no culture, but they do. All black people have their own culture, except that some are older than others, but they all branch out from the same tree. I know it's just common sense to work that one out but sometimes the simplest ideas are the hardest to grasp.'

Michael nods his head, deep in thought. 'Yeah, you're right: we all have a culture, even us Black British. You can't properly see it yet because we're still like toddlers in comparison, still need to rely on our parents and grandparents, but slowly we're learning to walk, to stand on our own two feet, evolving an identity of our own, a culture of our own.' He breaks into a wide smile. 'Hey, I really like talking to you. I don't feel like I'm in some competition. I feel like I could say the most stupid things in front of you and it would be okay.'

They sit quietly, watching the traffic go by and the people passing on the street.

'It's amazing how we're practically neighbours and yet here we are, God knows how many miles across the ocean, and this is where we finally meet. I can't believe I've only known you for'– he looks at his watch – 'thirty-five minutes.' A thought suddenly flashes into Michael's head and he glances at her left hand but can't see a wedding ring. He wonders how to approach the subject. 'So have you got any children?' he asks.

'No, but I hope Sunday – that's my boyfriend – and I will have some one day.'

'He's a very lucky man,' he says after a moment. And looks down at his shoes.

'What about you, O?'

'I don't have any children and I'm not presently involved with anyone. I'm a free spirit,' he says, but a shiver passes over his skin as loneliness descends on him. He tries to mask it with another smile, changes the subject.

'So how long did you say you've been in this city?' he asks.

'A day. And you?'

'Since this morning.'

'Aren't you tired?'

'No, I'm too excited to sleep. Well, since you've been here a whole day more than me that makes you the expert, so what is there to see?'

'Well, plenty, O. There's the Bay Bridge, Fisherman's Wharf. I was thinking of visiting Alcatraz, the National . . .' She tells him of some of the places she plans to visit over the next few days. He listens and likes the odd way in which she pronounces her words, the O that will suddenly appear at the end of a sentence, the elegant movement of her hands as she talks, and how her smile always reaches her teardrop eyes.

'I hope you won't mind if I tag along?' he asks.

She shakes her head. 'Of course not, O. To tell you the truth I would like the company.'

And so they become tourist buddies.

The next day, after Michael's conference, they meet again. Dinner at Fisherman's Wharf. It feels good. It feels right. They laugh, joke, share precious talk about people they know, about themselves. They're like kids on a school trip, all giggly and mischievous, like philosophers and anthropologists discovering the secrets of life, like an old couple comfortable in each other's company. Time passes much too quickly and the last night comes much too fast.

Ngozi looks in the mirror and places a silver earring in each of her earlobes. For the first time since meeting Michael she thinks of Sunday. 'You've done nothing wrong, O,' she says to her reflection, 'nothing,' then picks up her perfume bottle from the table to give herself a quick spray behind the ears.

'Four years,' she says – that's how long she and Sunday have been together. When it started, that night she sat across from him in the pizza place, she'd wanted it to be over, so she could return quickly to the assignments she'd left undone on her desk, but here she was, four years on with all that had passed between them. She's grown used to his crying after sex, although he rarely does it now, and the simplistic way in which he sees the world. But most of all she has a sense of loyalty to him, for without him she'd not have had the opportunity to start her software company, nor to recognize her own decency. Seeing herself through his eyes has made a peace inside her that she hadn't known she was craving. But being with Michael these last few days has opened a wound that she'd plastered over, ignored in the hope it would disappear, or get to a point where it wouldn't matter. But here it is now, the truth – there's no fire, has never been any fire, between her and Sunday. With Michael there's an energy, a constant bouncing off one another, and sometimes in the silences as they've toured the city, it has felt as though they could hear each other's thoughts, sense each other's feelings. It's as though they are somehow connected. Primal lust and loneliness were the original foundations of her relationship with Sunday. He filled the isolation of her early days in London. But with Michael it isn't about needs or wants or filling gaps. With him it's about being with someone who sets her alight, who makes her want to find out more about life, strive higher and do it with passion. They seem to understand each other. They are alike and yet not alike. They are different culturally yet there is a familiarity about him.

She hears a knock on the door, gets up to answer. It's Michael.

'You ready?'

'Yes, O,' she calls from behind the door. She emerges and locks the hotel room behind her.

'You look nice,' he says casually. *You look gorgeous*, he thinks.

'So where is this exclusive restaurant you made me get dressed up for?' asks Ngozi, walking in front of him towards the lifts.

'Just a few streets away,' he says and takes in the curve of her half-naked back shown off by her dress, before she covers it with her shawl.

'This had bettar be good, O,' she warns jokingly. They make their way out of the hotel lobby and on to the street and hail a cab. Fog is trying to creep its way out of the sky; tiny drops of rain can be felt on the skin as they get in the taxi. Outside it's beginning to rain harder. They dash into the restaurant out of the downpour. The room is aglow with warm candlelight. White tablecloths cover the tables. Sparkling wine glasses, napkins, silver cutlery, are set down precisely. A few eighteenth-century paintings of black faces whose eyes speak to them decorate the walls. Ngozi feels as though she's been transported back in time to the era of the paintings, a time of slavery, is uncomfortable with the voices coming from the canvases, looks around the room and sees mostly black faces, and relaxes. The spirits of the past fill the room. The brothers, sisters, taken away, speak to her in Igbo, telling her of the things they have seen, the suffering undergone, and they welcome her. 'My sister, my sister, *bia ke ne anyi*.' In this room they've just entered, Michael and Ngozi, in this room they belong.

'What do you want to eat?' Michael asks, as a waiter with locks comes to stand by their table.

She glances down at the menu: soul food. 'I think I'll have the chicken with corn bread and okra fritters.'

'Wine?' asks Michael.

'You choose,' she replies.

'Can we have some palm wine?' he says to the waiter.

'How did you find this place?' asks Ngozi, spreading a napkin carefully on her lap.

'I didn't – one of my colleagues told me about it. His sister's promoting it in honour of Black History Month.'

They make light conversation while waiting for the food to arrive. It's delicious and they leave their plates clean, sit back and relax, and the wine mellows them. A live band of piano and clarinet begins to play an old jazz tune in the corner of the room.

'Fancy dancing?' he asks.

He holds out his hand, Ngozi follows him on to the dance floor. Once they are close, the atmosphere between them changes. They fall quiet while they dance. He places a hand on her bare back and holds her gently. He can feel the beating of her heart as they sway to the music, smell her hair oil, a slight hint of coconut tantalizing his nostrils. Her skin is smooth yet firm. His sweaty palms slide down her back. He looks up and sees a man watching him; he imagines they are Sunday's eyes, her man's eyes. He brings his hand back up to where it should be. He looks up again and the man is still staring, and he imagines again they are Sunday's, boring into him, warning him not to get ideas. He tries to look away from the image

335

in his mind but cannot. Ngozi is busy talking to him about something but he doesn't listen; he's too tied up with the emotions she arouses in him. He feels naked, like he's making love to her under the gaze of an audience.

'So what do you think?' she asks.

It takes a while for him to realize she's asking him a question. 'Of what?'

'Nothing,' she replies.

They dance, close, until he can't take any more and excuses himself, blames tiredness for his lack of energy. They sit at the table in silence while the waiter brings the bill, then walk back to her hotel slowly through the cold and the fog, but the sky still isn't sure if it wants to rain again; it's holding back. Neither of them says a word. A cloud overshadows their last night, each of them lost in thought.

I should say something, thinks Michael. *I should tell her how I feel. It's just lust, man. Just lust – it'll pass. Don't complicate your life, her life, just for the sake of sex. Be the new you.*

You don't know this guy, thinks Ngozi. *Pull yourself together. You're imagining all these feelings, O. It's the different environment – it's gone to your head, O. Sunday and I have something going. It might not set me on fire, but it's worth more than a holiday fling. Don't complicate your life.*

'I—'

'Do—'

They both speak at once.

'You go first,' she says.

'I was just going to tell you that I've really enjoyed myself.'

'That's good,' she says with a smile.

'Friends,' he says.

'Friends,' she agrees.

'I'll call you this Sunday when I get back, about two in the afternoon.'

'Fine.'

'What were you going to say?' he asks.

'I was just going to ask if you want my home number in London.'

'Of course, I forgot I don't have your number. I've been meaning to ask since we met but we've been having such a good time, I kept forgetting.' She hands him her business card with her number scribbled on the back.

They reach the hotel and hover outside.

'I'll see you up to your room,' says Michael.

They make their way upstairs in silence.

I want you, he thinks.

I want you, O, she thinks.

The lift doors open. They reach her room. She opens the door. Walks right in.

Follow me.

He stands at the door, watches her looking for the light switch. His heart beats faster than the rain, which has just begun to pour again. He can make out her shape in the dark as she fumbles around. He feels the heat rise in him, is silent for fear of the wrong words, for fear that his voice might give him away. He takes slow shallow breaths.

Ngozi switches on the bedroom light.

Michael lingers outside the door waiting for some indication that she wants him. He gives up and steps inside. Ngozi is there facing him.

She waits for him to come to her. They hold each other's eyes.

The phone rings and they stand in shocked silence. It rings again. Ngozi hesitates, looks at Michael, his eyes say 'Answer it' and she does. It's Sunday.

Michael listens to Ngozi speaking in a language he doesn't understand and becomes aware of an isolation, a separation, and knows in that instant that once they return to London this spell will be broken. Reality will seep in between them, tearing apart any connections that have emerged in this foreign land, in this land that brings them together. He wants to kiss her and go on kissing her, but he doesn't want to spoil what they have, wants to be a gentleman for once in his life, doesn't want to face rejection, not from her, not from Ngozi.

'That was Sunday,' she says, putting the receiver down and looking over at Michael, hoping he might still kiss her.

He hands over her shawl and kisses her on the cheek.

'Safe journey. I'll call you when I get back to London,' he says, then closes the door behind him.

Their moment is gone.

22

Can't Be Real

MICHAEL PUTS HIS key in the lock of his new two-bedroom Victorian conversion flat in Brixton. The keys rattle as he opens then shuts the door behind him. He hears the squeak of his trainers against the wooden flooring as he makes his way along the hallway, and the rustle of the shopping bags as he lays them down on the kitchen worktop. His flat smiles back at him, glad to have him home, and he happily relaxes back into his old bachelor ways. Michael takes a beer out of the big stainless-steel fridge, pulls open the can and takes a sip. He has the newest gadgets and appliances, nothing is patched or cobbled together from second-hand stores or hand-me-downs like in the home Ms Lorez had made for them, but even so this flat still has meaning and love and Ms Lorez in it. It's the first home Michael has bought outright for himself, after five years of working hard at building homes for others. It's the physical proof that all the guidance, lying awake at night and fretting endured by Ms Lorez were not in vain. He makes a chicken sandwich, retires to the sitting room and turns on the TV.

He puts down the remote and leans back against the sofa to watch the game, but his mind drifts. He looks at his watch, twelve thirty, too soon to call, so leans back again. Three times he picks up the phone, three times he stops himself. He sits looking at the television, but he's not paying attention. He looks at his watch again: one o'clock. *I'll call as soon as it's two.* But time runs as slow as a Galapagos tortoise. Michael glances at the clock again. It's quarter to two. He leans back once again, stares up at the ceiling, waits for time to pass, secretly hopes that she will call him. He wonders what she's doing, if she thinks of him, if she dreams of him like he does of her at night, alone in his bed. He moves his right hand, settles it just under the elastic of his tracksuit bottoms, lightly scratches the scattering of pubic hair around his manhood, then delves deeper, grabbing it, squeezing it, then releasing it from his hold. His thoughts change from memories to fantasy. He needs to hear her voice.

Each digit he presses rattles his nerves like a cocktail shaker. The phone is answered suddenly.

'Hello?' says Sunday.

Michael pauses – the male voice throws him. It hadn't occurred to him that Ngozi might live with her boyfriend.

'Hello?'

Michael wants to drop the phone, but he can't. 'Hi, can I speak to Ngozi, please?'

'Who's speaking?' asks Sunday, suddenly alert.

'It's Michael. A friend. We met in San Francisco.'

Sunday puts the receiver down and calls Ngozi. Michael hears laughter. He imagines Sunday laughing at him as she recounts stories of their time together.

'Hello,' says Ngozi.

'Hi,' he answers.

And Ngozi turns her back on Sunday, who sits at the dining table sifting through papers, closes her eyes and savours his voice. 'How've you been, O?' she asks quietly.

'Fine,' he says, but inside he tries to keep the pounding of his heart in check. 'And you?'

'I'm fine,' she says. *I've missed you.*

'I thought I'd call and see if you got home all right and to thank you for a great time.'

'Yeah, it was great,' Ngozi says, breathing deeply. She swallows. Then there is silence, unspoken words.

Ngozi grips the receiver more tightly. Michael's voice fills her veins, her fingertips, her temples, her toes, they tingle. She's frightened by the effect he has on her.

Michael hears Sunday ask Ngozi a question in their language and feels alienated, but then hears a hesitation in her voice when she answers.

'What are you doing?' he asks.

'Paperwork.'

'I want to see you.'

'I can't.'

'What about tomorrow?'

'I can't,' she repeats more quietly.

'Why not?'

'I'm taking Sunday out – he's just got a new job. He starts on Monday.'

'I've missed you,' Michael says before he can stop himself.

'What am I supposed to say?' Ngozi feels Sunday's eyes boring into her back.

'What do you mean?'

Ngozi doesn't reply.

'Can I see you then?'

'No.'

'Where are you going tomorrow then?'

'The Hibesa restaurant in Clapham. Why?'

'Nothing. This conversation isn't going anywhere. I'll call you some other time,' says Michael.

'You're right,' she says.

He hangs up fast, angry with himself, with her, with everything.

'What was that about? Why is he calling you?' asks Sunday.

'Nothing. He just wants to thank me for a lovely holiday.'

'Don't you think that's strange?'

'No.'

Sunday says no more.

They both get back to their paperwork.

The following day at the Hibesa restaurant, Ngozi sits at a table opposite Sunday and looks up from her menu to see Michael walk in through the door.

'Ngozi, are you listening? Ngozi? Ngozi?' asks Sunday.

'Sorry.'

Michael's companion is tall and gorgeous.

Ngozi stretches her legs under the table and sits up straight in her chair.

'Hi,' says Michael, now standing beside their table. He looks over at Sunday, smiles and leans forward to shake hands. 'I think I spoke to you yesterday on the phone. What a coincidence.'

He says it in such a genuine way that if she didn't know better she'd have believed him.

Sunday reaches out and shakes his hand.

'This is Michael,' Ngozi says to Sunday. 'You know, the one I told you about, O, that I met in San Francisco? Who fights for black men who die in custody?'

'Yes, yes. Please take a seat,' says Sunday.

Ngozi looks daggers at him.

Sunday doesn't read them, but instead welcomes the interruption, the opportunity to delay telling Ngozi what he needs to tell her.

They, Michael and his companion whom he does not introduce, take a seat at the table.

Ngozi feels the heat in her cheeks, darts furious looks at Sunday, then at Michael, and the four of them sit in awkward silence.

'So I finally get to meet you,' says Sunday.

Michael sees Sunday look him up and down. When he's done, Michael holds his gaze.

'Yes,' Sunday continues, 'I'm glad to put a face to this Michael I've heard so much about.'

Ngozi shifts uncomfortably in her chair, watching the two men.

'You're doing good work. Very good work,' says Sunday.

'Thank you,' replies Michael.

Michael and Ngozi feel something unsaid; it gets under their skin, itches away at them. They're tense with it, on guard with it, but don't want to acknowledge it – after all, why should they when they've not done anything wrong? Sunday reaches across the table to put his hand over Ngozi's, lifts it to kiss it and hold it firmly in his, almost like a challenge to Michael.

Michael watches, then looks up to stare directly into Ngozi's eyes.

Sunday thinks about what he must tell Ngozi, about the girl his Auntie has introduced him to, that Auntie Bessie wishes him to marry. He feels the softness of her skin in his, kisses it again, squeezes it.

Ngozi feels Sunday squeeze her hand, but steals glances at Michael. *I love you, but I belong with Sunday. Sunday loves me even though I'm Osu,* but then after barely a moment Sunday places her hand back on the table and takes his hand away. She looks over to question why but Sunday looks away.

Michael stares across at Ngozi, then at Sunday, back to Ngozi and back again to Sunday.

'Ngozi tells me you're a doctor,' says Michael.

Ngozi darts an angry glance at Michael, lifts her shoulders, straightens her back, then places her hand back into Sunday's palm as if to challenge Michael, as if to tell him it can never be.

For the first time, amid all of this, Michael's companion makes herself known. She clears her throat and nudges Michael with her slender bare elbow.

'Well, we just came in to have a drink before going to the cinema.' Michael lifts his wrist to check the time. 'We'd better be going. I'll see you soon, Ngozi. Nice meeting you, man,' he says to Sunday.

'Nice meeting you both,' says his companion as they get up.

They leave, but in truth Michael runs, runs out of there, as fast as he can. And later that night when he gets home after dropping off his date, he locks the windows and the doors tight against the feelings, the love that knocks away and rattles to come inside.

But each morning as he rises she's the first thing on his mind. Every night, the last, the only thought, as he lies on his side wishing for sleep, turning over and over. In the waking hours, while listening to a colleague droning on about what should be important issues, there she is, interrupting his life. This dull ache never leaves him.

Three months later, Sunday finally plucks up the courage to tell Ngozi. He makes sure to move out all his belongings while she's at work, before coming back to tell her once she's home. At first she's shocked, but at the same time surprised at the sense of relief rising inside her.

'You really can't wait to go, can you?' she says.

'We'll talk,' he says as he opens the door and walks awkwardly out into the hallway.

'You know what, please don't come back!' she shouts after him as he scuttles down the stairs. 'I've already wasted four years of my life,' she says to herself. She stands in the hallway for a second, watches him as he hurries out of the building, then goes back inside the flat and slams the door. 'You gutless weasel.'

Ngozi leans against the door, feeling numb. She looks over at the window and imagines him getting into his car and driving away. She tries to squeeze out a tear, but at the same time, deep inside, feels an immense relief. After the first tear is shed, she simply cannot muster another. She thinks of Michael, of Sunday, and Michael again. *I've been so stupid, so blind to the truth.* The questions tumble over each other. *What should I do? Does he feel the same? Is it too late?*

She wants to know the answers, grabs her keys, skips out into the cold busy street with only a cardigan on. She opens the car door, doesn't notice the winter pinch, its teeny sharp teeth biting into her forearms, goosebumps appearing in protest. She starts the car, drives off as though she's being pursued. She halts outside Michael's house. *What am I doing? I've lost my mind. I've truly lost my mind.* She grips the steering wheel with both hands, then takes the key out of the ignition, places her palm on the door handle ready to open it. From the driver's seat she eyes the front door. Michael appears, emerging from his home with another woman. They laugh together as if they've done so many times before, then he bends and hugs her. Ngozi's heart drops. Watches as the two part ways. A lone tear falls, then another and another. She starts the car, stares at the road ahead, wipes her eyes and drives steadily home. The tears are flowing.

Early one summer afternoon, five months later, Sunday is out parading his pregnant new wife, visiting friends and elders. Michael bumps into them on the Tube, the Victoria Line to be precise, on his way to visit Stanford. He jumps on to one of the carriages at Brixton, just in time before the doors close, then smiles and congratulates himself on just making it. He sits in the first empty spot, to the left, among the single row of seats and notices out of the corner of his eye a couple dressed in African attire. He doesn't pay immediate attention to them until Sunday happens to catch his eye. For a second he's tempted to pretend he doesn't know him, but unfortunately there's too much recognition in Sunday's eyes so they throw each other a smile.

'How are you?' asks Michael from his seat.

'I'm fine.'

'And Ngozi?'

'I don't know, I've not seen her for months,' Sunday says, as if he has no wish to talk about her.

The news pounds in Michael's ears. 'What – you broke up?'

'Yes.'

'When?'

'Some months back.' And as if to shut him up, Sunday says, 'Meet my wife.' The young woman at his side, a slim pretty woman in her mid-twenties, leans forward and smiles back at him. Michael absorbs the information. At the next stop, Stockwell, he waves them a casual goodbye, gets off the Tube, changes for the Northern Line.

While he walks, he thinks and starts to question his feelings. There's something not right about the way he loves her. He doesn't trust it – it's a sick kind of love, an out-of-control kind of love, irrational for the length of time they've actually known each other. *Maybe I'm sick*. Lately he's started having strange and dangerous dreams. He wakes abruptly, his heart beating so fast he has to breathe in deep to calm himself down, his head filled with images of his fingers surrounding her neck, gripping her tight, slowly squeezing the life out of her. *I'm going insane*, he thinks and gulps in air, fills his lungs, expands his chest. 'Shit!' he says, gulping in more air to try and keep calm. 'Shit!' His hand travels to his chest and he stumbles. His head spins. 'Shit! Damn shit!' He wanders out of the Tube and staggers to the side of the pavement, holds himself up against a lamp post. 'What is this, just damn shit?' He struggles, gulps in more air to keep control. Without thinking he finds himself outside Uncle Fred's home.

Fred's out the back, gardening. He comes into the house to greet him. Uncle Fred senses something and doesn't speak, waits till his nephew is ready. They're silent together for a while, until Michael can calm the chaos in his heart, organize it into questions.

'Dad' – that's what he calls his Uncle Fred now – 'how do you know when you're in love?'

Fred takes a deep breath. Smiles widely. 'Well, son, that is a difficult one for me to answer. You see, it's different for everybody. Some people say they know when they're in love 'cause they want to see that person all the time. Others say it takes a while and you need to experience things with that person.'

Michael sits down on the armchair facing the garden. Closes his eyes.

'Then when did you know you were in love?'

'The minute I set my eyes on Eliza, but it took a while, mind you, for me to admit it to myself and give in to the fact that I was hers and she was mine. You see, your auntie there, she's a stubborn and crazy woman. Why you asking, son?'

''Cause I think I might be. I'm not sure.'

'If you're not sure then I don't think you are, 'cause when that love hit you, you'll know. You won't be able to sleep for thinking about that person, want to be with them all the time and if they do something to hurt you, you'd straight away forgive them.'

'I have all those feelings for her, Dad, and more, but how can I be sure? We've not known each other that long.'

'Sounds to me like you're scared, Michael. I knows how that feels 'cause I've been there. I was scared about Eliza, but I had to let go of the fear before I could let in the love. Let it go, son, let it go. It's only then you will know if you truly love her.'

'But what if I think I love her and tomorrow I find out I don't?' says Michael.

'What makes you so sure you're gonna live to see tomorrow? What makes you so sure about anything in this world, son? It's so easy to hold love in your palms and let it slip through your fingers – one minute you have it, the next she's gone. Trust me, I know a lot of my friends who didn't even know they had love till they let it go, and then it was too late. You ain't guaranteed tomorrow nohow. So when you're alone with time to think straight, take some time to throw away your fears, throw away your physical wants and needs, strip yourself of all your baggage and just look at her. Look at the good points and the bad points, think about the way she makes you feel when you're blue, look at the way she makes you feel when you're happy, and how honest you think her heart is. And when you've finished that, look at the direction in life you want to go and the direction in life in which she's heading. And if after going through all that you still want her from the bottom of your heart, then love her, son. Love her with all your heart as if today was your last. Don't let anyone tell you differently. You see, love between a man and a woman is easy to lose if you don't look after it and it usually happens just when you think you've got it all sorted. I know there's been times when me and Eliza almost lost it, but you see, we didn't give up trying. Sometimes, son, you've got to take a gamble in order to win. You ever read the Bible, son?'

'Yes, sir, but not since I was little.'

'Well, there's a parable in there, right? I'm not too sure how it goes. It's about this here man who says he want go visit some place else for a while, right, so he calls three of his sons – I think they were his sons – gives them a likkle bit of money each, then goes about his business. When he comes back from wherever he went, he calls them and asks each of them what they did with the money.

One says he buried it, the next says he spent it and the last says he invested it and he gives back the father more than he gave him in the first place. You see, that's what life is all about. God gives you gifts along the way and you have to invest in each one and let it grow. Sometimes you win, sometimes you lose, but you don't gain anything by doing nothing.'

23

The Battle

'WHY DIDN'T YOU tell me?' asks Michael. He's standing in the doorway of her apartment, his foot over the threshold.

She tries to push it shut, but Michael extends his arms and resists.

'I don't believe this, O,' she says, backing away from the door and almost tripping over a handbag in the middle of the room.

He grabs her round the waist before she falls and lifts her up. 'Why didn't you tell me you broke up with Sunday?' he says, stepping forward.

Ngozi glares at him, eye to eye, nostril to nostril. 'How dare you?' she says. 'How dare you knock on my door and ask questions after so many months?'

'Then let's not play this game,' replies Michael and the nerve at the side of his neck pulsates. 'I'm tired of playing games. Just tell me the truth. Tell me you don't feel what's between us. Tell me you don't want me. Tell me it's all in my head. Tell me it's just me going insane. Just tell me something and I'll walk back out that door and out of your life.'

Ngozi is stunned into silence. She sits on a chair and covers her face.

'Please, just tell me something!'

Ngozi begins to cry silent tears. Her shoulders quietly heave up and down. 'What do you want from me?' she asks.

'The truth,' he says, moving closer, 'just the truth.'

And suddenly she's angry, stands up and pushes him. 'What do you want to hear? How I can't sleep without thinking of you, without wondering where you are . . . which woman you're with. Please go – get out of here!' she cries, and pushes him towards the door. He stands firm as a rock, but she loses her balance, lands between the side table and armchair, hits her ribs on the table as she falls, and knocks the half-empty mug of tea which had been sitting there. So there she lies on the floor, rubbing her side, infuriated, the tears falling properly now.

'Ngozi.' Michael bends down, moves her hand gently out of the way and places his palm on her side. He pulls her body into his arms, absorbs her sobs. He begins to rock her body, soothes away the pain. 'Shush,' he says. He places his long fingers under her chin and lifts her face. His eyes look into hers, defeat bounces back, and somehow he knows, he understands. She's tired, tired of the game, tired of the pretence, of the battle, tired by life. The unpredictable nature of it, the ups and downs of it. He feels her feelings, tries to hold on to his own – after all, he is the man – but he also is tired, so very, very tired.

A solitary tear escapes from the corner of his eye, slides down his cheek, falls on to her hand. She feels the wetness, watches as it's followed by another, and another, his face set, the tears cascading down like two streams down a mountainface. Ngozi unwraps her arms, shifts her legs, draws him down on to the carpet, cradles his head to her breast and entwines her legs with his. They lie there and their tears release a tension, release some of the past. They fall asleep right there between the armchair and the side table, while the cold tea from the broken mug slowly stains and dries into the carpet beneath them. That stain will remain there for ever now, and

Ngozi will often get on her knees to scrub it away, but it will not budge. It will stay there to remind them every so often of the years they spent fighting this world alone and the afternoon when they first began.

Michael awakes to the sound of Ngozi's heartbeat which pulses in his ear. He can feel her soft breast under his head and her strong legs encircling his, and he's aroused. He moves to replace his head with his hand. The feel of it awakens Ngozi. She smiles, stretches, their eyes lock, and an emotion wells up in Michael. 'Dear God, I love you,' he says.

'I know,' says Ngozi.

'What do you mean "I know"?'

'I mean, I know you love me, but that's okay because I love you. It took some time for me to accept it, but I love you, O, Michael Watson.'

Michael laughs and Ngozi begins to laugh too. Then Michael becomes serious.

'So tell me, why didn't you tell me you'd broken up with Sunday?'

She hesitates. 'Because when I came to your flat to tell you, I saw you with another woman.'

'When was that?' asks Michael.

'Six months back.'

'But I've not been seeing any woman and definitely not six months ago. You must have seen me with my sister.' He goes to his jacket pocket and brings out a photo. 'Is this the girl you saw?'

'I think so.'

'Well, that's my sister, Marcia.'

'I almost died, O, when I saw her,' says Ngozi.

'Well, you know what that means?'

'What?'

'It means you have to marry me,' says Michael.

'I don't know any such thing – anyway you're a little bit fast, O.'

'I don't see the point in wasting time. I've seen what I want and it's you. We're both adults and we're crazy about each other.'

'You know, if you'd asked me that a year ago, I would have jumped and said yes. But—'

'But what?'

'The thing is, I've spent all my life being made to feel less than, not worthy, because of marriage, because my father would not marry my mother as she was *Osu*. I got into relationships I shouldn't have got into, and stayed in them much longer than I should have in pursuit of marriage.'

He frowns. 'Look, I'm asking you because I love you and I want us to be together.'

'I know, O, and I love you too, but I am finally in a place where I now realize that marriage wasn't the prize – all along it was me who was the prize, and if I had only known that, I could have avoided a lot of heartache. I've had a good last five months being okay with me and the freedom and peace of mind that it brings and I'm not yet ready to define myself in those terms, O. Can't we wait a little and just enjoy the now?'

He looks down. 'This is not how it went in my head.'

'Look, I'm not saying no. I'm just saying give me a little more time, time to enjoy being me and for us to get to know each other more. Ask me again a little later,' she pleads, stroking his face.

Michael smiles, draws Ngozi to him, and they begin to kiss slowly and then more urgently.

Ngozi drags her lips away, gets up, still smiling, goes to the bathroom and returns with condoms.

They store every kiss, every touch, every whimper to memory, and at the height of it, at the very tip of it, their hearts collide. There is a marriage in heaven. In years to come when their children and grandchildren ask them questions in relation to their beginnings, Michael and Ngozi will look at each other and smile privately, remembering this first night.

As they rest, the sun rises. The light seeps through the crack in the curtains and pulls Ngozi back to reality. Not wanting to move, she turns her head to Michael. 'Michael, it's almost seven o'clock. I've got a plane to catch tonight and I've got a lot to do.'

'Do you have to catch it?'

'I don't want to go, but I've got to go home for my sister's wedding and I need to see my mother.'

He feels a sudden sadness but understands the importance of her trip.

'When you're ready I'll take you to the airport,' he says finally.

Ngozi gets up from his side and pads barefoot towards the bathroom, while he remains on the floor and thinks of the time they will not spend together and how much he'll miss her. He thinks about his business and the boys he has to mentor and how much he has to do, but then it suddenly occurs to him and he gets up, makes a few phone calls still in his underwear, then pulls on his clothes.

'Ngozi, I'll be back later,' he calls. 'I just remembered something important I have to do. I'll be back about six tonight.' He slams the door behind him.

He runs back to his apartment to get his documents and heads out to see his travel agent and over to the Nigerian embassy to get a visa. It's hard work but he manages to pull it off, and in the evening, holding all the right documents in his hands, he goes to pick up Ngozi.

'Hurry, we don't have much time – we have to stop at my place to pick up my things. I'm coming with you.'

'WHAT?' exclaims Ngozi.

'I said I'm coming with you. Don't worry, it's all sorted.'

'That's not what I mean. You're not coming with me because I don't want you with me.'

'Yes, I am,' says Michael.

'No, you're not, O.'

They look at each other for a while in silence, their wills battle, but Ngozi lets him win.

When the apartment is tidy and the windows locked, he carries her suitcase out to the car. She casts one last look at her flat from the doorway, pulls the door to and double-locks it, takes a deep breath. Michael heaves her suitcase into the boot and they jump into their seats. Michael turns on the radio, and as they drive off they hear a line from a gospel song that makes them smile. It tells them to stay optimistic as long as they can keep their head to the sky.

24

Home

I SEE HOW strange it is for Ngozi to return to her father's land, the land where she was born, to see the father she spent so much time wanting more of, begging her for the same things he once denied her as a child. Now she has the power, and the battle rages within for revenge.

'My daughter, you look well,' he says. 'Life has been kind to you.'

Ngozi looks back at this man, her father, as she sits on the verandah taking in the day. The rest of the household have gone to the market and Michael has gone with them. She'd seen a figure in the distance and wondered who this old man was, walking so unsteadily towards the house. This is not the man her eleven-year-old self searched out to say goodbye to, to lodge his face in her memory, that day so long ago in the bus depot. As a child she'd dreamed of spitting words at him, to make him understand the pain he'd left inside her.

'They say you have done well for yourself,' he says.

Ngozi nods, and her disbelief quietens her. She'd not expected to see him, had resigned herself to that fact long ago, of never laying eyes on him ever again, but in a strange turn of events, here he is. 'What are you doing here?' she asks.

'Is that how you greet your father?'

Ngozi looks at him, really looks at him. Unlike her mother, he has not aged well – his skin is now leathery, as though beaten by the sun; his hair is grey with age and his eyes are sunken, the skin almost black beneath; his shirt is yellow where once it was white. In her youth Ngozi only ever remembers him dressed in crisp white shirts. 'What do you want?'

'I came to see my daughter.'

'And now you are finally concerned to come find me – now I am grown and can stand on my own feet? What do you want?'

'I see the house you have built for your mother. It is a good house. You were always a good daughter.'

Ngozi stares down at him from the verandah. A bird chirps on top of the roof.

'You know it was not my wish to stay away from you all. You are too young to know or even understand, but I was forced – they would not allow me to stay. I have always thought of you all.'

'Who is "they"?'

'You must understand that I was a young man, and young men in those days did not go against the wishes of their parents.'

'So you were worried about the wishes of your parents when you fathered the four of us?'

He falls silent for a moment. Then: 'Don't be so insolent, I am still your father, and no matter what, you are still my daughter.'

'You have never been my father.'

'I have always loved you children.'

'Loved us?'

'Yes, loved you.'

'You have a funny way of showing it, O. You loved us so much you left us to rot. For the world to have its way with us. Not even one visit. Not even a *kobo* to make sure there was food in our stomachs or clothes on our backs.'

'You don't understand – times were different then. I could not bring my disgrace out in the open. My parents were still alive. It was not the done thing.'

Ngozi opens her mouth to spit out more words at him, but as she does so she suddenly realizes there's no point. He's created his own story in his head. Everything is someone else's fault, not his, and no amount of standing, hands on hips, and shouting at this man can ever change the things that happened to her, the scars left behind by Mr Obindu or Mr MacDonald, 'cause he was never there to help protect her from this world. Neither would it change the lies invented in his head to justify his absence. Instead Ngozi closes her mouth, opens it again to ask, 'What do you want?'

'What makes you think—'

'What do you want?'

'I am sick. It's my heart. I need money to pay for the medication.'

That was yesterday, and today Ngozi sits pensively on the verandah, Blessing by her side, cutting okra for the soup their mother is making in the kitchen, half discussing her sister's wedding in two days' time, half pondering what to do about her father's request. She can taste revenge, but it's not as sweet as she'd thought.

Michael sits and leans back against the verandah steps, his face turned up to the sky. He takes in the birds calling, the trucks honking, the distant squeals of children in the village. The light breeze caresses his skin and the mixed scent of ripe mangoes, pawpaws and red cashew fruit tantalizes his nostrils. He listens to the two women in the background chatter in Igbo and it soothes him, calms his spirit. The heat of the day, absorbed in the concrete beneath him, rises into the cool evening like puffs of warmth on his skin. He inhales his surroundings until he almost believes they are part of him.

This is Africa, Nigeria to be precise. Two days of travelling and four nights of sleeping under its sky has taught him the squalor, the chaos, the pleasure, the smells and now the peace. And yet amid the poverty there is wealth, amid the chaos there is order, among the weakness there is strength, and among the bitterness is a sweetness. It's a place of contradictions, not as it first appears, nor as it finally appears to be. It's like a game of pass the parcel with a never-ending supply of wrapping paper – you can never truly get to the root of it or what is in it before it moves on. You take from Africa, from Nigeria, what you want to take, be it love or loathing, pity or pride. Life in England, the only country he has ever known, controls, conditions, tames, quietens the soul and he clamours instinctively for its regulation and semi-certainty.

Yet this is Ngozi's home. Will they, can they, make it? he wonders to himself. One day she will return to this land, to her people, and the question is, will he be willing to follow? He hears Ngozi's infectious laugh and smiles to himself. The answer is he can't let her go even if he wants to. He feels blindly behind him for her leg, places his hand on it and smiles more widely, for the sheer joy of finding her close to him. Nothing is ever certain about the future. He has her now, maybe or maybe not for ever, but at least he has her for now.

'Come, I want to show you something,' says Ngozi, breaking his thoughts.

'Where are we going?'

She signals with her hand. He follows her out of the compound and they walk for fifteen minutes over dirt tracks with large holes that blend in and out of the dust until they reach a main road. She hails a battered yellow cab.

Michael sits in the back with Ngozi on a tattered and torn brown plastic seat; the yellow foam weeps out from beneath it. He clasps the sides of the driver's seat in front to control the rattling as the cab manoeuvres around the uneven roads and the sweat begins to gather under his thighs, then the cab stops to allow in more passengers. Ngozi squeezes in closer to make room.

They reach their mysterious destination and climb out to be met with a dusty expanse where three yellow buses lounge in the far corner awaiting drivers. Ngozi walks purposely ahead of him and he follows.

'It's still here,' she says, pointing.

'What's still here?' he asks.

'My tree.' Ngozi walks over to it and embraces the mango tree like an old friend. He watches.

She leans with her back against the tree, scratches herself like a bear, looks out across the yard. She smiles for a moment, then turns serious. 'I used to sell fruit from this bus station, O,' she says. She holds out her hand for him to join her. He does so, bends down and kisses the side of her neck, then leans his shoulder against the tree, and watches the expressions on her face. He wants to hold her closer but senses her mood.

'I used to watch my father from here. He used to get dropped off by his wife and son over there.' She points to the far corner. 'Every day without fail. I hated him. Hated a lot of people around here – hated the way they looked at me, the lowest of the low. All these years, O, all I've wanted was revenge. Stored it away inside me for now, for this moment. I've hated him all these years, so many years.

'I didn't tell you – I saw him yesterday while you were out at the market. He isn't as I expected. He's old. He's always been so strong in my mind, but when I saw him yesterday he could hardly walk. Life has aged him. He needs my help, Michael, needs it badly. Here it is, the day I can have my revenge, Michael, I want my revenge, but it tastes bitter in my mouth.'

She kicks the ground in her open-toed sandals and a small puff of dust rises and settles. Ngozi sits down on the earth. He crouches down beside her, puts one arm round her shoulders. They sit in silence for a while, looking out across the yard. The evening sun is beginning to set.

'Sometimes it's better to let go of your demons. Life's revenge is the best revenge,' says Michael.

She's silent for a few moments, then, softly and without looking at him, she says, 'I love you, Michael.'

'And I love you, desire you, care for you, need you, Ngozi,' he replies.

'Please, I am ready. Ask me now.'

His eyes shine. He understands her words. 'Ngozi Nwosu, will you marry me?'

'Yes, Michael Peter Watson, I will marry you.'

And as she turns to him, he takes her gently in his arms, gives her a long, slow, deep kiss. And when it's over, they lean back and laugh. He takes her fingers in his, turns over her palm, as if trying to commit every detail to memory.

'I want to marry you here, before we go back. I want us to be married traditionally, like your sister. We can have a church wedding when we get back. That way we will always belong,' says Michael.

She cups his face in her hands and plants kisses across his nose and cheeks. 'I love you, Michael,' she repeats. The red dust still clinging to her wrapper, she gets up and walks across the yard.

'Hey, where are you going?' he calls.

'To face my demons,' she says over her shoulder.

He stands quickly and catches her up, and they walk slowly hand in hand to hail a cab.

25

The Cycle

MICHAEL SITS HOLDING his head in his hands and wonders if she's okay. She's not been well this past week and when he finally got the call, his heart almost missed a beat. He paces the corridor. 'Please, God, let her be okay,' he prays. 'Let her be okay.' He stands by the hospital window and looks down at the busy traffic crossing Westminster Bridge. He watches the ant-sized people hurrying below, hears the chimes of Big Ben. Memories of Ms Lorez on her deathbed come back to him. It seems to him a thousand years ago, but at the same time just like yesterday.

'She's okay now,' says the nurse bustling into the room. 'They've just finished sorting her out. You can go in if you want. Bed twenty.'

He exhales. 'Thank you.'

'How're you feeling, Sis?' he asks as he reaches her bedside.

There's a lack of lustre and colour to her face. A streak of grey seems to shimmer among her mass of wild black hair. She looks tired but draws herself up into a sitting position, a little grimace of pain around her lips, and in the midst of all the details he takes in, he notices the most important one – her eyes shine with a quiet happiness.

'I'm fine,' says Marcia, rearranging her pillow to be as comfortable as she can.

'Where's your man at?' he asks, looking around the ward.

'He's gone with the baby to get her settled.'

'You scared me, you know.'

'I scared myself – three weeks early and such a little thing as well.'

'So my little sis is a mother now,' he says.

Marcia smiles as widely as she can. 'Where's Ngozi?' she asks.

'Working. Got a new manager. She'll be down later.'

Marcia's man returns. There's worry in his eyes, an unspoken question. 'I'm fine,' she mouths.

'Leroy, my man,' says Michael, patting him on the back. 'How's fatherhood?'

Leroy turns to his spar and they hug.

'Tiring, but man, is she gorgeous,' he says, leaning over Marcia to kiss her on the cheek.

'It's a girl then?'

The two, Marcia and Leroy, nod their heads.

'You lot had me worried. But thank God, Sis, you and the baby are okay.'

Around the same time that Michael and Ngozi met in San Francisco, Marcia finally achieved the life goal she'd set herself and became a fully fledged doctor. But the problem was that after so many years immersed in work and study she found her mind was no longer kept busy, and so she had space to analyse and re-analyse, to dig up from where she'd buried it, deep inside, the death of her mother. It began slowly at first, the confusion. It disrupted her. She would say yes when she meant no, no when she meant yes, would open her mouth to shout for help, but no words came forth, and so she fastened her cloak of perfection ever more tightly around her.

At work, she perfected it, she became a flawless professional. But the clues, the giveaways, were in her private life, in the minor dilemmas like should she wear red or brown lipstick, should she use her big bag or her small bag, should she wear a white blouse or a blue blouse? These small decisions filled her with dread and left her drained, so that avoidance was the only option. And it showed in her appearance – she didn't wear lipstick, nor did she ponder over what to wear, but instead put on the first thing she could find and pulled back her hair until she was flung together like a midnight sandwich, almost as if, although subconsciously, her appearance cried out for her, but no one saw, no one heard. Until the day she was awakened from her troubled sleep by a morning phone call.

'Marcia, congratulate me – Ngozi and me, we are official.'

'What?'

'Listen, I don't have much time. You've got the keys to my flat – please can you go round and check on it every few days? I'm going to Nigeria with Ngozi for a couple of weeks.'

'Yes, but—' she said, confused, 'when did this—'

'Listen, I've got to rush off to get my visa and ticket for the flight tonight and I still have some phone calls to make. I'm sorry about dumping it on you like this. I'll tell you all about it when we get back.'

'Okay.'

'Love you, Sis.'

'Love you too, but—'

The phone went dead. That day, on her way back from work, it hit her as she stood in front of a cashier buying wine.

Which one, white or red? She held both bottles in her hand, put the red down on the counter, reconsidered, then the white, thought again, replaced it with the red.

'Please make up your mind,' said the cashier.

Marcia stared back at her, tears beginning to blur her sight. 'I can't.'

'Please, lady, can you hurry up?' said the customer behind her.

'I'm sorry,' she said to the cashier, still standing there.

'Lady, please,' said the customer again.

'Buy both,' said the cashier.

'I don't want both!'

'I'm just trying to help.'

'I don't want both.' And Marcia stood there, shaking with the crying.

'All right, all right, please, you're holding up the queue.'

She left both bottles on the counter, walked out of the shop. She heard the noise of the traffic passing by, saw the lights from the street lamps overhead, looked up and down the road, unsure which way to head, started walking, and as she walked, she thought of her family, the one before her father left, before Simon's breakdown, before her mother lay in her own blood on the bedroom floor. She felt the hole inside, deep inside, the hole that had taken up residence when her mother died. Which she could never fill, for there were no mother–daughter talks in her teenage years to fill it. No learning at the kitchen stove as she watched her mother cook. No gentle words of encouragement to soothe the embarrassment of her first period. No whooping across the stage of 'That's my baby!', as she went up to collect her certificate at graduation, for her mother would have clapped and cheered the loudest, 'cause being a doctor was their dream. For her, there was only the muddling through. Finding out things through books because she was too embarrassed to admit she just didn't know, and through other girls who neither had the patience nor understanding nor experience to tell her all she needed to know. The muddling through half-truths and big holes, hiding, masking her imperfections, leaving her with a lack of confidence in her womanhood. She remembered the day Simon killed her mother. The day she left the door open. But recently they'd been trying hard, she and Simon. And they were desperate with it, like two drowning people trying to grab hold of their last chance. They were building miniature bridges across the memory of that day, the day his psychosis robbed them of Ms Lorez. She thought of Michael, the changes to come in their fiercely close sibling relationship now he was to marry Ngozi. And as she walked along the pavement, the tears came streaming down, and within minutes she found herself knocking on the door at Auntie Eliza's.

'Marcia, are you okay?' said Leroy, noting her state.

'Leroy, is Auntie Eliza in?'

'No. No one's in except me. Are you okay?'

'I don't know.'

'You'd better come in.'

And so she did. Talked only enough to stop the crying. To get her to the place where she needed to seek help. Professional help. For she knew her problems were bigger than Leroy could understand.

'You can't live your life blaming yourself for your mother's death,' said the therapist.

Marcia sat opposite, a glass of water beside her.

'I know but . . . I just can't help it. If I'd only shut the door.'

'But you didn't.'

'I know, but if I—'

'But you didn't.'

Marcia nodded her head. 'I didn't. As you said, that's not what ultimately killed her.'

'Exactly. You've got to start finding a way to forgive yourself.'

'Forgive myself,' she repeated.

And gradually she came to an acceptance within, started that journey of forgiveness, forgave that eleven-year-old girl who'd left the door open, stopped hiding herself, the guilty one. And that's how her friendship with Leroy began. He'd check on her at home from time to time. And when she visited Auntie Eliza, sometimes they'd find themselves cleaning up in the kitchen, talking and sharing experiences as they tidied, gently laughing with each other and sharing little problems they had at work. Marcia liked talking to him, enjoyed his sense of humour. Sometimes, as they grew to know each other better, they'd laugh so much at each other's jokes that her sides would ache. Then one day as she went to leave, she stood up to give him her usual sisterly kiss. Leroy turned his head at the most unexpected moment and her lips landed on his. They froze, looked into each other's eyes, stunned by the electricity that shot through them. Then that peck became a kiss, a longer kiss. They never looked back.

Her thoughts are interrupted. 'What did you say?' she asks.

'I said, what're you going to call her? My niece, I mean,' asks Michael.

Marcia looks between her brother and Leroy.

'Delores,' she says. 'I'm going to call her Delores, after Mum.'

Michael nods his head in approval. Leroy takes her hand, strokes her fingers and communicates his understanding.

A few minutes later, Simon comes on to the ward. Michael stiffens. He's promised Marcia not to interfere in her relationship with Simon but he doesn't want to be here in this family reconciliation. Little Marcia, Simon's daughter, runs towards her auntie. 'Auntie Marcia!' she screams with delight. Michael sits, watches the interaction between his sister, Leroy, Simon and Little Marcia and he feels excluded, as though he's watching a family that he's not part of. He observes Little Marcia relay a story about school to her auntie. She looks just like Marcia when she was that age. Her shining, jet-black cornrowed hair glistens, her skin glows with health and she talks at top speed just like her auntie did.

The nurse brings in Baby Delores Watson Bailey in a cot. Even though she was born early, she's a healthy baby weighing in at 6lb 5oz.

'Michael, come and look at your niece,' says Marcia. She picks her up in her arms.

Michael reaches across to touch her, fondles her tiny hands, her tiny thumb.

'You can hold her,' says Marcia, as she lifts the pale-skinned baby to him. The little one has a full head of thick, dark curls.

Michael and Ngozi have been trying for a child of their own and so far have not been successful, but that is another story altogether. Holding that small baby in his arms overwhelms his spirit with the need to protect her.

He looks over at Little Marcia and feels the pain of what he's missed while she was growing, is sad that the child doesn't even recognize him. He hears her call Leroy 'Uncle' as they share a joke. He looks at the baby, looks at Simon and back again at Marcia. Can't he find it in his heart to build something out of the wreckage? Simon has changed – Marcia wouldn't be interacting with him if he hadn't. He knows he can never forgive Simon for his act, in madness or not. But wasn't she his mother too? He's watched Ngozi let go of the demons that haunted her. If she can do it, can't he find some way to work through the past? Wouldn't Ms Lorez have wanted them to try? If he and Ngozi have children, how can he not give them the opportunity of knowing their cousins? And deep down, does he not still love his brother? Does he not love Simon?

He looks down at baby Delores in his arms, remembers the brother he used to know, the one he looked up to, whom he followed around and worshipped as a child, and a feeling of hurt, of love, of pain, of need overwhelms him.

He hands the baby back to Marcia with tears in his eyes, and without thinking, turns and grabs hold of Simon. He doesn't know whether to hug him or hit him. He grabs him and sobs like a baby, sobs for the mother he lost, for the brother he lost. He doesn't let go.

At first, Simon doesn't know what to do but he hears his brother's sobs, feels his arms around him, so he hugs his little brother back with all the love he has in his heart. Begins to cry for the sheer joy of his brother's arms finally engulfing him. 'I love you, man,' says Simon. 'I don't expect you to forgive me. I ain't even forgiven myself. Please, let's try and get through. I love you, man. Let's just try and build from today.'

The two grown men stand in the middle of the ward hugging each other, gripping each other ever tighter. Michael, crying out the hurt of all those years. Simon, just holding him. While Marcia looks on at her brothers, tears rolling down her cheeks. *Mummy, I think we're finally beginning to find some sort of peace.*

About an hour later, Ngozi comes on to the ward; she's come to see her sister-in-law. Fred and Eliza Bailey wander in behind her; they've come to see their latest grandchild. All three take in the unforeseen spectacle.

Marcia asks a nurse who's hovering and smiling in the background, 'Please can you take a picture of all of us?'

They position themselves around Marcia's bedside.

'Say "Cheese".'

'Cheese!'

The Watson family is growing. There are now the five Watsons: Simon Watson, Michael Watson, Marcia Watson, Little Marcia Watson and Baby Delores Watson Bailey.

Somehow, they've grown and prospered, lost and loved, all under these white clouds and blue skies.

THEY, MICHAEL AND Ngozi, call to me. It's time for my children to be united. And I thank Chukwu that my soul has at last begun to find peace, a little more each day. But there still are parts of me, my own blood, scattered like kernels of corn from Sierra Leone to Virginia, from Virginia to Nova Scotia, from Nova Scotia to Rio, from Rio to London, from London to Jamaica, from Jamaica to the Bight of Biafra and back around again.

Over two hundred years we have searched, two hundred years since my death, and at last, they've begun to find each other. I pray that more will follow, that they won't blame me or each other, won't hate me for what has happened. It was not my choosing. I love them with such . . . I cannot find the words. I kiss Wind who is now by my side. I kiss him deeply and it is sweet, like the day our eyes first met across the deck, yet sad.

I think back to the girl I once was, before the day of my simple decision to stop at the shrine and give thanks for my blessings. To the young girl who raised her face to the sky, to the rain, and smiled with innocence into her future, who kicked up the dust as the bells at her ankles rang in her ears, kicked up the dust with freedom and joy. Her face lifted to the heavens, then down again and back at her friends, their virgin faces smiling back. I wish I could go back and change things, but I cannot. All that can be done is to move forward. For you to pass on a better baton than time and life allowed me.

We did not escape the consequences of my simple decision that day. But I tried to fight, tried to find you, waited here for you, but still I hear the damage echo down the generations.

I want you to know this, my child, that you were made in love. Your freedom fought for among the resistance and revolts of the Islands, and the sheer will and desire to be free. You will have to look to find this, but find it you will.

Wind takes my hand. I look up into his eyes again, those that willed me on. We breathe in and ready ourselves for life.

Acknowledgements

IT HAS BEEN a long journey to publication, and I would like to acknowledge those who have championed this book and without whose energy and support it would not have been published.

Firstly, I would like to thank my mother, who always had faith in this story and insisted it should be published. Thanks to my grandmother and the history lessons she gave me. To Kadija George, who appeared like a fairy godmother, giving positive advice and direction. To Uncle Rob and Sola for their support and encouragement, and especially Auntie Delores, who was the first person to read the novel in its entirety and fell totally in love with Michael. To Carole Welch, who sent me a letter over twenty years ago telling me that it showed promise but was not yet ready for publication, and who responded magnificently twenty years later, introducing me to Francine Toon. To Francine, who was very supportive and led me to Niki Chang and the Good Literary Agency. To my agent, Niki, who was one of the first industry professionals to read the full manuscript and responded immediately, bringing on board Arzu Tahsin, who gave me great editorial advice. To Olaudah Equiano, who left behind the information I needed to understand, in some small way, what it was like to be an enslaved Ibo in the late 1700s. To the International Slavery Museum in Liverpool and the Museum of London Docklands for their wonderful informative exhibitions. To my editor Jane

Lawson, who read and championed the book, totally understanding what it was about, and the rest of the team at Doubleday, who polished and buffed the manuscript and turned it into the book in front of you today. Thanks also to all my family and friends who have supported me throughout the years. But most of all, I thank God.

ROSANNA AMAKA was born to African and Caribbean parents. She began writing *The Book of Echoes* twenty years ago to give voice to the Brixton community in which she grew up. Her community was fast disappearing – as a result of gentrification, emigration back to the Caribbean and Africa, or simply with the passing away of the older generation. Its depiction of unimaginable pain redeemed by love and hope was also inspired by a wish to understand the impact of history on present-day lives. Rosanna Amaka lives in South London. This is her first novel.